Club
You to
DEATH

Also by Anuja Chauhan

The Zoya Factor

Battle for Bittora

Those Pricey Thakur Girls

The House that BJ Built

Baaz

'Quite simply, the funniest writer of contemporary popular fiction.' – TEHELKA

'Perhaps the best storyteller amongst India's writers of popular fiction.' – CARAVAN

'If there's one word that describes her writing, it's chic.' – THE TELEGRAPH

'The high priestess of commercial fiction.' – THE ASIAN AGE

'The mistress of words.' – VERVE

'A perfect read for just about anyone.' – VAGABOMB

'Chauhan is something of a rarity.' – INDIAN EXPRESS

'Her ear for dialogue is one of Chauhan's strengths.' – INDIA TODAY

'A distinctly Indian flavor.' – FIRSTPOST

The brazen style of humour, the settings, and the amusing concoction of Hindi and English make her stories richly Indian.' – THE HINDU BUSINESSLINE

'The only Indian writer of popular fiction really worth buying.' – MINT

ANUJA CHAUHAN

Club You to DEATH

HarperCollins *Publishers* India

First published by
HarperCollins *Publishers* in 2021
A-75, Sector 57, Noida, Uttar Pradesh 201301, India
www.harpercollins.co.in

2 4 6 8 10 9 7 5 3 1

P-ISBN: 978-93-5422-319-8
E-ISBN: 978-93-5422-322-8

This is a work of fiction and all characters and incidents described in this book
are the product of the author's imagination. Any resemblance to actual persons,
living or dead, is entirely coincidental.

Anuja Chauhan asserts the moral right
to be identified as the author of this work.

Typeset in 11.5/15 Adobe Garamond at
Manipal Technologies Limited, Manipal

Printed and bound at
Thomson Press (India) Ltd

MIX
Paper
FSC FSC™ C010615

This book is produced from independently certified FSC™ paper
to ensure responsible forest management.

For **Jaideep Singh**,
Strong, steady, twinkly-eyed,
We're still dealing with the loss.
Who always told the Ajays he met—
'You are a Jai, but I,'
(pause, deep chuckle)
'I am THE Jai, boss.'

1

Tambola Sunday

'I feel like a hooker, I say!'

Brig. Balbir Dogra is slumped low in the passenger seat of his old Maruti Swift, staring down at his phone in complete exasperation.

His daughter Natasha lifts her hand off the gear stick to pat his knee placatingly. 'That sounds *so* wrong, Daddy. But I think you mean you feel like you're available? Up for grabs? For sale to the highest bidder?'

'Exactly!' Brig. Dogra's chin juts forward, his face purpling with rage. 'My family's been members of the DTC for *decades*, and I've never seen such vulgar canvassing for votes during any presidential election! It's all so bloody crass!'

Natasha swings the old car onto Shantipath. It's a beautiful Sunday morning in February, and all the roundabouts are ablaze with flowers in Lutyens' Delhi.

'Did you get another WhatsApp message?' she asks.

The brigadier waggles his phone about agitatedly. 'Yes! Mehra keeps *on* messaging me! Even though it's clearly against the club by-laws! Inviting me to bawdy cocktail parties and whatnot! Practically offering bribes and kickbacks!'

The election for the post of president of the Delhi Turf Club, the capital's oldest and finest, is slated to happen the next evening between Lt General Mehra (retd) PVSM AVSM Yudh Sewa Medal and Mrs Urvashi Khurana, Padma Shri, homemaker and founder, lifestyle brand 'Chrysanthemum'. About two thousand permanent members residing in Delhi will be casting their vote, including Brig. Dogra.

'Why don't you just enjoy all the wining and dining and then vote for whoever you want?' His wife, Mrs Mala Dogra, suggests practically from the back seat.

The brigadier's eyes bug out. 'I'm not going a mile near these parties, I say! That poor sucker Suri went, and Behra Mehra cunningly recorded a video of him idiotically babbling "Jiggy Jiggy" as he jiggled a half-naked Russian belly dancer in his lap, and now he's blackmailing Suri into voting for him!'

'Your grandson's in the car,' Mrs Mala Dogra murmurs.

The brigadier's voice drops to a peeved mutter. 'And that wretched woman is no better! Bombarding us with gift hampers! Full of stinking cheese and candlesticks!'

'Ooh, I love Urvashi auntie's cheeses!' Natasha says at once. '*So* much better than tacky Russian belly-dancers! She has my vote for sure!'

'You don't *have* a vote, madam!' her father says dampeningly. 'Not till you become a permanent member, at any rate! And neither does your brother!'

Cuddled against his grandmother's bosom, five-year-old Dhan takes his fingers out of his mouth long enough to volunteer, 'Kashi mama don't wants DTC memmershi. He says it's full of sobs.'

'Snobs,' his mother corrects him automatically, then wishes she hadn't. The brigadier rises again with a roar.

'My son is a duffer, I say! My father got me green card-holder status at the DTC when I came of age, and I did the same for you and Akash! Now the fool's twenty-five – and eligible to apply for full membership – and he wants to let it lapse! He's just cutting off his nose to spite his face!'

'Good,' Natasha replies soothingly. 'Kashi's nose is way too big anyway.'

This doesn't have the desired effect. 'Don't joke, Nattu!' her father growls. 'We're talking about the Delhi Turf Club! The most exclusive club in the country! Regular people have to wait thirty-seven years and pay a seven-and-a-half-lakh waiting fee to get what I've got you and your younger brother for just *one* lakh!'

She glances at him affectionately. 'I *know*, Daddy, and I'm properly grateful for it. I took the full membership at twenty-five, didn't I?'

'But Kashi won't!' The brigadier sketches agitated quote marks in the air. '"The DTC is a symbol of privilege", if you please! "Of elitism and ossified class stratification!"' He drops back, disheartened. 'He wants to *give up* the membership.'

'He's *kidding*, Daddy, don't take him seriously.'

'He thinks he's the Prince of England,' Mrs Mala Dogra chimes in from the backseat. 'Abdicating his birthright. And that JNU ki Bangalan is his Meghan Markle.'

'Which makes you the queen of England, Mummy. Isn't that nice?'

Her mother looks appalled at this display of ignorance. 'It makes me a divorced, dead princess, Nattu. Don't you know any history?'

'Some would argue that the lives of the British royalty are more tabloid tattle than genuine history,' the brigadier puts his oar in.

His wife ignores this irrelevant remark. 'The point is that *she's* the one egging him on to do all this.'

Natasha wags an admonitory finger at her mother.

'Not nice, Ma! To imply that your phool-sa-boy can do no wrong, and it *must* all be the fault of the girl he's with! You should be happy Kuhu isn't status-conscious or money-minded.'

'Kuhu.' Mrs Mala Dogra rolls her eyes. 'Ridiculous name!'

'Money, status, where?' the brigadier broods. 'Arrey, the Turf is *not* a symbol of elitism! Look at us – four generations and a wheelchair stuffed into a rattling, eight-year-old Maruti Swift – how are we elite?! Elite people go to five-stars and seven-stars and whatnot! All the DTC membership gives you is cheap facilities and recognition that you – and your family – are old, established Dilliwallas! It helps in networking, and closing deals, and getting your children settled. Why, your rishtaa came through the club only!'

'Yes, Dad,' Natasha says patiently. 'But that *is* what privilege and ossification is all about.'

'He'll regret it,' Mrs Mala Dogra declares. 'He's only twenty-five now – so he thinks he's being very heroic and anti-establishment and socialist by doing all this, but when he's a middle-aged man and his children ask him why Natasha bua's kids have DTC membership and they don't – what will he tell them?'

'Kashi mama says he's going to be poor forever,' Dhan informs the car seriously. 'And if his chinnin want the good life, they'll just have to suck up to their boozy boujee bua.'

'Perfect!' Natasha claps her hands delightedly. 'I'd *love* to be boozy, boujee bua! We'll make all the little Kashi-lings really grovel before we sign them in for cheap daaru and dancing on Thursday nights, won't we, Dhanno?'

'Hands on the wheel, Nattu!' The brigadier frowns.

'For heaven's sake, Daddy, I'm thirty years old!'

'We should never have sent him to boarding school.' Mrs Mala Dogra's voice trembles slightly. 'He feels closer to his wretched friends than to us – that's why he's moved out to live with them in that dismal barsati in Nizamuddin.'

'But that's *healthy!*' The brigadier thumps the dashboard. 'That's normal! Besides, he can't commute from Noida daily! Do you want to smother the boy, Mala-D?'

'Don't call me Mala-D!' Mrs Mala Dogra hugs her grandson harder and sits back, disgusted.

Her mother-in-law, a fluffy, bird-like lady, dressed in a creamy chiffon sari and pearls, looks at her uncertainly, a question in her rheumy old eyes.

'Nothing happened, Mummy.' Mrs Mala Dogra pats the old lady's arm reassuringly. 'So exciting, no? We're going to the Club to play Bumper Tambola!'

As the old lady nods and breaks into a sweet smile, the Maruti Swift swings onto Aurangzeb Road and joins the long line of cars inching towards a set of imposing black wrought-iron gates monogrammed with the horse and jockey insignia of the Delhi Turf Club. A moustachioed guard, standing next to a gleaming metal sign that reads ENTRY FOR MEMBERS ONLY, notes the DTC sticker on the windshield of the dilapidated Swift, snaps to attention and waves them in.

The DTC's website declares it to be a world in itself – 'a haven of graciousness and elegance, merging the historical past with the modern present' – and on this particular winter morning, with the sun out, and the white colonial main bungalow gleaming in the middle of the sprawling thirty-two-acre lawns like a Fabergé egg in a bed of emerald-green velvet, the claim does seem to ring true. Pillared, bougainvillea-festooned verandas fan out from the main bungalow like fine filigree work; there is the glint of swimming pool turquoise, tennis court ochre, and skating rink peat in the distance, and a giant arch of multicoloured helium balloons sways airily across the East Lawn. A gay banner flutters below it.

'COME ONE COME ALL! ANNUAL CHARITY BUMPER TAMBOLA!'

'What's with the balloons?' Mrs Mala Dogra grimaces. 'Looks like a birthday party.'

'Some bloody lala trying for an out-of-turn membership, I say,' Brigadier Dogra replies. 'He sponsored free balloons to suck up to us. These baniyas are all the same.'

'Daddy!' Natasha throws him a reproving look.

'*I* like the balloons,' Dhan declares decidedly.

'So do I,' replies his mother firmly, as she swings into the senior citizen parking spot, right next to the main porch. 'Woohoo, Dadi, are you feeling lucky? We could go home millionaires!'

Brigadier Dogra's mother prods his back with her membership card. When he turns around, she holds up ten fingers, her eyes anxious and fever-bright.

'Ten,' she says. 'Ten.'

'Yes, I'll get ten tambola tickets, Mummy,' he replies gently. 'Five for you – and one-one for the rest of us. And Fanta-beer shandy and shaami kebabs for everybody!'

The old lady thrusts her membership card at him urgently, and he takes it with a slightly overdone cry of delight. 'Wow! Dadi's treat, everyone!'

Thank you, Dadi!!!!' all of them chant in a well-practised chorus. The old lady smiles proudly. The tension in her face eases and she sits back, satisfied. Paying for the eats is the sweetest part of visiting the DTC for her, and the family does not let on that they actually never swipe her card.

The brigadier produces a hat and pulls it low over his head.

'Behra Mehra and Urvashi Khurana are bound to be haunting the place, soliciting votes,' he mutters darkly as he exits the car. 'I'm going in incognito!'

'Mummy, they call the numbers so quickly – how will you tick five tickets at once?' Mala Dogra asks her mother-in-law, sounding worried. 'The stress will be too much for your heart.'

'Kashi and I will help Dadi,' Natasha says, turning around to wink at the old lady. 'And we'll all split the spoils.'

Mrs Mala Dogra rolls her eyes and sighs.

'That's *if* he shows up.'

In the dappled shade of an ancient peepal tree growing miraculously right out of the pavement at the edge of a scraggly park in Nizamuddin, a callow adolescent in a bright orange shirt holds a long, sharp blade to the throat of a young man about ten years his senior. They are watched by a circle of rummy-playing taxi drivers, a one-eyed shakkarkandi-chaat seller, several urchins and a skinny cow.

'Please don't kill me, Firdaus.'

This entreaty, uttered in a deep, smiling voice, causes the trainee-barber to pull his blade away, his expression reproachful.

'Why you're joke, Kashi sir? Would I kill my best client?'

'Your only client, you mean,' sniggers the chaat-seller as the puny Firdaus tips his victim's chair backwards to rest against the peepal's ancient trunk, stippled with the jointed names of lovers now long sundered. 'Akash sa'ab, better you than us!'

In reply to this sally, Akash Dogra, lathered to the cheekbones and tilted back till all he can see is the peepal's canopy (festooned with grimy string and a torn pink kite) lifts both hands in a fatalistic gesture to the Heavens. Seen from this angle, he is revealed to have thick, dark hair, a broad forehead, a large nose and comically panicked dark-brown eyes. As the blade scrapes away at his face, a firm but full-lipped mouth comes into view, and, gradually, a square, well-defined jaw and a column of muscular neck.

The 'barber' straightens the chair, twitches the striped towel away with a flourish and Kashi springs to his feet to a round of applause. He is a lean, muscular, young man, dressed in a cobalt-blue cable-knit sweater and khakhi chinos, both of which have clearly weathered several winters.

Surveying his visage in the mirror the barber is now holding up, he says briskly. 'Excellent job, Firdaus meri jaan. Just two nicks and a minor bloodletting!'

Firdaus grins a shy, shifty grin. 'Dekha?' he crows triumphantly to the onlookers. 'Kashi bhaiya fights such big-big cases, comes on TV and all, and gets his hajamat done right *here*! From *me*! When will *you* suckers latch on?'

The circle of drivers doesn't look very impressed.

'That is because Kashi sir is brave enough to risk a throat-slitting – and we are not!' one of them quips snarkily.

'You're drunk half the time, you'll kill us!'

'God knows if you even sterilize that thing!'

'C'mon guys, if you don't let him practice on you, how will he ever get better?' Kashi says as he hands Firdaus a folded note. 'Give him a chance to make you look handsome!'

'*You* were looking really handsome on TV, sir!' volunteers one of the drivers. 'On every single news channel last night!'

There is a general chorus of agreement.

'Nothing like that, boss.' Kashi, always awkward when praised, goes a little pink around the ear tips and gestures to the chaat-wallah for a plate of shakkarkandi chaat. 'Masala tez,' he says, as he drops down to sit on the low boundary wall. 'Nimbu zyaada.'

'Should we deal you in, sir?' asks another driver. 'Fancy a game?'

'Just one,' Kashi agrees, smiling. 'My Uber will be here soon. How much is the buy-in?'

He raises his eyebrows at the steepness of the stakes, but hands a note of the correct denomination to the 'banker', and pops a chunk of chaat into his mouth.

It is the first slow day he's had in months.

His client, Geeta Nagar Jhuggi Colony Dwellers, has finally been allotted a massive amount in compensation from the Supreme Court for the unauthorized demolition of their shanties thirty-six months ago. The Municipal Corporation has grudgingly coughed up the money. The judgement is a landmark one, and will set a precedent for several such cases all over the country.

Kashi fans out his cards (he's been dealt a pure sequence and two jokers) and gives a contented sigh. How pleasant it is to sit in the winter sun with no set agenda, with this sweet bunch of guys for company, relishing the nimbu-laced taste of smoky-sweet shakkarkandi, and thinking about how tomorrow he and Kuhu will be in Goa, finally taking a much delayed two-week holiday! Life couldn't possibly get better.

And then it does. His phone rings.

Kashi grabs it.

'Hey …' His voice is a deep caress. 'All set? Packing for Goa?'

The musical voice at the end is unusually sombre.
'Kash, there's a problem.'

Twenty minutes later, it is a rather tight-lipped and taut-jawed Kashi who steps into his Uber and sets off for the Delhi Turf Club.

When the grounds of the DTC roll smoothly up outside his left window, his face grows a little less stormy.

His eyes fill with a sort of resentful wistfulness – how much he had loved this place as a child! The tennis courts, the library, the pool, and later, as he grew older, the gym and the Thursday night bar scene. If somebody had told him then that there would come a time when he would go without dropping in at the Club for three whole years, that too while living four kilometres away from it, he would have just laughed in disbelief.

'Kashi baba! After so many days!' says the security guard after Kashi pays off the Uber and strolls in through the main gate. 'No more long tennis?'

They have a little chat about the state of the nation, then Kashi takes the shortcut through the Lady Darlington Swimming Bath, aka the swimming pool, passing a sign that declares: NO SERVANTS, AYAHS OR GUNMEN BEYOND THIS POINT. The place is practically still practicing apartheid, he thinks, as he crosses the stuffed leopards snarling inside glass cages in the main lobby. Founded in 1844 by bored British housewives, and stormed during the mutiny of 1857, it is still living with its head completely up its own arse – more a symbolic seat of power than the Red Fort would ever be, a citadel of rulers totally disconnected from the rest of the country, who, thanks to Kaya Skin Clinic and Blonde Highlights from L'Oréal Paris, have managed to become almost indistinguishable from the British who built the place. Like the pigs walking upright at the end of *Animal Farm*, Kashi had told his sister fancifully when she'd called to set up this meeting.

She hadn't been amused.

'Oh, stop being such a self-righteous little choot, Kashi,' she'd growled. 'You can't avoid the club forever! It's *too* conveniently located! Dadi loves it and she's *really* old now – and it's the only place Mom and Dad can afford to buy booze at, so cut the commie JNU shit and just meet us there! You can't spend your whole *life* hiding from Bambi Todi!'

He had stoutly denied hiding from anyone, of course, but as he now enters the sprawling, sunlit, dahlia-edged lawns at the back of the main bungalow, and inhales the well-remembered Sunday morning bouquet of candyfloss, tandoor smoke and strong beer, he has to admit that maybe his big sister had, as usual, stabbed mercilessly right into the throbbing crux of the matter.

He looks around warily. All of Delhi seems to be at the DTC today. The lawns are awash in silk cravats, pashmina shawls and designer sunglasses. People are sitting on white wicker armchairs around low glass tables, eating and drinking like the world is going to end tomorrow. Hotdogs, shaami kebabs, momos, French fries, kathi rolls, chhole bhature, paneer tikkas, beer, whisky, vodka, gin, you name it – fathers, mothers, toddlers, grandpas and grandmas, hot girls and hopeful boys are all going for it with full gusto. The only new addition to the scene are random bunches of multicoloured helium balloons on all the food stalls, bobbing on white satin ribbons secured with smooth, white pebbles.

That's a bit extra, Kashi thinks, amused. Actually, this whole place is frikking extra. And where is the Dogra contingent, anyway?

A knot of posh young women, dressed in body-con polo necks, miniskirts and Ugg boots, spot him and stop sipping their bloody Marys.

'Look!'

'Kashi Dogra! Wow, he *never* comes to the club!'

'*Cute!* Who's he?'

'Bambi T's ex. He left TVVS and went off to The Doon School in class seven.'

'Bloody Doon. All the cutest boys go off there as soon as their growth spurt hits. So Bambi dated *him*? Before Anshul?'

'Ya.'

'And after Anshul died, he never tried to slide back in?'

'*No*, ya. Anshul's death *devastated* Bambi. Besides, he's got a GF now. Some NGO type.'

'Damn. All the cute ones are taken.'

Meanwhile, Kashi, unaware of all this scrutiny, notices with interest that the old plant nursery next to the pool has been converted into what appears to be a gym. The view of

gleaming new machines through the grilled glass windows is
enticing enough to make him saunter over.

Entering the large sunny space, he emits a low, impressed
whistle. This new gym is *fancy*. There's a spaceship-ish
looking Precor multi-station with twelve different exercise
settings, a rowing machine, the mandatory treadmills and
cross-trainers, but as Kashi is a free weights guy, his eyes are
drawn to the extremely well-stocked dumbbell and bumper
plate rack, and a bench press so alluring it makes his mouth
water. Its body is solid yet sleek, the leather of the bench is
a deep supple red, and the Olympic-sized black, urethane-
coated plates are as smooth and lickable as butter. The bar
itself, resting in its grooved slot above the bench, is a textured,
matte silver that makes his palms itch and his fingers curl
instinctively.

There are benefits to the DTC membership after all.

'What's upstairs?' he asks the rather superior looking
trainer who has materialized silently at his side.

'An exercise hall, sir. We hold yoga, Zumba and mixed
martial arts classes there.'

'Naice, bro! But where have all the gym rats gone?'

'To the Housie, sir!' The trainer gestures resignedly to
the balloons tied in gay bunches to the window grills in all
four corners of the gym, and Kashi notices that they are all
stamped with the words BUMPER TAMBOLA. 'Cash prizes
worth fifty lakh.'

Shit, Kashi remembers suddenly, that's where the fam
must be!

He bids goodbye to the snooty trainer, ducks out of the gym and heads purposefully for the East Lawn. Hopefully, he won't get yelled at too badly – it's only half past noon after all, and surely they'll award him an A for effort for his clean clothes and the smooth shave Fridaus has given him …

'*Kashi?*'

Akash freezes.

'HEY, Kaaaaaasheeeeee!!!'

His feet drag to a halt.

Much to his disgust, his heart starts to slam against his ribs, loud and hard.

Pathetic.

Well, he knew this was bound to happen. The Delhi Turf Club is *her* turf. This is where she rules.

La Bambi.

Bambi Todi.

BT, bro BT, the Doscos would say with a shudder. Bad *bad* trip! Dogra ka BT ho gaya. Poor fucker. She sucked him and chucked him like a marrow bone. So much for her being a pure vegetarian.

Should he just … ignore her? Act like he hasn't heard? Like he's too busy and important, with grown-up shit to do, and cases to close, and a hot girlfriend waiting for him? Like he hasn't been stuck in some sort of sick, numbed purgatory ever since she dumped his ass three years ago?

Good idea. He unfreezes, and seeks to set one foot in front of another in the direction of the East Lawn.

But his body has a different plan.

Fuck off, boi, it says mildly as it turns around of its own volition and starts to walk towards Bambi's voice, which is still calling out his name like a siren on a rock.

And so Akash has no option but to resign himself to the inevitable, smile, and call out, as suavely as he can.

'Heyyy, Bambi Todi! How've you *been*?'

She throws out her arms then and does that mandatory little screaming dance of joy that girls always seem to do when they see you after a long time. It gives him ample time to walk over to her all slow and casual, like there is no angry, unsteady beat to his heart, no queer sort of gladness in his veins, no quickening of his pulse as he makes skimming, tentative eye contact with her, testing to see if the scar tissue he's managed to grow since they last met is going to hold up to the occasion.

How can such a small person create so much upheaval in one's internal workings, he wonders for the hundredth time. Bambi Todi is a five-foot package, the colour of powdered cinnamon, delicately and delectably curvy, with a bright smile and huge eyes, a small snub nose and masses of softly curling brown hair. She has tied a red-checked apron over her cut-off denim overalls, and is standing beside a table holding a confused but cheerful display of vegetables and fruit, a large mixer-grinder, and two shiny, bright red gumboots from which are protruding untidy bunches of bright yellow sunflowers.

Love, love me do!
You know I love you!
I'll always Beetroot!

So pleeeeeese, love me do! declares the bright hand-painted banner above her head.

Ghanta, you'll always be true, Kashi wants to say, but what emerges from his mouth instead is, 'You look like a picnic.'

He tries to say this casually, but it comes out sort of wobbly-intense.

She looks momentarily discomfited, then recovers, tucking a soft, unruly ringlet of hair behind her ear.

'Come buy some organic beetroot grown right here at the DTC,' she orders him in the clear sweet voice he remembers so well. 'C'mon, step up, show me the big bucks you've been earning since you left law school! It's all going to charity!'

'There's mud on your nose,' he tells her in a more natural voice as he digs into his pockets for his wallet.

She grins cheerfully. 'Perks of the job. I've spent the whole morning digging up the finest produce from the DTC kitchen garden with my main men here!'

She indicates her two assistants, also wearing red-checked aprons. Kashi nods at them in a friendly way.

'But where's Guppie Ram ji?' he asks. 'He's the resident garden fairy at the DTC, isn't it?'

The garrulous old gardener had befriended Bambi and Kashi when they were kids, picking out leaves and flowers and bird feathers for their science homework, helping them build a treehouse, and even organizing a most solemn burial for a dead baby squirrel once.

Bambi's face falls slightly. 'He died,' she says. 'Didn't you know?'

Kashi shakes his head. 'No. Shit.'

'You haven't been here for ages, have you?'

He nods.

There's a small pause.

In a resolutely gay voice, Bambi addresses her assistants. 'Guys, say hello to Kashi Dogra, mere bachpan ka dost!'

They smile at him.

'Sir, take juice?'

A disproportionately black wave of resentment sweeps over Kashi at this glib introduction. Mere bachpan ka dost? *My childhood friend?* Is that what you call somebody who was your 'best guy friend' right through high school, somebody you spoke to every night, sometimes from midnight to six in the morning, whom you claimed to love and promoted to boyfriend in college, whom you went to three-and-a-half bases with? He tells himself he's overreacting and manages to somehow bite down on the bile, but his eyes, when he looks up again after extracting some notes from his wallet, are decidedly cool.

'Sure,' he replies indifferently to the assistant.

'*Heyyy*, guys!! What's *upppp?*'

Kashi almost drops his wallet. A horde of ex-TVVS girls has descended on them, and he is suddenly drowning in a flurry of effusive, scented hugs, straightened hair and curious eyes.

He studied with these girls from nursery to class seven, but even then he has never been able to get their names straight. They're all called Pia/Kia/Tia/Sia/Dia/Lia – and so naturally, they'd ended up being nicknamed the Ghia-Lauki gang. They're in full attendance today – except for one, who had an arranged marriage with a major movie star a couple of years ago and vanished from the Delhi scene forever.

He hugs them all dutifully and listens as they tell him that they've been well, that they all did their graduation from the States and have come back to work in their family businesses. Two of them have got married. And Sia's having a birthday party soon with lots of the old TVVS gang from school. Bambi's already promised to come – would he like to come too?

Would I like to kill myself, Kashi thinks wryly. If the DTC is a bubble of privilege, then the old TVVS gang is a bubble within a bubble – a hardened Perspex shell, suffocating, unbreakable.

'Bring your girlfriend,' one of them adds slyly, which, Kashi notes with a little rush of exultation, makes Bambi narrow her eyes and flare her nostrils in a gesture he knows all too well.

'She's in Kalahandi,' he replies. 'We're doing the long-distance thing.'

'Awww, that *sucks*!' commiserates a Sia/Pia/Ria/Tia. 'Is the time difference really intense?'

'Ohmygod, Kalahandi's in *India*, Tia!' Bambi snaps. 'In Odisha. Why do you not know that?'

Tia widens her eyes. 'The point is why do *you* know that, babe? Been stalking him much?'

They all scream with laughter and walk away. Bambi glares after them disgustedly.

'Why are they always so *mean* to me?'

'Uh, you weren't particularly nice to them,' he points out.

She grimaces, looking slightly guilty. The insinuation that she's been stalking him hangs unaddressed between them.

'Oh, just buy some juice!' she says finally, sounding rather fed-up.

Kashi nods, moving in closer. 'Which one would you recommend?'

'Are you very happy with Miss Kalahandi?'

The question comes without any context, in typical artless Bambi Todi style.

'Kuhu.' Kashi corrects her automatically. 'Yes – yes, I am.'

'Then have the chukkandar juice.' She grabs a bunch of beets and drops them into the mixer. 'Beetroot is a fibre-dense superfood, packed with inorganic nitrates, and great for lowering blood pressure!' She adds some mint leaves, ginger, and sliced apple, shuts the lid, leans on it, and flips a button. As the mixer starts to roar, she shouts above it. 'Also, it turns all your um … body secretions pink! A nice little surprise for your next video call with the GF!'

Several people look around. Bambi giggles, and defiantly stares them down.

Same old no-fucks-given Bambi, Akash thinks resignedly as she turns the mixer off, pours the frothy concoction into a clear glass and offers it to him with a flourish. It glows a deep red in the winter sun.

Feeling like he's sliding backwards in time, he takes the glass from her.

'I recommend that you go buy a large vodka and spike it,' she leans forward and says softly. 'Oh, and get me one too. I'm bloody expiring over here!'

'Come get it with me,' he hears himself say impulsively. 'Can't your assistants handle the show for a bit?'

She hesitates, her eyes skimming about her stall, then coming back to rest on him doubtfully.

Why the hell is he persisting with this? He's done with her, she's dead to him. He had been perfectly happy and at peace only half an hour ago!

He leans in, his voice persuasive. 'Come *on*, Bambino.'

She hesitates, then shakes her head. 'This is the busiest part of the day ...'

'You need a break!' Kashi hears himself say firmly. His hands rise, as if to untie the apron from around the back of her neck, his fingertips tingling in anticipation of touching the soft, well-remembered brown hair.

Then he steps back and shoves his hands into his pockets. 'Just ten minutes? Maybe we'll win fifty lakhs!'

She closes her eyes and rocks on her heels for a moment, dithering, then gives a quick, decided nod, whips off her apron and grabs his arm. As she smiles up at him, sunshine on her face, he remembers the smallness of her and how incredibly manly that had always made him feel.

'Come!' she says.

2

Rasputin

A rapt silence rules over the East Lawn. More than a thousand people are bent over their tambola tickets, completely attentive. When Akash approaches the Dogra family table with Bambi in tow, Natasha's eyes widen speculatively, but she's too swamped to comment. Her hair has escaped from its neatly coiled bun and she looks a little crazy.

'Help me!' she whispers urgently, thrusting tickets in their faces. 'We've got ten tickets to mark! I'm barely able to keep up!'

Her son stops sucking on the straw of his Fanta long enough to look up at Bambi and state, with polite firmness, 'Nana's going to vote for Behra Mehra, not the stinky cheese lady. Move along please!'

'Dhan!' Brig. Dogra is appalled. 'Don't say Behra Mehra!'

'Don't say stinky cheese lady either!' adds his wife.

'Yes, of course, of course. The lady isn't stinky,' the brigadier explains earnestly to Bambi. 'The *cheese* is.'

Bambi smiles at him sympathetically.

'Have a lot of ladies been nagging you to vote for Urvashi auntie, uncle?'

He looks here and there in a harassed manner. 'No ... no ... nothing like that ...'

'*Hullo* Bambi beta!' Mrs Mala Dogra's voice is so disproportionately affectionate that the Dogra siblings look at each other and cringe.

But then—

'*Hullo* Mala auntie!' Bambi beams right back at Mrs Mala Dogra with equal effusiveness.

'Your parents aren't here?' Mrs Mala Dogra wants to know and Bambi's high-beam smile dims a little. She replies that her mother's in the US, visiting her brother, but her Dad will definitely show up for the voting tomorrow.

'Sorry I'm late, Dadi!' Kashi says as he drops down cross-legged on the grass in front of his grandmother's wheelchair. He studies her tickets. 'Wah, you're doing well!'

'Jaldi five and four corners and top line–bottom line are already over,' Natasha fills them in. 'But middle line and full house are still on!'

'Shusssh!' the brigadier hisses. 'Focus on the calling!'

Dirty stares are being directed at the noisy new arrivals from several of the other tables. Bambi and Kashi exchange comical looks and subside.

'Still in my twenties, twenty-nine!' intones the familiar voice of Club Secretary Srivastava. The bulldog-y old man has been calling out the tambola numbers for as long as Kashi can remember. *'Two and nine, twenty-nine!'*

This is followed by the rhythmic, well-remembered sound of the wooden number balls tumbling inside their wire-frame cage. It's a sound Kashi would've recognized anywhere in the world.

He doesn't have twenty-nine. Or thirty-seven or fifty-three, which are the numbers that are called subsequently.

But as he sits there in the grass next to Bambi Todi and stares down at the bright pink tambola tickets in his hands, he acknowledges that he is tingling all the way to the tips of his fingers with a sort of helpless, giddy exhilaration. Happy gas, Nattu would say, with a warning waggle of the index finger and a knowing shake of the head. Hugely addictive and very deceptive – as close to the real thing as broken glass is to diamonds. Never trust that shit, little bro.

Unfortunately, she had yet to give him all this gyaan when he was five years old and heart-whole, standing by the Lady Darlington Swimming Bath in his electric-blue swim trunks, all excited about his first swimming class. The inflatable arm band of the small, brown girl standing next to him – a pink-and-white polka-dotted affair, he still recalls – had gone phuss and she asked him to blow it up for her. When he handed it back, turgidly inflated, she had smiled at him, revealing the winsome gaps between her teeth. The hit of the happy gas had been so intense that as she watched open-mouthed, he had cannonballed into the water out of sheer animal excitement, causing a mighty splash that drenched her completely.

They'd ended up on the same school bus a year later. He had been sitting alone by a window when she walked over and sat down next to him like it was the most natural thing in the world. Ten years later, she had reached up and kissed him like that was the most natural thing in the world too.

'*Theme for a dream, sweet sixteen! One and six, sixteen!*'

His grandmother digs him in the ribs, dragging him back to the present.

'Sixteen,' she indicates, blinking and pointing a wavering finger at the ticket in his hand. 'We have that.'

'Awesome Dadi!' Kashi punches the ticket, then turns to look up at her curiously. 'But how are you able to hear the calling? Your hearing aid isn't even—'

She pokes him with a bony finger, directing him to look up. Her eyes are starry and her cheeks very pink.

'No listening, Kashoo, *looking!*'

Kashi looks up to the stage, and realizes that though the old tambola wire-frame cage and the brightly coloured number balls are still the same, and so is old Mr Srivastava, there has been at least one daring innovation to the ancient ritual that is the DTC Bumper Tambola. A dark, muscular and strikingly attractive man is holding up the numbers – drawn on two-foot-high, black-and-white placards – as they are being called.

'Hey, cool!' says Kashi.

'Thank you,' Bambi whispers. 'It was my idea.'

Kashi wonders uneasily whether the casting call had been hers too.

Probably in his mid-thirties, the man on stage is dressed in a fitted dark blazer, loose black dhoti pants, and has a muffler bundled tightly around his neck. His thick hair is pulled back from his high forehead into a messy man-bun that somehow emphasizes the chiselled, sensuous masculinity of his features and the hypnotic pull of his hooded eyes. As he puts down 1 and 6, and picks up 7 and 4 and holds them aloft instead, his movements have a smooth, fluid, slightly animal quality. He pivots from left to right, showing the numbers to each section of the lawn clearly. As he flashes white teeth in a smile that lights up his dark, exotic face, Kashi realizes that he knows him.

'Arrey! That's … Lokesh … no … Lambodar?'

'Mahadev.' Old Mrs Dogra smiles dreamily. Then she folds her hands and bows reverentially in the direction of the man on the stage. 'Om Namah Shiva.'

Natasha smothers a snort of laughter. 'He *does* look a bit like the hotter renditions of Shiva, actually,' she whispers. 'It's the hooded eyes, and the man-bun, and the cobra-like muffler. D'you think Dadi's nursing a crush?'

Bambi giggles. 'On Leo?'

Kashi frowns. 'His name's Leo?'

She nods. 'Leo Matthew. Isn't he decorative? He's part Jamaican, part desi.'

'Oh, but—' Kashi starts to speak, then goes silent.

'What?' Bambi prompts.

Kashi shakes his head. 'Nothing.'

Leo is holding up another number now. His muscles ripple beneath his tightly fitted coat. Old Mrs Dogra sighs gustily.

The brigadier lets out a short grunt. 'Ridiculous ape. Gigolo.'

'*Daddy!*' Natasha is scandalized. 'That's not nice.'

'Yes, Balbir uncle, Leo isn't sleeping with anybody for money as far as I know,' Bambi chimes in.

'I know a bloody Rasputin when I see one,' the brigadier replies tersely.

'What's bloodyrasp you teen?' Dhan asks interestedly.

'Dhan, finish your drink,' his mother snaps. 'Leo's a legit, highly sought-after personal trainer who conducts some classes in functional training, body combat and Zumba at the DTC gym. Daddy's just being appallingly regressive, that's all.'

'D'you go for his classes, Nattu?' Kashi asks.

'My mornings are spent at The Wonder Years,' she replies resignedly, 'wondering where my years went.'

'That's my school,' Dhan informs the table.

'Wonderful.' Kashi turns to Bambi. 'What about you?'

'I pay up regularly.' She rolls her eyes. 'But I barely go. They're at six-thirty in the morning – who is even awake then?'

On the stage, Leo is now holding up a 0 and a 2.

'*Runner's up, number two!*' says Mr Srivastava. '*Only two, number two!*'

'We don't have that either,' Natasha grumbles. 'On *any* of our ten tickets! How is that even possible?'

Right then there is a muted call of 'Middle line' and a portly man in a red-and-white striped sweater puts up his hand. The crowd wilts, then revives philosophically. There's still the Full House, after all.

On stage, Mr Srivastava's jowly face splits into a spectacularly dentured smile.

'Ah yes! A claim for the middle line, which today, is worth ten lakh! Come right up here, sir!'

'Who's he?' Mrs Mala Dogra nudges her husband.

He shakes his head. 'Must be somebody's guest. I don't know the fellow.'

As the man in the red-and-white striped sweater starts to walk to the stage, smiling shyly, a nasal voice sounds triumphantly from the far end of the lawn. 'Middle line! Middle line completed over here!'

The crowd murmurs, removes its designer sunglasses, and swivels around to look at this new claimant.

He is on his feet – a narrow-shouldered, wide-hipped man with thinning hair, a black shirt and yellow suspenders.

The brigadier raises his eyebrows.

'Here's a tamasha, I say!' he murmurs. 'That's Mukki Khurana – Urvashi Khurana's husband!'

His wife looks around interestedly. 'What will happen now, Balbir?'

He grunts. 'If they both have middle lines, they'll have to split the prize. Fifty-fifty. So five lakh each, instead of a cool ten. Still, it's something!'

On stage, old Mr Srivastava is looking unperturbed. 'And we may have a tie!' he exclaims. 'Yes, yes, come forward, let's check both tickets please!'

Both claimants hand their tickets to Leo, then stand beside the stage to await Srivastava's verdict.

There is a discussion between Leo and Srivastava. It starts off quietly, but becomes loud and growly really fast. Finally, the Club Secretary snatches the two tickets from Leo in a manner that is so aggressive that the latter steps back haughtily, crossing his arms across his chest.

'This is a shit show,' he says, quite audibly.

The crowd begins to bubble and boil.

Mukesh Khurana steps forward, snatches the two tickets from Srivastava and compares them. Then he grabs the mic from the old man.

'Cheating!' he cries in a shrill, aggrieved voice. 'Cheating! The two tickets are the exact-same!'

Consternation sweeps the crowd. Everybody turns to look at each other.

'But that's impossible!'

'The game's rigged!'

'Ya, but there's still no need to for Mukki to *shout*. He's not selling vegetables in Azadpur mandi, you know.'

'The gigolo has bungled it,' the brigadier says disgustedly. 'Too busy prancing around showing off his body to hold up the correct numbers properly!'

Kashi frowns. 'Dad, don't be rude.'

Mrs Mala Dogra shoots her husband a warning look.

He changes tack. 'Or maybe the first guy got a bogey,' he says placatingly. 'He anyway looks like a bloody doodhwala.'

His grandson chuckles delightedly. 'Bloodyrasp you teen! Bloody doodhwala!'

'Balbir, please,' Mrs Mala Dogra hisses. 'It's because you talk in that obnoxious way that Kashi thinks the club is snobbish!'

But Kashi's mind is on something else. He shakes his head, confused. 'What *am* I missing?'

'There can't *be* two identical tickets,' Natasha explains. 'Every tambola ticket is ... *has* to be unique. Like a lottery ticket. Two identical tickets implies either an error – or deliberate rigging.'

On the stage, old Mr Srivastava holds up both hands. 'One moment ... one moment ... we will just sort all this out ...'

'I was here first!' the man in the striped sweater steps forward with tentative aggression.

'So what?' Khurana starts snapping his suspenders menacingly. 'I also completed at the same moment you did!'

'But fastest finger first.' Sweater Guy sticks to his guns valiantly.

'We're not playing *KBC*,' Khurana retorts. He turns to face the crowd. 'Does Srivastava look like Amitabh Bachchan to you?' he asks with a loud neighing laugh.

Kashi raises his eyebrows. 'What a gem of a guy. Is his wife like this too?'

Bambi bites her lip. 'Urvashi auntie's really nice. I wish she were here ...'

'I was here first.' Sweater Guy turns to appeal to Leo. 'Wasn't I, bhaisaab?'

Leo nods and pats his back. 'Yes, indeed, you were.'

'And *even* though I was here first, I don't mind splitting the ten lakh with this gentleman!'

'Or you could arm wrestle,' Leo suggests half-jokingly.

'Can I please *speak*?' Bulldog-y old Srivastava struggles to re-establish his authority. 'I have been calling out the tambola numbers these thirty years—'

Khurana swings around to face him, providing the crowd with a perfect view of the magnificent wedgie he has given himself with all the suspender snapping. 'You've been rigging it for thirty years, you mean!'

'Hullo ... take it easy, uncle,' Leo steps forward, inserting his powerful frame between Khurana and the shaky old man.

It's like he's held a lit match to petrol-doused wood. Mukki explodes.

'*You* be quiet!' he hisses with disproportionate venom. 'Bloody item number!'

The crowd gasps. People turn to each other. Whispers turn to full-on babble.

'Well, that escalated fast,' Kashi says to the girls. 'Do these guys have history?'

Natasha and Bambi exchange glances.

'There've been some ... rumours,' Bambi admits. 'About Leo ... and ... uh ... Mukesh Khurana's wife.'

Kashi chuckles, amused. 'The lady candidate? Your Urvashi auntie?'

'Don't laugh,' Bambi whispers, worried. 'She's the star of Leo's Zumba class and her husband hates it.'

On the stage, Leo is holding up one hand, veins throbbing in his forehead.

'Watch your mouth, old man.'

'You watch *your* mouth!' Mukki draws to his full height, managing to reach almost up to Leo's nipples. 'This man is your known-to! You know him! You've rigged it so he wins!'

Leo shakes his head in exasperation.

'I don't know this man from Adam!'

'I don't know him either!' Sweater Guy says shrilly. 'I've never met him before in my life!'

'O ya, O ya?' Mukki, at a loss for words, makes up for it by snapping his suspenders again.

'It's like watching a chihuahua take on a Dobermann,' Natasha whispers, riveted. 'You've got to give it to Mukki – he's got guts.'

Kashi looks a little wistful. 'I'd love to go up there and O-Ya-O-Ya with him!'

His sister pinches his arm hard. '*You* sit here quietly!'

On stage, Leo seems torn between fury and laughter.

'Dude, what exactly is your *problem*?'

'Don't use that tone with me!' Mukki pants. 'Bloody outsider! Bloody PT master! *Hired help!*'

'Okay, that's it!' Kashi jumps lightly to his feet.

'Akash, don't get involved,' the brigadier rumbles warningly, but Kashi is already striding towards the stage, pushing up the sleeves of his navy-blue sweater to display well-defined, sinewy forearms. The Ghia-Lauki gang low-key cheer him as he passes. He flashes them a grin. Supreme Court regulars would have recognized that trademark cocky courtroom grin.

'Gentlemen! A little gentleness, please!'

His voice is deep, pleasant and authoritative.

The tableau on stage whirls to eye him belligerently.

'Tu kaun hai, bay?' Mukki snarls. 'Who the hell are you? Your middle line also came or what?'

This draws a laugh from the crowd.

'Go Mukki!' somebody hoots. A few people clap.

'Akash!' Leo is looking surprised and a little wary. 'You hang with *this* crowd?'

'My dad's a member,' Kashi admits sheepishly.

'Akash who?' Mukki glares from one to the other. 'Who the hell are you?'

'I'm Leo Matthew's lawyer,' is Kashi's cool reply. 'I've been studying your language and your demeanour from my seat in the audience, and I'm confident Leo can sue you, *and* your precious club—'

Brigadier Dogra chokes on his beer.

'—for libel, defamation, character assassination, manhandling and criminal intimidation. For *way* more than ten lakh.'

There is stunned silence both on the stage and off it. Then Leo chuckles deeply and holds up his right palm to Kashi, who grins back and slaps it.

'Har har Mahadevvv!' yells old Mrs Dogra, with sudden and supreme aggression, rising shakily to her feet. Bambi and Natasha leap up to placate her.

'Dadi, shhhh!'

'Everything's *fine*.'

Mukki's voice rises to a thin nasal scream. 'You will sue *me*? *You* will sue me? You will *sue* me?'

'It's not talaaq you know,' Kashi drawls, turning to face him. 'You don't have to repeat it three tim—'

But Mukki isn't listening. 'He's not even a *member*!'

'Which means he's probably a decent person,' Kashi retorts.

'O ya?' Mukki snaps his suspenders combatively.

'O ya!' replies Kashi, now hugely enjoying himself.

Mukki licks his lips. 'I know the best lawyers in this country! I know the whole gourmint! I know …' His eyes dart this way and that. 'I know *everybody*! Oho!' He chuckles pleasurably. 'I will screw you two *completely*—'

'Or we could just split the winnings fifty-fifty and finish this right here,' the man in the red-and-white sweater whom everybody has forgotten about interjects plaintively. 'Sharing kar lete hain na, bhaisaab?'

This appeal gives Mukki pause. He licks his lips again.

'Yeah dude, just *share*,' Leo's tone is patient and perhaps just slightly patronizing.

Again, it has a galvanizing effect on Mukki. He turns to face the much taller man, rising to his toes. 'I don't *share*,' he spits, breathing heavily. 'I've never shared *anything*.'

There is an odd, pregnant pause. Kashi, standing so close to Leo, senses an internal struggle taking place inside the large, powerful body.

It was like a horned, black Leo was battling a halo-ed, white Leo, he tells his sister later.

The horned Leo wins.

His handsome face curling into a sneer that's decidedly unpleasant, he leans in closer to Mukki Khurana.

'*That's what you think*,' he whispers tauntingly.

There is a collective gasp from the crowd.

Khurana utters a loud, wordless scream and charges in, fists flailing wildly. Leo throws one contemptuous punch, and drops him instantly to the ground.

'Darling, it was absolutely *appalling*. They were abusing and hitting each other in front of everybody.'

'How too delicious! I can't believe I missed it. What a day to go to the spa!'

The two Zumba buddies are tapping out WhatsApp messages thick and fast with exquisitely manicured fingers on their respective phones, while their two long, smooth cars speed down different roads in Lutyens' Delhi, set to converge at the DTC in about seven minutes for Leo Matthew's early morning class.

'Serves you right for wanting to look like a hoor on Election Day, Cookie! You should've sacrified the denting-painting and come for the tambola only. At least you would've witnessed the tamasha of the year!'

'Are you SURE you aren't exaggerating, Rosh?'

'Babe, I swear! Mukki Khurana said I've never shared *anything*, Leo said, that's what you think, and then Mukki screamed and went for Leo and Leo knocked him down!'

'He actually hit him in the face? Matlab dishoom dishoom? Full-on mukka-mukki?

'Haan haan, Cookie, I'm *telling* you! Khoon all over the kilim-kaleens.'

To underline her point, Roshni releases a series of fist emojis at the end of her message.

'Is he *maaaad*? Does he want her to lose the election?'

'Maybe he does, Cooks. The size of that man's ego is inversely proportional to the size of his cock.'

Cookie gives a loud snort of laughter. Unseen to her, her impassive driver winces slightly.

'I am SO disappointed in you, Rosh!' She adds a line of bright yellow crying faces for emphasis. 'How could you not get a video?'

'I KNOW!' Roshni punches out a line of little panda bears face-palming. 'It all happened too fast, ya. Otherwise you know me – would I ever let such a moment go unrecorded?'

'How come Leo's still taking his class like this whole kaand hasn't even happened?'

'That's Leo for you! I was SO surprised when he sent the message for the six-thirty class. You've got to admire the man's cheek.'

'Cheeks, you mean.' Cookie taps out at once. 'Butt cheeks.' She adds a little row of red hearts and panting faces.

'Dirty girl! Have you reached?'

'Ya ya, waiting in the parking. Hurry, na. I want to be in the front row today. If he has bruises, I can ask him about it. All innocently.'

And she signs off with an angelic halo face and a wicked wink.

Presently, the two friends emerge from their expensive cars and wave to each other. They are dressed in Nike trainers, Lulu Lemon pants and crop-tops the colour of summer sorbets. Their hair is pulled back from their faces in shiny ponytails and their eyebrows are finely plucked. Though both are in their early fifties, they could be taken, at a distance, for thirty-five.

Ro, the taller, thinner of the two, all tightened skin and nude lipstick, lets out a little scream. 'Oh my God, you're *glowing*! The gold facial has done wonders, babe!'

Cookie, smaller, rounder, pink-mouthed, responds with a wicked grin. 'This glow isn't from gold, it's from the gossip! Lovely, lovely gossip! Tell more!'

Roshni tightens her ponytail. 'Arrey, I already told you everything. Next episode will play out now. Urvi's coming for class. She responded with a thumbs up to Leo's message.'

Cookie gives a little gasp. 'Oh my God, she's going to brazen it out, is she?'

Roshni shrugs. 'What choice does she have? The election's today! It's her last chance to suck up to us! But yeah, you're right – it takes guts to show up like nothing's happened!'

They run down the pillared veranda to the gym.

'Leo's bike is here.' Cookie nods to the Hayabusa parked on the road on the other side of the veranda railing. 'Hurry, we'll get to see him changing shirts!'

They both laugh as they enter the gym.

An EDM track is pumping loudly on the speakers. Leo is clearly in the middle of his one-hour personal workout.

'Good morning!' Roshni calls out cheerily, more than usual perhaps – it's always a bit awkward to act naturally in front of somebody you've just been gossiping about.

There's no reply.

The two women exchange looks, smothering guilty giggles. Usually, when they walk into the gym for this class, Leo's wrapping up his workout, which he does alone every morning. In fact, there's been a lot of giggly talk among the DTC Zumba girls about how, if you come early enough, you can begin the day with a blessed darshan of him in all his sweaty splendour, bench-pressing like a beast.

'Leeeeo?'

No answer.

Bopping to the peppy beat, they look around the various aisles of the gym. The multi-station is unoccupied, and so is the row of treadmills. They swivel around to the rowing machines and ab-isolators but he isn't there either.

And then, as an insistent, electronic beat drop kicks in on the speakers, they spot him. On the bench press Kashi Dogra had admired the morning before. Lying on the deep-red leather bench on his back, with his legs stretched out on either side, his metallic neon green water bottle standing beside his sneakered feet.

Cookie grips Ro's arm. 'He's wearing the camouflage tracks,' she whispers. 'That means he must be wearing—'

'The tightie-whitie racerback vest!'

They both giggle and tiptoe closer.

Leo *is* wearing the sleeveless white vest. His smooth, brown, muscular torso is shiny with sweat, the veins on his forearms and shoulders are standing out clearly. His hair is pulled back into its usual samurai topknot. He looks like a life-size superhero action figure – or one of those gorgeous

American GI Joe dolls with every muscle lovingly etched and defined.

Except that a gleaming silver barbell stacked with a hundred and twenty kilograms worth of plates is pressed against his windpipe, pinioning him to the red-leather upholstered bench, cutting off all air.

The mighty chest is still straining upwards, fully inflated, but the head lolls sideways unnaturally. The sweaty corded neck is contorted to an impossible angle, and purpling with contusions. There can be no doubt about it – the glorious action figure is pathetically, irretrievably broken.

The dead eyes protrude from their sockets slightly, staring blankly at the two women.

Cookie and Ro emit ear-piercing screams.

'Leo?'

'*Leo!*'

They scramble forward, sobbing a little with shock and horror, struggling with nausea.

'He's still warm ... oh God, oh shit, what the fuck happened here, Ro?'

'Help me!' Roshni's voice is desperate. 'Maybe we can still help him – let's get the plates off ...'

They drop to their knees on one side of the prone figure, remove the clips that secure the plates in place and slide them off the bar. The freed bar rises up into the air, and can be pivoted off the broken body.

'Leo!' they call urgently as they remove it. 'Leo!

Cookie lifts one clammy, lifeless forearm to feel for a pulse. After a few moments, she shakes her head.

'There's nothing here, nothing. *I feel nothing at all!*'

Tears fill her eyes as she looks at her friend in the mirrored wall. They are both reflected there, suddenly looking much closer to their actual ages in spite of their girlish clothes and ponytails.

'He's dead. Quite, quite dead.'

'We need to call his family. Where's his phone? Where's his phone?'

'*There* – oh God, Cookie, it's asking for a fingerprint ID. Should we use it?'

Biting down resolutely on her rising gorge, Roshni gingerly lifts Leo's right hand and places his index finger on the phone screen. With a little musical sound, it unlocks.

'Ugh!' Cookie shudders slightly. 'Now remove the security lock while you're at it. Good, now go to Favourites.'

'It's a man.' Roshni says. 'Rax mobile.'

'Call him then!' Cookie says. 'And Rosh – we should call the Club president too.'

3

Jai Bhavani

'This is *nat* the way, PK,' ACP Bhavani Singh says mildly as he performs meticulous toe-touches as prescribed by the Canadian Air Force's *5 Basic Xercises* booklet in the central park of the Hauz Khas Police Colony. 'You cannat poke your nose in the girl's privacy like this!'

He is a soldierly looking man, close to sixty, with a square, homely face and spiky grey hair, and wearing a navy-blue tracksuit. Beside him, reluctantly performing the toe-touches too, is his subordinate, the much fairer, taller and younger Inspector Padam Kumar, resplendent in a bright yellow Brazil soccer jersey, who, being a single man in possession of a good future, is – following in the best Jane Austen tradition – in want of a wife.

'Mummy says there's nothing wrong in running little bit of background checks, sir.' A stubborn look settles on Padam's cherubic face. 'It is a question of marriage after all! I just used our database to check if she, or her family, have any criminal tendencies.'

'*Everybody* has criminal tendencies, PK,' Bhavani replies. 'You do too, or you would nat be snooping around, using the Crime Branch's official database for personal work!'

Padam Kumar's face reddens. 'I'm an *honest* policeman,' he mutters. 'I don't take any bribes or indulge in any shady deals—'

'You are nat doing the department a *favour* by being honest, PK!' Bhavani responds mildly. 'You are just doing your job!'

Which is all very well for you to say, Padam thinks petulantly, but it is an open secret that apart from you, most of the department is happily on the take!

Bhavani Singh moves on to doing sit-ups while continuing to speak.

He really is quite fit for an old man, Padam Kumar admits silently as he switches to sit-ups too.

'And it was nat just a matter of running a simple background check, was it – you have also had this girl followed by constables and checked out by police informers to find out if she has any boyfriends!'

Padam Kumar says, slightly out of breath, 'Sir, I thought ki just-for-this-once, there was no harm in using the department's facilities to get a clean chit on this girl. She is a very good-looking girl, and so she may have had many admirers and, after all, it is a question of my whole life, sir!'

Bhavani gives an exasperated little exclamation and pauses mid sit-up.

'Accha, so supposing the girl got a dirty chit,' he says. 'Matlab, you found out that she has had some boyfriends. *Then* what?'

Padam Kumar blinks. 'Then I would have caught her in a lie, sir,' he says virtuously. 'Means she is immoral, and untrustworthy – and not good enough to be my wife and mother-of-my-children.'

Bhavani smiles gently. 'But if she had come right out and told you that she has *had* boyfriends, then you would have rejected her, would you nat have, my good and self-righteous PK?'

Padam avoids his superior's gaze, checks his watch, and moves on sulkily to the third basic Xercise – the back extension. Bhavani sir has an English-teacher wife, two daughters and two granddaughters, so he has no choice but to be broadminded. But *I* still have a choice, he thinks mutinously.

As they lie on their stomachs and raise their arms and legs off the ground, alternately arching their backs and sinking back to the floor, he mutters, 'Sir, my family is very traditional ...'

'And you're *just* the man to modernize them!' Aggravatingly, Bhavani is not at all out of breath. 'The cost of the surveillance work you ordered on the girl is going to be deducted from your next pay cheque, and the only reason we are letting you off without a written warning is because we know you honour your mother. But you must learn to honour your future wife also! Or your marriage will be a *very* unhappy one.'

'Yes sir,' PK says miserably, wondering why *he* has to have such a weird boss. Anybody else in the Crime Branch would have understood and condoned his 'crime'. But not Assistant Commissioner of Police Bhavani Singh.

The older man isn't done yet. 'If you *really* want to get to know this girl better, take her for a walk in this nice weather we are having! Let her choose her own meal in a good restaurant, tell her about your failures and your fears and the women *you* have kissed, and then she *herself* will tell you all her secrets!'

As if! Padam Kumar thinks rebelliously as they get on their hands and toes to start on the fourth basic Xercise – push-ups. Why would I pay for an expensive meal for a girl I haven't even finalized yet? *She* should call me to her house and feed me! And *why* would I put such loaded information into my to-be wife's hands! But that's ACP Bhavani for you, he has no concept of the right and proper way of doing things.

Why can't I have a normal boss, Padam Kumar wonders gloomily. Or a *cool* boss. Like in all those *Dabangg* and *Singham* movies? The type who makes criminals piss their pants when he walks into the room? When Bhavani Singh walks into the room, all the crooks leap up grinning, and ask him how his granddaughters are.

'Remember you are nat superior to this girl, PK.' Bhavani is still holding forth. 'No human being is superior to another. *All* are equal.'

This is too much for Padam Kumar, who takes great pride in his badge, and his position as a crusader for law and justice.

'Sir, surely I am superior to a murderer, sir!'

'A murderer can go on to become a saint,' says Bhavani, rising red-faced and finally out of breath to start on the final basic Xercise – jumping jacks alternating with running on the spot. 'And a saint could slip off his pedestal and become a murderer!'

Padam Kumar has heard this particular line several times before. It's one of Bhavani Singh's four golden maxims, neatly penned by his wife (probably before I was born, Padam thinks peevishly) in multicoloured sketch pens upon the pin-up board in his cabin in the Crime Branch cell in Chanakyapuri.

THE FOUR GOLDEN RULES

1. Hitting people will loosen their tongues. Listening to them will open their hearts ♥♥♥
2. 'Every human being is capable of murder. Every saint has a past and every sinner has a future.' – Oscar Wilde
3. Routine work is God's work. Do it religiously.🙏
4. Never strain too hard. Breakthroughs happen organically, in their own sweet time. If you strain, you will only get haemorrhoids in the brain.

Galling though it may be for Padam Kumar to admit, this faded foundation has helped Bhavani achieve an impressive strike rate over the years. And it is generally agreed that in a workplace that is heated, aggressive and unrelentingly stressful, the genial older man is a walking, talking, low-pressure area. He exists in such a calm, unhurried, non-judgemental and totally receptive state that the hot winds of information come whooshing down on him of their own accord.

It is no wonder then that, when the chief receives an urgent phone call from the president of the Delhi Turf Club, he immediately thinks of Bhavani. A steady, mature hand is needed to deal with whatever the fuck is unfolding at the high-profile club, and ACP Singh is clearly the chap for the job.

•———•

Half an hour later, Bhavani is cloistered with the chief in the latter's office, while the still slightly sulky Padam Kumar cools his heels outside.

'What do you know about the Delhi Turf Club, Bhavani?'

'It's like an Amitabh Bachchan, sir,' Bhavani ventures, after considering the hallowed institution for a while. 'Ageing superstar, thoda irrelavent in these times, surviving mostly on reputation.'

The chief chuckles. 'The members would say that's sour grapes talking! But yes, maybe you have a point. There is still weight and snob value in the name, however! All the top faujis and civil services chaps, high-flying lawyers and business , politicians even, regard their DTC membership very highly!'

'Has something happened there, sir?' Bhavani asks.

The chief nods. 'I got a call from the Club President. He's an ex-home secretary of the Government of India. He woke up today to find a dead man on the club premises.' It's probably an accident, but it could be murder – the victim got into fisticuffs with a DTC member yesterday in full public view. Beat the other fellow up pretty badly apparently, so maybe that man decided to exact revenge. Go investigate it ... but gently.'

'Sir, isn't this the club that honourable defence minister sa'ab wants shut down for being anti-national?' Padam Kumar asks Bhavani in the car as they drive to the DTC a little later.

'Yes,' Bhavani Singh replies briefly.

There has been quite a storm in a beer mug with the DTC and the defense minister recently, typical of the hyper-nationalism dominating public discourse in these times.

From what Bhavani can recall, somebody had invited Gagan Ruia, the overfed son of defense minister Govardhan Ruia, for dinner to the DTC. Ruia Jr was wearing a pair of Gujarati mirror-work juttis, so the Club staff didn't let him enter the main dining hall – they had some only-formal-footwear rule for men, apparently. They requested him to either eat in the lawns, or change into closed formal shoes. Ruia had refused and left in a huff, and half and hour later, taken to Twitter to declare that the DTC was anti-national because it discriminated against 'Indian' attire in general and juttis in particular. He had waxed eloquent about the fact that his father, Govardhan Ruia, was a humble bhutta-seller from Kathiawar who had worn only juttis till he was twenty-five – and said he would not rest till the thirty-two acres of prime Delhi land leased to the DTC was reclaimed, and the whole place converted into a massive gaushala. Cows will graze on the sweet grass of all the turf and the tennis courts, he swore, and muscular bhakts will play bhajans on the flute for them, while demure lasses churn butter in the marble-tiled verandas! In about fifteen minutes all the news channels had been discussing the 'issue' using hashtags like #JuttiGate and #DTCMeriJutti.

It hadn't helped that a rather gaga old DTC member had pointed out that Ruia senior and his colleagues had all been assigned sprawling bungalows in Lutyens' Delhi and they were welcome to let cows graze on *their* three-acre gardens instead! The thirty-two acres of the DTC service five thousand members and their families, this member had said, whereas your three-acre gardens exists to serve only you and your porky son! Naturally, this incensed the IJP camp even further. They re-christened the Delhi Turf Club the Delhi Terrorist Camp right there and then, and have been baying for its closure ever since …

'So sir, *is* it anti-national?' Padam Kumar wants to know.

Bhavani sighs. 'The definition of anti-national is very, very broad today, PK.'

A messy murder on the DTC premises would suit the IJP admirably, Bhavani muses as his car turns into the imposing black gates of the Club and rolls down the tree-lined driveway. But it remains to be seen if today's incident is accident or murder …

Looking about the Club premises as he alights from his car, he feels his ageing superstar comparison is not too far off the mark. The main bungalow, almost one hundred and eighty years old, is gracious but, under the sparkling cream paint, somehow *exhausted*-looking. There are hundreds of

five-star hotels in Delhi now, and any number of housing
complexes with better pools and courts and other sporting
facilities than the Turf Club's. Agreed, the property is on
prime location, and the sprawling lawns are beautiful – but
they are not as well-maintained as they could be; there is
a slight air of seediness to the place – like it is holding out
defiantly to a new age, and a new set of rulers.

Very much in sync with this setting is the man who
comes hurrying up to greet Bhavani and Padam. Older than
Bhavani, with a receding hairline, bowed shoulders, and an
absent-minded manner.

'You must be Bhavani Singh!' he greets the ACP. 'Thank
you for coming at once! I'm Bhatti, Devendar Bhatti, Club
president.' He rolls his eyes ironically. 'For my sins!'

'Haha!' Bhavani smiles sunnily and grasps the proffered
hand. 'We have often heard of the garden at the DTC, but
we did nat expect it to be quite so beautiful, sir!'

Bhatti looks about the garden in a harassed sort of way,
blinking his watery eyes. His prominent Adam's apple and
receding chin make him look vaguely hen-like. 'Yes, yes, there
is a gardening committee … they are very … er … committed
… but what I want to show you is not very beautiful I'm
afraid …'

He leads the two policemen down the driveway, past the
Lady Darlington Swimming Bath and the No Ayahs, Servants
and Gunmen sign Akash Dogra finds so problematic, and to
the gym.

There is a knot of women of all ages and shapes waiting outside this building, toting water-bottles and yoga mats and whispering to each other furiously. But when they see the three men approaching, they quieten, push their sunglasses higher up their noses, and look at them expectantly.

'Buggered,' Devendar Bhatti mutters feelingly under his breath.

Bhavani Singh deduces correctly that this remark is not addressed to him.

'Is that the police, Bhatti?' a thick-set woman with a bouffant maroon boy-cut asks in an officious voice.

Bhatti stares at her for a moment, clearly unsure of whether to say yes or no. Then, reluctantly, he gives a small, jerky nod.

'Yes. There's been a most unfortunate accident, as you perhaps know—'

'Hullo there,' Maroon Hair cuts him short, holding out a hand to Bhavani. 'Good to know you've been called in.'

Bhavani Singh grasps her hand, bracing resignedly for a bone-crunching squeeze and receiving exactly that.

'Madam.'

'What's your rank?' she enquires bluntly.

Padam Kumar steps up. 'Bhavani sir is the assistant commissioner of police, madam.'

'Like an army colonel?' she demands.

'Like a captain, madam,' Bhavani says genially.

The lady juts out her maroon lower lip, which matches her maroon hair perfectly. 'That's too junior, surely!'

'Rank doesn't necessarily mean ability, auntie.' A slender girl in an ALPHA FEMALE sweatshirt steps forward, and smiles at Bhavani apologetically. 'Quite the opposite sometimes. Shit rises to the top and all that!' Then she winces. 'Oops! No offence, Bhatti uncle!'

Bhatti looks around finickily.

'Ladies, ACP Singh comes highly recommended by people in the know, and I can say with great confidence that we could *not* be in better hands.'

Maroon Hair looks sceptical, but changes tack.

'Are you going to go ahead with the election today, Bhatti?' she demands. 'I mean, if somebody has actually *died* it would be in terrible taste to carry on as if nothing has happened!' She hesitates, 'I mean, somebody *has* died, haven't they? I know Cookie Katoch and Roshni Aggarwal said so, but ...'

She trails off, managing to imply that Cookie Katoch and Roshni Aggarwal really can't be trusted.

'Later, madam, later,' Bhatti says testily. 'Bambi beta, why don't all of you get your workout on the jogging track today, huh? Or on the courts? I need to take these gentlemen through.'

He leads the two policemen into the gym, and gingerly indicates the exercise bench, not without a small flourish. 'And there you have it.'

The old ACP takes in the grisly sight quietly. The staring eyes, the straining chest, the twisted, contused neck.

No matter how many corpses he sees, the first sight of a body divested of the dignifying spark of life always depresses him. It is a jarring reminder that at the end of the day, in spite of all your dreams, worries, ambitions, successes or failures, in spite of all the EMIs you pay and the plans you make – plans of losing weight, plans of taking the kids out for ice cream, plans of revenge, of glory, of world domination – all roads eventually lead here – to a cold, crumpled stillness and the heat of the furnace.

Police folk use a lot of deliberately flippant slang for death – off ho gaya, ticket cut gaya, gauna ho gaya – but they're just kidding themselves. Seeing a freshly dead corpse is always an uneasy, unsettling, semi-spiritual business.

'It was quick,' Bhavani says finally. 'It looks bad, but it was quick.'

Sliding his hands into his roomy trouser pockets, he turns slowly to scan the gym – the gleaming machines inside, the sprawling lawns outside, visible through the windows.

'Who's he?' he asks.

'His name is Leo Matthew,' Bhatti replies. 'He was found by the two ladies they mentioned outside. Cookie and Roshni.'

'Looks like the barbell slipped from his hands, crushed his windpipe and broke his neck,' Bhavani Singh says. 'It is a fairly common gym accident, unfortunately.'

'You do weightlifting?' Bhatti jerks up an eyebrow. 'You look fit.'

'Oh no no no no no,' Bhavani says quickly. 'We just do eleven minutes of basic exercise – but *every* single day – for the past forty years. Nothing fancy like this ... with so much science and technology and special equipment to avoid injuries. And yet,' he pauses, 'and yet, the fellow has *still* ended up dead.'

'But he's fit, sir,' Padam Kumar says admiringly. 'What a deadly body he has built!' He raises an arm and points at the dead man's abs. 'One two three four ... *Seven* clearly defined abs!'

'Yes.' Bhavani shoots his junior a quelling look and continues to look about the gym. 'It's a company called Precor, we see.'

'It's very well reputed,' Bhatti replies. 'All this equipment cost a quite a packet, I can tell you!'

'Yes ...' Bhavani's eyes continue to roam. 'And where is the security camera? Ah, *there.*'

'It's placed at a good angle, sir,' Inspector Padam Kumar ventures. 'That should give us quite a clear picture of what happened. A movie director couldn't have placed it better.'

Bhatti's face lightens a little. 'I chose that placement myself,' he says. 'If there was any foul play, that camera would've definitely captured it! But there wasn't.'

'How nice,' is Bhavani's genial reply. 'But we would like to review the footage too. You have no objection?'

Bhatti shakes his head. 'Of course not. Of course not.'

Bhavani continues to study the space. 'Somebody celebrated a birthday party here?'

'Huh?' Bhatti is taken aback.

Bhavani indicates the helium balloons, some of which have come loose from their tethering and are hovering beneath the ceiling, their satin ribbons trailing below.

'Ah!' Bhatti's face clears. 'They're from the Annual Bumper Tambola we had yesterday.'

Bhavani is still looking around the room searchingly.

'But we should ask these Precord—' he begins.

'Precor.'

'Precor people to come over and give us their expert opinion at once. Just in case.'

Devendar Bhatti rubs his nose. 'Could he have been distracted or something? Ill or hungover?'

Bhavani Singh looks slightly surprised. 'He was a drinker? Doesn't look the type.'

They stare down at the ruined body for a while, their expressions sombre.

'Even then, it is possible he had some pre-existing medical condition that was worsened by the heavy weightlifting. Some sort of heart attack, or sudden clotting, or a tumour in the brain ...' He looks at his assistant. 'Get RML to do a full post-mortem, PK.' Turning back to Bhatti, he asks, 'Were there any witnesses at the time, sir? Anybody else using the gym?'

Bhatti shakes his head. 'No. He was last seen alive entering through the main gate this morning at five sharp. And the ladies discovered him, like this, at a quarter past six.'

'The ladies had also come to use the gym?' Bhavani Singh asks.

'Ah.' Bhatti's expression clears. 'But I haven't told you! This man is an instructor. After finishing his own workout, he would have started a Zumba class, from six-thirty to seven-thirty, attended by a group of about ten ladies.'

'What's a Jumba?' Padam Kumar wants to know.

'You've got me stumped there,' Devendar Bhatti admits. 'It's some sort of South American dance form, they tell me. Helps you lose weight and er ... tone up ... This fellow has a

YouTube channel, in fact. With lakhs of followers, I believe. It's called ... er ... *Lose it with Leo*. His name is – was Leo. Did I tell you that?'

'Yes,' Bhavani replies.

There is a short silence, which Bhavani Singh spends wondering what joy a man as intellectual as Devendar Bhatti, who has held such a powerful public office, gets from being at the beck and call of the members of what seems to be a highly entitled and eccentric club. To each his own, he supposes.

Finally he asks, 'Where's his phone?'

Bhatti puts a hand into his coat pocket, and fishes out a plastic ziplock bagged iPhone. Inspector Padam Kumar steps forward to take it, but Bhatti moves his hand out of reach.

'No need to go nosing about into it if it's just an accident,' he says, slightly defiantly. 'Let me hang on to it for the time being.'

Padam Kumar's eyes widen. He turns to look at his boss uncertainly.

Bhavani Singh holds out one large, brown palm. 'We will keep it just like that, sir,' he says easily. 'No nosing or prying till we get conclusive proof of foul play.'

He continues to hold out his palm.

Gulping like a cornered hen, Bhatti very slowly and reluctantly places the phone into it.

Bhavani hands the zip-locked bag to Padam.

'Keep it safe, PK.' Then he turns back to Bhatti. 'We will inspect this area minutely, get the Precor people to check for any tampering, watch the CCTV footage your security staff has, and of course, send the body to RML for forensic testing.

If all goes well, a clean chit can be given by this evening! Who is the next of kin?'

Bhatti looks harassed. 'We haven't quite figured out. Luckily, we happen to know the chap's lawyer. Young Dogra. Quite a well-known fellow. You could bring him in for background questioning, if required. He's a green card-holder.'

'He lives in America?' Bhavani enquires.

Bhatti looks blank for a moment, then gives a dry little laugh. 'Oh, green card-holders is what we call non-voting members at the club!'

'And why nat?' Bhavani smiles good-naturedly. 'The DTC is as great an institution as the USA, after all!'

Bhatti, not sure if he is being gently roasted by the homely old policeman, smiles uncertainly. 'Er … yes.'

'Can we talk to the ladies who found the body?' Bhavani asks next.

Bhatti nods again, not very enthusiatically. 'The ladies – yes. Certainly. I'll round them up for you.'

Bhavani studies the older man for a while. He definitely seems jumpy.

'Sir, there was some mention of an election?'

Bhatti passes a hand over his face.

'The Club elections, yes. They will have to be postponed I'm afraid. I need to send out an official communication … Meanwhile, you find what you can find, like a good chap! I'll also get them to allot you a guest cottage for the day. Make it your base, as it were.'

It was Bambi's sixteenth birthday. The ridiculously over-the-top Mexican-themed party was over. Everybody else had left. They had been playing *Call of Duty* on her bed, surrounded by torn wrapping paper, scattered presents and a shared plate of rich, eggless chocolate cake, when she chucked her controller aside, flopped backwards into his lap, smiled up into his startled eyes, and announced, in typical bossy Bambi fashion, that she wanted him to kiss her.

'You're the best bod on the Dosco squad so it has to be you. Don't say no to the birthday girl, Kash. It's rude. And don't worry – it won't complicate anything – we can keep on being just friends, and I'll never tell anyone.'

Thoroughly taken aback, his ears bright red with embarrassment, Kashi had stammered that what she was proposing was wrong for at least six different reasons. She'd shut him up with a kiss then, a sweet, warm, very clumsy kiss, which had gone on for far longer than it should have. Her body was under his, with her hands flattened against his bare chest by the time he found the strength to roll off and away.

'No!' he said forcefully, moving back when she tried to reach for him. '*No*, Bambi! No! Get *off* me. Stop it, *now!*'

She slunk away to her side of the bed and wrinkled her nose. 'You sound like you're disciplining a puppy.'

'Then stop acting like a puppy!'

Her eyes raked his face boldly. A lock of honey-brown hair fell across her face, making her look incredibly sexy and just a little demented. She tossed it back and met his eyes, straight on. 'Why not?'

He leaned forward and fired a counter-question. 'Are you in love with me?'

'Hai hai!' She had abandoned her sexy lounging pose, and sat up, genuinely horrified. '*No! Lame!* Who even *talks* like that?'

Hugging his pillow to his chest in his barsati in Nizamuddin, Kashi recalls how hard his heart had been thudding when he asked that question. And how, when she'd made it clear that the idea was ludicrous, it had seemed, for a moment, to stop.

He'd said curtly, 'You've spent the entire summer raving to me about Jaibeer Kanodia, and how he won't give you any bhaav and now, randomly, you want me to kiss you?'

She'd nodded serenely, not seeing any problem with this. 'Ya.'

'Well, I don't want to kiss you if you're going to be closing your eyes and thinking of Jaibeer Kanodia!'

Reaching forward, she'd smoothed his tousled hair. 'Maybe if you kiss me thoroughly enough I'll stop thinking of Jaibeer Kanodia. He's gonna pass out this year, anyway.'

Kashi had leapt off the messy bed and started looking for his shoes.

'You are truly the most selfish person I've ever met! I'm not a bloody rehab centre, you know. I'm a person with feelings. What the *fuck* is wrong with you?'

She'd sat up in bed, finger-combing her hair and rolling her eyes. 'Oh my god, Kashi, why're you overthinking this? Besides, I *have* feelings for you! I like you – I *trust* you.'

'Piss off,' he'd said tightly, and stalked out of the massive house.

After that, he couldn't get her out of his head. He'd dreamt the same damn dream every single night – he asked her again if she loved him, she answered with a yes instead of a no and he pulled her in close, wound his arms around her sweet, cinnamon body, pushed that frilly little birthday dress up her gleaming thighs and showed her what the best-bod-on-the-Dosco-squad could do.

And so of course, when he came home from Doon later that year, he'd ended up back in that pink bedroom, kissing her.

Later, she had told him that she'd made up all that stuff about liking Jaibeer Kanodia just to make him jealous. He'd accepted this explanation because he wanted to believe it, and thus had started the messy, magical hooking up years, every time he was back in town. On his nineteenth birthday, they'd gone official as a couple at his insistence, continuing to do the long-distance thing with no trouble at all while he studied law in Bangalore and she went to college in Delhi, till she told him, one fine day when he'd just started working, that her family was looking for a boy for her, and that she 'could never not do what they told her to'.

Numb with pain, Kashi had put a message on Jaipur House Soccer Squad and the Doscos had showed up at his parents' house in Noida almost immediately. They had drunk his father's whisky, eaten a shit ton of pizza, held forth with great eloquence on the themes of other fish in the sea, the joys of singlehood, and the fucked-upness of women in general and bloody Bambi Todi in particular. Much FIFA was played, *Pyaar ka Punchnama* watched and at 5 a.m., they marched him down to the Sector-44 swimming pool, stood him on the highest diving boards, completely naked, and made him shout, 'I declare Bambi Todi cancelled', before he leapt into the pool.

The love that had begun with a cannonball leap into a pool at the age of five had ended with this drunken, teary finale.

He had made a brief final appearance in the role of childhood friend at Bambi's glitzy, ill-fated engagement a couple of months later, and then dropped her entirely. And two years later, he had met Kuhu.

Thinking of which …

He rolls over onto his stomach, hauls out his phone and finally opens the email she'd sent him yesterday, right after they'd spoken on the phone.

From: kuhuban@gmail.com
To: akashdogra20@gmail.com▼

SUB: Goa

Kash, like I <u>tried</u> to tell you just now, the newly elected MLA wants the school ready in time for his mum's birthday, which is in two weeks. So all the deadlines have been advanced. The dude's funding the whole thing so I have to listen to him.

And like I <u>also</u> tried to tell you when you started being so cold and polite and you-do-you, he dropped this bombshell on me at the last minute.

And yes, you were right. I <u>could</u> leave my foreman in charge of the site for three weeks. He's entirely competent.

But here's the thing. I don't want to.

This school is my dream. These kids have become my family. I've put blood, sweat and tears into this project for months and I don't want to abandon it when it's almost done. And it's not fair of you to expect me to.

Are we Over?

Could you please let me know?

We have a tremendously loud machine here that cuts through reinforced concrete and steel rods like they were butter, and breaking up with you will hurt as badly as feeding myself into its jagged jaws. Just saying.

But fine, if you've decided what I did was unforgivable and you want a girlfriend with different priorities, then just let me know, okay? Don't let this drift and be 'kind.' You're always too kind.

Also, please please have fun in your three free weeks! I will feel SO guilty if you don't.

I missed your sweet, drowsy good-morning call today. I missed it like a limb.

I've ordered some books from Amazon which will be delivered to your place. Please COD 795 rupees?

Hugs,

Kuhu

He's frowning down at the screen, torn between resentment and remorse, when a voice speaks from the doorway.

'Behenchod, Dogra, get out of bed! You can't stroke your balls ruminatively under that razai all day.'

Kashi flips a middle finger. 'What are you, Walli, my mother-in-law?'

Kartik Walli leans on the door jamb. He's dressed for a corporate meeting – sharp jacket, shined shoes, slicked back hair.

Kashi grimaces. 'You look like a hooker.'

'I *am* a hooker. I've got a ten o'clock meeting at the head office and I'm already late. What about you?'

Kashi looks disgruntled. 'I'd taken three weeks off to go to Goa with Kuhu, remember?'

'Oh yaaa!' Walli chuckles. 'She cancelled! After you spent a whole month working on your abs!'

'Yeah.' Kashi yanks up his sweatshirt with a flourish and flexes. 'Should I go flash these guns at other women?'

'Hun*ter!*' Walli crows approvingly. 'Of course you should! Like who?'

There's an odd little pause.

Kashi lets his sweatshirt drop. 'I bumped into Bambi Todi yesterday,' he says casually.

'Wha—?' Walli's jaw sags. He scrambles into the room, sits down on Kashi's bed and starts to pluck at his razai with anxious fingers. 'Bumboo Todi? No, Dogra, you poor, sad, fucked-up choot, *no!* Stay away from bloody Bumboo Todi! BT, bro BT!'

'It *won't* be a bad trip, Walli!' Kashi says indignantly. 'I'm not a kid any more.'

'Dogra, mere bhai.' Walli's voice is hoarse with emotion. 'Bumboo Todi will just bumboo your ass agai—'

'*Stop* calling her Bumboo Todi!'

Walli holds up his palms placatingly. 'Okay, okay, sorry! But getting back on Bambi Todi's radar is a bad bad *bad* idea! You're *always* gonna resent her for putting you through so much shit, and she's *always* gonna despise you for putting up with it.'

'Behenchod, don't talk like a cheap therapist!' Kashi says irritably. He rolls away, reaches for his pillow, and hugs it pensively. His friend observes that his face has softened and his eyes have a faraway look.

'It was so *nice* meeting her again. It was *easy*, it was *chill* … maybe because we're both grown up now!' He turns glowing eyes on Walli. 'I think we're *finally* ready to be pals again.'

'Pals?' Walli scoffs disbelievingly. 'You – Kashi *chutiya* Dogra – are going to coax her – Bambi *tigress* Todi – to crawl obediently into a best-friend-sized cage and *stay* there?'

'Yeah,' Kashi replies doggedly.

'She'll bite your fucking head off, then have sex with your writhing body,' Walli says bluntly.

Kashi's eyes blaze with sudden, disproportionate fury. 'What the hell, Walli!'

They stare at each other for a hot, angry moment, then Walli shrugs and backs off the bed. 'Whatever bro, I have a meeting – haul your ass out of bed and shut the goddam front door.'

'Why can't Kalra do it?' Kashi mutters.

'He stayed the night at his chachi's.'

Reluctantly, Kashi wraps his razai tightly around himself, gets out of bed and hobbles to the door. Walli hovers impatiently.

'And let Kamala didi in, or the bins won't be emptied. *Again.*'

'Have a nice day, honey!' Kashi says sarcastically and shuts the door in Walli's face, cutting off the stream of abuses.

He stumbles back into bed and is staring moodily into the distance when his phone rings. He answers it.

'Akash Dogra?' a voice asks.

'Yes?'

'Sir, this is the Crime Branch cell, Chanakyapuri. We are calling from the Delhi Turf Club. Your client Leo Matthews has been found dead and we need your assistance immediately.'

4

Pinko Hathni

Sipping a cup of tea that is neither sweet nor milky enough, and longing for a spicy aloo patty to go with it, Bhavani Singh sits back in the smelly little room the DTC insists on calling a 'Command Centre' and addresses the eager young computer operator in the baseball cap.

'What's your name, beta?'

'Ram Palat, sir.'

'Why is there only one security camera in the gym, Ram Palat?'

'Sir, there are two – one for upstairs and one for downstairs. They are sufficient, sir! The placement is really very good!'

'Okay.' Bhavani nods. 'Are you ready to watch the footage, sardarji?'

This to a tiny, wizened turbaned Sikh in a blue blazer, emblazoned with a Precor ascot on its breast pocket, sitting on a chair with his feet not quite touching the floor.

'Yes,' the sardar replies in a fluting, bird-like little voice. 'By all means, let's watch!'

Ram Palat presses play.

'Yeh huee Leo sa'ab ki entry, sir ... sabse pehle he goes to the fridge, takes out a flask and drinks it till it's empty. Then he starts stretching ... phir twunty minutes fast running, uske baad ... push-ups ... bicep curls...' His voice trails away.

Bhavani sips his tea and watches the silent screen. It is the first time he has seen the dead man alive – and also the first time he has seen such perfected masculine beauty in action. Even on the silent, low-res, black-and-white CCTV camera footage, Leo's workout makes for hypnotic viewing. Watching him, Bhavani starts to feel decidedly bloated and unfit. Aaj se aloo patty band, he decides.

'It's coming, sir,' Ram Palat says eagerly. 'He is walking to the bench now. Look.'

Panting lightly, his chest moving up and down, Leo wipes his face with a hand towel, then approaches the bench press. The bar is already loaded and ready.

Hitching up his track pants slightly, he sits on the bench, then lowers himself into position below the bar. His sneakered feet rest on the ground, flexed lightly.

'He is lifting hundred and twenty kgs sir,' Ram Palat says in awe. 'I calculated.'

'Three-three plates of twenty kg each, stacked and balanced absolutely correctly.' Flutes the tiny sardar. 'No error so far.'

On the monitor, Leo raises his hands, curls them around the bar, and lifts it smoothly off the stand. He brings it down to his chest grimacing slightly. His chest expands, his arms ripple. His back and buttocks do not rise even a centimetre off the bench. He is completely in control of the movement as he performs his reps. One … two … three … four …

'Excellent technique!' the tiny sardar pronounces approvingly.

Ram Palat grips Bhavani's fat wrist urgently.

'Watch carefully now, sir. Here it comes!'

With a sense of impending doom, Bhavani watches as Leo pushes smoothly upwards again.

It happens really quickly. The trainer's arms are extended to the max, his elbows are locked. Then, inexplicably, the bar wavers and drops with sudden, sickening neatness to his chest. His body jerks up, then flops back. The loaded bar follows the pull of gravity, rolls down to his neck and settles against his straining windpipe. Slowly, the struggling stops and the powerful body goes still.

Bhavani frowns. 'Again.'

He pulls a chair to the monitor, and puts on his glasses.

'In slow motion.'

Ram Palat twiddles the knobs and they watch the clip intently three more times. Then Bhavani sits back with a dissatisfied grunt and takes off his glasses.

'Accident ho gaya rabba rabba …' he hums musingly. 'What do you say, sardarji?'

'Accident caused by human error, sir,' says the little Precor representative definitely. 'There was *no* gadbad with the equipment. I've checked it already. The bar, the bench, the plates.' He pauses, frowning, then admits, 'But I see nothing wrong with his technique either. Ekdum textbook correct hai!'

Bhavani frowns. 'Then ...' he looks around the smelly little room. 'Where's Padam? We need to chase forensics on this ...'

———◆———

Devendar Bhatti has assigned Guest Cottage No. 5 to the investigative team. It is a large, airy, high-ceilinged suite with heavy, white-painted teak furniture, its own veranda and garden. Floral curtains are drawn back to offer a view of flowerbeds blooming with rich maroon coxcomb, sweet-pea and dahlia.

When Bhavani hurries back to it, in search of the inspector, he finds him sitting upon the floral sofa, behind an old-school stainless-steel tea-tray and a plate of Marie biscuits, chatting cosily with a rugged young man, who looks vaguely familiar.

'This one is nice too!' the young man is saying, peering down into the screen of what Bhavani immediately recognizes from the virulence of its yellow cover to be Padam's phone. 'She has a karate black belt, and she can play Spanish guitar! Sounds like you're spoilt for choice, inspector!'

'She's not as fair as the one who can speak French and German, though,' Padam points out seriously. 'And she is two years older.'

'But that one had too many brothers, you said,' the young man reminds him just as seriously. 'They may create hassles.'

'That *is* true.' Padam frowns. 'What about the Chandigarh girl, sir?'

'She is nice too. Frankly I think they're *all* lovely!'

'You're too lenient a marker, sir.' Padam gravely rebukes the young man. 'After all, this is not a *date*, it is a question of my whole life. And my family's life. I'm the only son. Fair, six foota, police afsar – I can pick and choose, which means I have to choose carefully.'

'Sorry, sorry.' Much abashed at this reprimand, the young man bends over the phone with even greater concentration.

Padam sips his tea, mollified, then sights Bhavani standing in the doorway and does a double take, almost dropping his cup.

'Sir!'

'No, no, take your time, PK,' Bhavani says sardonically. 'We had asked you to chase forensics at RML, but we see you are busy with more important matters.'

'Yes, sir, no, sir! This is Mr Akash Dogra, sir! Lawyer of the deceased. He is waiting for you!'

The young man puts down Padam's phone and leaps to his feet at once, hand extended.

'Call me Kashi,' he says, his eyes twinkling. 'Inspector Kumar has been calling RML constantly, but in the middle, the Chandigarh party phoned, insisting on an immediate final answer, so PK enlisted my help.'

'O really?' Bhavani grasps the proffered hand, liking the young man instinctively and wondering again where he's seen him before. Then he turns to the hovering Padam. 'We need Dr Krishnan's report at once, PK!'

Padam exits, a little red-faced.

'Sorry to keep you waiting.' Bhavani gestures towards the sofa.

'Not at all, you must have a dozen things to do,' Akash Dogra says easily as he sits down. 'But do tell me – was it an accident?'

'Most probably.' Bhavani nods, taking a seat too. 'We are still figuring it out. You were the deceased's lawyer, we hear?'

'I didn't know him too well, actually,' Akash admits. 'I do some pro-bono work with juveniles – a bunch of boys were gathered up for underage drinking and rowdiness in Gurgaon once and Leo came to pay their bail and organize their release. He was an old boy from their orphanage and he still took an interest in its affairs. He said it was the closest thing he had to a home and a family. I liked how he handled them – he was kind, but also tough – I studied in an all-boys boarding school so I can appreciate these things. The boys really looked up to him.'

He pauses, looking down at his empty teacup and frowning. Bhavani senses he isn't done.

'And?' he prompts gently.

Kashi looks up. 'Only his name wasn't Leo that night. I thought about it after I went home yesterday and I'm pretty sure they all called him Lambodar bhaiya.'

'That is understandable, no?' Bhavani suggests softly. 'Lambodar is perhaps nat as ... upwardly mobile as Leo.'

Kashi nods again. 'Yeah ... yesterday when I saw him at the club, I realized he has a public persona here, which is different from the one I'd seen earlier. Smoother, suaver, sexier. He'd even told the ladies at the club that he was part Jamaican. But that night he spoke full-on Bhojpuri.'

'And you did nat like that,' Bhavani states. 'You feel people should have just one persona all the time. Their true persona.'

Kashi shrugs. 'Yeah. I do actually.'

Bhavani, reflecting privately that it is only people with great privilege who can afford to think like this, changes the subject.

'You have only met Leo twice then? We were told – perhaps there was some mistake – that you are his lawyer.'

'Oh that.' Kashi looks sheepish. 'Some bumptious asshole was leaning hard on him yesterday, during tambola, in front of everybody. I hate bullies, so I decided to butt in and say I represent him.'

Bhavani Singh's square, homely face breaks into a pleased smile.

'We recognize you now!' he says, snapping his fingers. 'You are *quite* a well-known vakeel! You got a jhuggi colony a big compensation, your picture was in the paper today!'

'A very small picture,' Kashi mutters, now looking even more embarrassed. 'Really tiny ...'

'ACP Singh?'

The young girl in the ALPHA FEMALE sweatshirt has popped her head into the cottage doorway.

'Bhatti uncle says both the gym trainers are here,' she says, looking at him in an oddly fixed manner. 'They're in the gym, with your men. You should go there.'

'Thank you,' Bhavani replies.

She tucks a strand of hair behind her ear and continues to look exclusively at him. 'No problem.'

There is an awkward pause. Bhavani notices that Akash Dogra, so gregarious thus far, is now looking down studiously at his empty teacup, while the tips of his ears slowly turn red.

Oho. A penny drops in the ACP's brain. This girl has come rushing to Guest Cottage No. 5 with the sole intention of ignoring Dogra pointedly. Interesting! He pours himself a cup of tea and sits back comfortably to see how the little love-scene will develop.

'So I guess I'll be going then!' Bambi says and starts to retreat from the room.

Kashi looks up. 'I'm sorry your instructor died,' he blurts out.

She stops.

'He was a great guy,' Kashi continues awkwardly.

She turns around.

'So he really is dead?' she asks apprehensively. 'It's like … pukka?'

Kashi looks confused and glances at Bhavani. 'Doesn't everybody know yet?'

She throws up a hand. 'No, I guess I do know … but I was sort of hoping—' She shivers. 'Ugh. Poor Leo. Well, this is better than living with ghastly injuries, I guess.'

'For sure,' Kashi agrees at once.

She takes a step into the room and confides, 'Actually I ended up missing most of his classes, because, no offense, they were *too* early in the morning for me – even though I live practically next door. That's why I'm not sadder, I guess.

Everybody else is inconsolable outside. They're all full-on *weeping* – imagining him dead or crippled. I'm clearly a *monster*.'

Her eyes belie her statement, however. They look curiously dazed, and her hands are shaking slightly.

Soothingly, Bhavani asks, 'So what exactly happens in a Zumba class? We are curious.'

'Hmmm?' Bambi looks puzzled.

'What happens in your Zumba class usually, Bee?' Kashi says patiently.

'Oh!' She gives herself a little shake. 'Well, ours began with Leo coming bouncing up the steps, all sweaty and pumped and radiating his usual *Sheila-ki-Jawaani* aura. Then—'

Bhavani interrupts, his eyes scanning her face keenly. 'Why do you say *Sheila-ki-Jawaani*?'

'Huh? Oh, the song you know. It begins "I know you want it but you're never gonna get it, *tere haath kabhi na aani*." That was just *so* Leo. He flaunted his hot bod at all the drooling aunties, but he also had this somehow *untouchable* quality.'

'Was he a gay?' Bhavani wants to know.

'No no.' Bambi laughs a little, very sure. 'He *liked* women, matlab that much I *know*—'

'I wonder how,' Kashi murmurs.

She has regained enough of her pep now to shoot him a dirty look. 'It was something else …' She shrugs. 'Like he had a chip on his shoulder or something …'

Bhavani nods encouragingly. 'Thoda … twisted tha, kya? Maybe inwardly resentful of his wealthy lady clients?'

Bambi laughs again. 'Maybe! He definitely got a kick out of seeing the rich old aunties grinding to stuff like "Give it to me, I'm worth it".'

'O really?' Bhavani sits up straighter.

'But he was cocky AF mostly. He totally had the upper hand ... he'd take his own sweet time finishing his personal workout, coming up the stairs only by six-forty, six-fifty sometimes, and they'd wait for him without a murmur! *These* ladies! Who are *so* sharp with their domestic staff for being even two minutes late! And sometimes he'd randomly cancel class saying he was unwell, and instead of demanding a make-up class, or their money back, they'd all put these cooing messages on the group – "So sorry to hear that!" and "Get well soon!" and "Awww take care". It used to really piss me off!'

'Sounds like Krishan Kanhaiya conducting a Raaslila,' Bhavani Singh says thoughtfully.

She lets out a loud snort of laughter. 'That's *it* exactly! They're *such* a bunch of sighing gopis!' Then she pulls up short, guiltily. 'I shouldn't laugh. He's dead. Oh God, he's dead!'

Her face goes pale. She gulps, swaying a little.

'Here, sit down.' Kashi leaps up and gets her a chair.

Bambi sits, smiling at him gratefully. Then she turns to look at the lounging Bhavani. 'Hadn't you better go talk to the trainers?' she asks doubtfully. 'They're waiting for you.'

'O yes.' Bhavani Singh says. 'Which way is the gym again?'

'I'll show you.' She rises to her feet.

'Bambi.'

She stops at once. Akash Dogra is staring at her, his gaze intense.

'Stay.'

Bhavani gives a little chuckle. 'We will find the gym,' he says. 'It is okay. You stay with vakeel sa'ab. Also, vakeel sa'ab – are you very much busy today?'

'Uh no,' Akash replies, still looking at Bambi. 'As a matter of a fact I'm free for three whole weeks!'

'Very good! Please wait here for us then! We want to finish our chat with you!'

He walks briskly out of the cottage.

A certain constraint creeps back into the room.

'Free for three weeks?' Bambi asks. 'Are the courts shut?'

Kashi considers this question for a longer time than logically required, then says. 'You didn't even say bye yesterday.'

'Sorry,' she says. 'The tambola broke up, and everybody started walking out, and I thought I could sell some juice if I went back to my stall.'

'Good thinking,' he says.

There is an awkward silence.

Yesterday was easier than today, Kashi thinks, vexed. Today is weird because we can't talk about how nice it is to see each other after three whole years. Shit!

'So how come you're here again today?' she asks finally. 'Rediscovered your fondness for the Club?'

He rolls his eyes slightly. 'They called me because now everybody thinks I'm Leo's lawyer.'

'Oh!' She giggles, then looks guilty.

'Bee, d'you think ... we can be ... umm ... friends again?'

It is now her turn to take longer than logically required to reply.

'Bambi?'

She covers the distance between them in two quick steps and wraps her arms around his waist. Her head rests on his chest.

Her breath comes in jagged little gasps as she says, 'I missed you ... so ... *much* after Anshul died.'

And so – finally – the name is out there, between them. Anshul Poddar. Anshul the glorious. Anshul the hyphenated. Entrepreneur–mountaineer. The wealthy arranged-marriage catch from the right community and class, who had wrested Bambi from Kashi's arms only to perish with a bus full of others in a freak landslide accident in Garhwal the day after their glitzy engagement.

Kashi sighs, closes his eyes and hugs her back. Looking down at the top of her head, he feels sick with shame as he recalls the moment when he'd heard the news of Anshul's bus plummeting into a Himalayan abyss. Because his one simple, savage thought had been *serves her right.*

Decency and sanity had prevailed later though. He had tried to call her. Even though all the Doscos had said it was a highly avoidable thing to do. But she hadn't answered his calls anyway, or replied to the text in which he'd asked her to call anytime, they could pull one of their ten-to-six all-nighters if she needed to get stuff off her chest ...

Three years of radio silence.

Over, just like that, with one simple hug.

Kashi sighs happily, then frowns. 'Fuck, Bambi, are you wiping snot on my sweater?'

—◆——◆—

'I din do anythin.'

The trainer protesting his innocence is a short, fair, muscular Manipuri dressed in tight, all-black clothes with blonde-streaked hair, bulging muscles and a paradoxically gentle face.

Padam Kumar looms above him, smiling a sinister cherubic smile. 'I didn't say you did, Tiger Shroff.'

'My name's Thinsuk,' he replies sullenly.

But Padam Kumar has already turned to the other trainer – a macho, moustachioed young Malayali with bright eyes and a military haircut.

'What about you, Rana Duggabuti? Your boss is dead – did you also not do anything?'

'It's Daggubati,' the Malayali, whose name is Thampi, retorts instantly. 'And he *wasn't* my boss.'

Padam Kumar chuckles. 'Lorrd of atty-tyoode! I like that!'

They're in the sunny exercise room above the gym. It has a wooden floor, one mirrored wall and huge windows which overlook the main lawns of the club. The trainers are sitting on a pair of rather trendy beanbags and Padam Kumar is standing over them.

He lets the silence lengthen, sneering down with tough, Singham-ish machismo at the cowering duo. *This* is how he'd imagined a career in the police force would feel. But then footsteps sound on the stairs and the pleasantly plain features of ACP Bhavani Singh appear at the landing.

'Hullo hullo,' he says amiably.

The tension eases out of the trainers at once, much to Padam Kumar's disgust.

Bhavani sits down, and sizes up the pair in silence for a while, smiling genially, drumming his fingers idly on the arms of his chair.

They're hiding something, he concludes. Outsiders to this city, one from the north and one from the south, they're radiating the classic mix of belligerence and fear that outsiders exude when faced with city cops. But there's also something more.

The question is, is this something more *relevant*? If they've been eating beef in their strictly Hindu rented flats, or peddling illegal steroids to Club members, then it may have nothing to do with the incident he's investigating.

He raises his voice, upping his jovialness a notch.

'So, you two and Leo ... you were ... friendly with each other, hain?' He looks attentively from one to the other.

There is a small, strangled silence. Then –

'I never got to see him,' Thampi says finally. 'He used to come very early in the morning and I never have the morning shift. Ask Thinsuk.'

Bhavani turns his patient, questioning gaze on Thinsuk.

The Manipuri shrugs. 'He was kind. A'ways busy, and in a hurry, but kind. I used to ask him for tips, because he was famous in the fitness community, and because his lifting technique was so good – an' even though he said, "People pay me good money for what I'm teaching you for free, Thinsuki," he a'ways helped me.'

Bhavani Singh tips his chair back into a more relaxed position.

'Money-minded, was he?'

Thinsuk looks sullen. 'We all have to be – living in this city! Leo was earning so much money – but spendin' a lot also. He paid big bucks to stay on top of all the lates' moves and trends. He had the bes' qualifications. He had heavy fuel consumption too – a'ways driving here and there for his classes on that Hayabusa.'

'O yes!' Bhavani Singh massages the lobe of his ear for a while. 'You say his technique was good – but it could nat have been too good if he ended up dead.'

Thinsuk looks just a little smug. 'That's true.'

'In the video, we saw that the bench press bar was already loaded for Leo when he walked into the gym at five. Who did that?'

'I did,' Thampi says sullenly. 'It was one of my "closing up" duties. Stack the bar with plates – a hundred and twenty kgs – for Leo the great. He was too busy and too important to load his bar himself. I even had to mix his pre-workout shake and leave it in there' – he nods at the clear-glass doored fridge – 'for him to drink during his workout.'

'And I put away everything afterwards when I arrived at six,' Thinsuk chimes in. 'The weights, the bottle, the towels. Apart from my regular duties – which are dusting and sanitizing the machines, laying out fresh towels, and setting out the water, and apples and juice.'

Unlike Thampi, Thinsuk's voice is matter of fact. He doesn't seem to mind that Leo hadn't helped with these duties. Bhavani nods, then asks casually, 'Why did the Club feel the zaroorat for a third trainer, waise? Don't you two know how to Zumba?'

This time resentment flares simultaneously on both the young faces. 'Of course we do!' Thampi asserts indignantly. 'But President Bhatti hired Leo because he has 1.01 million followers on his YouTube channel and Zumba training qualifications from Brazil. So President Bhatti felt he would be a better teacher.'

'And he was? Good? Effective? All the ladies were taking his class?'

Thampi says sullenly, 'The ladies just liked him because he knew good English and had trained abroad and all. They let him park his bike right here next to the gym veranda, but we have to park outside the main gate and walk such a long way!'

'But that may be because he only needed parking for one-two hours,' Bhavani Singh says tolerantly. 'And you fellows have what, nine-hour shifts?'

They nod.

'So now that he is dead what will happen? Perhaps President Bhatti will promote you to the post of Zumba instructor?'

Thampi laughs scornfully. 'Not if those women have a say!' he scoffs. 'They're much too snobbish to attend our class! D'you know Thinsuk and I are not even allowed to use that swimming pool outside because we may contaminate it?'

'I'm not saying they're unhygienic on *purpose*, babe,' Thinsuk mimics in a bitter tone, 'they just don't get enough water in the jhuggis to bathe daily, poor things.'

The imitation is cruel, but accurate.

Bhavani chuckles. 'That is pretty good!' he says appreciatively. 'You could be an actor – good-looking boy like you!'

Thinsuk goes a little pink.

'Tell us something,' Bhavani continues conversationally. 'This gym is new, is it nat? Who decided what-what equipment to buy for it?'

'President Bhatti, sir,' Thinsuk replies. 'And some of the members who use the gym regularly. And us.'

'O really?' Bhavani says blandly, even as his mind immediately starts to pluck on the possibilities of kickbacks and commissions. Had Thampi and Thinsuk received some money for recommending Precor over the others? Had that little Sardarji been in on the deal? Had the supplied material been substandard in anyway? Was that what had caused the accident?

As he is considering these possibilities, his phone rings. He extracts it from one of his roomy trouser pockets.

'Hullo?'

'Jai Bhavani,' comes a deep, well-modulated, south Indian drawl.

Bhavani's square face splits into a wide smile. He is very fond of the Tamilian head of forensics.

'Daaktar sa'ab!'

'What a good-looking corpse you've sent us this time, Bhavani. The girls are quite excited. Makes a change from the usual desiccated specimens we get.'

'My pleasure, my pleasure! So what information do you have for us?'

'Well, on the face of it, it looked like accidental traumatic asphyxia.'

'Speak English, daaktar sa'ab,' Bhavani entreats.

'A sudden force has compressed the neck and cut off the oxygen flow,' Dr Krishnan explains. 'I'm guessing that was the barbell.'

'Yes.'

'That *seems* to be the cause of death, but—'

'It was nat?'

'No, it was not.'

'A heart attack, or a tumour of some sort?'

'Nothing so innocent, I'm afraid.'

'Then?'

'Your man was drugged, Bhavani. He's awash with a particularly filthy sort of drug cocktail called "Pinko Hathni" that's been doing the rounds lately, though in areas far less posh than the Delhi Turf Club. No wonder he dropped a loaded bar on himself.'

'Pinko *Hathni*?'

'It derives its name from the fact that the extremely swift hit it delivers is like being kicked in your central nervous system by a sexy female elephant.'

Bhavani Singh isn't often at a loss for words, but all he can manage in response to this is a strangled-sounding 'Wah'.

'Could he have taken it himself?' he asks after a beat. 'As a ... a performance enhancer, of sorts?'

'It's not that kind of drug. If Usain Bolt took the dose your chap did before a race, he would speedily strip himself naked when the starting pistol went off, amble dreamily down the track marvelling at the contingent of psychedelic gorillas copulating in the stands, then go suddenly limp and drop dead.'

'Understood.'

'We checked the flask you sent with the body. It was empty, but it had traces of Creatine Monohydrate. That's a common pre-workout drink – a lot of these body-builder types take it just before they lift. It was laced with Pinko. So find out who filled it. That's your man. Or woman.'

Krishnan disconnects. Bhavani lowers his phone.

His face is entirely expressionless as he turns his genial eyes on Thampi. 'You mentioned preparing a drink at midnight and leaving it in that fridge for Leo.'

Thampi's face grows apprehensive. 'Yes, sir.'

Bhavani's voice is very gentle. 'Tell us how you did it.'

Thampi licks his lips. 'The way I always do – three tablespoons of the Creatine powder in water. It mixes really easily.'

Very conversationally Bhavani Singh asks, 'And Pinko Hathni? Does that mix easily in water too?'

'Pinko *what*?' Thampi's jaw sags ludicrously. 'No, I didn't, sir! I didn't!'

Bhavani spreads out his hands. 'No, no, it is completely understandable – the fellow is no better than you – your muscles are just as good, we can see that! But he gets paid so much more – he is making lakhs and lakhs and parking his motorcycle inside and flirting with the pretty ladies, while you stack his weights and clear his dirty towels. Over the months, resentment and khundak is building up and so one night, while you are making his wretched pre-workout drink, you take a tablespoon of Pinko Hathni and you' – he twists his wrist graphically – 'drop it into the flask!'

Thampi is now staring at Bhavani in horrified fascination. 'You're mad!' he says. 'Of course I did not! I'm not insane – I'm perfectly happy with my job – and if you see a photograph of my girlfriend Malathi – she is fifty times better looking than these dried-up Delhi women—'

'Yes, she's top class,' Thinsuk agrees, with perhaps too much fervour.

Thampi throws him a dirty look. '—then you would *know* that I would never do something like this!'

'You're just picking on him because he's an outsider!' Thinsuk says bitterly. 'It happens to us all the time – you're looking for somebody to pin it on and close the case quickly, so you're zooming in on us! All north-Indians behave like this!'

'Never!' Pained, Bhavani Singh holds up a stubby, rebuking finger. 'We *never, ever* niptao the case quickly. It is impossible to sleep well with a guilty conscience and the *one* thing that we love the most in the world is a good, sound sleep!'

'Then check last night's footage,' Thampi mutters. 'What use is that stupid camera, anyway? Why don't you check the CCTV recordings and see for yourself!'

Bhavani leans in. 'See what, Thampi? What are you so anxious for us to see?'

Thampi's head comes up, his clear dark eyes full of a desperate earnestness. 'See that I left ten minutes early last night! It was Malathi's birthday and I wanted to be with her at midnight! So I cleaned up the place, stacked the plates on the bar, made Leo's protein shake and put it in the empty fridge. And because Mukesh Khurana was *still* huffing and puffing on the treadmill, I requested him to lock up the place and drop the key off. *He* could have poisoned the shake – he *must* have poisoned the shake – everybody says his wife was sleeping with Leo, and he was *furious* because Leo blackened his eye in front of everybody only yesterday!'

5

Very, Very Over-Smart

'It *is* murder, sir. Quite clearly. A case of poisoning.'

Bhavani is pacing the veranda in front of the DTC gym, hung with baskets of hot pink petunias at regular intervals. The scent from them is sweetly cloying.

'Could the chap have taken it himself?' the chief wants to know. 'To enhance his performance? Don't these weightlifter types do that all the time?'

'It's a party drug, sir. So that is nat very likely. Of course we will examine all possibilities.'

'I'll send you back-up right away,' the chief says. 'This is going to be a high-profile maamla, Bhavani.'

'We know sir. An election was supposed to take place today. Gen. Mehra – woh surgical strikes waale – is standing for Club president. Against a lady who is rumoured to be having an affair with the murdered man, sir.'

'Good grief. So, she's a prime suspect then.'

'Her husband seems to be the man behind it, sir. He was at the gym five hours before the incident. Locked the place up and had every opportunity to doctor the drink. The CCTV footage should clinch it quite conclusively.'

'Good. Close it out fast. Have you got back-up?'

'Yes sir. A full team has arrived – they're combing the scene.'

'Good,' the chief repeats. 'Stay on top of things, Bhavani. Don't let 'em blow up.'

'Sir!'

Bhavani hangs up and looks at Padam who is hovering nearby.

'Yes, PK?'

'They want to show you something they've found on the CCTV, sir.'

A few minutes later he is back in the smelly little 'command centre', peering down at the computer screen, one hand resting on the back of operator Ram Palat's chair. An image is frozen on it, time code 11.45 p.m.

Young Ram Palat adjusts his baseball cap and explains the image animatedly.

'Sir, I've watched all the footage from ten till the time the ladies walk in at five-forty-five. Mukesh Khurana *is* doing his workout while Thampi prepares the protein shake and puts it in the fridge, but Khurana never goes anywhere near the fridge.'

'And then?' Bhavani prompts him. 'What's exciting you so much, Master Ram Palat?'

'Telling, sir!' The young operator's voice is alive with suppressed excitement as he presses play. 'And then at exactly eleven-forty-five, *a bunch of helium balloons floats up and covers the camera! Look!*'

They watch till the balloons he has described rise to totally obscure the view of the gym. Ram Palat turns to gauge the impact of this news on Bhavani and is not disappointed. The old ACP's eyes have started to gleam.

'O *real...ly?*' he muses slowly. 'Aise hi? By magic?'

Ram Palat nods excitedly. 'Exactly, sir!'

Bhavani rests his chunky buttock on the arm of Ram Palat's chair.

'Well done, mere sher. And then what happens? Do the security people spot the problem from this great command centre and rush in immediately to fix the problem?'

Padam Kumar clears his throat.

'Nikamme hain, sir, sab ke sab – lazy fellows. I just spoke to the two who were on duty here last night. They stammered out ki it was a very cold night and a long walk to the gym across the lawn, so they thought it's just balloons, let it be. And anyway, sir, at twelve-fifteen the balloons sort of scattered and floated away here and there on their own, and full visibility was restored.'

'And in those thirty minutes of missing visuals, somebody walked in and set the stage to poison the man!'

'Exactly, sir.'

Bhavani gives a small, vexed snort. 'So much for the finest club in Delhi!'

'Er ... yes, sir.' Ram Palat is looking decidedly abashed. 'And after that, apart from those loose balloons floating here and there a little, nothing else moves in the gym till Leo walked in this morning at five sharp!'

Bhavani absorbs this, his face grim, then straightens up.

'Let us go back to the crime scene.'

Crossing under the yellow tape cordoning off the gym a little later, he looks about the space, breathing heavily. The team inspecting the area eyes him warily, but continues with its tasks, dusting all surfaces and bagging the evidence.

'Four bunches of helium balloons with long trailing ribbons, tied at waist height, to the grills of the four windows, in the four corners of the gym. On the ceiling, in one of these corners, is the security camera! *Only the bunch tied to the grill of the window below the security camera* comes loose and floats up to the ceiling! How, bhai?'

One of the men from the back-up team speaks up hesitantly. 'Sa'ab, at the time of taking over of the crime scene, the glass shutter at that window was found shut. But not locked.' He points at the window below the security camera.

Bhavani goes very still. His eyes travel from the window grill, to the camera above it and back again, repeatedly.

'*So,*' he says softly, '*anybody* could have slid it open from the outside, reached in to loosen the ribbons securing the balloons, causing them to float up higher and cover the camera lens.'

'Yes, sir.'

'And once the job was done, he or she untied the balloons entirely so they floated off here and there on the ceiling!' Bhavani turns to the inspector. 'PK, we need to find out whose bright idea it was to have balloons as decorations at the Bumper Tambola.'

'Yes, sir.'

'For the time being, it looks like this Mukesh Khurana is our most obvious suspect. Get him in here for questioning, and go through the CCTV footage with Ram Palat from the rest of the Club *minutely*. Gates, corridors, restroom, gardens. Prepare a list of everybody who was in the Club between eleven-forty-five and twelve-fifteen.'

'Yes, sir.'

Bhavani heaves a dissatisfied sigh.

'Somebody has been acting very, very over-smart. We will have to change gears to catch this one.'

The Club president sticks his head into the gym, cocking it to one side like an inquisitive hen. 'ACP!'

Bhavani looks up.

'Bhatti sir.'

'So glad to catch you alone,' Devendar Bhatti says as he enters the gym and looks around gingerly. 'I've postponed the elections by a week. Hopefully, that should be sufficient time for this episode to die down! And I've ordered an excellent breakfast by Chef Suresh to be delivered to the Guest Cottage for you and your men. Bring me up to date, won't you? I see the body's gone.'

'We don't have good news, sir.'

Bhatti, in the act of dropping into a chair, freezes, then nods quickly and sits. 'Tell me,' he says crisply.

Bhavani Singh briefs him rapidly on his discoveries.

Bhatti's face sags slightly. 'So it *isn't* a bench press accident after all.'

'No, sir.'

'Pinko Hathni? What is it? It sounds vile.'

'It's a cocktail of ephedrine, heroin and fentanyl, sir. Hardcore stuff! They put in enough to kill an elephant. The protein shake masked its – very mild – taste.'

Bhatti's face lightens. 'I see. So the fellow was taking it to enhance his performance and accidentally took too much. Well, that clears things up!' He smiles at Bhavani, relieved. 'You've done a good job, ACP. I'll have good things to say about you to your chief today!'

Bhavani smiles genially. 'Thank you, sir ... but we think you have nat fully understood.'

He proceeds to tell him about Usain Bolt and the psychedelic gorilla sex. And the suspicious manner in which the CCTV footage seems to have been manipulated. But Bhatti shakes his head with stubborn hauteur.

'You police chaps are too suspicious! He had a filthy drug habit and he probably diddled his dosage. The balloons are just a coincidence. Write out the report the way I want it written and go.'

Ex-home secretary sa'ab believes he is still in office, Bhavani thinks sadly. Shooting out orders and expecting them to followed. His kingdom has shrunk to thirty-two thankless acres and even that will be taken away from him the moment this election is held. After that it's just memoir writing and lit-fests and funerals. Ah well, who are we to disillusion him?

Aloud, he says patiently, 'Sir, that is nat the way.'

Bhatti's nostrils flare. Now looking like a haughty hen, he says, 'Don't tell me what to do in my own club, sir!'

Bhavani sighs gustily. 'No, sir.'

There is a long, tense pause. Which the old policeman spends hunkered silently in his chair, staring down at his rather knobbly knuckles, radiating calm and sympathy in waves. It works. It always does. If Bhavani Singh were an Avenger, radiating calm and sympathy would've been his superpower.

'The government is at our throat, Bhavani,' Bhatti says finally, his watery eyes anxious. 'You must have read about it in the newspapers. They resent *everything* that existed in this ancient, cultured city before they came in from dhokla-land and conquered it. They want to tear all of it down and replace it with a shiny, new New Delhi!' He gives a short, indignant laugh. '*New* New Delhi! Like *Shri* Shri Ravi Shankar! With no history or culture apart from their own crude version of it! Typical nouveau ruler mentality! Naturally our club, with its traditional ties with the older regime, its illustrious members, and its traditions of independent intellectual thinking is high on their hit-list! They've got their eye on our land – which is not owned by us but only leased to us by the city corporation – and they want to throw us out. A messy murder on the premises will give them the perfect excuse. Do look at the bigger picture here!'

Bhavani, who had thought much the same thing on his morning drive to the Club, allows his expression to grow implacable.

'Sir, we are a small man and we can look only at the small picture. A murder has been committed and a murderer has to be caught. The forensic report has already been filed. It says poisoning. Please cooperate with us.'

Bhatti glares angrily at him. Bhavani gazes back doggedly. Finally, the older man mutters a peevish imprecation and flounces out of the room.

Well, we've certainly ruffled his feathers! Bhavani thinks, unperturbed, as he rises to his feet and sets off for Guest Cottage No. 5. He wonders if the offer of an excellent breakfast by Chef Suresh is still standing …

He needn't have worried.

When he walks into the cottage, he finds a fluffy masala omlette, six fat, crispy heart-shaped cutlets, a rack of thick, well-buttered slices of toast and a consignment of steaming hot idli-sambhar are all laid out in the DTC's monogrammed blue-and-white crockery on the coffee table. And Kashi Dogra lifting the lid off a tureen of creamy honey-laced oatmeal with every sign of great anticipation.

He looks up sheepishly when Bhavani enters the room.

'Just taking a peek,' he says apologetically. 'I recommend the oatmeal porridge. They do a great job of it here.'

And Bhavani recalls that he had told the young lawyer to wait for him.

Hmmmm. He has just been thinking that he needs to enlist an insider in this investigation. Somebody who understands the complicated ecosystem of the DTC. This intelligent young fellow, with his easy, friendly manner, his three weeks off and his link to the victim seems like a natural choice. The same members who would close ranks snobbishly when questioned by a Bhavani Singh, may open up to an Akash Dogra. He can be useful.

Bhavani smiles warmly. 'Please join us, vakeel sa'ab! There is enough for five people, we think so!'

Kashi's face lights up at once. 'I'd love to.'

They sit down at the table together.

'So who was bullying Leo yesterday?' Bhavani asks chattily as he spoons porridge into his bowl. 'What exactly was the jhagda-shagda about?'

Kashi looks up quickly, his gaze keenly appraising. 'Wasn't it an accident, then?'

Bhavani is impressed. The pleasant young man doesn't miss much.

He sighs and stirs his porridge. 'He was murdered,' he says bluntly. 'Poisoned.'

'What!' Kashi's face pales. 'Murdered? Are you sure? Why?'

Bhavani gets in two spoonfuls of porridge before he speaks. The lawyer is right. It is excellent.

'O yes, we are sure,' he says finally. 'And it has all been very over-smartly planned and thought through.'

Kashi leans forward. 'Tell me.'

But why are *you* so interested, vakeel sa'ab? Bhavani muses as he stirs his porridge again. Could you have more to do with this situation than you say?

There's no trace of these thoughts on his face as he brings Kashi up to date on his findings. The younger man listens intently, food forgotten, nodding now and then, his brown eyes kindling with fierce sympathy for the dead man.

'I'm not surprised actually,' Kashi says when Bhavani is done, 'that he got killed here. This place is *toxic*. And crawling with entitled snobs. They're all just so … smug and superior and … and … *insulated* from the real world somehow! You should have seen the hostility Leo was facing from the crowd yesterday. He was trying so hard to be helpful and charming, but the women were treating him like a decorative *object*, and the men just seemed to despise him. Khurana actually called him "hired help". That's why I went up there to defend him. Christ, what a bunch of bloodsuckers!'

His indignant outpouring seems sincere enough. Bhavani hears him out, then pushes his bowl away.

'We are worried they will now close ranks to hush the whole thing up. The gormint is anyway trying to shut them down …'

'Oh, the government's just as bad,' Kashi agrees unhesitatingly. 'Gagan Ruia's triggered because he wanted an out-turn membership and Bhatti was too much of a snob to give it to him! Now Ruia wants the place shut down out of sheer spite. That's why he showed up here in a pair of pompommed juttis and manufactured a controversy!'

Bhavani nods. 'Yes, vakeel sa'ab, and because Bhatti sa'ab is worried that this murder may give Ruia and party the perfect excuse to take over the Club, he wants our report to say that Leo had a drug habit and took an overdose accidentally!'

Kashi's eyes flash with anger. 'That's character assassination. And obstruction of justice. And also, just morally wrong. I'll file a public interest litigation demanding a probe if he does. And raise a huge stink. Tell him that!'

'We *will*,' Bhavani replies vigorously. 'Or better still, we will ask our chief to tell him!'

'Awesome!' Kashi says strongly.

Bhavani continues slowly, obeying a nascent, nebulous hunch. 'After that, will you help us, vakeel sa'ab? You have rightly observed that the members of this club are very snobbish. If you sit in on our interviews with them, they are likely to share information with us *much* more openly!'

'Oh!' Kashi looks slightly taken aback. 'Really? You think they'd talk to me?'

'Maybe your lady friend can also help from time to time,' Bhavani adds smoothly.

'Oh!' The hesitation on the lawyer's transparent young face clears up at once. 'Yes! Actually, that's a *great* idea! Bambi's the ultimate DTC insider – she knows everybody here. And she lives right next door!'

The old ACP smiles. 'Excellent.'

<hr />

Inspector Padam Kumar peers into the doorway on Guest Cottage No. 5 to find Bhavani and Kashi seated quite companionably behind the study table.

'Sir, we have located Mrs Roshni Aggarwal and Mrs Cookie Katoch. They were in the Anchor bar.'

'Drinking?' Bhavani raises his eyebrows and glances at his watch.

Padam's face is carefully non-judgemental. 'I er … think so … *yes*, sir.'

'Excellent!' Bhavani beams. 'Bring them in, PK!'

'Uh, testimonies extracted under the influence of intoxicants are not admissible as proof in a court of law,' Kashi says, as PK exits.

'Yes, vakeel sa'ab, but this is just an *informal chat*,' Bhavani replies cosily. 'Right now, they are unguarded and talkative and might point our nose in the right direction. That's all we need! Once they sober up and go home and speak to their husbands, they may button up and give us nothing at all!'

Presently, the two older women enter the room, walking slightly unsteadily, still in their gym clothes. Kashi jumps up to settle them into their chairs.

'You're Balbir's son, aren't you?' Cookie asks.

Kashi grins. 'Yes, auntie.'

'And Leo's lawyer too,' says Roshni. 'I saw you with him yesterday.'

Kashi nods. 'That's right, auntie.'

Bhavani clears his throat. The eyes of the two women swivel to him, apprehensively.

'We are very sad to say that your instructor was murdered, madams,' he says impressively.

The reaction he gets is most gratifying. They gasp; Cookie gives a little scream and Roshni flops into an almost-faint. Kashi makes solicitous noises and pours out glasses of water. Presently Roshni is sufficiently recovered to look Bhavani in the eye.

'Say swear.'

'Swear,' he responds gravely, his hand rising to pinch his Adam's apple. He then proceeds to share all the details, concluding smoothly with, 'Do you have any idea who it could be?'

'Mukki,' says little Cookie Katoch, then hiccups loudly.

Midway through Bhavani's narration, she had wandered off to the coffee table, helped herself to a large serving of the breakfast leftovers, and had been polishing them off with single-minded concentration. Her eyes widen when she feels everybody looking at her.

'These are really very good,' she says indistinctly through a mouth full of heart-shaped cutlet. 'You should try some, Ro.'

'You're supposed to be off carbs, Cookie,' bony Roshni reminds her pudgy friend. 'You're cheating!'

Cookie deposits another piece of cutlet into her mouth. 'I've had a terrible shock,' she says indistinctly, waving her fork about in a dreamy manner. 'A terrible, *terrible* shock. My body … *needs* carbs, ACP Brownie.'

Bhavani looks at her just a little reproachfully.

Cookie is immediately apologetic. 'I'm so sorry – but you *do* look so square, and chocolatey and walnutty and *dense*. I meant it in the nicest possible way!'

He smiles at her through the wafting scent of Bombay Sapphire. 'Please take all the carbs you need, madam!'

'Did you even *hear* what the ACP said?' Roshni demands of her friend. 'Leo's accident wasn't an accident – somebody murdered him!'

Cookie hiccups again. 'Mukki.'

Roshni gives a little scream. 'Stop *saying* that, Cookie!'

'Ooopsies.' Cookie covers her mouth. 'Sorry.'

She reaches for the ketchup in a vague sort of way. Kashi takes it from her and uncaps it, then pours a generous amount onto her plate.

'Why do you say that, auntie? That Mukki uncle did it?'

'Well!' She puts down her plate. 'For one thing, yesterday, at the tambola, when Mukki said, "I don't share. I've never shared anything", Leo sort of sneered and replied – "*That's what you think!*"'

'And that meant?' Kashi asks, being deliberately obtuse.

'That meant that Leo had been sharing Mukki's wife, of course!' Roshni sounds cross at having to explain. 'The implication's *obvious!*'

Cookie picks up the narrative again. 'And then Mukki gave a little scream and tried to hit Leo and missed, and Leo planted a big fat mukka on Mukki's face and Mukki collapsed like a bouncy castle when the electricity goes.'

'Very well explained, madam, very well explained.' Bhavani re-enters the conversation. 'Understood ... and so these two people – your friend Urvashi, and the Zumba trainer – they were having an affair?'

Roshni licks her nude-lipstick-ed lips and giggles. 'Everybody *says* so!'

Cookie pushes away her empty plate. 'Well, I *hope* she is!' she says staunchly. 'She needs some fun in her life, poor Urvashi!'

Bhavani tilts his head slightly. 'Why is she *poor* Urvashi?' he enquires. 'Is her poverty material – or spiritual?'

'Ah!' Roshni Aggarwal is surprised. '*What* an intelligent man you are!'

'Thank you.' He beams. 'So, Urvashi is poor because …?'

Cookie holds up one clarifying hand. 'Please don't misunderstand. Urvashi Khurana is our *hero*. Years ago, we were all in the same boat – more or less newly married – dropping our kids off to the same playschool, struggling to lose our post-pregnancy fat and regain our looks, homesick for our mothers' cooking and bitching about our mothers-in-law! We met for coffee and croissants every week and talked about starting our own businesses, and rising above being just Missus So-and-So, but Urvi was the only one who *really* managed to do it.'

'That's not true, Cooks,' Roshni interjects loyally. 'You have *ShivBling!*' She turns to face Bhavani. 'She's an *artist*, inspector, she makes these glorious, anatomically-exact Shivlings out of stone, metal and glass!'

'Her work's *amazing*, ACP!' Kashi chimes in. 'I've seen it!'

Cookie blushes. 'I think your parents won one of my pieces in the Diwali raffle draw a couple of years ago? I contribute one piece every year.'

Kashi nods enthusiastically and doesn't mention that his father had been thoroughly appalled by the thing, dubbing it 'a donkey's phallus' and draping it decorously in money plant before displaying it in the garden so that the modesty of Sector-44, Noida, would not be outraged.

'Still, my work's nothing compared to Chrysanthemum!' Cookie says modestly. 'Chrysanthemum is—'

'The lifestyle store?' Bhavani Singh is impressed. He is aware of Chrysanthemum – his wife has recently saved for three months to buy a bone china tea-for-two set from there to enliven the evening tea in their empty-nester home.

The ladies nod.

'It's a big success. She got a fifty-crore funding for it recently.'

'So aunties, then why do you say *poor* Urvashi?' Kashi endeavours to bring them back to the point.

'Because she's married to Mukki,' Roshni responds bluntly. 'The man's boring, and charmless and ugly. *And* he's passed on his ugly DNA to their two daughters, who, poor things, will never win a beauty pageant – what d'you say, young Dogra?'

'I think beauty pageants objectify women,' is his steady reply.

She dismisses him with a wave of her bony hand. 'Your generation is too politically correct! And that's why I say *poor* Urvashi. It was *heartbreaking* to see her valiantly trying to prettify those ugly girls – she might as well have wrapped Chantilly lace around two baby buffalos! Even now she keeps insisting they're late bloomers ... Arrey, they're twenty-six and twenty-four! Aur kitna late bloom karengi?'

'Ro, they're *quite* namkeen-looking!' Cookie objects. 'You're just being mean now!'

Roshni sniffs. 'People always say namkeen when they mean ugly.'

'Words can be ugly too.' Kashi's calm voice has a warning edge to it. 'Don't you think?'

There is a small pause.

Then Roshni shrugs and continues, 'Anyway, the *point* is that Urvashi, so beautiful herself, and a great connoisseur of beauty and style, condemned to live with Mukki and her two bhains-like daughters, *cannot* be blamed for gravitating towards Leo Matthew, also so beautiful, but in a delightfully *male* way.'

Bhavani, himself a plain man married to an extremely attractive woman, is reeling slightly at these sweeping statements. However, he manages to nod in agreement and look meaningfully at Kashi, who wades dutifully into the fray again.

'D'you *really* think they were having an affair, auntie?' he asks, fixing his brown eyes entreatingly on Cookie.

She responds to this direct appeal at once. 'See, all of us have – had – a bit of a crush on Leo. We giggle and talk about him, and of course all our pot-bellied husbands get jealous. It's all quite harmless. Urvashi doesn't giggle though. She's not the type – too dignified. But the thing is, she *really* enjoys the Zumba. Initially, she was just like any one of us – shy, you know, and self-conscious of all those Latino moves and Hispanic thrusts, and the way Leo would keep urging us to "throw a little hip into it!" But *then* ... maybe because she'd been doing yoga at home for years and is naturally flexible ... she started moving differently ... all Spanish and sexy ... She even began talking about becoming an instructor herself!'

'She started standing front and centre, too,' Roshni recalls. 'We used to all be really shy about standing in the middle of the front row. We would all hang back, and Leo would make fun of us for acting like backbencher schoolgirls, but then Urvi just started walking in and taking that place like it was reserved for her by right! And then Leo started praising her, and picking her every time he wanted to demonstrate a move with a partner ... Then she got all these new gym clothes ... and then *he* started asking her to stay back and help him fine-tune his yoga asanas because he wanted to be more flexible like her and then—'

'Have you seen *English Vinglish*?' Cookie interjects.

Bhavani Singh blinks at this random change in topic. 'Yes.'

Cookie beams. 'So it was like *that* only. The dancing *unlocked* something in her personality! She got this *glow*.'

'Please!' Roshni's bony face acquires a knowing expression. 'That glow was not just from *dancing*, Cooks.'

They both giggle.

But Bhavani Singh is not amused. A glow won't stand up in court, he gloomily. What he needs is proof of an affair and there seems to be none forthcoming. Then he remembers Leo's phone. Hopefully, there will be something in there ... pictures, messages ... With a sudden start he realizes Cookie is speaking to Kashi.

'See, if Leo and Urvashi were having an affair while that wet fish Mukki was balancing the account books of his stupid rich clients then it was really not anybody's business except Urvashi and Leo's, and perhaps Mukki's. But with the Club election coming along, it suddenly became *everybody's* business.'

'Why does Urvashi Khurana want to be Club president?' Bhavani asks abruptly.

This stumps the two ladies slightly.

'Uh, what?'

'Matlab, from what you've described, she's a busy, successful businesswoman, doing yoga and Zumba – *and* having an affair. *Where* does she have the time to stand for an election as well?'

Cookie's pudgy brow furrows. 'That's true …'

Bhavani smiles genially. 'So then?'

'You know, ACP, I think that she's a woman who likes a *challenge*,' Cookie says finally. 'Initially it was all about getting back into shape after her children were born, then it was about balancing work and home … Now that her girls are grown, and Chrysanthemum is all settled, she's restless again … And the DTC has never had a woman president before!'

'You'd never have asked that question if she were a man, officer,' Roshni says severely. 'You'd have just *assumed* that it's perfectly natural for a man to want to add another feather in his cap. But a woman's ambitions must always be questioned! *You're* being sexist!'

Genuinely abashed, Bhavani asks for forgiveness.

'So, what plans does Urvashi auntie have for the Club?' asks Kashi.

'A much bigger rainwater harvesting plant, for one!' Roshni says. 'That's why Mehra's so wild at her. She wants to put it where the kitchen garden is. Which is dedicated to his wife's memory.'

Kashi raises his eyebrows. 'That sounds insensitive.'

Roshni bristles. 'Not at all! She got it surveyed by the rainwater harvesting people and they said it's got the best catchment area. And she says they can replant the garden over it, once they're done. But he's *so* gussa about it!'

'Men have so much ego.' Cookie sighs.

Bhavani attempts to re-enter the conversation.

'Could you tell us something about Leo, also? What did you ladies talk to him about?'

There is the oddest little pause. The two women, so loquacious thus far, seem to have utterly dried up.

Kashi looks from one to the other.

'Err ... Cookie auntie? Roshni auntie?'

Slightly pink-cheeked and not quite meeting his eyes, Cookie says, 'We didn't talk to him too much, actually.'

Kashi's eyebrows rise. 'But why?'

'Oho, you won't understand, beta!' Roshni says. 'We said hello and goodbye and thank you and all that. And of course, if we did something wrong, he corrected us – but we didn't chit-chat.'

'It gets complicated if you chit-chat,' Cookie explains. 'People start taking advantage.'

'Ya, see, it's always awkward with these in-between types,' Roshni chimes in. 'People who are not quite your social equal, but higher than drivers or maids or the other trainers in the gym! Because such people are actually *quite* narrow-minded beneath their thin veneer of sophistication! If we talked too nicely he might have thought we were infatuated with him!'

'Which we were!' Cookie gurgles.

'But not *really*!' Roshni clarifies. 'We just liked *looking* at him!'

'*Baith mere paas tujhe dekhti rahoon*,' Cookie hums. '*Tu na kuch kahe aur mein na kuch kahoon.*'

Bhavani notices that Kashi is having a hard time dealing with all this casual objectification, and interjects smoothly.

'Can you tell us little-bit about his phone? We understand you picked it up and opened it?'

Roshni nods. 'I did it sort of automatically – I do it with my son's phone also sometimes, when his alarm is ringing and he is sleeping through it. Just grab his finger and press it to the phone to open it. I thought that would be the fastest way to inform his family.'

'That was good thinking on your part, madam,' Bhavani says. 'And you were lucky. That technique wouldn't have worked with a cold corpse. But clearly you got there just minutes after he died.'

She shivers. 'I still can't quite believe it. Somebody we know ... sneaking into our happy little balloon-filled gym, tip-toeing to the fridge we drink out of every day, clutching a lethal drug in their sweaty hands, opening the flask with their hearts thumping hard – because surely your heart must thump hard when you pull this kind of a stunt, officer?'

He nods soberly. 'O yes. Murder is always stressful, madam. Even for the most hardened killer. Let no one tell you otherwise.'

'One must burn a lot of calories while killing somebody, I suppose,' Roshni says thoughtfully. 'Your BMR must go through the roof! I wouldn't be surprised if one lost a few kilograms out of sheer stress!'

'I should probably kill somebody then!' her friend replies, staring ruefully down at her empty plate. 'Why did you let me eat all those cutlets? Especially after we missed our morning workout!'

'Cooks, we're going to have to find a new trainer, fast,' Roshni says seriously. 'I can feel the fat crawling up around my thighs already.'

And it's back to business as usual, Kashi thinks to himself. A man's dead, for fuck's sake, but they've already moved on. Wow! Is that an old person thing, a rich person thing, or a DTC member thing?

'You should start the Canadian army's XBX program for ladies, madam,' Bhavani tells the women meanwhile. 'It's just an eleven-minute workout and we do the gents' version of it every day! It can be done anywhere – no need for music or special equipment or an instructor!'

Cookie blinks at him. 'Well, music and equipment and a qualified instructor are kind of the point actually,' she replies. 'I mean, we're not some Hanuman bhakts doing rote exercises in a colony park!'

The old policemen blinks at this careless barb, yet continues to smile. But Kashi has had enough.

He says, rather sharply, 'Of course, now that we know that it was a murder, your handling of the phone amounts to evidence tampering, auntie.'

Roshni sticks out her tongue contritely, in a child-like gesture that looks odd on a woman in her fifties. 'I'm so sorry!' she says.

'Who did you phone, by the way?' Bhavani asks.

Her eyes widen guilelessly. 'The number one name on his speed dial. 'Rax something. But he didn't pick up. And there was no "mum" or "dad" or "babe" saved in the contacts.'

'That sounds so lonely!' Cookie remarks, with belated sensitivity. 'Poor Leo! How can you have no one to notify when you die? We should've gotten over his hotness and talked to him more often, Ro.'

'We just thought of him one-dimensionally,' her friend agrees. 'But clearly he was a whole person ... and we have no idea who that person was ...'

6

Cheeky Peaches

'Was that a good interview?' Kashi asks Bhavani after the ladies have tottered away to their cars, escorted by Padam. 'Did I help? Or make things worse?'

Bhavani sighs. 'No, no, you did well, vakeel sa'ab,' he says. 'But the main thing is that the good ladies were correct. We know nothing about Leo, or the person he was. There is no point talking to anybody else till we figure that out. And the answer to that question is right *here.*'

He gestures with one stubby finger to the black mirror surface of Leo Mathew's latest model iPhone, lying open and defenseless amongst the tea things on the cluttered study table.

'You wanna do the honours?' Kashi asks.

The old ACP sits forward, sighs, sends up a wordless apology to the dead man whose privacy he is about to violate and taps the phone gingerly. The screensaver blooms to life.

A zoomed-in shot of Leo Matthew's torso, smooth, alive and rippling with muscle. The words 'BODYBUILDING IS CHARACTER BUILDING' are tattooed into his sternum in simple black type.

'Hmm.' Kashi tilts his head to one side and considers the motto. 'I'm not sure I agree entirely. I mean, sure, bodybuilding teaches you discipline and is a great stressbuster. But it doesn't make you a kinder person, or a more empathetic person or even a more intelligent person.'

'It is an ape's motto.' Bhavani grunts succinctly. 'We are nat impressed by it at all! Now, what else does Matthew sa'ab have to say for himself?'

He fishes out a pair of reading glasses from his pocket, puts them on, then presses the Gallery icon and peers down at the screen.

'Not too many photos,' he murmurs. 'Now that is *very* odd. Such a vain man must have taken a lot of pictures of himself!'

'Maybe he was vain enough to have a fancy camera as well,' Kashi suggests.

'Hmm.' Bhavani considers the suggestion. 'Maybe. Let us see what he has on WhatsApp.'

There are eight groups with new notifications.

*Golf Links Girls

*Panchsheel Ladies Zumba

*Sundernagar Zumba

*Def Col Body Combat

*Vv Ladies Bollydance

*Saket Ladies Zumba

*Gulmohar Park Evening Zumba

Bhavani raises his eyebrows. '*Quite* the little Kishan Kanhaiya!' He presses his big square finger to the screen and randomly opens Golf Links Girls.

Where are you?

Late again?

Traffic jam?

Ditcherrrr!

Oho, is it your allergies? The pollen is crazy nowadays. TC!

Leo, this is unacceptable. I for one, will not be paying for this no-show class.

Get well soon!

We're starting without you. Join us soonest!

The other groups are all full of similar messages.

Kashi's forehead wrinkles. 'They're so *polite*,' he says. 'Except for that one terse lady. When I'm late for a consultation, everybody bites my head off.'

Bhavani opens the group he's most interested in. *Dtc Girls Zumba, last active at 5.40 this morning. He scrolls upwards to the beginning of the month.

LEO (admin)
Ladies please confirm your presence for class today – and also for the month of February. Please carry your fees of Rs 5,000 in cash with you. Kindly avoid delays and reminders.

Bhavani Singh lets out a low, impressed whistle. Five thousand rupees a month? This is a pricey class! And what is the full class strength anyway? He clicks on Group info.

There are sixteen women in the group. From the pictures, they seem like a mix of young and old. Going back to the chat, he can see that ten have put thumbs ups and confirmed for February.

Quickly, he does the math.

'Look at this, vakeel sa'ab! Your friend was taking eight different classes every month – charging each lady a fee of five thousand rupees. With roughly ten women in each class, toh' – he does some quick calculations – 'that was four lakh a month! For teaching this Zumba dancing! *And* he probably didn't pay any taxes either. All payments in cash only!'

'He's making more money than me,' Kashi says a little glumly.

'Except that he's dead,' Bhavani points out practically. 'So he isn't making *anything* any more. You're better off, don't you think?'

They continue to scroll through the group chat. It seems very businesslike – just timings, and a few messages from Leo about pending fees, running late, or calling in sick. There are a *lot* of Zumba videos on the group – full of shimmering, flat bellies and lithe limbs, all dancing energetically with wide smiles on their faces – and even a video of DTC GIRLS ZUMBA dancing to Shakira's 'Waka Waka', recorded by Leo.

'That must be madam Urvashi,' says Bhavani. 'She is standing front and centre, and she certainly is very beautiful.'

Urvashi is also very much the leader of the group, dressed in a simple, but gorgeously coordinated white-and-gold gym tights and matching vest. On her left is a sleepy-looking Bambi in a grey sweatshirt and baggy pants. On Urvashi's right is the maroon-haired lady, resplendent in red spandex. Cookie and Rosh, standing in the second row, are visible through the gaps.

When the music kicks in, Urvashi is absolutely electrifying – lissome, flexible, light on her feet and completely unselfconscious. Bambi is erratic, good when she remembers the steps, but blanking out sometimes – hopping about with a foolish, self-conscious grin on her face, till the group reverts to the main hook step that she has mastered. Cookie and Roshni give a fair account of themselves, but look utterly exhausted – the video has clearly been shot at the fag end of the one-hour class. And the maroon lady stomps gamely through the lilting song with robotic focus, managing to reduce the graceful, fluid steps to a series of PT exercises.

Kashi chuckles. 'Bambi's barely keeping up!' He stares down at the screen amused, as Bambi Todi forgets the steps and clowns around the floor.

'Focus, vakeel sa'ab!' mutters Bhavani, and abruptly exits WhatsApp.

Having spent thirty years in the Crime Branch, eighteen since the advent of the smartphone, he knows that almost every phone has its own little chamber of secrets. Shady deals, private diaries, bank accounts numbers and other financial details, archived chats, sexts, dickpics. You just have to keep digging till you find it.

He picks up the iPhone. It feels alive with its owner's essence, bursting with little secrets and insights. But it is proving to be aggravatingly bland.

He checks Call History.

The maximum number of calls Leo has received recently are from an individual called Rax, whose display picture shows a grinning, paunchy guy with a shaved head, probably in his mid-thirties.

Going back to WhatsApp, he checks Leo's chats with Rax.

TWO MONTHS AGO

> Lambu, come home. We'll drink beer and watch pondis. Get Vicky also. This new pondi I got will blow his holy little mind.

> Rain check, Rax. Working late. And you're WAY too old to watch pondis. Also, nobody calls them pondis anymore.

'Pondicherry?' Kashi wrinkles his forehead.

'Pornography,' Bhavani enlightens him. 'It is slang – from the nineties.'

'Ah.'

ONE MONTH AGO

> Hey man, can you lend me like ten grand? I'm in a bit of a sitch.

> PayTm-ed you. Check.

TUESDAY

Lee, I've got a lump. On the side of my neck. It's my lymph nodes, I think. I'm sick, man.

> No, you're not. Stop feeling yourself up.

FRIDAY

Haha, fucker, thanks for taking me to the doc! So good to know I'm not dying! Hey, you wanna come over tonight and watch pondis?

This last message has been seen-zoned by Leo.

'Clearly a clingy, childhood best friend,' Kashi pronounces.

Bhavani nods. 'Agreed.'

They move on to the second most frequently called number. This proves to no-nonsense looking young woman called Sho. She has short pink ombre hair, and is cuddling a belligerent looking orange cat in her WhatsApp DP.

ONE WEEK AGO

Leo, here's the edit. It's lo-res, obvio. Approve and I'll upload the high-res.

> I saw. It's so good, Sho! You're a genius!

FIVE DAYS AGO

Dude, can you please reply to one or two of the comments on the latest video. The ladies are clamouring for some love.

Done.

TWO DAYS AGO

Sho, I can't shoot this week, can we manage with a rerun?

Are you nuts? Your sponsors will lose their shit! Get here by 9 sharp, wearing those teeshirts and trainers they sent you! It's going to be a great shoot - I splashed out on some fancy lenses and I'm dying to try them out!

YESTERDAY

I know why we named the damned show Lose it with Leo. The 'it' refers to my sanity, my self-respect and my money. Die, you dog.

They look at each other.

'She means it figuratively,' Kashi says.

'We know,' Bhavani replies. 'She sent it after he didn't come for the shoot, and didn't return her two missed calls.'

Kashi peers down at her DP. 'She sounds nice. Strong, and responsible. D'you think they're in a relationship?'

'Not any more,' Bhavani replies whimsically.

They move back up to the edit Sho has sent – the thumbnail is Leo's handsome brown face frozen mid-move on the screen. The powerful neck is tossed back, the trademark messy mane of hair is on full display, as are the very white teeth, parted in a warm, wide smile.

Bhavani presses play.

'*Uno! Dos! Tres! Cuatro!*' Clad in just a pair of cream cotton pyjamas and a Hawaiian flower garlard, Leo dances to a vibrant salsa beat at the edge of a landscaped swimming pool. His movements are effortless, his coordination with the music bang-on. The flowers bounce against his sculpted brown chest and rippling abs, emphasizing the sinuous fluidity of his moves.

Bhavani starts to hum and sway tentatively to the beat. 'Too good, ya!' He smiles. 'This Zumba is quite zabardast!'

Kashi doesn't look too impressed. 'Let's look at the third most favourite caller.'

This turns out to be a man called Naaem. He's very smiley-faced, and encased in a too-tight jacket.

ONE WEEK AGO

NAEEM
Sir, this is really a superfine opportunity. The Rosetta Fern membership is far superior to anything Club Mahindra of Sterling can offer you. In just 8 lakhs all inclusive, you and your partner can have a time share vacation of seven days in a year, every year for twenty years! This is a limited opportunity, please avail.

'How much we would love to take our Shalini on a European holiday!' Bhavani sighs. 'Her English is better than the Queen's also!'

Kashi wonders if he should mention that England is no longer a part of Europe, then decides not to bother.

Bhavani taps the DP of the fourth most frequent caller. He's saved as Vicky, and turns out to be a dark, smiling man in a Roman Catholic cassock, standing in a Mother Mary grotto.

Kashi utters a small exclamation. 'Hey, I know this guy! He runs that orphanage through which I met Leo. It's in Haryana somewhere.'

There are no WhatsApp messages to or from Vicky. Clearly, he and Leo prefer to just talk.

'He looks to be the same age as Leo, nahi?' Bhavani asks.

'Yes.' Kashi nods. 'Didn't Randy Rax talk about a Vicky? He said the pondy would blow his holy little mind. The three must be school friends!'

'Good people to talk to,' Bhavani replies. 'We'll get PK to set up meetings straightaway. Oh look, here are some messages from Urvashiji.'

There is a very prim exchange of birthday greetings between Leo and Urvashi, several music videos – Shakira's 'Waka Waka', Nora Fatehi's 'O Saki Saki', Bruno Mars's 'Uptown Funk', and a final one Kashi isn't familiar with. 'Secrets' by The Cheeky Peaches.

The two blue ticks beside the message reveal that this last song has been seen by Urvashi, but she hasn't reacted to it. Nor has she reacted to his next – and final – message, which is a link of some sort.

'That is a really old song,' Bhavani Singh says surprised. 'Matlab, from *our* times!' He has a hazy memory from when he was young, of a girl band in the seventies – a blonde, a redhead and a brunette, belting it out in glittering catsuits. 'Why would he send her that?'

'Never heard of it,' Kashi replies. 'Maybe they were practicing a retro dance or something?'

They continue to scroll though WhatsApp.

'Here's a bunch of messages from Bambi,' Kashi says, amused. 'Leo keeps asking her if she is going to sign up for Zumba next month and she keeps making excuses and trying to wriggle out of it …'

He looks so relieved, Bhavani observes privately. What a fellow! If he likes her, why doesn't he just tell her?

Something catches his eye. He frowns and quickly puts out one hand, staying Kashi from scrolling further.

'Stop, vakeel sa'ab! See, Leo has sent that old song to Bambiji too! She's replied with two question marks and a comically scared face. And then he has sent her …'

He pauses, then continues, his voice low and musing, 'He has sent her *this* link. Odd.'

He plucks the phone out of Kashi's hand and clicks on www.badshahpurchildrensvillage.in.

Immediately, a bright blue banner flutters across the screen.

WELCOME TO THE BADSHAHPUR CHILDREN'S VILLAGE! JESUS IS LORD! DONATIONS WELCOME! it proclaims as it settles over an image of laughing children gathered before a red-brick building standing in what appears to be rural Haryana. A priest in a white cassock stands in the middle of the group, smiling.

'Vicky!' says Bhavani at once, pointing at the priest. 'Whose mind will be blown if he watches pondys.'

'Father Victor Emmanuel,' Kashi says slowly. 'That's the orphanage I met Leo at.'

They stare at the screen, their minds computing this new information.

'He sent Urvashi some link too,' Bhavani recalls suddenly.

He checks, working the phone, then looks up at Kashi, his eyes glowing with excitement.

'Urvashi Khurana, Roshni Aggarwal, Bambi Todi and the surgical strikes walla Gen. Mehra have *all* received the Cheeky Peaches song. Only Bambi has replied. The others haven't said anything. Two blue ticks, but radio silence. And *all* of them, one hour later, have been sent the Badshahpur link by Leo. Again, no response at all. Just two blue ticks.'

'Bambi, two aunties, and a general,' Kashi says slowly. 'Surely that's odd? Why does Leo even *know* the general? He doesn't do Zumba!'

Bhavani frowns. 'Good point.'

'My Dad isn't too hot on Gen. Mehra,' Kashi continues. 'He was Dad's junior in the IMA, but he got a bunch more promotions. Dad says he's a kiss-up.'

'He *is*,' Bhavani agrees. 'When we were young, we were taught that an officer should be loyal to the Constitution of India, nat the gourmint of India, but this Gen. Mehra clearly bunked those lessons.'

'He's insanely popular though,' Kashi says.

'Yes,' Bhavani is starting to look extremely satisfied. 'And a man with a reputation to maintain can easily be blackmailed.'

Kashi looks confused. *'Blackmailed?'*

The old ACP chuckles, nodding. Crime Branch regulars would have noticed that his homely face had started to shine with the luminous, beautifying glow of a Bollywood heroine in the 'after' part of a face cream commercial – this always happens when he achieves a breakthrough.

'Yes, vakeel sa'ab, blackmail! What we have here is three rich ladies and one gent with a reputation to maintain. And they've all been sent *this* song! What other conclusion could we possibly draw?'

'I don't understand what you're getting at.' Kashi frowns. 'Sure, Bambi's rich, but she's never done anything *so* shady that somebody could blackmail her for it. Besides, she's the kind of person who needs to regurgitate *everything* that happens to her on a daily basis or she gets physically ill! I doubt she'd have a deep dark secret. She's just not made that way.'

He looks up at the policeman with defiant, hostile eyes. Back off, they are saying quite clearly.

Bhavani backtracks smoothly. 'Well, maybe he was wrong about Bambiji. She is the only one who has sent a casual, puzzled reply. The others have gone as still and silent as if a snake has sniffed them. It's suspicious.'

'I don't see why,' Kashi insists stubbornly. 'I don't know how you're getting blackmail from all this, anyway!'

Bhavani smiles. 'That is because you are too young to have heard *Secrets* by the Cheeky Peaches. *Listen.*'

He taps the screen.

An insistent back beat, the thrum of a string guitar, and a husky female voice:

You think your secret's safe,
You think you left no trace
You're sure, that no one knows
You're smelling ... like a rose
But fate has a way of catching up with sinners
At the end of the day there are no free dinners
And I will make you pay
Oh, I will make you pay
P p p p p pay
P p p p p pay
P p p p p pay
P p p p p pay
Oh yeah, you better be worried,
Cos I know where the bodies are buried.
Pay, pay, pay and stay worried,
Cos I know where the bodies are buried.

Bhavani, watching Kashi's face over the pulsating iPhone, sees the confusion clear as the young lawyer's mind wraps itself around the only, inevitable solution.

The song ends.

'Kyun?' demands Bhavani. 'What do you think now?'

'He seems to have been blackmailing the rich to give to the poor,' Kashi admits slowly. 'Like Robin Hood. The kind of wild, romantic scheme that's a socialist's wet dream. Not bad for Lambodar/Leo!'

The traffic pile-up at the Delhi–Badshahpur Toll Gate is almost a kilometre long and half a kilometre wide. Vendors criss-cross the eight lanes of slow-moving, smoke-spewing, drearily honking vehicles, selling peanuts, jasmine strands, cucumber slices and wedges of coconut to jaundiced looking commuters, who watch with envious eyes as the smartly painted police Gypsy coasts through the ninth lane – reserved for VIPs – and disappears down the highway.

'I've always wanted to do that!' Kashi Dogra grins. 'Perks of the job, eh, Bhavaniji?'

Bhavani Singh chuckles genially. 'As you say, vakeel sa'ab, perks of the job!'

The Gypsy makes good speed on the open road, empty except for the occasional tempo traveller or bus. For a while, both men stare out at the dusty road, which bifurcates a classic Aravalli ridge landscape of grey-green thorned keekar trees spreading out as far as the eye can see.

'I met my girlfriend on this road,' Kashi says, after a while. 'Exactly a year ago.'

'O really?' Bhavani looks at him, surprised. 'You have a girlfriend? We thought—' He checks himself, shaking his head.

'You thought, what?' Kashi's tone is slightly challenging.

Bhavani shrugs. 'We thought that if you had three weeks off, you would want to spend them with your girlfriend. But it's none of our business.'

Kashi's lean cheeks flush. 'Oh that,' he says, a little awkwardly. 'We had a Goa holiday all planned – which is why

I had taken the three weeks off in the first place, but then she cancelled at the last minute.'

'That is *nat* nice,' Bhavani says sympathetically. 'We hope she is *nat* unwell? Did you get your money back?'

Kashi nods. 'Yes, all that part of it is okay, but ... we uh, well, we had a bit of an argument when she called to cancel on me.'

'So you are sulking,' Bhavani states, shooting a sideways glance at the younger man.

There is a longish pause.

'Yes,' Kashi admits ruefully.

'Young couples fight all the time,' Bhavani says comfortingly. 'It is all part of getting to know each other better.'

'Kuhu and I already know each other well enough.' Kashi is immediately defensive.

Bhavani smiles reassuringly. 'We're sure. We're sure.'

'Our tuning is *amazing*,' Kashi continues doggedly. 'We complete each other's sentences.'

If Bhavani thinks Kashi is protesting too much, he doesn't let it show. Instead, he asks, 'What does she do? Your girlfriend?'

Kashi's face clears a little.

'She's an architect. In fact, the day I met her, she was driving out very early in the morning on this very road to see how the light of the rising sun hit the plot of land she had been commissioned to build on.'

'Wah! It's good to see young women focusing on their curryars,' Bhavani remarks admiringly. 'We have two daughters and they are curryar-minded too. Your girlfriend sounds really committed.'

'I'm committed too,' Kashi says at once, and then is utterly mortified. Why the hell did he say that? The ACP was clearly talking about commitment to a career, not to a relationship!

He has Kalra to thank for that first meeting. The two of them had gone to see a late-night screening of the new *Creed* movie, and the fucker had been texting Walli while driving, about how foul it was, and crashed the car into a barrier on a lonely stretch of the Vasant Kunj ridge at three in the morning. Kashi, asleep beside him, had woken up with a godawful jerk to the sight of Kalra, his nose all bloody, bent over in pain, screaming, 'My cock, my cock!'

It had turned out to be his leg, not his cock – but he was definitely unable to walk. The two of them ended up sitting in pitch darkness by the side of the forest road, besides the totalled car. Kalra's phone had got smashed in the crash, and Kashi's had been dead anyway. Their best hope was that Walli, wondering why Kalra had stopped texting mid-rant, would be alarmed enough to come looking for them.

Just when Kashi had started thinking it made more sense to leave Kalra there and start jogging to civilization for help, a car had driven up, its beams shining on their bloodied faces. They had waved frantically. The car had slowed down uncertainly, the driver clearly in two minds – the Badshahpur forest road is notorious for rapes and muggings. Kashi had leapt to his feet, run forward and beaten his hands on the glass, shouting for help.

That settled the matter. The car accelerated, and sped off.

'I'm dying!' Kalra had groaned thickly, collapsing to lie on his back on the road. 'I'm dying, Dogra!'

Then, as Kashi had watched, holding his friend, helpless with fury and frustration, the car executed a three-point turn, drove back and stopped nearby. The window on the driver's side had lowered an inch.

'You guys need help?'

It was a hesitant female voice, slightly musical, very wary. At that moment, it seemed to Kashi he had never heard a more beautiful sound in his whole life.

'My friend's hurt!' he yelled hoarsely. 'We need a ride!'

There was a long pause.

'Don't drive off!' Kashi begged, panicking. 'Please! Our phones are smashed! And the signal's shit, anyway!'

'Okay, but we can *never* tell my mother about this,' the girl had finally said in a tight voice. 'Get in.'

Needing no second invitation, Kashi had half-carried, half-bundled the bloodied Kalra into the backseat, then clambered in beside him and slammed the car door shut.

'If you pull out a knife or a gun now,' the girl said, in the same tight voice, 'and this spirals into some ghastly rape and robbery, you'll have destroyed my faith in the human race forever. Remember that.'

'I'm speaking perfect English, bro,' Kalra groaned in reply. 'Do I sound like a fucking rapist?'

'That's fucking classist,' she'd shot back at once. 'You're clearly an elitist asshole.' She met Kashi's eyes in the mirror.

He glimpsed narrowed eyes behind black-rimmed glasses, a belligerent nostril and a tiny nose piercing. 'Are you an asshole too?'

'No no, I'm just thankful you stopped for us,' he had hurried to assure her. Then he couldn't help adding, 'Though you *do* realize you took a terrible risk! *Never* stop like that again! And you shouldn't be driving alone, on such a lonely road, so late in the night, anyway!'

'Okay, Mummy,' she had replied, now disgusted with both of them. 'Jesus, what a pair of creeps.'

'Sorry,' Kashi had muttered contritely. Kalra had just moaned in pain.

She'd changed gears, got the car to move. 'The Spinal Injuries Institute is closest,' she'd said curtly. 'Brace yourselves for the ride.'

And that had been that.

Now, Kashi stares out of the window at the passing wilderness, and feels like a total heel.

Then he reaches for his phone, types out a message, and presses send.

> Nice try, Bannerjee. We're definitely not Over. Suck it up.

'Well, at least this young lady likes to wake up early!' Bhavani chuckles besides him. 'Your *other* young lady, she doesn't like to wake up early, no?'

Kashi looks up from his phone, confused.

'Arrey, for the Zumba!' Bhavani reminds him.

The tips of Kashi's ears redden. 'She's not my *other* young lady,' he says shortly. 'She's just a … a bachpan ka dost.'

And then he remembers how hurt he'd been when Bambi had used exactly this phrase to describe him to her juice stall assistants, and starts to feel wretchedly guilty.

'I'm just ...' he hesitates and goes quiet.

Missing something, he admits to himself. Something he wasn't even aware he was missing until he met Bambi Todi again. The memories, and the level of comfort and familiarity they share is insane, and then there's that trustful, peculiar softness of her, the open vulnerability, the total access pass – the whole combination is a potent package.

Basically, when Kuhu turns her eyes on him and smiles, he feels like the sun has come out from behind a dark cloud, but when Bambi Todi does the same thing, he feels like the sun itself.

Besides him, Bhavani Singh, seemingly unaware of Kashi's internal churnings, gives a satisfied little grunt. 'Ah! There is the Badshahpur turn-off ...'

Twenty minutes later, they are driving through a large, rather ramshackle gate on a kachcha road, into the compound of the Children's Village.

A game of basketball is in progress on the newly cemented court. As they alight from the Gypsy, several of the boys raise their arms and wave at Kashi, who waves back. A lean, dark man in his mid-thirties breaks away from the group of players and strides towards them, letting down the cassock that he had hitched up around his waist.

'Kashi!' he greets the lawyer. 'How are you, men? Good to see you again! What's happening?' His gaze travels to the quiet, homely stranger standing beside Kashi, and his face grows slightly apprehensive. 'Has ... has something happened?'

'This is ACP Bhavani Singh,' Kashi says formally, looking at the priest with troubled eyes. 'We don't have good news I'm afraid, Father Vick ...'

In his little office, lined on three sides with metal filing cabinets, Fr Victor sits behind a metal desk, a crucifix and a portrait of Mahatma Gandhi on the wall at his back, and stares at his guests, his expression stunned.

'Dead! Dead yesterday morning! Lambu! I can't believe it! I just spoke to him on Saturday!'

'We saw your call history on his phone,' Bhavani replies.

'You have his phone?' Fr Victor looks startled. 'Yes, of course, you would have his phone ... what am I thinking ...'

'My men tried to call you.'

Fr Victor turns to look at the policeman in an uncomprehending sort of way. 'They did? I'm sorry, I didn't see ... Mornings are so busy here ... all the boys have to be bathed and dressed and fed ...'

'Of course, of course,' Bhavani murmurs.

'How ... how did it happen? An accident? That accursed motorbike!'

Victor listens intently as Bhavani explains the details. Then breaks down and asks for permission to go away and pray. Bhavani nods very solicitiously, and grants it.

The priest returns after twenty minutes, his eyes bloodshot, but his expression calmer.

'This is going to hit the boys hard,' he says sombrely. 'They're all so fond of their Lambodar bhaiya. They work so hard to impress him, and they're all hoping he's going to give them a big leg-up career wise and so on ... He's the big success story around here, for sure—' He looks up at Kashi, '*You* know that, men!'

'Yes of course.' Kashi's voice is reassuringly steady. 'I've personally seen how much the kids idolized him – but right now it's you I'm thinking of Fr Vick – you two were,' he pauses (that damn phrase again!), 'childhood friends, right?'

Fr Victor nods, his eyes still stunned. 'We grew up right here in BCV – Lambu, me, and our friend Rax. I was the good boy – always did what I was told and so on. Rax was born with a misshapen leg – and the Brothers used to say that his mind was even more twisted than his twisted body. And Lambu ... he was the tallest and the strongest boy in all of Badshapur, all of Harayana perhaps! We were a good, tight team and we watched out for each other, and all the little fellows too. When we got older, I went off to the seminary, Rax got an accounting job in a sports store, and Lambu got placed as a waiter in a small café in Mangalore.' He gives a short, unsteady laugh. 'He used to get angry if anybody called him a waiter – he said he was doing hotel management, if you please! But he did well ... he was noticed by the senior people, and soon he got a job as a cleaner on a cruise ship! It was the lowest paying job on the ship, but Lambu always knew how to talk to people and charm them – and soon he was cleaning on a bigger, better cruise ship – and then he wrote to me that he was learning dancing, and that they let him work out in the gym for free …'

His gaze grows distant. They all sit quietly for a while – the only sound in the room is Bhavani Singh steadily working his way through a cup of tea and a packet of Parle-G biscuits.

Fr Victor draws a deep, shaky breath, then continues.

'When he came back for my ordination ceremony, I couldn't recognize him, men! His hair was long, and he had this accent, and he moved differently – the dancing had *opened* up something inside him! He was different inside his head too – he said watching people spend his entire month's salary on a bottle of wine on the cruise ships had changed the way his brain was wired. He was nicer in some ways – but he was also …' Fr Victor's voice dips, '*darker* in some ways. It troubled me.'

He goes quiet for a while, seeing things they can only sense.

'I spent the day I received my holy orders feeling jealous of my best friend. I resented the amount of money he was clearly earning, his dashing looks, his expensive clothes, the motorcycle he showed up on, his casual sexual conquests – not that he boasted of them or anything, but I could sense a certain smungess in him. It made me feel small on what should have been my big, glorious day. We fought.'

He falls silent. Outside, the basketball game seems to be getting more boisterous.

'Rax tried to stop it, but not wholeheartedly. He is essentially a mischief-maker – the kind of person who *enjoys* it when people around him fight. The Lord makes some people like that. Lambu was hurt and angry. I was self-righteous and envious – both terrible things for a priest to be. It was horrible.'

'But it got better,' Kashi says.

Fr Victor nods gratefully. 'Yes! We lost touch ... six years went by ... but I remembered Lambu in my prayers every single day! Perhaps, he too thought of me ... Rax was the only point of contact between us, and Rax ... is Rax. "Blessed are the peacemakers" was a psalm he'd always laughed at! Just enjoying the importance of being the guy in between, and doing *nothing* to heal the schism! Anyway, then I was transferred back here and one blessed day, out of the blue, Lambu came to see me. He said he knew a lot of rich people who wanted to do good works – donate money and volunteer and so on. He said he wanted to contribute in some way too; BCV was his home and that Rax and I were his family.

'I was so relieved I can't tell you, men! My prayers to the Lord to heal the rift between Lambu and me had finally been heard! And then, what *blessings* poured down on us from above! Lambu's clients were generous – too generous! We have done so much good work with the money he has been sending us! The new wing for the younger boys, the laptops for the senior boys, the new basketball courts ... it has *all* happened through Lambu's donors!'

Bhavani Singh puts down his teacup. 'Would it be possible to see your list of donors, Father Victor?'

It is a very pale, taut-jawed Kashi Dogra who arrives at Bambi Todi's 6, Aurangzab Road home that evening. The guards at the gate aren't impressed when he emerges from a ramshackle UberGo – they make him wait for a while. Finally, after a short exchange on the intercom with somebody inside, their manner changes and they allow him in with a deferential bow. He strides quickly through the familiar driveway and garden and into the portico, pressing the bell above a massive marble Ganesha impatiently.

Still as smug and loathsome as ever, he thinks as he surveys the Ganesha with undisguised hostility. They have a history – at the age of eight he had knocked the trunk off that thing with a cricket ball, and it had to be stuck back with Araldite. The faint crack is visible even now. Bambi's mother had pretended not to care, but she has disliked him ever since – which is cool, the feeling is mutual. He hopes she isn't home; he really doesn't want to meet her or drink any of her foul mocktail concoctions. All he wants is a quick, no-bullshit conversation with Bambi. *She* must be home – there's no way they'd have let him in if she wasn't.

She is. She answers the door herself, dressed in a Red Riding Hood–type flannel dressing gown, loosely tied over a short white nightie that leaves her smooth, creamy thighs bare. She beams at him, looking more like a cinnamon-sugared cupcake than ever. Kashi struggles to hold on to his anger.

'Oh my God! Kashi Dogra in the house!' She holds out her arms in enthusiastic greeting. 'How long has it been since you came ho—'

'Can we go up, please?' he cuts her off abruptly. 'I want to talk to you.'

'Oookay.' Bambi pulls a face, then grabs his wrist and leads him up the marble staircase. 'Cmon! I've redecorated since you were last here – what d'you think?'

She throws open her bedroom door and turns to him with a smile. He registers a cool mintiness where there once used to be a lot of hot pinkness, then locks eyeballs with her.

'Was Leo Matthew blackmailing you?' he asks quietly. 'Why? And don't even *try* to lie to me – you know I'll know at once.'

Staring down at her with angry, entitled eyes, he watches as a live, breathing girl turns into a statue. She goes so stony and still that for a moment, Kashi is reminded of the marble Ganesha downstairs. Suddenly scared, he gives her a little shake.

'Bee!'

'Hmm?'

'Talk to me!'

She blinks. Her eyes lose that scary blind look and focus on him – which should be good – except that they're blazing with anger.

'Why?' She gives him a little push. 'Who the fuck are *you*?' Another little push. 'What makes you think you can just barge into *my house*, and demand I tell you stuff I haven't told a single human *soul*?' It's turning into a series of little pushes punctuating her words, each slightly harder than the one before. 'What makes *you* so special, huh?'

Backed against the closed door now, Kashi grasps both her hands, which are flattened against his chest, into one of his.

'But I'm ...' His voice falters, his eyes are troubled. 'You're my ... You used to tell me *everything*, Bambi!'

'*Used* to.' She nods, breathing hard, her voice bitter. 'But you're "very happy with your girlfriend" now, na!'

His jaw sets. 'That's not fair, Bam.'

She gulps. 'I *know*!'

Breathing as hard as her, he leans in to urgently say, 'Fuck all that. Tell me what's going on.'

She shakes him off. 'No. This whole "friends" idea was silly. We should just let it go.'

The pain in her voice is raw.

Kashi grabs her hands. '*Tell me*,' he says steadily. 'Tell me what's been happening, Bambi, *why* did your Zumba trainer send you that stupid, threatening song and *why* have you donated half a crore to the BVC?'

She sits down on the minty green bed with an ungraceful thump.

'It's Mammu. She steals things.'

When Kashi just looks at her blankly, feeling absurdly anticlimatic, Bambi explains, 'It's kleptomania. She started small, just stuff from the hotels she used to stay in – low risk, easily explained away, not at all a biggie – but then she started getting more ambitious. I don't understand it too well, but apparently the greater the risk of being caught, the more of a high you get out of doing it. She's been desperately unhappy for a while—' She gives a bitter little laugh. 'Paapu's some sort of a manwhore apparently.'

'Bambi!' Kashi reaches for her, appalled – she used to be such a daddy's girl, the man could do no wrong according to her.

She backs away, but holds on to his fingertips, pulling him to sit beside her on the bed. 'Never mind *him*. Let me tell you about her. Ya, so anyway, she went to some fancy-ass party, and while everybody was singing happy birthday to the birthday girl, she slunk off and picked up two gift boxes from the gifts table and snuck them into her bag, and Leo took a video of her doing so.'

Kashi cocks a quizzical eyebrow.

'Whatthefuck was he doing lurking around the gifts tables with his camera out? What a dog!'

Bambi gives a rather manic giggle. 'Yeah, I think he suspected her already – he had this way of knowing things about people.' She gives a little shiver. 'It's bloody scary.'

Kashi gives her a quick side hug. 'Then what happened?'

She stares down at their inter-laced fingers. 'Then he sent me that stupid Cheeky Peaches song. That's what you saw on his phone, na?'

Kashi nods. 'Yeah.'

'Naturally, it freaked me out a bit. Had he cottoned on to Mummu's problem? But I brazened it out, acted like I didn't know what he was talking about. So then one day after class, he slithered up to me and showed me the video.'

'And Bambi Todi ki phat gayee,' says Kashi whimsically.

'Naturally! Especially as those little boxes had really expensive earrings inside them! Like diamonds and shit. Anyway, he showed me the video, which was bad enough –

seeing Mammu with that crazy gleam in her eyes, furtively sweeping loot into her handbag – but the lecture he gave me after that was even more fucked up. He was such a bloody hypocrite! He said this was an opportunity to do *penance* and give back to the disadvantaged, and how the rich have a responsibility to the poor – and that he'd delete the video right away if I donated some money to this orphanage he was into. As if Todi Corp doesn't give back at all!! I wanted to tell him ki listen, behenchod, we have a *huge-ass* CSR wing and we do a *lot*!'

She pauses, breathing hard.

'He thought he was Robin Hood,' Kashi says defensively. 'He had a pretty shitty life, Bee.'

'He thought he was *God*,' she says vehemently. 'Bypassing the legal system, handing out "justice", granting absolution … Like, what *the fuck*?'

Well, seen from Bambi's point of view, Leo Matthew does seem to be a bit of a choot, Kashi has to admit.

'So then …?' he asks.

She shrugs. 'I sanctioned a sum of fifty lakh to his stupid orphanage from our CSR funds, what else? I did it in bits, so nobody would question the decision – we're not some lala family-run business, you know.'

'You didn't tell your folks?'

She rubs her eyes tiredly, looking like the child he remembers so well. 'No ya, Kashi – you've no idea, my home life is hell. Mammu's anyway refused to get treatment for the kleptomania and gone off to her brother's place in LA. She's been holed up there these past three months. Paapu's never home either. We're all just looking for reasons to stay the fuck out of this house.'

There is silence in the room for a while.

Sensing his disapproval, she adds defensively, 'Besides, you know, it *was* for a good cause and all. Like, that orphanage is *legit*. Maybe it'll help him get some brownie points in Heaven.'

'Well, you can't let it go any more,' Kashi says decisively.

She grimaces. 'Why? Leo deleted Mammu's video once I transferred the money.'

'I know,' Kashi replies. 'There was no such video on his phone. We checked it out thoroughly today.'

She breathes a sigh of relief. 'So then it's all cool.'

Kashi grips her hands. 'No it isn't.'

She looks confused. 'Why?'

'You weren't the only person Leo was blackmailing, Bambi.'

Bambi's pretty mouth falls open. 'What?'

He nods grimly. 'And his death wasn't a gym accident. He was murdered. His protein shake was poisoned.'

'Shut up!' Her eyes are huge. 'What are you saying! You mean one of the people he was blackmailing offed him? Oh my God, Kashi, who all did he even send that song to?'

'All people with secrets, I guess,' Kashi replies grimly. 'Seems like he was running a proper blackmailing ring. And one of them got sick of Leo yanking their chain and decided to take him down. We have to find out who.'

7

A Snake in the Garden

'You left the milk on the gas,' Bhavani Singh's wife looks up from her book to tell him when he emerges from their bathroom later that night in his half-sleeved vest and striped pyjamas. 'It curdled.'

'So give us paneer bhurji for breakfast tomorrow,' he replies as he pulls on his warm 'sleeping' sweater. 'Shalu, do you know what is Zumba?'

She shuts her book, amused. 'Why? Who's doing Zumba in Chanakyapuri?'

He stands by the dresser and just looks at her for a while. The sight of her soft, bright face, loose, brown hair and familiar red-and-purple batik kaftan is so restful to the eyes after a long, hard day.

'All of us,' he informs her as he clambers into the bed. 'From the constables to the commissioners. We are all real hip-cats in the Crime Branch.'

Shalini gurgles with laughter. 'Bhavani, nobody says hip-cats any more!'

'Oho, Shalini ma'am thinks she's so up-to-date because she teaches teenagers!' he says teasingly, as he eases his pillow out from behind her. 'But let us tell you, Shalu, that retro is cool now! You remember that old Cheeky Peaches song – "Secrets"?'

'Cheeky Peaches!' she exclaims. 'We used to like that band!'

'Well, we had a dead body today.' Bhavani sighs as he sinks back against the pillows. 'He died because of the Cheeky Peaches.'

'What? *What?*' Shalini puts away her book and turns to her husband attentively. 'Tell!'

The Crime Branch would frown upon their cases being discussed so freely in the marital bed, but Bhavani and Shalini have always shared everything. Food, fears, colds, chores, sweaters, socks, dreams and information. It had made them a formidable combination as parents, always united before their two strong-willed little girls, and now that the girls are settled and they themselves are much older, it is the glue that binds their marriage.

Shalini listens, absorbed, her chin resting on her fisted hand, as he fills her in on the main points, ending with the call he has just received from Kashi while in the bathroom, confirming that Bambi was indeed being blackmailed by Leo.

'Kleptomania isn't that bad,' she says finally.

He nods. 'But the others probably had worse secrets. He was playing a dangerous game.'

'But the murderer played it safe,' she says. 'We've heard of Pinko Hathni. The kids are popping it at all the parties – a really tiny, white pill, like a homeopathy ki goli, which acts two minutes after you've consumed it. Which is why another nickname for it is Maggi.'

'That school is a den of vice.' Bhavani shakes his head.

'We love our school,' she says at once.

'And they love you!' He snorts. 'That's why you get so many flowers from those horny boys on Teacher's Day!'

She laughs. 'We don't care for flowers, Bhavani. Except pink Oriental lilies. Now, they are something special!'

'At a hundred and fifty rupees per stick!' he replies ruefully. 'We agree, they are indeed something special!'

'Not stick, Bhavani, stalk,' she corrects him laughingly. 'Accha, wait, we'll get you a glass of cold milk.'

Bhavani always has trouble sleeping the night after a corpse-sighting. Plain, iced milk, with a little cardamom, helps.

'No need to get out of bed now.' He puts a hand on her arm. 'It is too much trouble for you.'

But Shalini is already on her feet. 'It'll be more trouble for us if you toss and turn all night,' she says plainly. 'You shake the whole mattress! We won't get a wink of sleep – and even if we do, we'll dream we're on some sinking ship, being tossed about on the high seas, and about to end up in a whale's belly.'

When she returns with the milk, she finds him scrolling through a sleek iPhone 11 and raises her brows. 'That's his phone? An expensive toy!'

'Not just a toy if he was using it to record people doing shady things and then blackmailing them! More like an … investment, wouldn't you say?'

'Drink your milk,' she replies.

He chugs down the milk, then picks up the iPhone again.

'But there's nothing *on* it,' he says grumpily as he hunches over the device, scrolling this way and that. 'Our technical people have checked it out thoroughly. Maybe he had *another* phone.'

'So get his house searched tomorrow.' Shalini wipes the milk moustache off his square, homely face. 'And put that thing away. Sleeping with a corpse's phone will only give you nightmares.'

* * *

'Aren't those gauraiyas, sir? We thought they were extinct!'

Thus, Bhavani Singh, with determined cheerfulness, to Devendar Bhatti the next morning, in what appears to be a large vegetable garden at the rear of the club. Padam Kumar and he have tracked the Club president down with a certain amount of difficulty to this pretty, enclosed space, full of neatly laid-out vegetable rows. Bhavani identifies carrots, potatoes, several sweetly scented herbs and, under a huge, spreading jacaranda tree, a wide bed of beetroot, easily identifiable by the deep red stems from which their light green leaves spurt. Bang in the centre of the beds is a rocky, dappled birdbath, in which tiny house sparrows hop and splash gaily, entirely oblivious to the documented fact of their extinction.

The entire garden is ringed by a rustic wooden fence abloom with bright yellow zuchini flowers, and rises, at one point into a gated arch. Framed within this gateway stands the ex-home secretary of India, clutching a red plastic basket half-full of muddy, reddish-orange carrots in one hand and a humble iron khurpi in the other. Bhavani notices that he looks less like an indignant hen today and more like a slightly guilty hen. Maybe he isn't supposed to be purloining the DTC's veggies …

'Well, they were certainly *almost* extinct,' Bhatti responds stiffly, waving his khurpi in the vague direction of the gaily hopping sparrows. 'But we built all these nests, and put out water and seed, and made them feel welcome, so they came back.' There is a pause and then adds, tetchily, 'As did you.'

'Yes, sir!' Bhavani says brightly. 'Enquiries are going well, sir.' He has decided that the less he shares with the Club president, the better.

Bhatti makes a small, snorting sound.

'Take Bhatti sa'ab's basket, PK,' Bhavani tells his subordinate. 'And dig up some more vegetables for him. Was it carrots you were wanting, sir?'

'Beets,' grunts the old man. 'They're damn good here. Red as blood.' He addresses PK, 'You understand beets? Chukkandar.'

Padam Kumar, resplendent in a pink Rajasthan Royals jersey today, nods, but not very happily. Squatting resignedly down in the vegetable beds, he plunges the khurpi into the beetroot patch. As he inhales the sweetish, overripe scent of organic compost rising from the damp earth, he shudders quietly. Tea leaves and eggshells and rotting banana peel and jhootha leftovers and what-not! Why people just can't use honest, government-backed urea fertilizer is beyond his comprehension.

Meanwhile, Bhavani and Bhatti sit down on a stone bench under the jacaranda tree.

'I still say it was suicide,' Bhatti maintains stubbornly. 'Or if it *wasn't*, then Behra Mehra did it.'

'O really, sir? The general? Why, sir?'

There is a longish silence.

'My stint at the Home Ministry didn't end too well,' Bhatti says finally. 'My boss and I didn't see eye to eye. My values were secular, while hers were rabid.'

Bhavani blinks. Bhatti sa'ab is clearly going to be taking the long route home. So be it. He settles his buttocks as comfortably as he can upon the stone and stares down at his knobbly knuckles, radiating sympathetic attentiveness.

'Anyway, I had hoped, after serving my time in the seething snake pit that was North Block, to retire in peace and have some good times with friends and family here in the DTC. I love this place – I grew up here and I suppose I idealized it when I was too busy to visit it regularly.'

'And now, sir?'

'And now, ACP, I realize that every paradise has a snake in it.'

Bhavani looks about the garden perplexed.

'Snake, sir?'

'Yes! There was a snake in the Garden of Eden and there is a snake here too!'

He stares at the policeman, panting a bit. The slightly obsessive gleam in his eyes makes Bhavani speculate uneasily about paranoid delusions and early onset dementia.

He nods soothingly. 'Understood sir!'

'No, you haven't understood anything,' Bhatti says irascibly. 'Let me explain properly! We hold elections for the post of Club president once every two years. Traditionally, the presidency alternates between the defense chaps and the bureaucrats. So it was the faujis' turn this time, and that slick sycophant Behra Mehra was more or less the agreed-upon candidate, damn his eyes! He's a big darling of the press, a great war hero – Amitabh Bachachan played him in the disgracefully jingoistic *Jhelum Bilge*. So he was sitting around smugly, waiting for me to bugger off while he wrote his acceptance speech and planned his tie and socks combination, when Urvashi threw her hat into the ring and queered the pitch!'

He gives a dry chuckle of laughter. It's an odd, gleeful laugh.

'She doesn't give a damn about our alternating fauji-and-civil tradition! *And* she has some bloody good plans too! Tax-saving ideas her hubby's come up with, and a brilliant scheme for a new rain-harvesting plant. The fact that Chrysanthemum just received a fifty-crore investment helped sway the voters in her favour too! Naturally Mehra's chaddis got into a twist!'

He stares at the rows of vegetables pushing quietly upwards in the winter sun, and slowly his face darkens.

'Unfortunately, Urvashi's husband, like the husbands of so many other good-looking, capable women, is her weakest link. And so Behra Mehra and his supporters, crafty trench fighters that they are – launched an attack on her, *through* him. They started taking Khurana out for drinks and suggested to him that she was having an affair with our dead boy on the bench press.'

Bhavani nods sombrely. 'Yes sir, we heard about that-all, a little. You suspect that these people wound Khurana up like a cuckoo clock till he went cuckoo and killed Leo in a fit of jealousy, sir?'

'Well it sounds terribly melodramatic when you put it that way,' Bhatti admits, 'but now that you say that it *is* murder, after all – that's my theory, yes. My theory B, I mean. My theory A remains suicide.'

'So the snake in this particular paradise is …?' Bhavani mumurs.

'Mehra, of course!' Bhatti explodes, bits of spittle flying out of his mouth and hitting a startled butterfly. 'The so-called hero of the so-called surgical strikes! He struts around like he polished off a nest of terrorists himself, but all these generals do is send out young men to die, while they themselves sit safely in Army HQ, massage the egos of their political masters, strike heroic poses before the press cameras, and negotiate fancy posts for themselves post-retirement in exchange for agreeing to reduce the pensions of their brother officers!'

Bhatti's voice has risen to a squawk and his Adam's apple is bobbing alarmingly.

Bhavani attempts to soothe him. 'Sir, the surgical strikes are well documented—'

Bhatti's eyes bulge. 'Pakistan has never acknowledged them! They say they never happened! *Never!*'

'Yes, but we are not Pakistanis na, sir,' Bhavani points out gently. 'We are Indians.'

'You're a fool,' Bhatti says bluntly. 'If that chap becomes DTC president, this whole place will be overrun by uncouth Gujarati riff-raff, wearing chappals and pyjamas and demanding we only serve veg food ...'

He rants on in this vein for a while. Bhavani lets him. Padam Kumar, still industriously harvesting the beetroots, thinks privately that the defence minister is right – the DTC *is* a den of anti-nationals.

When Bhatti finally stops, Bhavani says gently, 'Sir, but *even* if Mehra instigated Khurana, the point is that, according to your theory B, Khurana is only the actual murderer, sir.'

Bhatti stares at him with glazed eyes for a while, panting lightly. Then he continues as though Bhavani hasn't spoken at all.

'On top of that, he's constantly harassing the girl who works at the Daily Needs here! Sweet, simple child, young enough to be his granddaughter! It started when his wife was alive and her husband was around! Now his wife is conveniently dead and the husband has conveniently vanished! That's the kind of low life that fellow is! Urvashi Khurana is worth *thirty* of him!'

Bhavani is wondering how to compute this new angle, when an angry female voice pierces the barrier of the rustic wooden fence, making them all jump.

'Helllllooo … bhaisaab! You can't just waltz in here and dig up beets for free! You need permis—'

Bambi Todi appears in the arched gateway, her small frame rigid with outrage, glaring accusingly at Padam Kumar in his muddied pink jersey. Then she spots the two old men sitting under the jacaranda tree and relaxes, smiling.

'Oh hi, Bhatti uncle. ACP Singh! I didn't realize you guys were hanging here.'

—❦—

'So Kashi filled you in on my … uh … *dealings* with Leo, huh,' Bambi says hesitantly to Bhavani a little later, as they walk back under the shade of the neem trees to Guest Cottage No. 5 together.

He nods solemnly. 'You've been through a tough time, Bambi ji.'

She shrugs her slender shoulders. 'That's okay …' Then she turns to him impulsively. 'But I hear I wasn't the only one? He was squeezing other people too?'

Bhavani's homely face grows inscrutable. 'That's classified information.'

She pulls a face. 'You told Kashi – but not me.'

'Vakeel sa'ab is partnering us unofficially in this investigation in his capacity as Leo's lawyer.'

'Ghanta.' She snorts. 'I was there when he decided to be Leo's lawyer and there was nothing legal about it!'

He looks down at her smilingly. 'Even so.'

'I'll worm it out of him.' She grins outrageously. 'He tells me *everything*.'

O really, thinks Bhavani wryly. We wonder if he's told you that his roof-builder girlfriend and he have perfect tuning and they complete each other's sentences.

Aloud he says, 'Thank you for being so frank. The information you shared with him last night has put us on the right track really fast.'

'And yet you don't trust me,' she complains.

'Actually,' he says, his expression growing thoughtful, 'we would like to enlist your help today.'

Bambi's eyes widen with excitement. 'Oooh, tell!'

'Are you aware of a young lady who works at the Daily Needs store?'

Her face closes down a little. 'Ganga? Of course. I only got her the job.'

'Bhatti sa'ab alleges the general is obsessed with her,' Bhavani says. 'He hinted at some sort of a chakkar between them. What do you think?'

She says, rather curtly, 'I think the general's name was on Leo's list of blackmail victims.'

Bhavani smiles. 'You're a smart woman, Bambi ji. But please answer the question.'

Bambi pulls to a halt. 'Look, ACP, I'm *very* protective of Ganga. She's had a crap life with an abusive husband and she's finally finding a little peace now that he's deserted her. She's single, Mehra uncle's single, and in life I just try to stay as non-judgemental as possible! God knows I can't afford to point fingers, what with my klepto mum and all!'

So the general and this girl probably *do* have an arrangement, thinks Bhavani. But if everybody knows about it already, and they're both single, then how is that even a motive for blackmail and murder?

'Fair enough,' he tells Bambi. 'Also, we want to interview the Khuranas separately. One at a time. But we want to make it look like it happened casually. Could you help?'

Bambi's face grows troubled. 'So Urvashi auntie was being blackmailed too? Ugh! I don't know why I thought this would be fun ... You're just going to keep poking and prying and digging with a blunt stick into people's lives, aren't you? Just like Leo!'

'Yes,' he says gently. 'But we're not doing it for cheap thrills or to hurt people or to make money. We're hunting down a murderer, Bambi ji. Surely, that makes it worthwhile?'

She shakes her head violently. 'No! Don't you see? It means that somebody I *know*, somebody who is *part* of this club – which, unlike the *shitty* house next door, is my *safe* place, my *strong* place, the closest thing I have to a home – is a killer! And that makes it much *much* worse!'

Tears stream down her cheeks. The tears she had been so embarrassed about not being able to shed yesterday.

Bhavani puts a fatherly arm about her small shoulders.

'Bambi ji, we have not been privileged enough to go inside, but from outside your home looks like a palace! If *that* is a shitty house, then our home in Police Colony is a bear cave!'

She sniffs loudly and unselfconsciously. 'Don't patronize me, ACP. I'm sure you're very happy in your bear cave in Police Colony.'

'But that is because we are a bear,' he says whimsically. 'And you are a princess.'

She gurgles. 'You're sweet.'

'Mrs Cookie Katoch says we are a walnut brownie,' he says. 'If we keep coming to the DTC, we will get an inflated head soon.'

* * *

'So the fellow's been poisoned to death, I heard?' Mukesh Khurana's nasal voice holds a distinctly gloating tone. 'Well well, I won't pretend to be heartbroken about it!'

Nobody prepared Bhavani for the unloveliness of the accountant and he is recoiling slightly. For reasons best known to himself, Khurana has chosen to wear a brown tweed cap pulled low over the forehead, which makes him look rather unintelligent. He is also sporting his favourite suspenders, today over a fearsomely cabled sweater, and has tied a shiny, navy-blue cravat around his pudgy neck. It doesn't improve matters that his eye is blackened and swollen. The whole effect is unaesthetic in the extreme.

None of this visual overload seems to be affecting Bhavani on the surface.

'So *nice* of you to not be a hypocrite,' he says warmly. 'So, matlab, frank and refreshing!' He throws his hands into the air in a gesture of speechless admiration.

Khurana glows purply under this praise. 'O, I am ekdum frank!' he says airily. 'Ask anybody!'

Bhavani smiles and tries out a little frankness of his own. 'Khurana sa'ab, humne suna ki there was some kind of khat-pat between you and the deceased in the East Lawn on Tambola Sunday?'

Mukki laughs thinly and points at his blackened eye. 'You call this a khat-pat? It was assault – pure and simple! And now he's dead! Chalo, he got what he deserved!' He utters a loud neigh of laughter.

'You are saying he had it coming?' Bhavani Singh murmurs encouragingly.

Khurana seems to swell up before his eyes. 'Aji, the fellow was a bloody troublemaker! Slithered in out of nowhere, shaking his bum, and made all the women unsatisfied with their husbands! None of us were getting any action in the night any more because the chap wanted only well-rested, "fresh" maal for Zumba at dawn! And not just Zumba – he was giving them all "personal training" too, if you please, touching their upper arms and bellies and hips, and tsk-tsking about how soft it all was! Sab kuch ekdum cool and professional on top, but underneath oho, underneath it was all salsa and lalsa and goodbye Guru ji ka khalsa! Naturally we chaps got hassled.'

'Naturally, naturally,' murmurs Bhavani, as Khurana sits back, breathing heavily. He adjusts his cap which makes him look even more ape-like, then winks at the policeman.

'But I'm a chap who's all for healthy competition, ACP. Matthew had raised the bar for sure, so I just told myself: Mukki beta, you'd better raise your game too! Your wife's a lovely woman and you've always been a plain chap, but you owe it to her to at least stay in shape!! So what I did was, I zoomed in on Thampi. He's a smart, respectful fellow and he knows all the tricks of the trade. I took him aside and I told him my goals. It's been seven months now, and just see what he's done with me! Wonders!'

He flexes his biceps. Bhavani dutifully makes wordless noises of appreciation. Mukki beams.

'And so yesterday, when the chance came for a direct confrontation with that item numbar, I played it on the front foot. I wasn't going to back down in front of that ape! Urvashi pretended to be angry with me later, but I know she was impressed. A woman wants a man to *be* a man, you know – she may *say* that she doesn't, but at the end of the day, she'll never respect you if she thinks you're weak – either mentally or physically.'

'You are so right!' Bhavani applauds the noble sentiment, then leans forward and asks invitingly, 'So what exactly was the argument about, Khurana sa'ab?'

Khurana's face purples. 'The whole thing was disgraceful! The tambola was clearly rigged!'

'Rigged?' Bhavani's voice holds just the correct amount of concern and wonder. 'How?'

Khurana puffs out his chest. 'That all I don't know! But the entire admin department of the Club, starting from that wretched Srivastava, is corrupted! The bloody clerks are all on the bloody take!'

'The clerks?'

'Yes! Take this cottage we're sitting in, for instance! It's empty, isn't it? That's why you're sitting in it! But if you go online and check, it says *all* the guest cottages are booked for the next six months! *Why?*

'Why, sir?'

Khurana's eyes bug out. 'Because the booking clerks want a bribe, that's why!'

Bhavani makes distressed clicking noises with his tongue.

Khurana continues, 'Urvi wants to clean up all their shady rackets, that's why they're shitting bricks at the thought of her becoming president!'

'Sir, but the argument wasn't only about the tambola, was it?' Bhavani says blandly. 'There was some talk of sharing – or not sharing … Can you please tell us about that?'

Mukki stares at him suspiciously for a while, then decides to give him the benefit of the doubt.

'There has been some talk … about a chakkar between my wife and Leo,' he admits huffily. 'The typical stuff – people can't stand to see a well-adjusted couple, so they say all kinds of things. I should have known better, of course, but I was already angry about the obvious rigging, and I'd had a few beers, so when he made that vulgar crack, I hit him.' He adds with a touch of pride, 'Quite hard, actually. You must have seen the bruises on his face, eh?'

'O yes!' says Bhavani Singh, who had seen nothing of the sort.

Khurana smiles smugly. 'That's why I didn't file a police complaint. Yesterday, people kept telling me to file a case of assault and battery, but I thought, what if they see the injuries on his face and book me instead, eh? What then?'

'Indeed, sir.'

Mukki adjusts his cap again, looking gratified. 'I'm smart that way. Large-hearted too! I didn't want to destroy the fellow's life! He must be having a hand-to-mouth existence – running from here to there, making ladies dance! So I thought, I've taught him a sharp lesson and that's enough!'

'You were so large-hearted with Thampi also, sir,' Bhavani adds smoothly. 'You let him leave early for his girlfriend's birthday …'

Mukki nods. 'Yes, I still had ten minutes to go on the treadmill, so I offered to shut the place down for him. It was a bit irregular, I suppose, but he looked so desperate that I said theek hai yaar, tu ja. I've been young, I remember what it's like to have a girlfriend with a birthday! I finished with the treadmill, shut off the lights, locked the door and left. Then I dropped the keys into the locked box at the reception. All that must be on the CCTV camera – your fellows must have checked it by now?'

He looks at Bhavani with wide-eyed innocence.

Bhavani shakes his head gravely. 'Unfortunately, sir, a bunch of gas balloons came loose, floated up and blocked the camera for half an hour, starting from quarter-to to quarter-past midnight.'

'What!' Khurana's jaw sags. 'What nonsense! Bhatti's famous "command centre" took half an hour to react? All the guards were warming their bums on their heaters, I suppose! I *told* you this place is slackly run!'

'Er … sir, what were *you* doing when this happened?' Bhavani asks. 'Matlab you were right there, inside the gym – didn't you notice that the balloons were obscuring the camera?'

Khurana eyes bulge fearsomely. 'I don't even know where the camera is, damnit! I was doing my workout!'

Bhavani sighs. 'Well, sir, it doesn't look very good for you, frankly!' He holds up his fingers one by one. 'Your wife is rumoured to be having an affair with the victim; you had an argument with him yesterday; he knocked you down—'

'I hit him too!'

Bhavani continues inexorably. 'And then you were the *only* person in the gym, *alone* with the prepared protein shake, during the time when there was no camera visibility.'

Khurana leaps to his feet, snapping his suspenders threateningly. 'That doesn't prove anything!'

Bhavani continues to sit, looking up at him serenely. 'Agreed, sir. But you have to agree it looks bad.'

'Well, I *didn't* poison the bugger,' Mukki blusters. 'I'm a straightforward man – if I ever wanted to finish off a fellow, I would shoot him in the chest, while looking him in the eye! I would definitely *not* tiptoe about, stirring a damnfool drug into a water bottle like a woman!'

Overall, Bhavani is in agreement with what Khurana is saying. The fellow has all the symptoms of someone with high blood pressure in any case – Bhavani can visualize him firing a gun, swinging a club or even throttling somebody at the spur of the moment … but not this simple, cool, almost elegant murder.

He says pleasantly, 'Sir, please don't misunderstand. We don't think you committed the crime—'

Mukki grips the table hard. 'Then what *do* you think, Inspec— What was your damn rank again?'

'ACP.'

'Ya, so what *do* you think, *ACP*?!'

'We think somebody is trying to frame you, sir.'

Khurana goggles at him for a moment, then collapses dramatically on the opposite seat.

'Thank you!' he declaims gratefully.

'You're welcome, sir,' Bhavani replies.

There is a small silence.

After a little while, Khurana sits forward. 'Do you how *tough* the CA exams are?' he demands. 'They are much more difficult than getting into the bloody army! Or the police, for that matter,' he can't resist adding, a little snidely.

'Yes, sir.'

'And yet this fool Mehra thinks that *I'm* the fool! That just because my wife is beautiful, he can pull off a poora-ka-poora *Othello* on me! He's trying to play that over-smart Narad muni-type character – what was his name?'

Bhavani grimaces with the effort of trying to remember. 'Oho, our wife would've supplied the name at once,' he rues. 'We know who you mean, of course. Aago? Ego?'

'Ego! Ya, he's been trying to play that chap Ego, and now he's trying to make it look like I killed my wife's so-called lover in a fit of jealousy. But I'm too sensible to do that! I know my wife has eyes only for me.'

'Of course she does, sir. And you may not be a pretty boy, but you have a nice manly way about you, sir.'

Mukki pinks up and says 'Thank you' with so much surprise and sincerity that Bhavani feels a twinge of remorse at resorting to such blatant flattery.

'So then, sir, *who* killed your wife's lov— Er … we mean Zumba trainer?' he asks the accountant. 'Gen. Mehra himself? Isn't that rather far-fetched?'

'No, it isn't,' Mukki says at once. 'These damn faujis have no respect for human life. Killing a human being is like slapping a mosquito for them.'

Bhavani, who has spent a troubled night after seeing Leo's lifeless body, and who knows many men in uniform who feel the same way, manages to stay unprovoked.

'Motive is a bit weak, sir,' is all he says, mildly. 'He wouldn't kill Leo just to frame you and prevent your wife from getting elected! There would have to be something else. Do you know of some other issue between them, sir?'

'My wife thinks Mehra's preying on the girl in the Daily Needs.' Mukki offers doubtfully after a longish pause. 'She's been quite vocal about condemning it. But then she ...' He sighs, 'She can be a little too protective about these young girls sometimes.'

'But it's an avenue worth exploring,' Bhavani suggests.

Mukki nods. 'Oh, yes.'

8

Selective Hearing

'This whole thing is terribly unfortunate.'

Dressed in a natty, tightly tailored blazer with monogrammed buttons and a baby-blue cravat that sets off the hazel of his eyes, Lt General ('Behra') Mehra, PVSM, AVSM, Yudh Sewa Medal is definitely an improvement, aesthetically speaking, on Bhavani's previous interviewee.

'*Terribly* unfortunate,' the general repeats.

Bhavani, who has chosen to adopt a slightly stupid expression for this encounter, agrees at once. Beside him, Kashi Dogra, inducted into the meeting to be a social lubricant, nods soberly as well.

They all maintain a minute's silence for the departed soul, then Mehra looks up, his hazel eyes keen.

'Chap was poisoned, I hear?'

The other two nod again.

'Fine thing to happen at the fag end of Bhatti's tenure! He must be so cut up. But why have you asked to speak to me? I didn't even know the fellow!'

'O really, sir?' Bhavani says innocently. 'He had your number saved on his phone, actually!'

'He must've had a thousand numbers saved on his phone, ACP,' Mehra says testily.

'Mehra uncle!' Kashi leans forward. 'Can I just mention that the ACP is a big fan!'

Slightly mollified, Mehra cocks an eyebrow at Bhavani. 'Seen me on TV, eh?'

Bhavani beams. 'Of *course*! During the surgical strikes briefings – and afterwards. Why, sir, you did all the work – you were the brains and the balls of the whole operation! The IJP just took credit for all *your* hard work!'

Mehra strokes his moustache modestly. 'That's the army way, ACP. We don't hog credit. Never have, never will.'

'Amazing! Sir, to answer your question, we are speaking to you because Leo Matthew sent a few people this song on WhatsApp, and we feel it may have a bearing on the case.'

Mehra frowns. 'A song? What song? The chap sent *me* a song?'

Bhavani nods. Kashi, who has 'Secrets' cued, plays it on Leo's phone.

Behra Mehra listens with polite curiosity, humming a little at the catchier parts. When the song ends, he cocks an eyebrow at Bhavani.

'Yes? It's a very old song. What about it?'

'Any reason why he would send it to you, sir? Along with a link to an orphanage in Badshahpur? An orphanage to which you subsequently made a substantial donation?'

Mehra is openly bristling now. 'I assume you're implying he was blackmailing me. Because I have a secret. And because I "think that no one knows" and I am smelling err ... "like a rose". That's the theory isn't it?'

Bhavani does not respond. There is a small, uneasy pause and then the general throws back his head and laughs uproariously.

'I don't even remember receiving this WhatsApp message, ACP! I get so many messages! It's the curse of being well-known! People keep sending you all kinds of things all the time – I certainly never opened this video or heard this song.'

'There are two blue ticks on it,' Kashi points out.

'I will give the answer I always give my grandchildren! Yes, baby girl, I opened it, but because I did not have my reading glasses with me, I did not actually *read* it!'

'But you don't need to read it, sir,' Bhavani insists doggedly. 'You just have to *listen.*'

'Well, I didn't listen,' is the rather sharp reply. 'I don't listen to stuff I don't want to hear. Everybody knows that.'

Kashi chuckles. 'Tell the ACP why they call you Behra Mehra, uncle.'

'Yes, sir, we were wondering!' Bhavani picks up the cue at once. 'Because your hearing seems excellent to us!'

The general grins, flashing yellowing teeth. 'It is. What happened is that back when I was a second lieutenant, posted in Poonch, we had a small insurgency situation. These six

Pakis had crept in and taken over our bunkers during a snowstorm, and I was sent up there with four of my men to flush them out. So we went in there, but they got wind of our arrival somehow, and we lost the element of surprise. There was a shootout and I lost two of my men – we downed three of the Pakis though, and the other three ran for their border. We gave chase, but when we reached the LOC, my superiors starting yelling at me through the walkie-talkies to stop – we weren't to cross the LOC or it would be a violation of the border agreement we had with Pakistan. But the fog of war had descended on me, ACP – those chaps had killed two of my men… There was no way in *hell* I was going to let them get away with it!' He stops, panting. His eyes are glazed; he is seeing things Bhavani cannot.

'So then, sir?' Bhavani asks breathlessly.

'So then, I held my walkie-talkie a little away from my mouth and said, "Reception poor, sir! Repeat order, sir!"'

Bhavani's jaw drops. 'No!'

Mehra chuckles. 'O yes. My superior repeated the order. I held the walkie *even* further away from my mouth, and again said, "Reception quality poor, sir! Repeat order, sir! UNABLE to hear order, sir!"'

'That's *too* good, general sa'ab!'

'He bleated out his wretched little order for the third time – that we were to return to our station with our tail between our legs – and for the third time I replied, "Unable to HEAR, sir! Order UNCLEAR, sir!" And then I dropped my walkie into the snow, dove across the LOC and downed those three escaping Pakis. And *that*, ACP, is why they call me Behra

Mehra,' he finishes with a flourish, face flushed, eyes alight, clearly expecting applause.

Bhavani dutifully bursts into enthusiastic clapping. 'Wah! Wah, general sa'ab, wah!'

These damn faujis have no respect for human life. Killing a human being is like slapping a mosquito for them.

Mukesh Khurana's words had been a sweeping generalization, of course, but they do seem to ring true for Behra Mehra, AVSM PVSM Yudh Seva Medal.

Mehra ducks his head modestly. 'I applied the same tactics in 2016. You might have seen the movie *Jhelum Bridge*?'

'Yes, sir, of course! You were played by Amitabh Bachchan in the movie! It was *too* good, sir!'

'Thank you! The IJP was really keen to milk my popularity after the surgical strikes,' Mehra continues. 'Offered me a ticket to contest the election from my native place! But I'm a simple creature, ACP. A bit of tennis, a round of golf, some drinks – that's good enough for me!'

'So *humble*, sir!'

They stare at each other in rapt delight for a while.

Finally Bhavani drops his gaze and says in a much more matter-of-fact voice, 'And your donation to the charity mentioned in the WhatsApp link, sir?'

Behra Mehra furrows his forehead.

'Somebody mentioned the place to me – said they do good work – so I made a donation and asked them to say prayers in the memory of my wife, who studied at a convent school, and was a big fan of Mother Mary and Mother Teresa. That is all.'

'Who mentioned it to you?' Bhavani's voice is very casual.

The general's is equally casual as he replies, 'I can't remember off-hand.' He goes quiet.

As the silence threatens to lengthen, Kashi says quickly, 'Any leads for the ACP, Mehra uncle? You know everybody at the DTC ... surely you can point our nose in the right direction!'

Mehra sits back comfortably.

'There's a world of suspects out there if you look beyond me! From what I've heard, this Leo chap led a colourful life! Any number of jealous husbands out for his blood! Any number of jealous women competing for his affection!'

'Then these women would kill each other, wouldn't they? Why would they kill him?'

'Oh, Hell hath no fury like a woman scorned ... blah di blah,' Behra Mehra says vaguely. 'What I mean to say is, go digging into his past. He seems a bit of a mystery man to me, frankly – no parents, no girlfriend, no background, no foreground! Isn't that what they say in all the mystery novels – the psychology of the dead man points an unerring finger to the criminal? I've seen all sort of crazy things in the army, and I'm sure you've seen all sorts of crazy things in the Crime Branch!'

'That is true, sir! Sir, we wanted to ask you about the ... young lady called Ganga who works in Daily Needs.'

Observing Mehra's expression closely as he asks this question. Bhavani decides that while the general is surprised by it, he doesn't look rattled in any way.

Shrugging slightly, he says, 'My ill-wishers have been busy, I see. What that disgusting rumour has to do with Leo's death I cannot imagine, but I will gladly answer your question.'

'If you don't mind, sir ...' Bhavani looks hugely relieved.

Mehra inclines his head graciously.

'Young Ganga and I are buddies. We got friendly during an extremely taxing period of my life – my wife of thirty-seven years was grievously unwell, and I had taken on the responsibility of the weekly shopping. Ganga assisted me in picking out my daily needs very sweetly. She had a no-good husband – chap came and went, I believe – drank like a fish, and was a terrible provider. She was lonely; I was retired, my children had moved abroad. To cut a long story short, we hit it off. She started visiting us at home. Meeting her cheered my wife tremendously! We all played teen-do-paanch, drank a little whisky. Then my wife died and I ... I leaned on her a little. Like a father would, on a daughter. But then her husband got wind of it. There was a bust-up, I punched his face in, and that night he walked out on her. Left her for good. We always agreed he was a bad lot – me and my dear departed Savitri.'

'So sorry for your loss,' Bhavani says gravely, as if the general's wife has died that day and not three years ago.

Mehra's hazel eyes grow wistful. 'She was a saint,' he says. 'A real saint! Loved gardening! In fact, the kitchen garden here is dedicated to her memory. There's a beautiful, engraved plaque: Shrimati Savitri Mehra Udyaan.'

'So nice,' Bhavani replies. 'We were there this morning with Bhatti sa'ab. But we did nat observe the plaque.'

'Bhatti wouldn't have shown you. He doesn't like me. Because he made such a hash of being home secretary while I was such a success in South Block! Defence Minister Jagmohan Ruia is my very good friend even today. In fact, the party offered me a Lok Sabha ticket. Did I tell you that?'

'Yes. Uh, general sa'ab, one last question. You must have heard all these rumours about Mrs Khurana and Matthew … Do you think Mr Khurana could have been upset enough to poison him?'

Mehra thinks hard, then exhales noisily. 'Look, the chap's unhinged,' he says bluntly. 'Desperately sick. I wouldn't be surprised if he's on medication for schizophrenia and bi-polar behaviour! I know everybody's been saying I've been winding him up about Matthew and his wife, but believe you me, Khurana did not need *any* egging on from my side to perform any of his recent antics – he's *always* been like this – there's *always* some chap or the other he's jealous of! Wife's a real looker, you know! Not much difference between him and young Ganga's husband, if you ask me, frankly! His wife should not be volunteering for public duty with such an ill man on her hands. In fact, she shouldn't be running a business either. Her primary duty should be to her home and husband.'

Bhavani looks confused. 'We were told he's a highly successful chartered accountant? With his own firm?'

Mehra leans in earnestly. 'Chap like that would be right at home with numbers and accounts! It's black-and-white stuff – with clear rules and consequences. It's the human side of things that he would find incomprehensible!'

'You think he did it, Mehra uncle?' Kashi asks.

Mehra shrugs carelessly. 'He's the most obvious answer to your little problem,' he says. 'And in my experience, the most obvious answer is usually the correct one.'

This is the beauty and wonder and miracle of the institution of arranged marriage, Bhavani Singh thinks as Padam Kumar ushers Urvashi Khurana into Guest Cottage No. 5, that a wet fish like Mukesh Khurana can score a wife like this!

Because this a special woman – tall, finely made, with a short mop of chic, loose curls he can only describe as French-looking, and a glowing complexion. She is dressed in a pepperminty woollen firan, white track pants and embroidered leather juttis.

'Good afternoon,' she says gravely in a soft, exquisitely modulated voice. 'I believe you are the ACP?'

She reminds him vaguely of those elegant ladies in the Pakistani TV shows his wife likes to watch. There's something *refined* about her, so much so that she makes you want to be refined too. Bhavani notices that Padam Kumar has put on his most cultured face, smoothed down his pink Rajasthan Royals jersey, and is coyly pushing forward a chair.

Bhavani gestures towards it invitingly. 'Yes, madam.'

She takes her own time sitting down, then looks at him with serious and complete attention.

'And you wished to see me. Why?'

Her sheer classiness is extremely intimidating, but Bhavani Singh ploughs in doggedly, his plain face as grave as hers.

'Madam, your role in the proposed election for the Club president and the fact that your husband was ... umm ... assaulted by the murder victim on Tambola Sunday do accord you somewhat special status,' he says stolidly. 'Also, the rumour that, forgive us, you and Leo Matthew shared a somewhat special relationship.'

A ghost of a smile gleams in the grave eyes. 'Please don't apologize, ACP. I'm well aware that there are various nasty rumours doing the rounds – in clear contravention of the Club's election by-laws, by the way – of my lurid affair with dear Leo! Please ask me anything you like.'

Bhavani gives a quick nod.

'Thank you, madam. So first just the routine questions we are asking everyone. What exactly was the relationship between Leo and you, then?'

'We learnt from each other,' she replies composedly. 'We met three times a week for the Zumba class at the Club, after which I helped him with his yoga practice. People who lift a lot of weights – like Leo did – can become inflexible and stiff, so we were working on that. Sometimes we messaged – usually to share videos or music we liked. That's it.'

'Like this song, madam?'

He taps on Leo's phone. 'Secrets' fills the room.

Urvashi smiles. 'Yes,' she says calmly. 'That one too – it's so cute and retro.'

His eyebrows rise. 'No other reason, madam?'

She looks amused. 'Like what?'

'Like blackmail, madam,' Bhavani says steadily.

She gives a perfectly pitched, exquisite little laugh. 'That's ridiculous, ACP!'

'Is it? Because right after that song he sent you *this* link, madam. To an orphanage – and subsequently you sent a substantial donation to them.'

Now it's her turn to raise her eyebrows. 'Badshahpur? But that's where Leo grew up! We had a long talk about it once … But please could you not tell the Club ladies he grew up there? He was terribly embarrassed about his humble roots.'

Inwardly impressed by how unflappable she is, Bhavani says, 'We will do that – but, madam, if he was so embarrassed, how come he opened up to you?'

She turns her clear open gaze on him. 'I didn't fetishize him, ACP.' Then, seeing his uncomprehending expression, she explains. 'I didn't see him as a sex object – I didn't giggle about his abs or his shoulders. I just related to him as a person, a fellow athlete, and spiritual seeker.'

'Understood, madam!' Bhavani nods. 'And the other ladies in the Zumba … Don't mind, but are you implying that they saw him as just a fetish?'

She plays with the rings on her fingers. 'I don't want to criticize anybody, ACP. Our Zumba class is really very sweet, and the ladies there are mostly harmless – but they are sometimes remarkably immature for women over fifty. It's like they have purposely infantilized themselves. I find that kind of thing ridiculous.'

'But they're all very supporting of your candidature in the election.'

She shrugs. 'That's what they *say*. Building up a business from scratch for the past sixteen years, I've learnt that people don't always mean what they say.'

'And these ladies …?'

She squares her shoulders. 'I think they don't wish me as well as they claim to. I think they wouldn't mind seeing me fail.'

'But surely they wouldn't go so far as to poison Leo to do it!'

She shrugs. 'They wouldn't have to. I think the whole Club is in agreement that winding up my husband would be enough to get the job done.' Her voice is very bitter.

They sit in silence for a while.

'Madam, the tambola yesterday was your show of strength, you organized everything – and beautifully! Why didn't you attend it?'

She sighs. 'Well, little Bambi had the thoughtful idea of having somebody hold up the numbers for the benefit of the hearing impaired. Leo was really eager to do it – he was quite awed by the Club you know, though he tried to hide it. He only got to see it very early in the morning, when nobody was about, so being on stage in the packed lawns during lunch was a big deal for him. When Leo was nervous he tended to … overcompensate. Strutting and flexing and putting on an accent. I didn't think Mukesh would like watching that, and I certainly didn't want to be around to see Mukesh watching that! *Especially* with all these wretched rumours flying about. Besides, I was exhausted from all the canvassing I'd been doing – not asking for votes *directly*, of course, so crass, but talking about how much I loved the Club and wanted to serve and so on! So I went into that grubby parlour next to the pool and got a pedicure! Of course I regret doing it now – if

I had been there I could have stopped the scene from getting so ugly!'

She shudders slightly.

'Madam, we will keep this very confidential, of course, but is your husband on any kind of medication for a mental condition? Has he been diagnosed with something?'

Her eyes lose all dreaminess and blaze with sudden anger. '*Of course not!* Mukesh is absolutely sound mentally! Who has been suggesting such a thing?'

Bhavani throws the general under the bus deftly. 'Mehra sa'ab did mention something of the sort ...'

She makes a small scoffing sound. 'Of course. Our local Donald Trump! How could it be anybody else?'

'Donald Trump, madam?'

Her beautiful eyes glitter with anger. 'He's an oaf and a chauvinist! And a lecher! Always hanging around the Daily Needs, harassing the poor girl there! And he wants to hold a beauty pageant at the Club every year! A "Miss DTC" contest if you please!' She gives a fastidious little shiver. 'Naturally, all the randy old men are delighted – imagining themselves as judges, surrounded by pretty contestants, all buttering them up!'

'But, madam, he is a war hero.'

She snorts. 'He *would* thrive in a war situation! All crude machismo! Always boasting about how he got his nickname – let me tell you, officer, it *suits* him! The man has selective hearing! Anything that doesn't agree with his particular view of the world – women's rights, aesthetics, people with special needs, LGBTQ rights – he acts like he has never heard of it! He's a human bulldozer!'

She pauses for a moment, too overwrought to continue. 'Actually, *all* these male presidents – even the *best* of them, like Devender Bhatti – they just can't see the DTC for the shining jewel it is. The building is historic. The *legacy* is historic! They see it as a cosy place to hang with their buddies and swim and play tennis and consume cheap whisky and chicken tikka and leer at each others' granddaughters—'

'And you, madam, how do you see it?'

Her eyes start to glow in her almost translucent face. 'I see it … oh! As a place of tremendous beauty and influence and soft power! You see, ACP, beauty has the power to *refine*. When people are surrounded by everything aesthetic, they begin to have a genuine, *civilized* exchange of thoughts and ideas! That is my dream for the DTC – that it will be *so* beautiful that the best minds will gather here to have free and fearless discussions about art, music, literature, governance, policy—'

Bhavani's eyebrows rise internally. The good lady is clearly living in some sort of dreamworld.

'But President Bhatti told us the Club has to toe the government line or they come for all your licences and permissions!' he points out, cutting her off mid-speech. 'All this free and fearless exchange of ideas won't work with them! They'll cut your water supply or something, madam!'

'Oh that!' She shrugs, her expression growing inscrutable. 'That can all be *managed*.'

'O really?' Bhavani is greatly interested. '*How*, madam?' She smoothens the folds of her firan carefully.

'The IJP government is oafish, ACP. They're crude and violent and just plain illiterate – but even the crudest minds can be sensitized and refined by consistent exposure to beauty, kindness and yogic meditation. Those are the three tenets on which I have built Chrysanthemum, my lifestyle brand.'

It sounds more like religion than a brand to Bhavani, but he nods enthusiastically. 'O yes.'

'People come into the store with money, but no taste. It has been *my* task to open their eyes … *sensitize* them to good aesthetics, to refinement, to *class*. Of course I use the word 'class' not in the crude, literal sense!'

'Of course, of course.'

She fixes her clear glowing eyes on his sympathetic face.

'I hope to do the same with the elite of Delhi! We began all wrong with the IJP government, I feel! We got their backs up. Most of them just have an inferiority complex because they're small-town bumpkins who resent us for being well-educated and well-off for a hundred years or more! If we had been less patronizing and less snobbish and just … *nicer* generally – half of the nonsense that's happening in this city and the country would never have happened!'

A vision of the Club as Urvashi Khurana would like it to be rises before Bhavani's eyes. Scented candles, soft cushions, pools of water, the best wines, right-wingers and liberals appreciating Korean cinema or the latest Booker Prize–winning novel together in hushed voices, while the High Priestess of Beauty strides softly through her domain in robes of embroidered white, scattering goodness and light.

'Wah!' he declares. 'Your vision is beautiful, madam!'

She smiles graciously. Then her tone grows a little matter of fact. 'Instead of despising this one for being uncouth and that one for being a lala, if we give a few, judiciously chosen, influential or wealthy people out-of-turn memberships ... educate them about beauty and *civilized* society, then at least all our licensing and financial woes will be sorted ...' She gives the tiniest of shrugs, letting her voice fade away.

Bhavani starts to understand the secret behind Chrysanthemum's success, and why Urvashi Khurana is tipped to win the coming election. It is because she exists simultaneously in a beautiful fantasy la-la land – and a very practical lala land.

'Madam, one last question: who supervised the placement of the balloons in the gym yesterday?'

Her chin rises. Her husband has clearly told her about the loose balloons that had floated up and obscured the camera.

'I did.'

The words hang in the air like a challenge. Bhavani lets them.

Then he leans in and looks the beautiful woman in the eye. 'Things are not looking good for you, madam,' he says gently. 'Or your husband. *You* decided that balloons should be part of the décor of Tambola Sunday. *You* instructed that four bunches of gas balloons be placed in four corners of the gym! One of those bunches floated up to block the *sole* camera in the gym at the *exact* moment when your husband was there alone, and could have poisoned the flask of Creatine Monohydrate Thampi had prepared for Leo. It is common knowledge that Leo had hit your husband hours before, after a very public disagreement. And now this song has surfaced! Along with evidence of your payouts! A *very* good case can be made by from joining all these pieces, that you, Urvashi Khurana, were having an affair with your Zumba instructor, that he started blackmailing you with some intimate photos or videos or something, that you finally told your husband about it, and then the two of you conspired to kill the blackmailer to save your standing in society and that you succeeded.'

She glares at him, white-faced, tight-lipped and absolutely furious.

He stares back. For a moment it seems to him that she may crack, may break down, may let him in and confide in him, but the moment passes.

'Intimate photos?' she says finally, with a small, scornful laugh. 'Do you think I am a *schoolgirl*, ACP Singh? Or a pathetic, middle-aged woman having a midlife crisis?' Her chin comes up proudly. 'I'm an independent, successful, self-made businesswoman and I think with my *brain*. I would never, ever put myself in somebody's power like that! And as far as your four bunches of balloons are concerned, anybody with even a *minimal* knowledge of Chrysanthemum's design principle would know how fiercely committed I am to four-cornered symmetry! It is at the *core* of all my designs!'

He sighs and sits back. 'So it is your stated position that you were not being blackmailed?'

'Yes,' she replies. 'And if you do your homework properly, you will find that I have been donating money to Badshahpur for decades, *much* before Leo Matthew arrived on the scene.'

This is brand new information for Bhavani. He can't stop his mouth from falling open.

'*O really?*'

'Yes, *really*,' Urvashi retorts, faint triumph in her voice. 'Do check. And check my WhatsApp history with Leo too. He has sent me *several* songs – not just this one. Our conversations were almost exclusively about music and dance and exercise.'

'We will do that at once,' Bhavani says. 'My apologies if I have in any way offended you …'

Urvashi inclines her head graciously. 'You're a thorough man, that much at least can be said for you.'

'Thank you! But, madam, don't mind, but just for one minute, a short time ago, we felt that there was something you wanted to share with us …'

She doesn't deny this – just looks at him with careful and total concentration for a moment, then shakes her head decisively. 'It's got nothing to do with all this. Can I leave now?'

9

An Eye in the Wall

The final interview for the day, with a very sober and wary Roshni Aggarwal, begins on an uneventful note. She says vaguely that Leo had sent her many songs, 'Secrets' being just one of them. When questioned about her donations to the Badshahpur Children's Village, she gets suddenly emotional.

'Ab what to hide from you,' she says, tears spilling from her mascaraed eyes and spilling down her bony face. 'You are the police, you know everything anyway! My son … has some … *problems*. And when your child has problems, you try to bribe the Gods, so that these problems will go away. Donating to Badhshahpur, a place where Leo did some volunteer work, was one such bribe for me.'

And that is all she has to say on the subject.

By lunch time, Bhavani is alone in Guest Cottage No. 5, all his interviews done for the day. He sinks into the floral couch, puts his feet up on the coffee table, rakes his hands through his hair, and thinks furiously.

They are all lying. They *have* to be. Bambi has already confirmed that Leo was a blackmailer! But how had Leo cottoned on to Bambi's mother's secret? Did he have some inside information? We will have to instruct PK to interrogate all the staff at the Todi house …

His mind turns back to Roshni Aggarwal. Roshni's 'secret' must be connected to her problematic son. Stands to reason.

Picking up his phone, he calls the criminal data base team at Tis Hazari. 'We want information on an Aryaman Aggarwal,' he says. 'Take down his details.'

Presently, he hangs up, his mind now on Behra Mehra.

Mehra's 'secret' is probably to do with young Ganga and her estranged husband. Where is that fellow now? Have he and Ganga broken it off entirely? Or does he still get drunk and visit her? How to find out? He can ask Bambi Todi, but she … she is clearly biased towards the girl. He drums his fingers on the table, then sits bolt upright, his grey hair rumpled.

'PK!' Bhavani Singh roars. 'PK!'

The inspector rushes into the cottage. 'Yes, sir!'

'Interrogate all the staff at the Todi house next door. Find out if any of them were friendly with Leo Matthew.'

Padam Kumar snaps to attention. 'Yes, sir!'

Bhavani looks him up and down, taking in his height, his broad shoulders, his fair complexion, and the innocent ruddiness of his face. Yes, PK will do. He will do very nicely, actually.

'And one more thing.' He smiles cosily at the unsuspecting inspector. 'There is a kirana store inside the club itself, called Daily Needs. Go in there and strike up a conversation with the young lady behind the counter, one Ganga Kumar. Find out, very subtly, who and where her husband is.'

Padam Kumar baulks. 'But, sir, how?'

'Arrey, you are meeting a lot of girls nowadays, aren't you?' the ACP replies, a touch irascibly. 'Go meet this one too. She is separated from her husband. Maybe you will fall in love with her. Maybe that is why the Fates have conspired to bring us here!'

'A separated woman!' Padam Kumar gasps. 'What are you *saying*, sir!'

Brushing off these protests, Bhavani waves the scandalized inspector out of the cottage, then sits back to muse on Urvashi.

What could *her* secret be?

Hadn't she protested too strongly against his suggestion of intimate photos? Insisted too vehemently that she wasn't a pathetic middle-aged woman having a mid-life crisis? Because it did make sense for Leo to have been blackmailing her – with the DTC election and Chrysanthemum's Rs 50 crore funding on the line, the stakes for her had been super high.

It's just a question of gathering proof. He presses the intercom.

'Haan, Ram Palat, suno.'

He gives the young computer operator some instructions. Then he hangs up, sits back on the floral couch, puts his feet up on the coffee table again, crosses his hands over his stomach and closes his eyes.

'Enough,' he murmurs. 'Easy does it, Bhavani. Do nat strain. If you strain, all you will get is haemorrhoids of the brain ...'

Meanwhile, Padam Kumar trudges down to Daily Needs, feeling rather awkward and resentful.

Trust Bhavani sir to make a joke out of everything! He can't meet just *any* girl! One with a vanished husband, at that, belonging to God alone knows what caste, having what astrological chart, and what background!

But when he reaches the store, he perks up slightly. The girl behind the counter, placing a palmful of jasmine flowers into a lapis lazuli bowl before Saraswati ji is as graceful as Saraswati ji herself. She is dressed in a meticulously pleated cream sari, with her black hair oiled and combed into a smooth plait, and gold studs gleaming against her glowing dusky skin. Padam Kumar checks her on the mental shade card he carries inside his head, calibrated from Ajay Devgn to Alia Bhatt, and decides that though she is not as fair as *he* himself is, she is definitely not on the Devgn side of the scale either.

This important point settled, he smiles at her, and then, as she smiles inquiringly back, he experiences both a mild electric shock, and an epiphany. She looks just like the girl at the end of the *Jungle Book* movie – the girl who drops her waterpot to get Mowgli to speak to her.

'Huh hulloji,' he manages to say.

'Hello.' Her voice is low and musical, and clearly, she is not uncomfortable with English.

'I ... am ...' He licks his lips and looks about the shop. A display of Valentine's Day cards catches his eye. 'I am with Archie's Gallery, akchulli. We are doing a survey. How much interest do you get in consumers for Valentine's Day?'

Her eyebrows rise. 'This is a kirana shop,' she replies. 'We don't get much excitement on Valentine's Day. Some of the younger crowd – green card members or dependent children – come in and buy chocolates and a few cards or a single-stemmed rose. That's it.'

Padam Kumar nods, starting to feel quite pleased with himself. 'I see, I see ... and you, ma'am? What are your plans for Valentine's Day? Do you, uh ... have a date with somebody special?'

She doesn't reply, just crosses her arms in front of her chest and stares at him steadily for so long that his face starts to turn red.

'Should I call security?' she says finally. 'Or would you prefer to leave quietly with your dignity intact?'

'I ... uh ... no, no, I'm not a ... You are misunderstanding!'

Her eyebrows rise even higher. 'Really? You're from Archie's Gallery? Can I see some ID?'

Stung to the quick at being taken for some sort of cheap Lothario, he sullenly pulls out his police ID and lays it on the counter (though not without a flourish).

The change in expression is dramatic. Her face pales. She seems to shrink. Eyes wide with apprehension, she looks at him as one would a poisonous snake.

'What ... what do you want?'

'Nothing,' Padam Kumar says, now feeling rather flustered and foolish. Bhavani sir didn't specify if he should reveal his identity to the girl or no.

She stares back at him, uncertainly, dark eyes wide.

'Is it ... about the murder?' she asks. 'Because I don't know anything about it!'

'Are you married?' He gathers the shreds of his dignity to ask.

Her hand goes to her bosom, brings out the mangalsutra half hidden in the folds of her saree and holds it before her like a talisman. 'Yes.'

Padam Kumar feels an entirely disproportionate amount of disappointment at the sight of the black and gold beads.

'Okay,' he says curtly, then turns on his heel and walks out the shop, his cheeks flaming red.

DIRTY TRICKS CLUB?

Elections at the uber exclusive Delhi Turf Club, once a dignified affair, have been turning murkier and murkier in the last decade. This year's election has already been in the news with stories of one of the candidates for president, Lt Gen. Mehra (retd) PVSM AVSM Yudh Sewa Medal, holding large, lascivious parties with fancy alcohol and fancy women to woo the two thousand-odd permanent members of the club, doing the rounds.

And now his opponent in the election, Chrysanthemum founder -president Urvanshi Khurana is in the news too, after her trainer, with whom she was rumoured to be having an affair, was found dead in the Club's gym. A connection with the upcoming election cannot be ruled out.

Businessman Gagan Ruia, who was not allowed to enter the formal dining room at the DTC recently because he was wearing traditional Indian shoes, said, 'It is clear that the rot runs deep in the DTC's systems. It needs to be placed under some kind of government control.'

From: d.bhatti@dtcdelhi.in

To: dtccorecommittee@dtcdelhi.in ▼

SUB: DTC CORE COMMITTEE MEETING

Dear Members,

PFA the attached clipping from the India Post's 'Gossip and Gupshup' section. We need to come up with an action plan to deal with this brewing crisis.

Equally importantly, a date needs to be fixed for the postponed Club elections. That will be the main agenda of today's core committee meeting.

Please be at my residence at 12.30 p.m. sharp. I shall be serving snacks and lunch.

Warm regards,

Devendar Bhatti

President

'What do *you* think we should do, Balbir?'

The core committee is sitting in Devendar Bhatti's large, well-lit living room, sipping Scotch or nimbu pani as per their medical restrictions, in pleasant anticipation of more solid sustenance to follow. Their average age is sixty-five-plus.

'I think you should postpone the election by a couple of months, sir,' Brig. Dogra says at once. 'I mean no offence to either candidate, but any one of them *could* be involved in this thing up to their eyeballs, and our by-laws state quite clearly that *nobody* embroiled in a criminal case can stand for Club election till they are clean-chitted.'

'Or we could hold the election with two new candidates,' murmurs Bambi's father, industrialist Pankaj Todi – a short, fat, very fair man with a smoothly shaven head, long-lashed, beautiful eyes and fleshy lips. 'Gen. Mehra and Urvashi can take their chances next time around, when this whole jhamela has blown over. What d'you say, Bhatti?'

Bhatti looks at Todi with open hostility. '*You* are the reason we are in this situation in the first place,' he says. 'If you hadn't brought that clown Gagan Ruia to the Club, then he couldn't have kicked up such a fuss about his ruddy juttis, and we would still be flying under the government's radar like we've been doing for seventy years!'

Todi's jaw drops at this blunt attack. 'But I was just trying to … *help* the Club,' he says. 'Matlab, being on good terms with the current dispensation is important, isn't it?' He looks appealingly about the room.

There is a subdued, but unanimous murmur of agreement from the rest of the gathering.

Bhatti's Adam's apple bobs up and down agitatedly. 'Crass commercialism!' he says slightly incoherently. 'Populism! Majoritarianism!'

Behra Mehra puts down his drink and sits forward. 'You're being a little naive, Bhatti,' he says smoothly. 'Like it or not, the IJP is firmly in the saddle now, and going to be calling the political shots for a while. A good club president would understand that it pays to be on their right side.'

Bhatti makes a sound that is half-snort, half-squawk. 'And you're that "good club president" I presume? Because Gagan Ruia's father and you are as thick as thieves!'

Mehra bows. 'I have been privileged enough to serve under Ruia bhai, and yes, we do have a good equation. I think that can only help the Club.'

'He does have a point, Bhatti,' rumbles Balbir Dogra. 'It *would* be in the interests of the Club to have a sycophant like Mehra as president. I'd vote for him.'

Mehra, not sure if he should be insulted or pleased, wisely decides to turn his famous deaf ear to this remark.

Bhatti gives a finicky little nod. 'Very well. I shall anyway be spending more time at the IIC once my term is done! So, coming back to the point – should we postpone the election by two months or choose two fresh candidates as Todi suggests?'

'Postpone by two months,' Mehra says decidedly. 'The lovely Urvashi is, of course, forever young and beautifully immortal' – he bows gallantly in her direction – 'but I may not even be alive two years from now! I want to take my chances this year.'

'Well, you've blown up so much dosh on expensive parties, it makes sense for you to collect on it now, when it's still fresh in people's minds,' Balbir Dogra says bluntly. 'In two years these buggers are quite capable of demanding a whole new round of parties from you.'

Mehra throws back his head and laughs, baring large, yellow teeth. 'Brilliantly put, sir!'

'The general overestimates both my youth and my beauty.' Urvashi smiles tightly. 'I too, would like to contest this year – if you could continue for perhaps a month or two more, Devendar, I would be *so* grateful.'

There is a general chorus of agreement from around the room.

'Very well, very well, at your kind insistence, I will continue in this post for two months more.' Bhatti smiles thinly. 'Ah, here come the snacks!'

A rather elderly looking bearer comes in with tray of appetizing-looking starters. Sizzling, crispy kebabs, loaded, multicoloured canapes and garden-fresh vegetables served with a creamy dip. Everybody digs in.

'*Amazing* dip, Bhatti!'

'Is that mutton? Or beef? It's buff! You're serving buff with an IJP government in power, you crazy bastard!'

'You're welcome not to eat any,' Devendar Bhatti says with a sly wink.

'Give it here! Oh, *delicious*! Try some, Urvashi!'

'Thank you – I am enjoying these delicious vegetables! So very fresh!'

Bhatti's face brightens. 'All the vegetables here are from the DTC's organic kitchen garden!'

'Set up by Todi Corp when my wife was on the horticulture committee,' puts in Pankaj Todi.

'*And* me,' Behra Mehra says at once. 'I was on the horticulture committee with her! We set up that garden together!'

'Then you can both take a bow,' Urvashi says smilingly. 'These beetroot canapes are delicious! *Such* a deep, rich red colour! What's the secret ingredient?'

Todi and Mehra look at each other hesitantly.

'What?' Urvashi asks, lowering a half-eaten ruby-red canape from her mouth. 'What *is* it?'

The general nudges the industrialist. 'You tell the lady, Todi.'

Pankaj Todi pats his fleshy lip with a napkin then leans forward. 'Well, good old Guppie Ram – the old maali you know, God rest his soul – was sometimes sighted er … *irrigating* the vegetables with his personal, patented fertilizer!'

Urvashi's eyes widen suspiciously. She puts the canape down. 'Matlab?'

'Matlab, the chap was a raging alcoholic and not above pissing into the plants!' Behra Mehra says.

'*Ewww!*' Urvashi puts her plate away, looking queasy.

The two men roar with laughter.

But Devendar Bhatti is not amused. 'Urvashi, please, the man's been dead for a year or more. There is no way he could've urinated over this current crop of beetroot! It's such a deep red because the gardeners put so much onion peel in the compost, that's all! Urvashi!'

But she has already put a hand to her mouth and rushed out of the room. The men all look at each other.

'How can this lady run the club?' Todi asks in a low voice. 'Seriously? She's much too delicate!'

'You're a crass fool, Todi!' Devendar Bhatti snaps angrily. 'Urvashi Khurana is a highly intelligent woman with a strong sense of aesthetics—'

'Which is why she married Mukki!' Somebody sniggers.

'*And* unlike you, Todi the toady, who can't think beyond toadying up to the Ruias, she has a great vision for the club!' Bhatti concludes forcefully.

'What's her great vision, I would like to know?' Mehra demands. 'All she wants to do is set up a new rainwater-harvesting system!'

Urvashi re-enters the room, perfectly composed, and takes her seat.

'Did someone say rainwater harvesting?' she enquires as she picks up her Scotch and soda and gives it a rather militant swirl. 'You, general?'

'The Club doesn't need a new rainwater-harvesting system.' Mehra picks up the cudgels at once. 'The current system is quite adequate.'

Urvashi's clear, beautiful eyes start to sparkle. 'Are you *serious*? The current system is a joke! The new one will halve our water bill!'

'You just want to make me look small!' Mehra roars. 'That garden is dedicated to my dead wife, madam! It's named after her – The Shrimati Savitri Mehra Udyaan!'

Her eyebrows rise. 'I assure you I have no such intention! It's just that the assessment team recommended the kitchen garden – because it's low-lying, and perfectly accessible to all the run-off pipes. They say it's the cheapest and best spot. And so, though we all know how much you loved your wife—'

His eyes bug out. 'Are you being sarcastic, madam?'

'What?' Urvashi draws back, startled. 'No! No at all!'

'Because I will *not* tolerate any disrespect to my spouse!' Behra Mehra waggles a celery stick in her face.

Urvashi's eyes kindle. 'Well then, general, you should think twice before disrespecting *other* people's spouses! What the *hell* do you mean by telling the ACP that Mukesh has a mental health issue?'

There is a collective intake of breath at this. Mehra looks a little ashamed of himself.

Backing down a little he mutters, 'I was just genuinely *concerned* ... for Mukesh. He behaved so *oddly* during tambola that day.'

Urvashi gives a short, disbelieving laugh.

There is tense silence.

'What do you want?' Mehra says finally, offensively. 'An apology? For voicing genuine concern about your husband's mental state?'

'Yes.' She nods, as regal as a queen. '*And* for spreading rumours about my affair with Leo Matthew! A double apology!'

Mehra licks his lips. 'Well, you aren't going to get it.'

'Just do the gentlemanly thing and apologize, Mehra,' Bhatti says testily. 'You've no business gossiping about Urvashi.'

'Well she has no business to trying to desecrate a garden laid in my wife's memory!'

'Yes, but if you win the election, she won't be able to!' Bhatti sounds quite fed-up. 'So why not just beat her in a fair fight and leave it at that?'

Urvashi gives a tinkling little laugh. 'Gen. Mehra hasn't fought fair in his *life*.'

The general stares. 'What do you mean by that, madam?' he demands. There is actual foam on his lips.

Urvashi looks amused. 'Exactly what I said,' she says coolly. 'You prefer to have an unfair advantage over people.'

He leans forward. This is his game face. The one that Amitabh Bachchan had so much trouble replicating in *Jhelum Bridge*. '*What* are you alluding to?' he hisses.

'Oh, so many things! But most recently, poor little Ganga Kumar whom you have been pestering with your unwanted attentions.'

There is a collective gasp from the room.

Mehra gets to his feet, shaking a little.

Urvashi continues to sit, smiling composedly.

'Leave it, Mehra.' Pankaj Todi puts a restraining hand on his friend's arm. '#MeToo ka jamana hai. Don't get into a battle of words with a woman. Save your fire for the election.'

'As will I.' Urvashi looks around the room, her eyes flashing. 'I know I don't have the votes of the old boys' club in this room – but there *are* some women members, *and* other people, who want the DTC to be more than some sordid adda where old men get drunk and hit on hapless young women! I *will* get those votes, and then, when we have sensible leadership—'

She turns her gaze on the general, '*Then we will dig up the kitchen garden.*'

Balbir Dogra frowns. Urvashi's voice seems disproportionately threatening. What's with this obsession with the kitchen garden?

Behra Mehra holds up one shaking finger. 'Over my dead body.'

Urvashi tips her glass to him in a polite salute. 'Oh, I hope not.'

My inner thighs are still so sore,
But the man responsible is no more,
Leo, you were the best trainer, ever,
Heaven just gained a stronger Core!

These immortal lines on Cookie Katoch's Facebook wall, accompanied by a candid, laughing photograph of Leo and her, flexing their biceps, starts an unofficial but desperately fierce contest among Delhi's poshest ladies to put up the best possible 'mourning' post for Leo, featuring a trainer–trainee photograph and a heartfelt paragraph describing how close the two of them had been.

'Babe, I haven't seen something as nuts as this since Wendell Rodricks died!' Cookie confides to Roshni smugly. 'Everybody was hunting through their photo galleries then, remember, trying to dig up a pic with him? Some of them toh were shameless enough to just photoshop it! Of course, *I* had a genuine pic because Wen and me were just too close, na, and now it's the same thing happening all over again, but with Leo, and in gym clothes!'

And Roshni, who had never unbent enough to click a candid pic with Leo, has to swallow her bile and agree with Cookie that what is happening on FB is *too* vulgar.

Pictures and videos of Leo trend on Facebook all day – flexing with a bride-to-be here, doing a side plank with a grandmom-to-be there, pulling a crazy face at the end of class somewhere else.

Alternately wiping tears of genuine grief and scanning each other's photographs mercilessly for signs of underarm sag, back fat or belly pudge, all of Delhi's chic set spends a satisfying day scrolling through each other's timelines and coming to terms with their 'grief'.

Lose It with Leo posts a sober little video by the evening, featuring a handsome, laughing image of the trainer, and sharing the details of the funeral mass which will take place at the Sacred Heart Cathedral at Gol Dak Khaana the next day. Cynics and statistics both assert that a large online following does not translate into a large following IRL, especially in such cold, foggy weather, but come the next morning the huge church is quite decently half full.

Bhavani, huddled into the second-last pew with Kashi and Bambi, watches over the proceedings with indolent interest.

Altar boys are readying the church for mass. The organist is tuning up, talking to the choir in hushed voices. A woman Bhavani recognizes from her pink ombre hair and no-nonsense air as Sho is walking around with a camera, shooting the congregation – presumably for the final episode of *Lose It with Leo*.

Bambi scoots in closer to Kashi. 'My money's on Mehra,' she whispers. 'Out of us four blackmail victims, I mean. He either did it himself, or he chaabied Mukki into doing it.'

'Where's your feminism?' Kashi demands sternly. 'Four people got sent the song, and you zoomed in on the only man on the list? Are you saying a woman can't be as good a murderer as a man?'

She makes some laughing reply, which he counters immediately. Their voices grow lower and more intimate.

Vakeel sa'ab and Bambiji are looking very happy today, Bhavani thinks as he watches from the sidelines. Well, well, good for them! And meanwhile, the early rising girlfriend is busy constructing a roof in Kalahandi! Things are going to get terribly complicated for young Kashi soon ...

His mind shifts to complications of his own. He had had an in-depth briefing from Inspector Padam Kumar earlier that morning.

'Sir, we interrogated all staff at the Todi residence on 6, Aurangzeb Road. Guards, drivers, maids were *all* clean-chitted, but we managed to establish that an old drunk gardener, now deceased, used to be quite friendly with Leo! Yaari-dosti, drinks and all! He got him sports shoes and fancy watches and let him drive his fancy motorcycle even! We're guessing ki he was the Leak. And that this was Leo's modus operandi – to cultivate servants and staff of rich people, and pump them for dirt on their employers! We are now checking to see if he had similar contacts in the other three households.'

'What about Behra Mehra?'

'Yes, on that, sir, the men we had posted outside Daily Needs have reported that General Mehra visits the shop every day and lingers to chat with the young lady for twenty-twenty minutes at a time.'

And that is Mehra's motive, quite neatly sorted, Bhavani muses, as his eyes scan the congregation covertly. He was sweet on young Ganga, perhaps had a hand in the disappearance of her husband even, and Leo found out about it through his cultivated network of domestic staff.

He starts to hum the Cheeky Peaches song speculatively.

'...*but fate has a way of catching up with sinners*

At the end of the day there are no free dinners
And I will make you pay
Oh, I will make you pay
P p p p p pay …'
Bambi gives a little shiver.

'Don't ACP, you have no idea how that song haunts my dreams.'

He smiles at her sympathetically. 'It won't any more, Bambi ji. Good thing you told the whole problem to vakeel sa'ab – we have already facilitated the returns of all the missing valuables and made up a convincing story in which nobody gets blamed!'

'Yeah … about that …' She smiles, a rather wry, twisted smile. 'My father's really angry with me for allowing myself to be blackmailed. He says I should have come to him.'

Bhavani's eyes are sympathetic. 'Why *didn't* you go to him?'

She bites her lip, looks around the church, then lowers her voice. 'My parents are getting divorced. I was worried he would use this information to get out of it without paying Mammu her fair share.'

'And now he will?'

She sighs. 'And now he will.'

He pats her hand comfortingly, looks about the pews for Roshni, and spots her amongst a gaggle of DTC Zumba girls. She is sitting next to Cookie Katoch, who, for reasons best known to herself, is attired in a maxi dress patterned with large, magenta and turquoise flowers.

'But where's the Jamaican choir?' He hears her say plaintively. 'Why are only all these converted desi Christians about?'

Roshni and the rest of her friends shush her and she subsides.

Bambi giggles. 'She really bought that Jamaican story! It was *such* a bunch of lies!'

'So you're the *big Dick*, I hear?!'

It's a high, excitable voice, very carrying and a little unhinged, and it makes everybody turn around. A bald, bright-eyed, satyr-ish character on crutches, easily identifiable as Randy Rax, has just limped into the church and snuck up behind Bhavani, emitting a strong odour of cheap alcohol mixed with Moov.

The old policeman inclines his head genially. 'We're the ACP in charge of the case, yes.'

'Oh, *we*!' Randy Rax gives a mock-reverent little wriggle. '*We* as in royalty? Or We as in schizophrenia?'

'We as in polite Hindi,' Bhavani replies genially.

Randy Rax winks. 'Well, I know *nothing* about politeness, ACP! Does ACP stand for A Colossal Penis by the way?'

'Rax, stop it!' A mortified looking Fr Victor hurries into the church, clearly in search of the errant Rax. He turns to Bhavani Singh. 'Forgive my friend, he just likes to be outrageous.'

Randy Rax has moved on to Bambi now. 'Well, huh huh *hello* there, poppet!' he almost-shouts. 'You're a pretty one! Are you one of Leo's? Leo always had a harem around him! I used to call him a Haremzada! *Haha!* Isn't that a good one?'

'It's a deadly one,' Bambi tells him lightly. 'You've got a great sense of humour, Rax.'

He leers at her, then taps the side of his nose. 'But that's not the answer to my *question*!'

'I'm part of the harem, I guess,' Bambi says ruefully. 'But then, so is this whole church, isn't it?'

'O!' Rax's eyes widen in gleeful delight. 'Even *Jesus*?' he screeches. 'Even, Gawd-help-us, Mother *Mary*?'

'Rax.' Victor's voice is sharp. 'Just, please, respect the occasion, please.'

Rax cringes extravagantly. 'Are you with the poppet?' he asks Kashi conspiratorially as he lowers himself into the pew beside them. 'Cuckolded by the mighty Leo, like many, *many* men before you?'

'I'm Akash Dogra,' Kashi says smilingly. 'Hullo, Rax.'

But Rax is busy observing the congregation, his eyes bright and inquisitive.

'So this is Delhi high society!' he whispers loudly. Spittle sprays freely from his mouth. Several people in the pew in front of him wince as droplets land on the backs of their necks. 'Are they *all* members of the Delhi Turd Club?'

'Please can you watch him, Akash?' the harassed Fr Victor appeals to Kashi. 'I have to start the mass.'

'Yes, of course, Father Vick.'

The priest rushes away, relieved. Behind him, Rax rises again to his feet, leaning heavily against the back of the pew in front of them.

'Lots of hot chicks!' he announces in a loud, satisfied voice. He raises one shaky arm and points directly at a woman seated a few pews ahead. '*That* one has the biggest tits!'

The congregation gasps. Kashi gets to his feet and clamps a large hand over Rax's mouth.

'Chup!' he says firmly.

Rax giggles. 'I'm being violated from behind!' he splutters, wriggling against Kashi's palm. 'That too in church! This is *better* than any of my fantasies!'

'Just sit down,' Kashi says grimly. 'Your friend is dead – do you think you can show some *respect*?'

Rax nods, and Akash slowly releases him. Immediately, he lunges forward and bellows, 'And *that* one is the prettiest! I *think*. But I can't tell till she removes her sunglasses. Excuse me, take off your glasses please!'

The lady he has picked out for this high praise is Urvashi Khurana. She is seated a few rows ahead, to the left, wearing a sober white chikan salwar-kameez and the aforementioned dark glasses.

Instead of being offended, Urvashi takes off her glasses and smiles at Rax.

'Thank you, young man,' she says in her exquisitely pitched voice. Then she pats the place next to her. 'Why don't you come and sit with me?'

Randy Rax needs no second invitation. He lurches forward eagerly, clambering over several hapless people in his rush to get to the coveted spot.

'Do pardon my odour,' he says loudly to her as she wrinkles her nose slightly, 'I applied the Moov to mask the booze – because this is church, you know! So now I smell of Mooze.'

She smiles and holds out her songbook, not at all rattled. 'Do explain the ceremony to me. I've never attended a mass before and I don't want to make any mistakes.'

As Rax takes hold of the songbook with clammy hands,

Urvashi Khurana looks over his head at Kashi, and flashes him a conspiratorial thumbs up.

'Real classy,' Kashi whispers to Bambi.

'Yeah,' she says serenely. 'Urvashi auntie's like that.'

The organ sounds, the church choir starts to sing and everybody rises to their feet. Father Victor, his simple white cassock now covered with the ceremonial robes of the Holy Mass, walks into the church with the red-and-white–robed altar boys before him.

Reaching the pulpit, he waits for the song to end, then intones in a low reverential voice, 'In the name of the Father and of the Son and the Holy Spirit!'

And the mass begins.

◆——◆

'It's going to be a *great* final episode.'

Sho has tied her pink ombre hair back into a ponytail and is packing her camera and lenses away, speaking more to herself than to Bhavani. The church is almost empty.

'How nice,' he replies genially.

She smiles, then puts out a friendly hand for him to shake. 'Shonali Jha. You're investigating Leo's death, I believe.'

She has a smoker's voice, deep and husky, and a firm but relaxed grip – she doesn't need to prove anything with her handshake, clearly.

'Yes. We were waiting to speak to you only. Didn't want to disturb while you were working. Leo's phone records reveal that you two were very close.'

Sho chuckles. 'Really? I haven't the faintest memory of what I talked to Leo about on the phone. Were there any dirty pics?'

'No,' Bhavani says calmly. 'Should there have been?'

She rolls her eyes. 'I don't know … maybe in the early heady days. I bet there're none recently!' She throws back her head and laughs. It's a warm, comfortable laugh.

'You two were … a couple?'

She shakes her head. 'No. We weren't even friends-with-benefits – more like colleagues-with-benefits. Is that even a thing?'

'An office romance,' Bhavani suggests trendily.

She chuckles. 'Only there's no office, and no romance! Just work, and a weekly deadline, and some … er … benefits. Am I embarrassing you?'

'Nat us, but perhaps all these murtis of saints and virgins …'

She looks about the church ruefully. 'Don't they hear lurid confessions all the time? But you're right – let's go outside. I want a smoke anyway.'

A little while later they are standing in front of a Mother Mary grotto, ablaze with sweetpeas, larkspur and bright red poppies. Shonali's hair is candyfloss pink in the sun. She puts her heavy camera case on the ground and lights up.

'Leo hated my smoking,' she says. 'He said it was going to be the death of me.' Her voice breaks a little. 'I'll laugh at your funeral, he used to say.'

You are more affected then you let on, Bhavani thinks, as the woman next to him shudders and struggles to control her tears. You are genuinely grieving.

He sighs sympathetically.

They stare in silence at the small statue of Mother Mary in her blue and white robes.

'What do you want to know?' she says finally, abruptly, gripping the railing around the grotto and turning to face him. 'How can I help?'

Bhavani spreads out his hands. 'Just ... a general picture – of your friend and colleague ... that's the most important thing – and also, if there's anything you think could be useful, or pertinent to the case.'

'I'm a trained film-maker,' she says. 'With a fairly fancy degree! But when I became a single mom – long story, totally irrelevant – I had to find a way of earning money while being with my son. So I started shooting birthday party videos for my friends and their kiddies. Luckily, they were all really wealthy and they wanted to help me.'

She takes a long drag and exhales – no fancy tricks or sexy pouting, just matter-of-fact exhalation.

'I met Leo at a little girl's birthday party – I think the mother went to his Zumba class, and she'd asked him to come by and show the little girls some of his fancy moves. Later, I sent him the video I'd shot that day – he'd given me his number. We went out for a drink, which turned into dinner, which turned into coffee at his apartment, which turned into breakfast – which turned into *Lose It with Leo!* I wasn't in love with him or anything – I'm beyond all that now, I save all my love for my son and my mum – and Leo, he was very cynical about conventional relationships. But yes, I guess we were ... comfortable with each other. I'd like to help catch his killer.'

'Thank you for sharing such an intimate story with us, Shonali ji,' Bhavani says softly. 'You have been very honest – tell us, when you say he was cynical, what do you mean?'

She looks thoughtful. 'He didn't respect the usual boundaries – as in hands off because somebody's married, or like, be polite because somebody's old, or don't do that, that's against the law ... Things like that.'

'He steered his way with his own unique moral compass?'

She nods vigorously. 'Yes! That's it, exactly! The laws of Leo! Not the laws of society!'

'The laws of Leo,' Bhavani Singh muses. 'So interesting that you say that ... and what about the laws of ... er ... your YouTube channel? The paperwork?'

'We split everything fifty-fifty,' she says crisply. 'Ad revenue, as well as in-product placement. It was perfectly fair – I made him look damn good, you know!'

'O yes, you did! His fans clearly adored him!'

She chuckles. 'Aren't they *hilarious*? Leo's horny auntie army! I'm actually thinking about tracking a few of them down and shooting a video where they finally meet Leo!' Her face falls. 'Except that ... I can't any more. Fuck!'

She stares blindly at the grotto for a while. Ash drops from her cigarette.

'It's going to be *hell* cutting this final episode,' she says finally. 'I'm going to cry like a complete chutiya.'

Bhavani pats her arm sympathetically. She stubs out her cigarette savagely and lights a new one.

'Shonali, please don't mind – but was your relationship with Leo an exclusive one?'

This makes her laugh – a rich, husky, slightly hysterical laugh. Her pink hair ripples in the sun. A few matrons, rushing for the next mass, turn around and stare at her disapprovingly.

'Of course *not*! I did my own thang if I wanted to and, I'm sure, so did he!'

'And these ladies ...' Bhavani pauses delicately. 'You would know who they are?'

'I didn't *stalk* him, if that's what you're suggesting!' Shonali says, amused. 'I'm too busy. So no, I won't be able to name them, or even recognize them – but I got the impression that he was, you know, dipping into his pool of hot cougar clients a little!'

'Cougar?' Bhavani is confused.

'Attractive older women.'

'Ah!' Bhavani leans in. 'What gave you that impression? Please think carefully and tell us.'

She looks amused. 'Oh, I don't know ... just the way he'd look so smug and full of himself on some days. Purring like a big black cat who'd got the cream! And sometimes' – she stubs out her cigarette, laughing a little – '*sometimes* he would ask to borrow my camera. I got the impression he was shooting some uh ... intimate pics, you know?'

Behind them the church bells start to toll.

'O *really*?' Bhavani says, very slow and soft.

He stares at the innocuous looking camera case on the ground between them, and when he looks up at her again, she is startled by the glow on his face – transforming his plain features so that he looks almost De Niro-esque.

'How do you store footage shot on this camera, please?'

ॐ

You are cordially invited to
SHIVBLING

A charity sale of exquisitely crafted, Swarovski studded Shiva lingams by contemporary artist Karishma 'Cookie' Katoch. All proceeds shall go towards building a medical clinic for migrant labourers.

Shri Gagan Ruia has kindly consented to light the holy lamp

ॐ

at 12.30 p.m., the Rose Garden, Delhi Turf Club.

Jai Bholenath!

Some eyebrows are raised when a large contingent of DTC Zumba Girls travels from Leo's memorial service at the Sacred Heart Cathedral straight to Cookie Katoch's exhibition at the DTC, but Cookie herself is not at all conflicted.

'Oho, it's for a good cause, ya. Leo himself would have wanted me to go ahead with the exhibition! We had both been working so hard together to get my weight down to seventy kgs for it!'

And so, dressed in Jamaican finery with her well-buttressed cleavage on display, she awaits her invitees in a garden strewn with mighty lingams, all lovingly sculpted out of rose quartz, lapis lazuli, malachite, marble and glass. And soon, Delhi's richest socialites are trickling into the sun-dappled Rose Garden, knocking back sparkling white wine, dipping bits of focaccia bread into warm olive oil, and wah-wahing at the beauty and anatomical correctness of the sculptures.

Mrs Mala Dogra sneaks a look at the discreetly displayed price tags, then tugs at her daughter's dupatta.

'I don't have my reading glasses,' she whispers. 'Does it really say *thirty* thousand?'

'It says *eighty* thousand,' Natasha whispers back. 'And it's going to charity! Stop checking the price tags, Ma. It's bad enough that our khataara just broke down in front of everyone!'

Because the old Maruti Swift had wheezed to a defeated halt in the driveway of the club after its long journey from Noida, Mrs Mala Dogra had had to disembark, and with great dignity, request the ACP and his young inspector to push it up to the porch.

'But eighty thousand rupees is obscene!' Mrs Mala Dogra whispers back.

'Yes, Mother, they are clearly obscene,' a voice agrees from behind them. 'What's with the engorged veins and shit?'

'Kashi!' His sister whirls to glare at him. 'Where were you?'

'I got held up by VIP traffic,' he says wryly, nodding towards the entrance. 'Look who's here.'

Gagan Ruia, the defence minister's son, tall, fair and overfed, has just stridden into the garden, dressed in a crisp white pyjama-kurta, and woollen jacket (and his infamous pompommed juttis), with both palms joined reverentially over his head.

'Jai Bholenath!' he intones. 'Jai Bholenath!'

'Ugh!' Nattu pulls a fastidious face. 'They let him in here again? After JuttiGate?'

'He's come to inaugurate the exhibition apparently,' Kashi replies. 'Cookie auntie must've insisted on a real dick.'

Nattu giggles. 'Look who he's with.'

And Kashi realizes that Gagan Ruia has been escorted into the Rose Garden by Bambi's father, industrialist Pankaj Todi. They are twinning in crisp white.

'Are they tight?' he asks Nattu curiously.

She nods. 'It was Bambi's dad who signed him in that night when he made such a fuss about his stupid juttis,' she says. 'Gagan Ruia was his guest. Didn't you know?'

'No, I *didn't*,' he replies. 'I know you think I'm obsessed with the Todis, and I track their every move, but I don't, okay.'

She chuckles. 'Liar. Ooh, look, mushroom canapes! C'mon let's score some.'

A chunky brown hand reaches for the canapes at the same moment they do. It is ACP Bhavani Singh. He is looking about the exhibits somewhat bemusedly, but his expression lightens when he sees the Dogras.

'Oh, vakeel sa'ab, is this *your* family?'

Kashi is surprised. 'You guys have met?'

Mala Dogra smiles. 'The ACP was *too* kind! He helped us with the car when you were nowhere to be seen.'

'Ma, that's not fair,' Kashi protests. 'He has a *police* car! Naturally he didn't get held up in the roadblock!'

His mother sniffs, unconvinced. 'Somehow you and your father are never there when we're in trou—Oh, hello, Cookie!'

Cookie Katoch has descended upon them, gushing vaguely and dispensing effusive hugs.

'Hello, dear! Hello, dear! Please do pick up a lingam!'

Hai, hai, Mala Dogra thinks to herself. One's quite enough for us, thank you!

Aloud, she says smilingly, 'I was just asking my son which sculpture he likes *best*.'

Cookie turns eagerly to Kashi.

'Uh ... um ...' Kashi knits his brow. 'They're all unique in their own way ... but I do like this green one here! It's so ...' His fingers shoot up into the air, as if in search of words, '*Green!*'

'Just like grass,' adds the hovering ACP helpfully. 'And this nice chutney.' He points at the crystal bowl full of basil pesto.

'It's called dipping sauce,' the bearer corrects him importantly.

'O really?' Bhavani replies, beckoning him closer. 'We'll just dip into it again then ...'

Cookie continues to hold forth. 'The greens stone is malachite. You have a good eye, Kashi beta, this is one of my *best* pieces. It has a twin – but in lapis lazuli – a deep, rich blue. I had presented it to Bambi and Anshul at their engagement. In fact I asked her to lend it to me, just for this exhibition, I wanted to exhibit that one too, but she said ki she has no idea where it went. Which is a real loss to the art world, of course, but I didn't want to nag her about it, especially after that engagement ended in such a tragedy, you know.'

'We didn't know,' Bhavani replies, with great interest. 'What tragedy?'

'Oh, ACP Brownie, it was all *so* sad ...'

As Cookie lowers her voice and starts to fill him in on the story, Kashi moves away. He is in no mood to listen to the grand doomed saga of Bambi–Anshul.

As he walks past, Roshni Aggarwal summons him to her side imperiously. Surrendering to the fact that today is his day to hang with boojie, boozy aunties, Kashi goes over obediently. She promptly thrusts somebody at him – sullen, paneer-fair and dead-eyed, with worked-out arms, a soft belly and skinny legs. Kashi remembers him vaguely as a senior from TVVS.

'My son, Aryaman,' Roshni says, smiling a little anxiously.

Of course, Kashi recalls unenthusiastically, Aryaman Aggarwal, Roshni auntie's hot mess of a son, is a notorious stoner. It is rumoured that he'd been badly beaten up by his drug dealer once, and left with injuries that had affected his brain.

'Hey Arya!' Kashi smiles.

Aryaman looks at him with dull, vacant eyes. 'Hullo,' he says finally, reluctantly.

Roshni gives Aryaman a little push. '*Talk* to Kashi, Arya!' she says brightly, as if her son is five years old. 'He's become a very well-known lawyer. You'll have fun!'

And then she walks away.

Kashi and Aryaman look at each other for a while.

'So, man,' Kashi says finally. 'What d'you think of the uh ... exhibits?'

Aryaman doesn't bother to reply.

Kashi shrugs philosophically and sips his wine. Across the garden, Cookie is still talking earnestly to Bhavani. Seems like she's giving him the Bambi–Anshul debriefing in great detail.

He isn't wrong.

'The Poddar boy was really *very* good-looking, ACP Brownie!' Cookie is saying into the old policeman's attentive ear. 'And altogether too good to be true! In fact, I told Bambi's mother ki check-up kar lo, perhaps he is secretly gay or *important* or something! Not that our Bambi wouldn't attract the *best* offers – but you know in India, in the Marwari community especially, for *every* twenty gorgeous girls there seems to be only one dhangg ka ladka, just one decent boy, and all the girls have to fight for him! People keep saying ki pre-natal sex determination and female feticide is a big menace in our society and the number of girls born is dwindling and kya kya, but to me it seems like somebody is systematically tracking down all our tall, fair, strong, handsome, intelligent boy fetuses and bumping them off in the womb only! Maybe it's a Pakistani conspiracy.'

Bhavani agrees with her, then inquires in a low murmur about the Kashi–Bambi angle. What exactly is going on there?

Cookie giggles. 'Oh yes, those two! Quite the lovebirds when they were little! Why, once I saw them in the squash court, all squashed up together ...'

She proceeds to give him details that would've made Kashi's ears burn if he could've heard her. Luckily, he can't.

The party rolls on.

Above the Rose Garden, the sky starts to get a bit thundery. The intrepid bits of female cleavage, shoulder and thigh that had braved the late February chill begin to goose-pimple all over the lawn.

And then Bambi Todi bursts into Rose Garden, and things immediately get sunnier.

'*Heyyy* guys!' she says as she plucks a glass a wine off a passing bearer's tray, drains it in one gulp and comes to stand between Kashi and Aryaman Aggarwal. 'Wow, I needed that! I didn't know church services were *so long*.'

'It's been *so long* since I saw you, Bambi.'

Oh wow, thinks Kashi, startled, I couldn't get a word out of the fucker and now suddenly he's all chirpy!

Bambi beams at the drooping Aryaman.

'I *know*, Arya! We used to meet so often at the club when we were younger!'

A gleam briefly illuminates Aryaman's dull eyes. 'Swimming,' he says.

'*Yes!*' she replies encouragingly. 'Tennis.'

'*Yes!*'

'Hooking up on the library roof.'

'Uh huh!' She shakes her head, her eyes dancing. '*That* must've been with somebody else! Uh ... refill please!' She waves her glass at a bearer.

Aryaman continues to look at her blankly for a while, then finally, his eyes trail away.

'I've seen that guy before,' he remarks. 'The one in the fucktard shoes. Who's he?

This, because Gagan Ruia is walking up towards them, his juttis chwing-chwonging noisily.

'Bambi! What an amazing artist your Cookie auntie is!'

'Pick up something then!' she challenges him gaily. 'Cookie auntie's put me in charge of bullying people into buying! All the proceeds go to charity.'

'Oh daffynitely,' he replies at once. 'Come help me choose, na!'

He puts out a hand appealingly. She hesitates, then takes it and walks away.

'Well, he's *daffynitely* hot for her!' Aryaman sneers softly. 'What a guy!'

And Kashi has to agree. Ruia Jr looks smitten for sure, staring down adoringly at Bambi as she points out the finer points of each smoothly polished piece. Kashi averts his gaze.

Near the bar, Cookie Katoch's husband, dutifully present to support his wife, is holding forth to a rather inebriated, pot-bellied male audience.

'Bhai, it is really high time that the DTC replaced its tambola kit! Srivastava insists ki it is an antique piece, but if you ask me, calling any toota-phoota old thing an antique is just being pretentious! I told him ek naya set mangwaate hain, there are so many options available in the market today ... If the Club is short of funds, then *I* will sponsor it personally, but he is just refusing to listen! And Bhatti is supporting him!'

'That is because Bhatti is quite a toota-phoota antique piece himself!'

'A lot of the members here are antique pieces too.'

'Not me.' Katoch guffaws loudly. 'I have a young and perky "member"! Who d'you think all these blingy lingams are modelled upon?' He winks.

Everybody cracks up, with Katoch laughing the loudest.

Meanwhile, in another circle, the DTC Zumba ladies are scarfing down focaccia and champagne and mourning the loss of their trainer.

'Those lashes.'

'So long. And that hair.'

'So thick. Talking of thick, babe, we need to find a replacement trainer ASAP. How are Thapa and Thambi? Any good?'

'You mean Thinsuk and Thampi,' Urvashi Khurana corrects the speaker gently. 'Mukki trains with Thampi. He says he's good for sculpting and strength but not for cardio.'

'Leo was *great* for cardio. Just looking at him set my heart racing!' Cookie Katoch sighs.

Everybody follows suit.

'He was so sweet, na? Noticed *immediately* if anybody was slacking off, or having some gynaec issue or using the wrong technique – paid so much attention to each and every one equally!'

Roshni pulls a wry face. 'You make him sound like a gigolo.'

'Are you mad!' Cookie grabs another piece of focaccia and soaks it liberally in olive oil. 'Leo would've made a *terrible* gigolo. Asking you to lay off carbs all the time, and tsk-tsking over your flabby triceps, and saying he was terribly, *personally* disappointed in you if you "finished" too soon! I like my gigolos plump and non-judgemental, please.'

This makes everybody scream with laughter.

'He was so good with Arya also,' Roshni Aggarwal says wistfully. 'I had really high hopes that he would pull him out of his dark place …'

The ladies murmur sympathetically.

'Don't worry so much about Arya, Roshni,' Urvashi tells her friend. 'He's making such an effort to improve himself – it's *too* commendable! My God, I was such a *mess* when I was his age! What temper tantrums, what selfishness and drama – my poor parents were constantly at their wits end!'

'Lies,' Cookie Katoch declares roundly. 'All lies. You must have been the goody-goody head-girl type since the day you were born!'

Urvashi smiles at her fondly. 'Oh, it's taken me a long time to get to this place, Cooks. You've no idea.'

Roshni's tight face softens a little. 'Maybe my boy *will* get over his … problems too. I'll speak to Thampi, Urvi.'

Urvashi squeezes her friend's hands. '*Great.*'

'*Oi Cookie!*' Katoch calls out from across the garden in a ringing voice. 'Congruchulations! *All* your pieces have been sold! Young Ruia just bought the last and most expensive piece!'

'Oh my God, girls!' Cookie gives a little scream of delight and reaches out to hug her friends. 'Thank you *so* much for coming to my exhibition!'

And then Bambi Todi comes running up to the ladies, dragging Gagan Ruia behind her. 'Group hug!' she shouts. 'Three cheers for Cookie auntie and all her ShivBlings!'

The ladies crowd in, laughing and smiling as Ruia produces his phone. They pout and shout and pose as the camera clicks repeatedly. The bonhomie is palpable.

And yet, muses Bhavani Singh, munching his final mushroom-and-bacon canape of the day and wiping his hands on a napkin monogrammed with the DTC's horse and jockey logo, and yet, one of this group of laughing, privileged people is a cold-blooded poisoner ...

—◆—◆—

Bambi Todi, very buzzed from all the bubbly she has consumed, rushes into the Ladies to wash out the red wine somebody has sloshed onto her white jumper. She whips it off and lays it under the running tap in the wash basin. Wearing just a skimpy lace bra and jeans, she stares slightly unfocusedly into the mirror and smiles – a smile that Nattu would no doubt have called a chutiya smile.

Three times, she thinks dreamily. After ignoring me completely for three whole years, Kashi Dogra has managed to bump into me three whole times within a week! Sunday, at the Bumper Tambola, could've been a coincidence. Monday – okay so the cops called him in. But today? First at the memorial service, and now he's hanging around at Cookie auntie's penis exhibition! And he says he wants to be friends!

I can do friends, she thinks seriously, as she finger-combs her damp hair. I can totally do friends. I *need* a friend – especially with things so fucked up at home, and Leo dead, and the cops sniffing after poor Ganga and everything! And of course he has a girlfriend and shit, but I won't intrude on the GF's space – I will fully respect her superior claim on him. I'm more than happy with just friendship ...

Because if they're friends, then even boring conversations at the DTC become fun because they can both look up to meet each other's eyes across the room in silent, shared laughter ... They can redeem shitty web series by ranting against them together late in the night ... She can reach across the table and pick up food from his plate and pop it into her mouth ... She can fiercely contest points on a game of tennis and watch him throw down his racquet and lose his shit ... She can edit his Instagram DPs for him so he looks hotter – not that he needs help looking hot any more given how lithe and muscly he is, with the shock of unruly black hair that falls onto his broad forehead, blatantly soliciting a pushback from female fingers ...

It's like a part of her had fallen asleep once she let Kashi Dogra leave her life and now that he's back, he's casually flicked on a switch – and all the old connections and emotions are flickering back to life. Memories she'd suppressed, jokes she'd forgotten, smells, songs, feelings, sensations, even the noise the rain makes when it comes pelting down on the roof seems hyper-real now!

This is how paralysed people must feel when they start walking again, she thinks. Walking, then running, then dancing, then kissing ... No! No kissing. Strictly no kissing. There's the GF in Kalahandi and Bambi will be a *good* friend and not intrude on the GFs space ... no, kabhi nahi, *never*.

She raises cool, wet fingers to her hot cheeks, shakes her head at herself sternly in the mirror, then bends down to see if the stain has washed out from her sweater, when a sudden sound makes her whirl around.

This is the small wooden cloakroom next to the Rose Garden, meant mainly for little kids with unpredictable bladders who can't make it to the main bungalow in time, and it has just one commode and basin. Bambi is quite alone in here.

Silence.

She does a slow three-sixty turn to take in the whole space. Nothing. For some reason – probably the alcohol or all the idiotic obsessing over Kashi – her heart is thudding extra hard and the hair at the back of her neck is standing on end.

She pulls a face at herself in the mirror. 'Stupid girl!'

Then goes back to scrubbing her jumper with great dedication. It's a favourite and it goes with everything.

And then, as she's scrubbing, she sees it in the mirror. Quite clearly.

An eye.

The white of it, slightly veined and bloodshot, the dark brown of the pupil, and a bit of hairy lash.

Looking at her through a small gap in the wooden slats. There is a small knot in the wood, which has created a gap just wide enough for somebody to peer in.

And somebody *is* peering in at her as she stands there scrubbing her sweater, wearing just a skimpy, lace bra and jeans.

Furious, Bambi whirls around and bangs the wall hard.

'Fuck off!' she yells. 'Fuck off, you fucking pervert!'

The eye vanishes. Breathing hard, Bambi bends to press her eye to the gap, but there is nothing to be seen. Just a dark, empty veranda and a swinging screen door.

10

The Hottie-Culture Committee

Inspector Padam Kumar heads for his boss's cubicle very cockily on Monday afternoon. He has met a very attractive new candidate for the post of Mrs Padam Kumar over the weekend, an encounter which has quite erased the memory of the embarrassing scene with Ganga. And after a fruitless search of Leo's spartan bachelor digs that went on for almost two days, his men have, early this morning, finally struck gold with a custom-built, beautifully concealed storage compartment in the dead man's Hayabusa – recovering a hard drive full of recordings from Shonali's camera.

They are still sifting through all the footage – but there is one particular recording that he is sure Bhavani sir will be interested in seeing right away.

He enters with a hasty step, his cherubic face glowing.

'Sir!' He waves a pen drive at Bhavani excitedly. 'See *this*, sir!'

'Show, PK, show!' Bhavani greets him, clearing away the remains of his lunch at once. 'Quite a breakthrough you have had with the motorcycle compartment. Fantastic! Stick that thing in and press play!'

Saying which, he settles down in his chair to watch, his chin in his hands, his fingers still smelling of chhole bhature and his eyes scanning the computer screen with keen anticipation.

Ten seconds of static and then a wiry, ancient man appears on the screen, wizened, whiskered, the colour of dark chocolate, dressed in a bright, oversized, striped T-shirt. He is toying with a glass half full of what appears to be neat whisky. The camera seems to be placed on a dining table and is recording surreptitiously.

'You're my type of guy, Lambodar! I *like* you! You've got a big heart, and a pair of big balls! The first keeps you happy, and the second makes you rich!'

The man's whiskered face splits into a wide, white smile. His teeth are surprisingly good. His fingernails, as he puts his glass down, are filthy with grit. He puts more ice into his drink, stirs it with one dirty finger and knocks it back. Then he slams the glass down and stares almost straight into the lens. His eyes are red-rimmed, slightly glazed and have the milky beginnings of cataract.

'The things I could tell you!' he says with a chuckle. 'Oh, the things I could tell you, Lambodar!!'

'Tell na, Guppie Ram ji,' Leo's deep voice says persuasively. 'I want to learn from you – you're such a smart guy. You know I grew up in an orphanage – you're like a father figure to me.'

The old man chuckles. 'You're no West Indees,' he says knowingly. 'I've heard you gas to the Club ladies that you're half West Indees but you're *not*! Maybe you've sailed on many ships and swum in many seas, but I've seen your kind of face in my community again and again – you can grow your hair down to your arse, get as many piercings as you like and change your name to Matthew or Thankyou – but I *know* those features – and those aren't features that come from abroad. Oh no! They come from *right* here – they belong to a certain caste, and that certain caste has certain tasks to perform. They've been performing them for centuries, and if they stop, evvvverybody will soon be drowning in their own shit!'

He points a peremptory finger at his empty glass. *Pour, bitch.*

Leo's hand enters frame and refills it liberally.

'You're right, of course.' Leo admits easily. 'And I'm not ashamed of who I am. I'm *proud*. But you know what snobs these women are – if they figure out my roots, I'll end up losing half my clients. But Guppie Ram ji, tell me more about what you were saying before. How you've spent your whole life cleaning up the filth of the so-called high castes …'

'Yes, I have.'

'And you've helped clean up after some crimes too …'

The old man's face grows vaguely wary. 'Arrey, naee naee naee naee naee!' He wags his whiskery old head. 'I *promised*. I promised – and I'm a man of my word!'

Leo's voice grows even more persuasive. 'Aww, c'mon, Guppie Ram ji – tell me! I've already guessed half the story anyway from all the hints you've dropped! It happened three years ago, didn't it? You'd spent a few days preparing a composting trench, a really deep, four-foot trench, when you got a phone call in the middle of the night …?'

The old man nods, and assumes a more official tone. 'I dug up that trench at the orders of Gennil Mehra's hottie-culture sub-committee. He was the head, and Missus Aggarwal, Missus Khurana and Missus Todi were all members of it too.'

'And late at night you got a phone call …?' Leo eggs him on gently.

The old man nods. 'Yes. I was told ki there had been an accident, there was a mess, and could I please come and help clean it up? So I went along … and found that the "mess" was a body. But he was definitely a *very* bad persons – an *evil* persons – and he *deserved* it! So I agreed to help. We wrapped him in a bedsheet and dragged him out to the trench together … there was jabardast fog that night, so nobody saw us … I made the trench a little more deeper and … rolled him in. What a thump he made when he landed! Then I layered kitchen waste and dirt and topsoil over him nicely and left him to the earthworms. It was almost dawn by the time I finished. Of course, I was given money also – but more than that, I did it for the friendship! Who says rich, high caste folk and people like me can't be friends, eh?'

'*You* only said,' Leo replies. 'And I told you you were being too cynical!'

The old man looks reflective. 'Yes, perhaps you're right, Lambodar. Perhaps I am being too cynical. That night I really felt I was not being *used*, or given orders, or being *paid*. I felt that what we shared, we two, when we buried the body, was love ... and dosti – and equal-equal trust. Yani ki friendship!'

He lapses into a rather pensive silence.

'Here's to friendship, then!' Leo refills the glass again.

The old man knocks it back. 'To friendship.' He blinks solemnly.

'But who are we really drinking to, boss?' Leo presses. 'Let's put a name to it! Or a gender, at least – was it a man or a woman?' His voice is eager. Too eager.

The old man's face closes down at once. His head vanishes from the camera's frame as he gets to his feet abruptly, and all that is visible is the bottom of his tee shirt and the beginning of his pyjamas. His dirty-nailed fingers fumble at the waistband.

'Paishaab,' his says hoarsely. 'Toilet. I have to do toilet. Where is it, Lambodar?'

Static fills the screen again – Leo has clearly turned the recording button off.

'That's it?' Bhavani cocks an interrogative eyebrow at Padam Kumar.

'For the time being, sir.' The inspector nods fervently. 'Though of course we are still looking through the rest of the files!'

'Know who the man is?'

'Yes, sir! An old gardener called Ram Gopal aka Guppie Ram, who died a year ago! He looked after the DTC garden!'

'Excellent,' says Bhavani. 'He's talking about the kitchen garden, of course. Where we found Bhatti sa'ab digging carrots the other day.'

Padam Kumar gives a superstitious little shudder. 'I didn't like that place, sir! The soil was too smelly, too black, too sticky. Full of jhoothan and garbage that should be thrown away. I can fully believe ki uss chyawanprash mein laash hai!'

'Rubbish! Composting is a very good and hygienic way to garden, PK. It's completely organic.'

'Organic is a good name for it!' Padam Kumar snorts. 'All the dead man's organs are in there! Layered in kitchen waste and topsoil as lovingly as a biryani! No wonder the beetroot is so red!'

His big breakthrough has clearly made the inspector more outspoken than usual. Bhavani smiles.

'Well, well, maybe you're right, PK! But great work! Take your chaps out for a drink tonight.'

Padam Kumar goes a little pink. 'We were all just following your lead, sir! You said find the hard disk, and we found it. Sir, should I start on the paperwork required to get us permission to dig?'

Bhavani nods, delighted at this show of enterprise from his usually sleepy inspector.

Padam Kumar bounces out of the cubicle energetically, a man on a mission. Bhavani settles back in his chair and plays the recording again, taking painstaking note of all the little details. The grilled windows behind Guppie Ram, the bottle of Teacher's whisky, the digital clock on the wall … but that thing that strikes him most is the voice of the unseen Leo. Perhaps because of his association with the Badshahpur orphanage, his healthy, wholesome charisma and his massive fan following, Bhavani has unconsciously slotted Leo Matthew as an essentially good, Robin Hood-ish character.

But the voice speaking so easily and cajolingly to the inebriated Guppie Ram is not a 'good' voice. It is soft and cunning and opportunistic. A serpent's voice.

Impulsively, Bhavani logs onto *Lose It with Leo* and stares at the image on the home page fixedly. The instructor has been captured in all his glory – frozen mid-movement with his mane of hair flung back, and his lithe, sinewy body on full display.

This man had been playing a dangerous game, wielding sexual charm, sympathy, information and the moral high ground like a weapon. How many rich, powerful people had he hurt, humiliated, antagonized? Yes, the money he extracted from them had gone to an orphanage, but surely he had also been doing it sadistically, to exert power over them, to watch them squirm and sweat and suffer endlessly?

He was different inside his head too, Father Victor had said. *He said watching people spend his entire month's salary on a bottle of wine on the cruise ships had changed the way his brain was wired. He was nicer in some ways – but he was also darker in some ways. It troubled me.*

Bhavani minimizes all the screens and frowns down at his brown knuckles.

Of course, the old gardener *could* have been lying, he muses. Or exaggerating. For the fancy alcohol, and for all this attention from the glamorous trainer. But in that case, would Leo have ended up dead underneath a loaded barbell? No, it stood to reason that he had been onto something solid.

Love ... and dosti – and equal-equal trust.

Whom would've old Guppie Ram enjoyed receiving that from?

Gen. Mehra, the hero of the surgical strikes? Helping him could have made Guppie Ram feel like a crack soldier himself, even as he went about performing his sordid mission! But then, whose body had it been? Who was the 'evil persons' who *deserved* to be eaten up by the earthworms in the composting trench?

Ganga's husband, of course. A wife-beating villain who totally had it coming. And who had vanished three years ago. Yes, it made sense.

What about the hotties on the 'hottie-culture' committee? They too would have been aware that the composting trench was available that night – a highly convenient place in which to bury an inconvenient body ...

Roshni Aggarwal? Could her ghastly son have killed somebody in a drugged-out state? He was clearly a mess. Could she be the provider of *'love ... and dosti – and equal-equal trust'*. At a pinch, yes.

Bambi Todi's kleptomaniac mother had been in the US at the time of Leo's death so she was out of it, but what about Urvashi Khurana? Her beauty and grace could certainly have charmed the old man. But whose body could she have asked Guppie Ram to bury? Who was the 'evil persons' in *this* scenario? Some enemy of her weird husband, perhaps? Or perhaps some ex-lover who was threatening to talk?

Leo had said that this happened three years ago – and Guppie Ram hadn't contradicted him.

Bhavani gets up and starts to pace up and down his cabin. We will have to pull back and focus on what had been happening at the DTC roughly three years ago, he thinks. But first, we will have to dig up the Shrimati Savitri Mehra Udyaan and see if there really *is* a corpse layered like biryani beneath the carrots and the radish and the blood-red beets …

◆ ─ ◆

'I feel so bad for her, Kash.' Kuhu's voice is drowsy. It's late in the night and they have been talking for over two hours now. He has done most of the speaking – updating her on what's been happening in his life since he met his family at the DTC for Tambola Sunday. 'Your Bambi Todi. I mean, she's been through *so* much shit! First her parents made her break up with you, then her Prince Charming died, then her mother was revealed to be severely psychologically damaged! *Then* her dad turned out to be a real slut, which blows a hole right through the whole marriage-within-our-own-community-only recipe for marital bliss, doesn't it? Which sucks big-time for her because she'd accepted it as the gospel truth her whole life! And then, when she *finally* got her shit together, somebody started *blackmailing* her about her klepto mom! And then *he* gets murdered! How is she even *managing?*'

'That's the nicest thing about Bambi,' Kashi responds in an equally sleepy voice. 'She's tiny. But she's tough. She's got the most amazing coping mechanism of anybody I know.'

'Walli and Kalra are worried about you.' Kuhu sounds like she's turning onto her side. He knows exactly how she would look – the dark curls, the thick, straight black brows, the dips and curves of her firm, strong body. 'They both messaged me today. Kalra dropped some dark, garbled hints about how while I was so busy building homes for other people, my own home was being destroyed. And Walli entreated me to watch you better. His exact words were "Bannerjee, apne saand ko baandh".'

Kashi bursts out laughing. 'Horndogs. Anything to slide into your DMs. They're both in love with you.'

'No they're *not*!' she protests immediately. Kuhu always has a hard time believing anybody could be in love with her. 'They just don't trust poor Bambi, clearly. Or you.'

You shouldn't trust me either, I'm not as safe from her as you seem to think.

Aloud, he says. 'Any other girlfriend would be jealous.'

Kuhu gurgles with laughter. 'Oh, I *am* jealous. Of this doughty, crime-fighter cop you've described. You sound totally besotted!'

Kashi laughs.

'I do love the guy!' he admits. 'He's so *organic*! Just sits there radiating sympathy and nodding and staring at his hands and people spill their guts to him! It's a masterclass in interrogation!'

'And you're going to help him catch a killer? Be the bumbling Hastings to his Poirot?'

Kashi frowns. 'I think Inspector Padam Kumar is his Hastings.'

She laughs. 'You're too smart to be Hastings, huh? Well, you're certainly having fun on your three weeks off!'

Kashi flips over onto his stomach with a little groan of longing. 'I was planning to have *so much fun*, babe, till you stood me up!'

'Ewww. Don't be cheap. Did my books come?'

'They did indeed. They look boring AF.'

'They're *not*,' she retorts. 'They're fascinating. All about how to create natural air-conditioning – with water channels and cross-ventilation and high ceilings. Like the Mughals did. And the ancient Egyptians.'

She holds forth enthusiastically on this topic for a while and he imagines her sitting up now, her razai sliding down to reveal the firm, moulded shoulders, the animated gestures, the clear, passionate eyes.

'I miss you,' he says, with sudden, strong fervour. 'You make everything simple. That's *your* nicest thing. You make all the complications go away.' He headbangs his pillow in a fit of mock-frustration. 'What the hell are you doing in Kalahandi, Bannerjee? Get into this bed with me *now*!'

She sighs, wistfully. 'I'd love to! You know I'd love to. But the *roof*, Kash! I need to cast the roof!'

'Arrey, balls to the bloody roof!' he replies, rearing up to sit bolt upright. 'Why do they need a roof? Let it be an open-air school! The first open-air school in Odisha! You'll win an award for innovation! You can thank me in your acknowledgement speech, then!'

'I'll thank you in my acknowledgement speech, *anyway*. I've got it all worked out. D'you wanna hear what I plan to say?'

'What?' Kashi growls, half-sulky, half-mollified.

'Okay listen carefully.'

He can practically smell the sweet Kuhu scent of her – soap and shampoo and freshly baked bread – as she curls up in her razai again and whispers with shy importance.

'*I*

can soar so high,
because you,
are my sky.'

Kashi's heart turns over in his chest. The happy gas buffets him so hard he feels like he's floating. Not because of the words – his parents have been milking the whole Sky equals Akash thing in his birthday cards his entire life – but because she is just so damn incredibly *adorable*.

'That,' he says, when he is finally able to speak, 'is the cheesiest thing I have ever heard in my life, Kuhu Bannerjee.'

'Fuck *you!*' comes the instant response. 'I'm an architect, not a humanities major, who went to law college and can fling around a bunch of flowery Latin words every time I open my mouth! Just say thank you nicely and clap for me for winning the award!'

'Oh, I'll *clap* for you!' he promises. 'I'll clap so hard I'll bring the roof down!'

She gurgles triumphantly. 'But there *is* no roof, stupid! *That's* why I'm winning the award.'

Kashi hits himself on the forehead with his pillow. 'You think you're *so* smart.'

'Yes,' she agrees. 'I am. Now let's see if *you're* smart or not – was this a make-up call or a break-up call?'

'Uh, I was kind of hoping it was a make-*out* call ...' he says meaningfully.

'That,' she says happily, 'is cheesiest thing *I* have heard in my life, Akash Dogra. Good night.'

⚊ ▪ ⚊

Bambi Todi is working her way through a ring of steamed veg-momos with complete concentration. There is a little red chilli sauce on the corner of her mouth. A little snot drips from her nose. Sensing Kashi's gaze, she looks up, and wipes her nose with the back of her hand, eyes slightly glazed with slick satisfaction.

'Momos are the *best*.'

'Agreed.' He smiles.

They're sitting on the veranda that looks out at the tennis courts of the DTC, sweaty and flushed from a hectic game of doubles – Kashi and Gen. Mehra, verses Bambi and Brig. Dogra. The older men are still at it, playing a highly competitive game that has just gone into a tiebreaker.

'I'm a momo snob, I think,' she says. 'I judge people for preferring dim sum and dumplings and wontons to momos. Bloody chutiya fakers.'

'Did Anshul like momos?'

The question is out before he can stop it. His face reddens.

'I just asked because he was a mountaineer,' he hastens to clarify. 'I mean, he must've done a lot of the whole Mountain Maggi and Thukpa thing.'

She reaches out and lightly touches his hand. 'Kashi, it's been a while. I can talk about it without bawling my eyes out.'

Then she pushes away her plate. 'But why am I talking to you about momos? I have *big* news.'

'What?'

She leans, lowering her voice.

'Bhatti's having a *cow*. Because ACP Bhavani Singh and the Crime Branch are trying to get a search warrant to dig up the' – she sketches quote marks in the air and adopts an official tone – "Shrimati Savitri Mehra Udyaan.'

Kashi's jaw drops. '*What?* The kitchen garden? But why?'

She shakes her head, her eyes huge. 'He won't *say*,' she whispers, apparently as mystified as him. 'But I'm guessing it's because he suspects something's *buried* there.'

''*Cos I know where the bodies are buried*,' Kashi hums in a sinister voice.

Bambi giggles, rather guiltily. 'Exactly!'

As they stare at each other, half-excited, half-petrified, Kashi feels a thrill of excitement. Goosebumps rise on his arms. Then a thought strikes him and he sits back frowning.

'Why didn't the ACP tell me though? I thought I was assisting him in this investigation!'

'He didn't tell me either,' she admits. 'Though I've been helping him too! I only found out 'cos I went across to dig up some beets and it was all cordoned off with yellow tape and PK's men were guarding it, looking officious AF.'

Kashi crosses his arms. 'I think I'm a little offended.'

She nods. 'Me too. Sly Bhavani. Cutting us off from the inside info after using us to *get* the inside info! Matlab, I'm the only one who came clean about the blackmailing – he should *trust* me!'

'That's true,' Kashi agrees.

'*Except ...*' Her voice trails away. Then she looks up, her eyes resolute. 'Kashi, I didn't quite tell him everything.'

His heart gives the oddest little bump. He knows this look well. He groans softly. 'What *now*, Bambi Todi?'

She rolls her eyes, looks around the buzzing, noisy veranda, and leans in. 'Walk me to my car?'

He nods and leaps to his feet quickly. 'Sure.'

She gets to her feet too and they start to walk towards the exit.

'Oye! Master Dogra! The waiter still has your card!'

Brig. Dogra, in a red headband and tennis whites, is leaning across the net worriedly.

It is now Kashi's turn to roll his eyes. 'I *know*, Dad,' he yells back. 'I'm coming back.'

'Good!' the brigadier bellows. 'Because as soon as I've pulverized Mehra, I plan to beat you in straight sets!'

This cocky statement is met by a chorus of cheers from the older gents on the courts.

'Done!' Kashi yells back and strides out of the veranda. 'He's *unbelievable.*'

'He's just happy to be hanging out with you again,' Bambi says. 'This three-week break of yours is like a huge bonus for him!'

Kashi shakes his head. 'He's appallingly competitive. He's having a blast playing with Mehra uncle nowadays because Mehra uncle is so desperate for his vote that he's letting him win. He's figured it's the only way to bribe my dad.'

'Aww! So *cute!*' Bambi replies, a little mechanically.

'Never mind my dad,' Kashi says grimly as they emerge onto the driveway. 'Gimme the tea.'

She nods and exhales, shivering a little in the cold.

'Okay, so I don't know if you remember, but back on that last night we spent together, you accused me of being a brainwashed inmate of the Maaru matrimony cult.'

It certainly had been part of the last conversation they'd had, three years ago. Bambi in shorts and a sloppy loose tee, sitting cross-legged on tumbled sheets in her pink bedroom, smelling of his sweat, talking to him earnestly.

'Kashi, you and I have always been more friends than lovers. *That's* our secret superpower – friendship. And it fucking kicks *ass.* But I need a man in my life who will be more lover, less friend. Anshul is *that.*'

'*I* could be that,' he had insisted hotly. 'Your parents have brainwashed you into believing that you can only ever marry a Marwari man or your marriage will fail. It's like you're living in some freaking *cult.* An educated girl like you! It's pathetic.'

Tears had filled her eyes, and rolled down her cheeks. 'Don't be mean to me, Kashi. I can't bear it when you're mean to me!'

And of course he couldn't bear it when she cried.

Hugs, kisses, fevered caresses, tears. He had sneaked out of her house in the early hours, feeling absolutely drained.

He pushes away the memory with an effort. 'I remember,' he says steadily.

'Yeah well, thanks to Manju's kleptomania and Pankaj's manwhoring—'

'Don't call your parents by their first names, Bamb!' He is actually a little shocked.

'Manju's stealing and Pankaj's sluttiness,' Bambi maintains determinedly, 'I am *out* of the cult! For good!'

Kashi applauds. 'That's awesome! Congratulations!'

She grins. 'I told them I'll find my own life partner, fuckyouverymuch, and then I started dating again.'

Why didn't you call me?

The words leap to his lips but die unsaid.

'*Really?*' he remarks, managing to look no more than mildly interested, though blood has started to pump hard against his temples. 'Uh … anyone I know?'

'Uh, well …' She looks sheepish. 'A couple of TVVS guys … Not our batch though! Some randos … I thought I'd found a nice guy for a while, he reminded me a little of you – same socialist agenda – but then he started *blackmailing* me.'

She stands back, somewhat guiltily, and waits for him to react.

'Wait … *What?* Kashi looks at her blankly for a moment, and then his jaw drops. '*Leo!*'

She nods embarrassedly. 'Stupid, wasn't it?'

Kashi is still just staring at her, computing this brand-new information. 'You! And Lambodar!'

She looks confused. 'Who's Lambodar?'

He shakes his head. 'Never mind! But he was … what … *ten* years older than you?'

She nods. 'That was part of the appeal, I guess. And part of the revolt against the matrimonial madness. He was older, wilder, Christian, working-class, poorish ... All qualities designed to drive my parents nuts.'

'I can see the appeal, I guess,' Kashi manages to say with a credible attempt at casualness. 'I'm all for this revolt against the cult – but, *wow*!' He shakes his head again. 'I'm still trying to wrap my mind around this – you and Leo! *Fuck*, you hide your secrets well!'

She rolls her eyes. 'I've had to learn how to.'

'So all this talk of an affair between Leo and Urvashi auntie, that's all just *talk*, then?'

'I wouldn't know.' She sounds cross. 'God, what a thing to ask me, Kash!'

'Sorry, don't get pissed,' he apologizes quickly. 'But Bambi, really – what the fuck?'

She hunches her shoulders. 'Cut me some slack, okay? My fiancé died, my dad's a womanizer, my mother's a klep—'

'Yeah, yeah, that's exactly what Kuhu said,' he says without thinking.

Her eyes widen. 'You've been discussing me with your *girl* friend?'

He looks a little caught out. 'Umm ... is that a problem?'

'Uh ... no, I guess not,' she replies hesitantly.

There is an awkward silence.

Finally he says, 'Look, could you please just date slightly less complicated people?'

'Oh yeah?' She turns to face him, eyeballing him challengingly. 'Like *who*?'

The tips of his ears redden. 'Like … uh, non-blackmailers?'

She stares at him resentfully, a thousand words seeming to tremble on her lips, then looks away with a toss of the head.

'Anyway, *that* was the thing I didn't tell the ACP,' she says in a more collected voice. 'That before Leo cottoned onto Mammu's squalid secret, there was a brief phase where he and I were … dating. I didn't really think it was relevant.'

They've reached her car by now – a bright red Mini Cooper, which probably costs more than what Kashi earns in an entire year. It is covered in fallen neem leaves and looks almost bridal.

'Whoa, nice car!'

'Yeah,' is the unenthusiastic response. 'It was a happy dead-fiancé anniversary present from my parents last year. To cheer me up. These trees are shedding like crazy.'

Kashi starts to brush them off, then notices a white pamphlet stuck between the windshield and the wiper.

'What's this?' he asks as he pulls it out. 'Did you get challan-ed or something?'

She shakes her head, as he smooths the paper out against the bonnet of the Mini Cooper. It isn't a pamphlet. It's a regular A4 sheet, with words printed on it in thick black ink.

'It's some sort of *letter*.' Kashi whirls on his heels to look all around the parking lot. 'Who could've left it here?'

'I don't know.' Her voice is curiously subdued.

He looks at her, puzzled, then picks up the paper and reads it.

Bee, be patient.

You and I were made for each other.

Nobody else can take your place in my life, or mine in yours.

Mehendi laga ke rakhna, doli saja ke rakhna, and all that jazz.

Wait for me.

The A to your B

'What the fuck!' Kashi looks up from the sheet, startled. 'What's *this*?'

'Damn,' Bambi mutters. 'I thought these had stopped.'

'Matlab?' Kashi's voice grows sharp. 'You've got these before?'

She nods awkwardly. 'For a while now. Every time I go out on a date with anyone.'

'But you're not dating anyon—' he pauses. 'You mean *me*?'

She nods, going slightly pink. Kashi goes slightly pink too.

'But that's … *insane*,' he says. 'The A to my B? Made for each other? Are these supposed to be from … *Anshul*?'

She shrugs uncomfortably.

'Haven't you told your folks? Or the cops?'

'What?' She laughs uncertainly. 'Don't be silly, Kashi. It's probably the Ghia-Lauki gang. It's the kind of thing they think is funny.' She stops, then adds reluctantly, 'At least that's what I thought till a little while ago.'

'Till Leo died, you mean,' he says.

'Yeah,' she says. 'Till Leo died.'

They stare at the paper.

'You don't think' – the words seem torn from her – 'that he's *alive*, do you?'

The hope in her voice smites his heart. His voice is gentle when he replies. 'Bamb, Anshul's *dead*. His bus tumbled into an abyss on the Manali–Leh Road three years ago. His dad identified the body. There was a cremation. We all saw the ashes, remember?'

A stubborn expression settles on her face. She juts out her chin a little. 'Then who's sending me these?'

Kashi spreads out his hands.

'I don't know. It makes absolutely no sense. Maybe you've picked up some psycho stalker.'

She shivers.

His lips tighten. He yanks opens the car door for her. 'Get in and go straight home. In fact, let me get in with you. I'll walk back here from your place.'

She's too cowed to argue. As they drive towards the main gate, she says, 'Kash, should I tell Bhavani about this?'

'Yes!' The word bursts out of him like he's talking to a moron. '*Please* do! About you dating Leo, and the letters too! You should have told him all this right at the *start*, Bambi!'

'But supposing …' She trails off, then shrugs forlornly.

'Oh my God!' Kashi's expression grows concerned. 'You really believe it's Anshul?'

'I don't know what to believe!' Her voice has a hysterical edge. 'Suppose it really *is* him? Out there, alive, perhaps scarred or crippled and too insecure to meet me? I don't want to get him into trouble!'

He leans in, and there is raw emotion on his face.

'Bambi – no,' he says forcefully. 'Don't go there. You're opening yourself up to *so* much pain and disappointment if you start thinking it's Anshul! You've clearly picked up some sadistic stalker – or as you said, it's the Ghia-Lauki gang!'

She stares down at the letter, then crumples it up with a savage little laugh. 'It would *so* serve those cows right if I gave this to Bhavani and the cops came and arrested them ...'

'Never mind all that,' Kashi says grimly. 'Focus on what's important. Give Bhavani the complete low-down before something even more fucked up happens.'

The neem trees lining Aurangzeb Road are alive with fluttering gauraiyas and starry white neem flowers are twirling to the ground like confetti when Ganga Kumar drives her zippy little Maruti Suzuki Alto through the monogrammed gates of the DTC, happy Bollywood music playing on its speakers.

The sun is out today. Feeling very fresh and feminine in her floral kota sari, she exits the car and trots down to the little Daily Needs store. Her cleaning lady has already opened the place and dusted the shelves. All Ganga has to do it set a match to the diya under Saraswati ji ki murti, and wait for customers to arrive. Not that anybody will show up before 9 a.m., but Ganga loves the quiet time in the empty store before the rush begins.

'Good weekend, didi?' her cleaning lady asks.

Ganga smiles back at her cheerfully, a slightly secretive twinkle in her large, brown eyes.

'Yes! And yours?'

'Terrible,' reports the cleaning lady's little son happily, before she can speak. 'I got cuff!'

'Cough,' says Ganga automatically, as she frowns down at him. 'That's a nasty cough, Chhotu. There's balgam rattling around in your throat.'

He nods proudly. Snot dribbles from his nose. He wipes it off on his sweater sleeve and smiles at her. 'Didi, let's make lemim tea?'

'Ooookay!' Ganga laughs as she sets the match to the brass lamp below the Saraswati idol, and places a handful of jasmine flowers in the lapis lazuli bowl. 'Actually, today we'll make honey-tulsi tea! Specially for your cold.'

He hunches. 'I don't like tusli.'

'Nonsense,' she tells him firmly. 'C'mon, let's get some! We'll get some carrots too, hmm?'

Chotu likes carrots. He grasps her hand and together they emerge into the winter sunshine and walk down to the kitchen garden. They pass the tennis courts, very busy at this hour, cut through the cluster of guest cottages and come out near the rustic wooden fence of the kitchen garden. As they do, they hear the steady *beep-beep-beep* of a hazard horn, and the sound of a heavy engine reversing.

Ganga falters, then stops.

'It's the police,' says an old sweeper, who happens to be leaning on his long-handled broom near the path.

Chhotu gives a little wriggle of excitement, phlegm rumbling wetly in his throat. 'Police!'

'They're digging up the kitchen garden,' the sweeper reports with relish. 'They're saying there's a laash there.'

Ganga's hand goes to her bososm. 'What!'

Chhotu starts jumping from foot to foot. 'A laash! Didi, didi, let's look! I've never seen a laash! Didi, come!'

She gives him a little shake. 'No, Chhotu! Let's go back!'

But he shakes off her hand and goes sprinting down the path. Ganga gives an exasperated cry, picks up her sari pleats and chases after him.

They both arrive breathless and panting, within seconds of each other, at the kitchen garden.

'Oh!' Ganga's lips part in a little exclamation of surprise.

The gate to the kitchen garden has been cordoned off in yellow tape marked POLICE LINE DO NOT CROSS.

Beyond the cordon, a sinister-looking, mustard-yellow earth mover with massive, whirring wheels and a long, slender neck ending in an iron claw is feeding upon the ground like a giant, fantastic bird. The erstwhile pretty, peaceful garden appears dismbowelled – spilling entrails of trailing roots, squelchy, dark dirt, snails, and muddy vegetables. There is a rich, overripe smell of dankness in the air. An earthworm wriggles by Ganga's foot and she steps back with a gasp of horror.

'Chhotu, let's go back.'

But the excited child shakes his head, wriggles out of her grasp and ducks through the cordon. Ganga curses and follows him determinedly.

Inside the wounded garden, a crew of stubbly, sunburnt workmen, all wearing orange helmets and neon green jackets stand at the lip of a dark hole, talking and gesticulating over the sound of the earth mover. They all seem to be working under the supervision of the tall, handsome policeman who had come into Ganga's store the other day – but today, he looks more intimidating, with his moustache very clipped and his dark sunglasses glinting in the sun.

Ganga grabs the collar of Chhotu's shirt and yanks him backwards, out of the sight of the police crew. They both land with a thump on a lichen-covered rock at the edge of the garden, half obscured by the tulsi leaves they had come to pluck.

Chotu squirms angrily. 'I *want* to watch!' he hisses.

Ganga finds she has lost the will to fight him. A peculiar paralysis has gripped her limbs and all she can do is stare, with a thumping heart and a sick, horrid sort of fascination as the slender neck of the mighty machine dips gracefully into the ground and the clawed head emerges, loaded with a mouthful of dark earth. The necks swivels, groaning a little, and the head dribbles out its gritty load. Then the neck swivels back to its original position, and the head bends again to take another voracious bite out of the ground.

Ganga and Chhotu are not the only audience. The plump grey-and-brown gauraiyas are watching as well, their heads cocked to one side, their eyes bright and inquisitive as they hop about in the wake of the digger, pecking for worms and insects in the huge upended mound of rich, brown earth.

Above and behind them, in the branches of the ancient neems, several yellow-eyed, hook-nosed cheels swoop down too to observe the proceedings with haughty, soundless interest.

The digger gives a low keening groan and dribbles out what look like the swollen mishappen limbs of hastily buried corpses onto the muddy ground.

Ganga gasps in horror.

'Didi, it's just *mooli*!'

And indeed it is nothing but a load of muddied white radishes.

'Oh,' she says faintly.

Chhotu shakes his head in disgust at her squeamishness.

The neck swivels back into the hole in the ground, and suddenly, the workmen begin to shout hoarsely. The neck freezes mid-air, hovering, as the crew discusses something animatedly, until the tall, fair policeman blows a whistle and the claw descends slowly, almost tentatively into the darkness.

Her nerves electrified by some sudden instinct, Ganga covers Chhotu's eyes with her hand.

'I want to see!' he cries, struggling.

'Shh!' She places a hand lightly over his mouth.

And then has to bite down on her lower lip to strangle the scream of revulsion rising from her own throat.

Because the giant claw has just risen from the hole in the ground again. And this time something is dangling from it. A macabre, mocking thing, with stick-like white limbs, a semi-dismembered pelvic girdle, and what are clearly ribs. A thing with a gleaming bald pate, two hollow, staring eye sockets, a dark hole where a nose should be and two rows of yellowed teeth bared in a wide, grisly grin.

11

A Gun in the Mud

Hai hai, Rosh, did you hear?

They just dug a MURDA LAASH out of the DTC kitchen garden! Out of the freaking BEETROOT PATCH! I've been eating those bloody beetroots for years! There's a BUNCH IN MY FRIDGE RIGHT NOW L L L

No wonder they're so fucking RED!

Oh god, we're all cannibals! And we thought we were strict jain vegetarians!

Roshni? Wth, reply ya!

I can see your blue ticks.

Whatever, reply when you can. I'm going to bury the beetroots in my garden and say a prayer over them. Or should I BURN them? Like a cremation?

Call me, babe, I'm giving such good gossip and you're not even replying. I thought we had a special bond now. How many other people have you discovered a dead body with????

Roshni is staring down at Cookie's messages on her phone blankly, when Aryaman walks into the room. He looks heavy-eyed with sleep – and in dire need of a shave, a haircut and a purpose in life.

'Ma, can I get some dosh?' he says dully. 'I want to order a new router. The one I've got is too slow.'

'Maybe *you're* too slow.' Her words come out with so much suppressed violence that he blinks, vaguely surprised.

'What'd I do now?'

Roshni stares at him mutely for almost a minute, then says, 'The police have dug up the DTC kitchen garden and found a dead body buried there.'

'Huh?' Aryaman looks at her blankly. *'No way!'*

'Yes way.' She copies the teenage lingo ironically. 'Has your brain processed that information yet? Or should I wait half an hour for it to reach?'

He looks injured. 'You're using language that demeans me. The therapist said you should use language that builds me up.'

She takes a deep, calming breath. 'Arya, did you hear what I said? A *body* has been found. *Dead.* In the kitchen garden. By the *police.*'

'But who told them to go digging there?' he asks, puzzled. 'Were they looking for vegetables and dug too deep?'

She throws out her arms. 'How the *hell* do I know, Arya!'

He draws back. 'Why're you looking at me like that, Ma? Do you think I—'

'Shhush,' she cuts him off fiercely. 'Actually, don't tell me *anything.* Don't speak another *word.*'

They stare at each other in silence for a while. Then his eyes skitter away guiltily.

She draws a deep breath. 'It's my own fault! *I* was the one who had bete-ka-bukhaar, and kept hankering for a son in spite of having such lovely daughters! Your sisters are both so, so much better than you—'

He cuts in. 'Yes, Ma, we all know how much you love your daughters and what a little shit I am! Are you going to give me the money for the new router or not?'

She stares at him in speechless fury for a moment, then lunges forward, moving with Zumba-honed speed, grabs him by the shoulders and shoves him against the bedroom wall.

'What the hell, Ma!'

'Back to your room,' she says roughly. 'No internet. No money. No wandering around. Just go *back* in there and let me handle it.'

—◼︎————◼︎—

'Urvi?'

Urvashi Khurana is sipping a cup of chamomile tea, swinging gently in the white wicker daybed on the terrace of their beautiful Vasant Vihar home, staring out at the silk-cotton trees, which are in full, riotous bloom.

'Hmmm?'

'You heard?'

She looks around. 'What, Mukesh?'

He says hesitantly, 'Did you know?'

Her beautiful face grows inscrutable. 'Did I know what?'

He blunders forward. The bruise around his eye, the mark of the dead Leo, has still not faded entirely.

'About the body! In the kitchen garden! Did you know it was there?'

'Oh that,' she murmurs and sips her tea.

Mukesh stares down at her. The silence lengthens.

'And if you did – who told you?'

She turns more fully towards him and gives a light musical laugh. 'No, Mukesh! How would *I* know?'

'Leo.' He continues doggedly, '*He* knew for sure! That's why he got offed! Matlab, it's only logical! You two were as thick as thieves. Always exercising together!'

Urvashi puts down her teacup. 'How *many* times, Mukesh Khurana?' Her voice has a pained edge to it. 'How many times have I asked you to exercise with me? Yoga, tennis, cycling, walking, *anything*! And how many times have you told me no?'

'Don't make this about my fitness!' He is immediately defensive. 'You ghumao things, and twist my words, and somehow always manage to put me in the wrong! Don't I go to the gym and train with Thampi?'

'You could train with *me*.' Urvashi's calm is definitely stirred now. 'I'm a qualified yoga instructor, for heaven's sake!'

He shakes his head, stubborn. 'I can't learn from you.'

Her face grows bitter. 'Chauvinist.'

'No!' The word emerges like a maddened bellow. 'I am not a chauvinist! I'm *proud* of your achievements – and your work ethic. I'm proud of our girls!'

Urvashi stares at him, bewildered, hands on her hips. 'Then what's the *problem*, Mukesh?'

There is a pause. Mukki is clearly trying to gather his thoughts.

'Problem *yeh* hai, Urvi,' he says finally, slowly, 'that you have been wanting that kitchen garden dug up for *months*! You *claimed* it was for the rainwater-harvesting plant – but that could have been placed somewhere else also! So my question is – did you know there was a body in there?'

'Of course not,' she says crossly.

'That snoopy item number didn't tell you anything?' he asks her. 'Your Leo?'

She rounds to face him, pale. 'Show a little respect for the dead, Mukesh!'

He lets out a loud, neighing laugh. 'That's a good one! Respect for the dead? How much respect did the police show for the dead – digging up some peacefully sleeping corpse today?'

'Just what are trying to imply anyway?' Her voice is icy-cool. 'Why am I being interrogated in my own home, by my own husband?'

He's walking agitatedly about the room now, whirling around every time he reaches the exquisitely papered walls.

'You have secrets from me! You've always had secrets from me! A husband and wife shouldn't have secrets!'

'Can we please stick to the point? Which precise secret are you alluding to?'

'You're trying to phasao Mehra!'

'Mehra is trying to phasao *you*,' she says coolly. 'He was clearly in cahoots with that club secretary, Srivastava, who rigged the tambola to start a fight between you and Leo. They've been keying you up for *ages*, going on about a non-existent affair between me and Leo. And you succumbed to their chaabi-ing and fought with Leo – then went to the gym five hours before the murder! They *all* think you poisoned Leo's protein shake. That square, smiling policeman definitely does.'

'I didn't kill him!' Mukki bellows agitatedly. 'I would never poison a man! I'd take him in a fair fight!'

'A fight between you and Leo couldn't possibly be fair. He was so much younger and fitter than you,' she says pityingly.

Mukki deflates slightly. 'I know.'

He stops pacing, and sits down beside her on the daybed with a dejected thump.

'I've made a total mess of things, haven't I. You won't win the election now, because of me ...'

She turns to face him. '*I* believe you're innocent,' she says earnestly, 'but they may not – and so—'

'And so you're trying to get them to suspect Mehra? Is that the game? If it is, then it's a damned dicey game, Urvi ...'

⚫────⚫

It is a very exhausted Bhavani Singh who pushes in the small gate and enters the house in Police Colony several hours later. Shalini, back from school some time ago, freshly bathed, and sipping a cup of tea in the jute swing-chair, takes one look at his face and gets to her feet.

'I'll get the cold milk.'

He shakes his head, his eyes tired but twinkling. 'It's Friday.'

She smiles understandingly and goes into the house. When she emerges, carrying two iced whisky-sodas, he is sitting in the rope swing and staring at the jasmine hedge, his mind clearly miles away.

She hands him his drink, and sits down on a moodha beside him.

Bhavani glugs it down like he's drinking plain water. Shalini raises her eyebrows, then takes his glass and hands him her own.

'We found the skeleton exactly where Guppie Ram said we would.'

She gasps. 'Bhavani! That's a huge breakthrough!'

'Yes.' He sips her drink slowly, savouring it this time, and his expression changes. 'What is this, Shalu, why did you give us the Johnny Walker? The VAT 69 would have been just fine.'

'Nonsense!' she says firmly. 'You've had a tough day. Spoil yourself a little.'

'Chalo theek hai.' Bhavani sinks back into the swing with a sigh of satisfaction. 'Like you said, it's a big breakthrough. President Bhatti can't talk about self-inflicted drug overdoses any more! Leo was clearly murdered – that too because he *knew* about a previous murder! It's all starting to add up!'

'Fantastic,' she replies. 'So this was the body Leo was alluding to in the "Secrets" song!'

'Yes.'

'How easy will it be for you to identify the remains?'

'Krishnan is on it,' Bhavani replies. 'He said he would phone as soon as he has something concrete. We will nat hold our breath though – it is a Friday night.'

The call comes when Bhavani is finishing his 5BX workout in his tiny garden the next morning. He picks it up while running on the spot.

'Jai Bhavani,' says the sardonic Tamilian voice.

'Daaktar sa'ab!' Bhavani beams, waving with one arm even though Krishnan can't see him.

'You're panting like a carthorse, Bhavani. Call me back.'

'No, no,' Bhavani puts the phone on speaker. 'Tell us please – we want to know everything.'

'Well, there's not much to tell,' Krishnan replies. 'We work best with taaza maal, and your offering wasn't exactly daisy fresh.'

Bhavani waves all this aside. 'What can you tell us about the body? Could the cause of death be ascertained?' he demands. 'Poison, like the previous time? Or something more violent? A blow to the head, a bullet in the back? Stab wounds?'

'It's a thirty-something male. But the man was in a compost heap, Bhavani,' Krishnan says wearily. 'All the soft tissue has decomposed or been chewed through. We've pieced the bones together, and there doesn't seem to be any injury.'

Bhavani's jumping jacks grow a little half-hearted. 'So you have nothing for us?'

'I didn't say that,' Krishnan replies. 'There is *one* interesting thing. Are you done with your silly bunny-hopping yet?'

'Yes, yes.' Bhavani has reached the end of his workout, and is wiping his face with a hand towel. 'Tell us, please!'

'I think he may have been wearing some sort of costume jewelley – there are shards of some sort of blue stone in the mud that came with him.'

Bhavani is conscious of a tremendous feeling of anti-climax. 'A blue stone? Like a neelam? A sapphire?'

'Perhaps. We've washed it out nicely and it appears to be bluish. There are several large shards. About as big as sugar cubes.'

'And that is ... *it* ... daaktar sa'ab?' Bhavani knows he's sounding petulant but he can't help himself. 'We sent you a tractor-trolley full of evidence and this is all you've got?'

'Send a fresher corpse next time,' Krishnan replies. 'I'm not an archeologist.'

A bright red Mini Cooper drives up to the Crime Branch's Tees Hazari office around noon, and a curvaceous yet slender young woman, all sweet smiles, doe eyes and softly curling brown hair emerges from it and enquires with pretty diffidence for ACP Bhavani Singh's office.

An eager crowd of volunteers leads her to the office at once. She thanks them with a sweet effusiveness, then sticks her head into the door.

'Psst, ACP!'

He looks up startled. 'Bambi ji!'

She grins, walks in and takes the seat opposite him. 'Nice cabin! You're quite a big shot, huh?'

He wriggles modestly. 'In a very small well.'

She fiddles with the pictures on his desk. 'Oh, is that your family? They're all so pretty!'

'Thank you.' He twinkles. 'The girls have grown up and moved out though. It's just mama bear and papa bear in the bear cave now.'

She gives a peal of laughter. Several people sitting just outside the cabin turn around. Bambi pulls a comically contrite face and leans in.

'How's your new corpse?' she whispers.

Bhavani smiles wryly. 'It is our *old* corpse, actually. Nothing but pearly bones. Therefore not very talkative.'

'Oh! Then maybe it's got nothing to do with Leo's death at all?'

He nods. 'That is a possibility too.'

She smiles at him encouragingly. 'I'm sure you'll get it to talk! I mean, there's modern science and all now! Forensics!'

He waggles his head ruefully.

'You've been watching too many Hollywood shows.'

'Not me! I watch CID. You're *much* better looking than ACP Pradyuman, by the way.'

He gets the feeling that she's just making conversation.

'What is on your mind, Bambi ji?'

'Nothing,' she says quickly. Too quickly. 'Tell me, am *I* also on your list of suspected murderers?'

'Of course,' he replies steadily. 'You were being blackmailed – and your blackmailer's dead.'

'Oooh!' Bambi shivers excitedly. '*So* thrilling!'

'Yes,' he agrees gravely. 'But unfortunately, your *motive* is not very strong. We don't think your mother's kleptomania is such a shameful secret that you would commit murder for it.'

She cocks her head to one side, eyes dancing. 'And so we come to the reason of my visit to you today. I'm really sorry for not telling you this earlier – and please don't get mad at me – but I was dating Leo for a while. Before he started blackmailing me.'

This is brand-new information for Bhavani. He studies the impishly lovely face before him – the sparkle in the soft, brown eyes (is that why her parents named her Bambi? His daughters used to love Bambi the deer when they were young, but that Bambi had been a sweet, peaceble creature) is somehow brighter and almost dangerous today. Bambi Todi, he decides, is on some sort of mission.

'We won't get mad at you,' he says. 'And yes, that certainly changes things. Because now your motive is ...?'

She gives a little gurgle of laughter. 'Unrequited love, the fury of a woman scorned, and perhaps a sex tape or two.'

'Ah. Yes, that would put you right on top of the heap of suspects.'

She chuckles. 'Knocking Mehra uncle from the top spot?'

He smiles. 'We never said he was at the top spot.'

There is a small pause.

Then she looks up, and something about her face makes him think that *now*, finally, they are coming to the real purpose of her visit.

'There is one more thing I wanted to tell you,' she says. 'It's all tied up with me dating Leo, and it's ... well, it's *these*.'

She pushes a sheaf of A4-sized sheets across the table. The paper is thin and crumpled and the thick letters are printed in black ink. They are all variations of the same theme.

Bee, be patient. We put rings on each other's fingers and promised to marry and one day, we shall. Mehendi laga ke rakhna, doli saja ke rakhna, and all that jazz.

Wait for me. The A to your B.

Stay faithful to me ... The A to your B

Save all your kisses for me ... The A to your B

He shuffles through them for a long time, then quirks an eyebrow. 'What is all this, Bambi ji?'

She hesitates. 'It's a longish story, ACP. I don't want to distract you from your work.'

'Nat at all!' he says cozily. 'Please! Begin your Satyanarayan ki katha!'"

'Okay.' She takes a deep breath, then pulls up her legs to sit cross-legged on the chair comfortably. In a voice that is light, almost frivolous in tone, perhaps to distance herself from the story she is telling, she begins –

'I don't know if you've ever heard of a fun, fearless, handsome, young mountaineer–tycoon called Anshul Poddar. His family was from Kolkata and he was living and working in Delhi. My parents and his got in touch with each other through a network of Marwari friends and they decided that Anshul and I would make a wonderful couple. A meeting was organized, and it turned out that they were absolutely right. Anshul and I got along like a house on fire! Our engagement was announced literally a week after we first met. We would talk on the phone all day, go for long walks in Lodhi Garden, then come back to the DTC for drinks, dinner and dancing. We were blissfully happy.'

'How many years ago was this?' Bhavani asks.

'Three years – almost exactly.' The light, frivolous tone is fading fast. There is wistfulness in her voice now. 'My parents wanted an elaborate engagement party, and would have liked a little time to plan it, but Anshul was leaving soon on a mountaineering expedition. His team was going to travel by bus, then cable car, then helicopter, to reach the Nanda Devi base camp. The whole expedition – preparation, ascent and descent – would be about a month long. His mother said they'd rather have the engagement before he left – "Because, beta, whenever he comes back from these expeditions, he is burnt black by the sun and snow and looks like a purple bhoot. Your photos will be *ruined* and all your friends will think your parents have married you to a yeti."'

Bhavani chuckles. 'Good advice by the mummy ji.'

'Yes.' Bambi looks sad. 'I really didn't mind either way, but Anshul agreed with his mother – he was definitely a *little* vain. But I don't mind a slightly vain man – they understand good grooming and fitness, don't you think?'

Bhavani, not sure where he stands on this one, murmurs a non-committal response.

Bambi continues, 'My parents pulled out all the stops for the last-minute engagement. It was held at the DTC, we booked all the guest cottages. It was a brilliant party. Anshul and I had rehearsed a dance – it was a big hit. Everybody said we were the perfect couple.' Her eyes grow pensive. 'Even Kashi came – he's my childhood friend, you know?' She looks up at him inquiringly.

'We know,' Bhavani replies gently.

'Even *he* said that Anshul and I were meant to be!'

'How nice.'

'My lehenga was bright yellow and gold. The colour of mustard fields at dawn.'

This seems to be the high point of the narrative. She falls silent, her eyes very far away. Bhavani stares down at his knuckles, radiating respectful sympathy. Finally, she draws a long shuddering breath.

'Anshul didn't want to leave me that night. He kept insisting that I come with him on the expedition – that he could climb Nanda Devi with me strapped to his back.' She laughs shakily. 'He could have done it too – he was tremendously strong. And *so* tall – much taller than Kashi!'

She stares down at her fingers. 'Finally, he left. I was so tired, and had drunk so much wine that I went to sleep as soon as my head touched my pillow. When I woke up … ten hours later …'

Her eyes rise to meet his, stunned, bewildered, blind eyes. 'He … was *gone*! Forever. It was sleeting, the road was slippery, the fog as thick as soup. Perhaps their driver had been drinking to stay warm, nobody really knows. Their bus went off the road, and plummeted into a ravine. Everybody died.'

She stops. Tears fill her eyes and spill onto her hands.

'We're so sorry,' Bhavani says gruffly.

She nods, wordlessly.

There is a longish silence.

Then Bambi looks up, resolute. Her lips twist into a wry little smile.

'I'll spare you the grim details. Let's just cut straight ahead to two years later, when I finally felt healed enough to meet new men. The first time I went out on a date, I found *this*' – she places her finger on one of the letters lying between them on the table – 'stuck to the windshield of my car the next morning.'

Bee, stay faithful to me … The A to your B.

'I can't tell you what I went through, Bhavani ji. I couldn't decide if it was somebody playing a sick joke, or something else … I called Anshul's parents to confirm if they had *indeed* retrieved his body from the wreckage of the bus. It had plunged into a river … Anshul was so strong, and such a good swimmer, perhaps …' Her voice breaks, she wipes her nose with the back of her hand, look heartbreakingly like a small child. 'Perhaps … he had *survived*?'

Bhavani's voice is deep and soft with genuine sympathy. 'And what did they say, Bambi ji?'

She closes her eyes and shakes her head. 'They said that he was definitely gone.'

'We see ...' Bhavani clicks his tongue sympathetically. 'You have truly suffered, Bambi ji.'

She sighs, and sits forward, resting her elbows on his desk and cupping her chin in her hands.

'I decided it was all a silly prank. I know some pretty silly people – they don't like me very much because I don't fall neatly into their definition of what a pretty, rich Delhi girl should be – this could be their idea of fun ... So the next time a letter came, I ignored it, and the time after that.'

'You never went to the police?'

'No.' Her face grows inscrutable. 'I thought ... I mean, I know it's silly and melodramatic ... but—'

'You think they are really from Anshul and that is he is alive,' he says calmly.

She looks troubled. 'I ... I don't quite know. But ... Well, like I mentioned earlier – he *was* vain. He talked a lot about how good-looking our children would be. If he got ... burnt ... or scarred very badly, or crippled in some way that he couldn't climb mountains any more, or do any physical activity, it could have destroyed his mind.'

Bhavani sits back in his chair. 'You think he has maybe lost his memory, or his reason, turned into a crackpot stalker and murdered Leo out of jealousy.'

It is a statement, not a question. Bambi gives a hysterical little giggle. 'Well, when you say it as baldly as that it sounds utterly *idiotic*.'

'But that is why you have come to us, is it nat? That is what you suspect?'

She colours, bite her lip and nods. 'Yes.'

'And now you think, don't you, that because you have been socializing with your er ... childhood friend Kashi Dogra again ... that the vakeel sa'ab is in danger too?'

'You understood!' Bambi's face lights up with relief. 'You're so smart! Yes! I'm worried *sick* for Kashi!'

'What about you yourself?' he asks. 'Do you feel like you are being followed, sometimes?'

She looks startled. 'Why?' she asks worriedly.

He shrugs. 'When you go here and there, shopping or to the beauty parlour, or partying—'

'I *do* have a job, you know,' she says wryly.

He nods placatingly. 'Or, indeed, to the office, do you feel that somebody is *trailing* you? Is watching your every move?'

She hesitates. 'It sounds so silly ... but somebody *was* spying on me in the bathroom at the DTC. I saw an eye through the wall. Quite clearly.'

'When?'

She tells him about the whole incident, adding at the end, 'But that could be entirely unrelated to all this, no?'

He nods. 'Yes, it could. By the way, how did this latest letter arrive?'

'It was stuck to the windshield of my car, as usual.'

'We see.' He lapses into silence. 'Bambi ji, you did the right thing by coming to us.' His face looks uncharacteristically grim.

Bambi looks at him apprehensively. 'What ... what are you going to do?'

'You have given us a lot to think about,' he says. 'So we will … *think* about it.'

Inspector Padam Kumar is thoroughly disgruntled. The DTC case is causing havoc with his search for a bride. Just look at today only! It is a sunny Saturday morning, a perfect day for seeing girls – for visiting some nice family, drinking tea, savouring homemade snacks, being respectfully charming to the older folks, and teasingly big-brother-ish with the younger brigade. All the while stealing thrilling little glances at the prospective bride, assessing her beauty and her health, the jolliness of her nature, the competence of her cooking, and comparing them with the other finalists he already has in his kitty, smug in the knowledge that there is no way she could possibly reject *him*, an only son, six-foota, fair, with a full head of hair and a secure police job!

Instead, he's standing ankle-deep in the marshy, Chyawanprash-y mire of the DTC's wretched kitchen garden, sifting through every square inch of mud from the hole in the ground where the accursed body was found, because Bhavani sir has some notion that there may be a clue in there.

Clearly, the colourful chart on Bhavani sir's softboard which says 'Work hard, but not too hard' applies to him only. Everybody else on his team is expected to strain till they get haemorrhoids everywhere, not just in the brain!

Sifting through the mud is messy, back-breaking work. The men are using long spade-like tools that end in a heavy iron mesh. They scoop up the squelchy mud in it, dredge it through the mesh and then look at what's left. All they've found so far are vegetable tubers. Their initial enthusiasm, and the hope finding some vital clue – a key, a button, a watch, a cell phone, anything that could have survived the worms and the germs – has long since dissipated.

It's a fool's task, Padam Kumar thinks bitterly, and I'm the fool who's been delegated to do it!

What makes things even worse is that this place has become some sort of tourist spot. In spite of all the yellow police tape they've put up, somebody or the other keeps wandering up to the site, eager to gawk at the place where the laash was found. Some claim to have lost a golf/tennis/cricket ball, some come from the kitchen with tea and snacks, and some just want to scavenge free vegetables unperturbed by the fact that everything growing in the garden has been fertilized by a laash. It doesn't help that there's a big parking lot just opposite. People keep walking past, messing with the sanctity of the crime scene.

Padam Kumar sighs and sips his tea. The DTC's tea is supposed to be very good and all, but frankly, he's had better. He should really have done what his mummy had suggested. Carried a thermos of sweet, strong, milky tea from home.

Overall, this place is hyped, Padam decides, looking about the sprawling property with dissatisfaction. Haan theek hai, the location is very good, but it seems to primarily be full of skinny old people, chubby children and noisily squawking birds. And you can get better food in the food court of almost any mall. *And* the décor reminds him of those haunted inspection bungalows they're always showing in scary movies. Stuffed tigers and moose heads and mouldering fireplaces!

He dips a biscuit into his tea and chews on it sullenly.

A little child comes skipping happily along the path accompanied by that Ganga girl who had been so withering to him the other day. She is holding her sari pleats fastidiously high in one hand to avoid the mud that has scattered all over the path. Padam Kumar, feeling his cherubic cheeks grow hot, turns away hastily and harangues his men.

'Speed it up! Speed it up! Is this a picnic, or what?'

'*He's* having biskut-chai and accusing *them* of picnicking!' Ganga says to the child quite audibly as she passes. The child chuckles.

Padam goes even redder. Much to his humiliation, he hears his men laughing behind him. He opens his mouth to utter a hasty retort, but realizes that they're not laughing, just talking excitedly, bent over one of the meshes.

Another false alarm, Padam thinks irately. They've probably found a ballpoint pen cap, or a Kurkure packet or a stick that's shaped like a knife or something.

He glowers down at them, disproportionately angry with Ganga, with himself and the world at large.

Then a constable straightens up. He beckons excitedly with both hands. 'PK sa'ab! PK sa'ab! Come and look!'

They're going to *make* me walk, Padam thinks bitterly. I can't just stand here in this sunny spot and drink my tea. No! I have to pick my way through the filth and descend into that accursed hole again …

Shaking his head, he picks his way over the uneven muddy ground to the lip of the hole.

'What?'

But then the excitement in the eyes of the squatting men causes his own heartbeat to quicken. As a thrill pierces his heart, Padam Kumar thinks – could this be it? Could Bhavani sir's hunch be right after all?

'What is it?' he asks, and his tone is quite altered from the surly one he'd used moments before.

'Sa'ab, look.'

Triumphantly, they hold up a mesh trowel for him to inspect.

Padam drops to his knees, suddenly unmindful of the dirt and squelch. 'Clean karo,' he says crisply.

With slightly trembling fingers, the men brush aside the mud and loose grit around the object till it is easily identifiable.

'Ohhh teri!'

Their gazes lock in a moment of shared triumph then drop down again to feast on their trophy.

It is rusted, partly decomposed and covered in a greenish mould, but every man present can identify it for what it is.

A standard-issue army revolver.

LOVE'S SURGICAL STRIKE

NEW DELHI

In a shocking development, the nation's much-loved hero, Lt General Mehra, PVSM AVSM Yudh Seva Medal, the mastermind of the 2016 surgical strike into Pakistan was revealed to have a less than exemplary personal life today, when he was apprehended and taken in for questioning for the murder of Leo Matthew, a celebrity personal trainer who was found poisoned and crushed to death beneath a loaded bar at the gym of the posh Delhi Turf Club.

Shortly after Matthew's death, the Crime Branch team that was investigating the incident made some discoveries that lead them to dig up the organic kitchen garden on the club premises – which is, interestingly, dedicated to Gen. Mehra's late wife – where they unearthed a second corpse.

ACP Bhavani Singh of the ChanakyaPuri Crime Branch remained tight-lipped, but our sources speculate that the body is that of one Ajay Kumar, the estranged husband of young DTC employee Ganga Kumar who is allegedly in a romantic relationship with the widower general.

It is further alleged that three

```
years ago, the General
fatally shot Ganga
Kumar's husband post
a heated argument,
and buried the body in
a shallow grave in the
kitchen garden. Leo
Matthew somehow got
wind of this and began
blackmailing him.
    It   is   being
speculated that
this is what drove
Gen. Mehra, who was
anxious to be elected
president of the Delhi
Turf Club, and is very
low on funds, to take
the extreme step of
poisoning Matthew.
    The   police
identified the General
by his licensed,
standard-issue service
revolver, which had
been wiped clean of
prints and thrown into
the grave along with
the body.
```

'I can't *believe* this.' Pankaj Todi shakes his head over the newspaper in his opulent dining room the next morning. 'General Mehra? Such a great man! A hero! How little we know our closest friends!'

Bambi, who is pretty shaken by the article herself, is finding this reaction of her father intensely irritating.

She looks up and says coolly, 'Well, you *knew* he's a bit of a predator as far as women concerned. And you knew he'd killed people in hand-to-hand combat – he tells that Behra Mehra story to anybody who will listen! If you put those two things together, then this seems fairly logical.'

Todi stares at her in disbelief. 'Those are entirely different things, beta! Killing enemy soldiers during a war—'

'Killing is killing,' she says harshly. 'Let's not kid ourselves.'

'And what d'you expect the man to do when his wife is too unwell to have physical relations with him?'

'Cheating is cheating,' she concludes firmly.

She looks at her father with decidedly judgemental eyes. He lowers his own hastily and reaches for a toast.

'Perhaps you are right,' he admits. 'In *which* case,' he continues thoughtfully, 'we should probably distance ourselves from this man. His good days are clearly over.'

If he'd been hoping to placate his daughter with this statement, he's in for a big disappointment. Bambi lets out an angry exclamation.

'Typical! When people's good days end we should discard them as if they're past-their-expiry-date vegetables!' Her voice is trembling as she attacks her bowl of diced papaya savagely. 'Like you're doing with Mammu?'

Pankaj Todi purses his fleshy lips worriedly. 'I have not discarded your Mammu, beta. Our relationship has merely *changed* a little – I may soon cease to be her husband, but I will *always* be her provider, friend and well-wis—'

'Oh please!' She fidgets with her fork agitatedly. 'You call Mehra uncle your *friend*, you invite him to all your parties – when the surgical strikes happened, you boasted to everybody that he was your buddy! And now you want to drop him! Why?'

Todi's liquid eyes harden. 'Because now I realize that though he appears strong on the surface, he is weak! The way he allowed himself to be pressurized – by that *same* bloody thug who pressurized *you*, don't forget – is utterly disgraceful! There's no mention of that orphanage in this article, though. I am going to sue those bastards and get our money back.'

'What?' Bambi is appalled. 'You can't do that! The children must've been so happy with the money! It went from the company's CSR account. And that nice Father Victor didn't know that Leo was blackmailing people!'

Pankaj Todi stares at his daughter in disbelief. '*Obviously* that Father Victor must have known! And just calling yourself father-father, and wearing a white robe doesn't make you holy! The two of them are childhood friends – the orphanage is *obviously* only a front – a money laundering scheme! But don't worry – now that this case had become so high profile, they'll panic and cough up our money quietly enough.'

He goes back to reading. Bambi glares at the raised newspaper in frustration for a while, then slowly goes back to eating her papaya.

Pankaj Todi rereads the article. It is accompanied by two photographs. One of the general looking very smart in his full army regalia, and one of Ganga and her husband on their wedding day. She looks thin and sallow and weighed down by her finery, but the husband seems to be reveling in his, his French beard perfectly manicured, his teeth flashing in a wide smile.

'It's really so sad.' Pankaj Todi sighs. 'A man with such great distinguished accomplishments, bought down by a weak obsession for a young woman. And *what* a young woman!'

Bambi puts down her fork and looks up. 'What d'you mean?' There is a dangerous edge to her voice.

Todi lowers his paper warily. 'Hmm? Matlab ki she is not exactly a *Playboy* centrefold, is she? Just an ordinary sort of girl.'

His daughter glares at him in disgust. 'And if she *did* look like a *Playboy* centrefold? Would it have been okay to kill two people to get with her?'

Pankaj Todi spreads out his hands. 'Bambi, don't be difficult. That's *not* what I meant!'

Bambi points her fork at him. 'Ganga is a good, clean sensible girl – and she *isn't* having an affair with Mehra uncle!'

'I really think you should stop calling him Mehra uncle now,' her father says firmly. 'And please distance yourself from him at once. No more playing doubles tennis with him!'

Her eyes widen in disbelief. '*You* play doubles tennis with him too!'

'I *used* to, but I won't any more,' he replies, looking harassed. 'In fact this is all your fault – you believed that sly Ganga's stories when she came up to you three years ago, even though your mother and I *told* you she was talking rubbish! If you hadn't got her that Daily Needs franchise at the Club in the first place, none of this would have happened!'

'Oh my *God*!' Bambi pushes back her chair violently and gets to her feet. 'Everything is *always* the woman's fault according to you! You make me *sick*.'

'Bambi—'

But Bambi has already stalked out of the room.

It takes her precisely seven minutes to walk across the road to the Daily Needs store inside the DTC, where Ganga is taking care of an unusually large number of customers all at once, including, Bambi notes savagely, Pia and Dia, two members of the Ghia-Lauki gang.

Bloody cows! They're shopping for nothing but gossip – they wouldn't be seen dead *anywhere* except at DLF Emporio and La Marche and Nature's Basket!

They've walked into one of the many aisles of the store, whispering and giggling.

'Babe, look, how strange, did you know there are *Indian* brands of sunblock too? Here's something called Lotus!'

'Chhee, such tacky packaging! And here's a foundation called MACK, with a K! And it's only two hundred rupees! Might as well be called MUCK!'

They both laugh.

'Ohmuhgawd, *Indian* cream cheese! Haw, such wannabe Philadelphia packaging! Ideal for dips and cheesecakes, it says. Should I pick it up?'

'Why not – if it's ghast, just give it to your maids.'

Bambi's lips tighten. She marches over to the girls and yanks their trolley away.

'Niklo. Git. Now.'

Their eyes widen. '*Excuse* me?'

'You heard me,' Bambi replies, her eyes glittering with anger. 'The stuff you're after isn't available here – so leave now and things will stay pleasant.'

They exchange looks, then turn back to face her.

'Babe, relax, we just thought we'd shop here for a few weeks because poor Ganga's going through such a hard time currently! She needs the business, and we need the uh … cream cheese. It's *really* none of your biz, Bambi Todi.'

'Is anybody else waiting for service?' Ganga's voice speaks up pleasantly, in her slightly halting English. 'Do come up to the counter. I'm free now.'

Snatching back their trolley, Pia and Dia move triumphantly to the front of the store. Bambi grabs a packet of sanitary napkins and follows them, glowering at them as they hand over their cards, daring them to utter a word out of place to Ganga.

'How are you?' Pia asks.

'Well,' Ganga replies serenely.

'You must be so worried about Mehra uncle,' ventures Dia.

Ganga smiles blandly. 'Aren't we all?'

They nod uncertainly wondering how to proceed. Just then, a tall shadow darkens the doorway and all the women turn around.

Inspector Padam Kumar is standing there, his cherubic face grim.

Pia and Dia gasp in horrified pleasure. Bambi, noticing with a sinking heart that there is a female constable accompanying Padam, moves forward to stand in front of Ganga protectively.

'Whuh ... what do you want, inspector?'

'I want Ms Ganga,' Padam Kumar replies steadily. 'For questioning.'

He nods at the constable, who steps forward, walks around Bambi and inclines her head at the pale-faced girl in the cream sari.

'Please come with me.'

12

The Ghia-Lauki Gang

'Your name is Ganga Kumar?'

'Yes.'

'Age?'

'Twenty-three.'

'Are you married?'

'Yes, I am married. My husband has abandoned me several times, but as far as I know, he is still alive.'

'When did he contact you last?'

'Two years ago. He wanted me to PayTM him some money. I refused.'

'Who got you this job at the DTC.'

'Bambi didi. Bambi Todi.'

'How did you meet her?'

'*She was looking for a maid. She interviewed me for the job, but when she found out I had such good marks in class twelve, she said I was too smart to work as a domestic. She also noticed that I was badly bruised, as my husband was abusive. So she got me this job – to manage the Daily Needs store at the Club.*'

'*And where did you meet Gen. Mehra?*'

'*At the Daily Needs store. His wife was very unwell so he used to do his shopping himself. She used to give him a list. He was always very confused about the items on his list, so I started helping him.*'

'*Did he ever meet your husband?*'

'*Did he ever meet your husband?*'

'*Please answer the question. Did he ever meet your husband?*'

'*Yes.*'

'*We have here, a record of a police complaint made against your husband by Gen. Mehra, which states that your husband had beaten you, and when Gen. Mehra tried to stop him, he had assaulted Gen. Mehra too?*'

'*That happened almost three years ago. Ajay suspected me of having an affair with a rich man and attacked me, and I phoned Gen. Mehra to say I was in fear of my life.*'

'*Why phone Gen. Mehra? Why not phone your family – or Bambi didi, who had been so kind and got you a job?*'

'*I don't know. I must've thought … that the general would look scarier to Ajay than Bambi didi! He is a war hero after all!*'

'*Yes he was. In fact, is it normal for such a senior, well-known,* successful *man to be on such close terms with a young woman from his provisions store?*'

'*It felt extremely normal to me. If you knew the general well, you would never ask such a question!*'

'*Ganga Kumar, are you having sexual relations with Gen. Mehra?*'

'*I most certainly am not! He is like a father to me!*'

'*Why did your husband, on the night before he disappeared, accuse you of having an affair with the general?*'

'*Because he was a sick man, with a filthy, suspicious mind – just like yours!*'

'*Why do you still continue to wear a mangalsutra?*'

'*I wear it because my father paid for it – not my husband. My husband paid for* nothing *during the wedding. I wear it because it makes me look respectable and because it stops horny men from making passes at me!*'

'*What about the rumour that it was given to you, in secret, not by Ajay Kumar at your wedding, but two years later, by Gen. Mehra?*'

'*That is absolutely* untrue!'

END OF INTERVIEW.

━┥━━┝━

'You've potted a big one this time, Bhavani!'

The chief's voice is bluff and congratulatory.

Bhavani's reply is glum. 'We haven't potted anything, sir. That article should never have been published. We *still* don't know who leaked the information!'

The chief's voice alters slightly. 'Oh, agreed. That article definitely jumped the gun slightly – ha ha, jumped the gun, that's funny.'

The smile Bhavani dredges to his lips in response to this sally is so constipatedly perfunctory that the chief purses his lips.

'Something worrying you, ACP? Care to explain why you're suspicious of Inspector Padam Kumar's prized discovery?'

Bhavani sighs gustily, his homely face deeply unhappy. He rakes his large square hands through his hair, making it look crazily rumpled and leans forward.

'That gun feels ... *wrong*, sir,' he says earnestly. 'Somehow, we feel like somebody is forcing our hand, and leading us up the garden path, first by the discovery of this gun, and then, by the quick publishing of this article.'

The chief sighs. '*What* feels wrong about the gun, Bhavani?'

'Sir, even forensics admits, after we questioned them *thoroughly*—'

The chief pulls back. 'Bhavani, you've been bullying them.'

'—that it *could* be artificially aged, and hasn't really spent three years at the bottom of a composting pit!'

'Yes, but it *could* very well have been in there for three years too, right?'

A sheepish look settles on Bhavani's features. 'Yes, sir,' he admits, sitting back.

'So your pet theory is that somebody planted the gun on the crime scene *after* the corpse was discovered?'

'Yes, sir!' Bhavani sits forward eagerly. 'It's a highly porous location, sir! People walking up and down all day. Somebody is trying to scapegoat the general! We're sure of it!'

The chief shakes his head. 'I think you're trying to complicate what seems to be quite a simple case. Or else you're a fan of Gen. Mehra's.'

'No, sir.'

'What d'you mean no sir, dammit!'

Bhavani looks slightly surprised. 'We mean we're not trying to complicate a simple case. And we're not a fan of Gen. Mehra. Personally, we think the surgical strikes were highly exaggerated.'

'Keep your voice down,' the chief growls. 'And tell me quickly – who do *you* suspect?'

Bhavani perks up.

'We have some theories, sir. Guppie Ram said the person whom he helped that night accorded him '*Love … and dosti – and equal-equal trust*. Somehow, we can't see Gen. Mehra doing that, he's too full of himself, but in spite of all her wealth and elegance, we *can* see Urvashi Khurana pulling it off.'

'What about that Aggarwal woman?'

Bhavani ponders. 'She could do it too. Not as well as Urvashi Khurana, but she could.'

'That's weak, Bhavani. Very weak.'

The ACP doesn't reply. Various bit and pieces of information and conversation are floating through his mind.

Wait for me. The A to your B

I'm a straightforward man – if I ever wanted to finish off a fellow, I would shoot him in the chest, while looking him in the eye!

There was an eye looking at me. Through the wall.

A much bigger rainwater-harvesting plant – she's obsessed with it!

We think he may have been wearing some sort of costume jewelley – there's the crushed remains of some sort of blue stone in the mud that came with him.

My son … has some … problems. And when your child has problems, you try to bribe the Gods, so that these problems will go aw—

'Look Bhavani,' the chief interrupts his musings. 'I'm under a *lot* of pressure from the top on this. The lurid media coverage hasn't helped. So please *do* something! Thoda zor lago. Strain a little harder, and arrest somebody *fast.*'

Bhavani's face grows stubborn. 'We don't believe in straining, sir,' he says stolidly. 'Straining gives you haemorrhoids not results.'

'Oh *really*,' the chief's voice drips with sarcasm. 'Well, you're going to have to take a few health risks in the next few days, in that case. I can't buy you much time.'

Bhavani's face clears up at once. He beams at his superior. '*Thank you*, sir!'

'Theek hai, theek hai,' the chief waves away this effusive response. 'Might I ask what you plan to do next?'

'Of course, sir. Our most immediate plan is to send vakeel Akash Dogra and Bambi ji to a TVVS party.'

'Can you imagine, Papa humay Disneyland le ja rahen hai!' Kalra's voice is delirious with joy. 'After all these years! I can't believe it!'

'Shut up, Kalra,' Kashi says gruffly. 'Act like a grown-up please.'

'But I *can't*, Dogra.' Kalra, dressed in a white polo tee and denim bermudas shakes his head dreamily. 'This drive to Chattarpur has reactivated all my randiest thirteen-year-old fantasies. That's why we friended this fucker in class seven, isn't it, Walli?'

'Correct!' Walli, in his tightest red shirt and partying black pants, rubs his hands together with glee. 'We were two hopeful young small-town chomus, and Dogra was the Delhi buoy who was gonna invite us over in the summer and take us to farmhouse parties with swimming pools full of hot TVVS chicks! It's taken twelve years but he's *finally* opened the gates to hook-up paradise!'

Kashi, sitting between his friends in his cleanest vee-neck navy-blue tee, turns to give them a dirty look each.

'I'm not your fucking pimp, guys. These girls are my childhood *friends* – and remember, you're technically gate-crashers—'

'Balls! We heard Sia on the phone! She said' – Walli puts on a cooing 'female' voice – '"Bring along some hot Doscos, Kashi!"'

Kashi glares at him, 'She said that as the merest formality! Secondly, remember, it's not just a party – we're doing this at ACP Bhavani's instructions—'

'*We're* doing this to protect Bannerjee's interests,' Kalra says piously, 'You've been using these recent unfortunate deaths to get close to Bambu Todi again—'

'Yeah, what kind of sicko cuddles up to his ex at funerals?' Walli chimes in. 'Not cool, Dogra!'

'So we're tagging along to make sure things don't get too hot and heavy! This is not a pleasure trip for us – we're sort of on-duty only!'

Kashi glares at the grinning pair at a total loss for words, then sits back.

'Uptown Funk' plays uncontested on the speakers for a while.

Stylin, wilin' living it up in the city,
Got chucks on, with Saint Laurant,
Gotta kiss myself, I'm so pretty!
I'm too hot (hot damn!)
Call the police and a fireman
I'm too hot (hot damn!)

As the Uber turns on to Aurangzeb Road, Kashi picks up his phone and dials a number.

'Hey. We're outside. Come.'

Walli and Kalra wink at each other.

'Hey.'

'We're outside.'

And then both together, moaning. *'Come!'*

They collapse into waves of laughter, then sober up quickly as Bambi emerges from the massive gates, wearing a tight little body-con black dress, her soft brown hair a mass of loose, floating curls.

'She got *even* hotter,' Kalra says, awed, peering out of the window. 'I didn't think that was possible. Dogs, you said she's single and not too picky, right?'

Quickly, he looks at Walli. 'There's not enough space, fucker, get in the front seat.'

Walli protests, but Kalra practically shoves him out, then smiles up at Bambi.

'Hey, Todi! Get in here!'

Bambi smiles. 'It's ... Kalra isn't it?'

'Madam, jaldi karo, please,' the Uber guy says in a surly voice.

Bambi gets in and the ride resumes.

Wedged in between Kashi and the door, Bambi reaches out to shake hands with both Kalra and Walli. They exchange artificially effusive greetings and then a slightly constrained silence descends on the car. 'Uptown Funk' reigns supreme again.

> *Girls hit your hallelujah (whoo)*
> *Girls hit your hallelujah (whoo)*
> *Girls hit your hallelujah (whoo)*
> *Cos Uptown Funk's gonna give it to ya!*
> *Saturday night are you in the spot,*
> *Don't believe me, just watch!*

'This is a frickin' all time low,' Bambi mutters to Kashi after a while. 'You and me partying with the Ghia-Lauki gang! My social cred is utterly destroyed.'

'You *have* no social cred.' He smiles down into her eyes. 'All you do is work and vegetables.'

She winces. 'Wow, harsh!'

'You made me drink a glass full of that beetroot juice,' he reminds her. '*That* was harsh!'

'Shit!' She looks stricken for a moment, then recovers. 'It was really good beetroot, okay? And beets grow really shallow, you know – I doubt the roots touched what was … uh … *lying beneath.*'

'I'd rather not talk about it, if you don't mind,' Kashi replies.

'Sorry,' she says contritely.

Walli pipes up from the front seat. 'Uh, Dogs … why are we going to this party again?'

'We are going,' Kashi raises his voice to explain patiently for the nth time, 'because ACP Bhavani wants us to zoom in on a bugger called Aryaman Aggarwal and get him to talk.'

'About what?'

Kashi throws up his hands. 'Anything! I've already shown you guys his Insta pics. If you spot him, point him out to Bambi and me – and we'll take over the convo. Kindly do *not* exceed your brief. That's *all* you need to do tonight.'

'Hello, we wanna *do* more than that tonight!' Walli says meaningfully.

'Yeah, yeah, yeah,' chimes in Kalra. 'Set us up with some nice friendly girls with very low standards, okay, Todi?'

Bambi looks at their hopeful faces in disbelief, then turns to smile at Kashi. '*So* nice of you to let your animals ride in the car with us. You're *such* a kind guy – must be all the nice TVVS values you picked up in your childhood.'

As all three Doscos protest loudly, the Uber turns off the main highway and plunges into the darkened lanes of Chattarpur.

'So what do we do with Aryaman once we find him?' Bambi whispers to Kashi.

He flashes her a mock-sinister grin and whispers back, 'We charm him with our worshipful juniors vibe, and try and figure out *who* he could've bumped off and dumped in the kitchen garden.'

'What!' Bambi gives a delighted little gurgle of laughter. 'But that's *wild*! Like a whodunnit movie! Bhavani thinks Arya's the murderer?'

'Or his mum, more likely.'

'*Ah.*' Bambi takes a while to digest this.

'You don't think it likely?' Kashi asks.

Bambi shrugs. 'He's an official *weirdo*. He's had a bad rep for years, but even then, killing a whole human being and burying them sounds a little too high-energy for him. He's pretty lethargic. As in, constantly stoned.'

'Well, he would have had Guppie Ram ji's help,' Kashi replies.

She gasps, wide-eyed. '*What?*'

He nods. 'Yeah, that's what the ACP said – they've found a video recording of Guppie Ram ji talking mysteriously to Leo about a body he helped somebody bury in the kitchen garden.'

'What? OhmuhGod, Kash! They dug up the kitchen garden because of something *Guppie Ram ji* said? *He* was their source?' She shakes her head. 'Wow, didn't you tell them that

Guppie Ram just like, made shit up all the time? Remember when he told us a huge-ass cobra bit him, and he sucked out the poison himself, and it turned his tongue blue, when actually he'd just been eating jamuns?'

'And he said Katrina Kaif and Johnny Lever were sitting in the Rose Garden and we both went running like idiots to see, and it was just gorgeous Urvashi Auntie and ugly Mukki uncle!' Kashi recalls. 'Yeah, he always exaggerated the fuck out of stuff.'

She nods. 'Which is why he was nicknamed Guppie Ram. His real name was Ram Gopal.'

'But they really did find a dead body there, Bam.'

She shrugs. 'Even if they did – it doesn't prove that Guppie Ram's story of helping somebody bury a murder victim there was true! He could've just found a couple of old bones there while he was digging about the garden! And then he made up a whole story just to take the piss out of Leo. I can *just* see him doing it!'

'*Hey!*' Walli calls plaintively from the front seat. 'I think we're circling the same area again and again. Provide some direction, bro!'

They reach the party house fifteen minutes later, guided more by the loud house music than the GPS. It is a poolside rave at Sia Kapoor's farmhouse in Chattarpur, a location Bambi and Kashi remember well from a bunch of over-the-top birthday parties Sia had thrown in their childhood.

'I *hate* Sia Kapoor,' Bambi mutters as the guards at the gate wave them through. 'She hugs me so hard every time she sees me – it's like she's trying to stab me to death with her super-pointy boobs.'

'I like her already,' Kalra says happily. 'But this farmhouse is so extra, bro! Is her dad an arms dealer?'

Bambi frowns. 'He makes steel, I think,' she says doubtfully. 'She is *so* going to pass out when she sees me. I haven't attended any of her dumb parties for years! Listen, I hope you guys are wearing costumes underneath? These guys just throw you in the pool randomly sometimes. But it's heated, so that's okay.'

Saying which, she tugs her dress lower over her luscious little butt, flat palms the massive double doors and walks into a huge lobby.

As anticipated, the Ghia-Laukis do almost pass out at the sight of Bambi Todi entering the party hand in hand with Kashi Dogra. Sia Kapoor, lounging in the lobby on a fibre-glass couch, dressed only in a flame-orange bikini and too many pearls, staggers to her feet, clearing mascara out of her eyes.

'Ohhhhmyyyygawd!!!' she screams. 'I am so dhanya! I am so blessed! I wish I had rose petals to scatter at your feet, ya! Look who's *heeeeere*, guys! Bambi Todi and Kashi Dogra and some cute *Doscosssssss*!'

Slapping palms and kissing cheeks all around, they enter the massive beach-style farmhouse, all hung about with fairy lights and exotic tropical blooms. Bollywood music is pumping on the speakers and there is a huge glass bar where, back in the old days, a bouncy castle used to be.

'*So* not my scene, bro,' Bambi mutters fervently into Kashi's ear, and he registers the last word with a slight shock. He's not sure he is spiritually evolved enough to not resent being *bro*-ed by his ex.

'Mine neither,' he whispers back. 'D'you want a drink?'

She nods. 'Sprite. Can you bring it to the pool? Where'd your friends go?'

They look around, and realize that Walli and Kalra have already been swept up into the party – one is at the centre of a group of lonely looking girls who are clearly hanging onto his every word, and the other is being applauded for potting a difficult shot by a gang of jocks at the pool table.

'Hmm, nice,' Bambi concedes, reluctantly impressed. 'At least they don't need babysitting!'

Saying which, she twists her hair into a casual topknot, then reaches down, grabs the edge of her black dress and pulls it up and off in one smooth move. She chucks it on a chair already festooned with assorted garments and walks to the pool dressed in a black-and-pink halter-topped bikini and a slim black anklet.

Kashi stares at the slender, cinnamon body till it dives gracefully into the crowded pool to a chorus of welcoming whoops, then turns around to get his drink. The tips of his ears are flaming red and his throat is dry.

'Two Sprites, please.'

He walks with the cans to the pool, and looks around for Bambi. She is sitting right across the pool, with her feet dangling in the water in the centre of a gaggle of joint-smokers, giggling and splashing and holding forth in a high-pitched voice that he can immediately tell is not very natural.

'*Shut uppppp!*' she is saying to a muscular man with shiny, emerald-green fingernails. '*You* – and *all* the other gay guys were the ones with a crush on Jaibeer Kanodia! I just said I was crushing on him out of sheer queer pressure!'

'Well, we turned out to be right about him, didn't we?' the guy retorts. 'JK *was* on the spectrum! He came out with a vengeance and is currently the hottest mechanical engineer in the Bay Area!'

'Bam, your drink!' Kashi holds it up from across the pool.

She takes a drag from somebody's joint and stares at him with strangely shining eyes. Then she raises one solemn arm.

'Guys gimme a beat.'

They oblige at once, and she turns back to look at Kashi, swaying a little.

'Un-dress! Un-dress! Un-dress! Un-dress!'

'Unbelievable.' Kashi mutters under his breath. She always claims to hate this scene – and she even *does* – but whenever she ends up with this crowd she feels the need to be the absolute throbbing heart of the party.

Staring across the pool, Kashi feels a sudden intense dislike for the entire chanting group, including Bambi – so rich, so privileged and so utterly spoilt.

Then he remembers his Goa abs, lurking under his vee-neck tee.

Very deliberately, he raises his arms and tugs it off.

The gang across the pool whoops loudly.

Locking eyes with Bambi across the water, Kashi unbuttons his chinos, drops them and kicks them aside.

'I can die now! Maine Kashi ke darshan kar liye!' he hears somebody declare as he dives into the pool and the water splashes around him, shutting off all sound.

Reaching the other side, Kashi pulls himself up and sits down beside Bambi, shivering a little. The night air is definitely a bit chilly.

'Arya at eleven o' clock,' she whispers in his ear urgently.

Surprised at her totally sober voice – she has clearly been fake-inhaling the joints – he looks as casually as he can in the direction she has indicated. Yes, there he is – across the pool, sitting with his legs dangling in the water and staring at the waves like a zombie.

'No hurry,' Kashi whispers back to her. 'We'll get to him in a bit.'

'So you guys are like, back together now?'

Sia Kapoor is very drunk. She's lying on her back on the Italian mosaic floor by the poolside, her long legs propped up on a deckchair, surrounded by most of the people Kashi and Bambi went to junior school with.

There's a chorus of general snickering at her question, and some low-key cheering. The TVVS batch of 2012 has always been unhealthily obsessed with Kashi Dogra and Bambi Todi – it's the price you pay for pairing off early, when the rest of the class is still hanging out in clearly demarcated 'girls' and 'boys' groups.

Bambi is sitting next to Kashi, their thighs almost touching through their towels, but at this question she straightens up like she's received an electric shock, saying hotly, 'Oh, for heaven's sake, Sia, get a li—'

Kashi's arm descends around her shoulders, holding her firmly to his side.

'Yeah,' he says calmly. 'Bam and I are friends again. We're gonna stay friends for life.'

This is met with a cheer that is not low-key at all. The TVVS gang appears disproportionately pleased. Sia Kapoor's face spasms oddly. She looks, suddenly, close to tears.

'I'm *so* glad,' she says fervently. 'When I see you guys together, I feel like everything is okay with the world. And the world is just so fucked up, you know? There's like so much *competition*, and all these pushy chicks from *Ghaziabad*, and horrible men who stare at you if you're showing even a little side-boob, and my favourite boy bands keep splitting up, and my favourite brand of mascara just got discontinued, and it's *so hard* to remember to eat healthy and sleep on time and work out, and *then* there're *pandemics* and *terrorists* and *crippled people* and poor migrant workers whose kids spend their whole year looking forward to eating just *one* McDonald's vanilla cone on their birthday!' She lets out a long, shaky breath. 'It's too sad, ya – school was really the best time of my *life*!'

'Wow, that's deep, Sia.'

'You have so much *soul*.'

'C'mon, I'll show you some midget porn. That'll make you laugh.'

Sniffling, Sia allows herself to be led away. The group, considerably sobered, breaks up and wanders off to get a drink or swim. But Kashi and Bambi continue to sit and stare at the dancing water.

'What are you thinking?'

'I'm thinking ...' he says slowly, 'that my girlfriend won't like us sitting like this. And so ...' Very reluctantly, he lifts his arm off her shoulder and slides a little further along the deckchair. Continuing to hold on to her hand, he grins at her. 'This is safe, I think.'

Bambi sticks out her tongue. 'You'll never be safe from me, Kashi Dogra.'

His brown eyes glow. 'That,' he admits, 'is probably true.'

He stares at her across the space that divides them, feeling suddenly, idiotically happy.

'Hey, I read up on that case you won,' she says. 'Good *job*, Kashi!'

He gets the uncomfortable look he always gets when people praise him, and glances away at the pool. 'Thanks.'

Bambi continues to stare at him, her eyes warm and approving. 'You got all those jhuggi dwellers their rights – it was *awesome*.'

'I had a lot of help,' he replies. 'I worked with this really committed NGO – they did all the research.'

'I want to help people too.'

He turns to throw her a smile. 'Cool!'

She hugs her knees. 'No, no, I'm serious! I have this whole *plan* and shit!'

'Tell me.'

She hesitates, then shakes her head decidedly. 'No. You'll judge me.'

'T'fuck!' He laughs. 'When have I *ever* been judgemental about the shit you do, Bam?'

It is she who turns away to gaze at the pool now. 'You don't know half the shit I've done, Kash.'

A cool gust of wind swoops down on the poolside, causing goose-pimples on their flesh. Bambi gives a little shiver, rubbing her palms on her bare arms. 'Where's my dress?'

A little later, towelled and dressed, they start looking around for Aryaman Aggarwal. When they finally spot him, he is passed out on a deckchair, under a pile of damp towels, lying flat on his back, staring up at the stars blankly.

'Shit!' Kashi pulls back. 'The guy is wasted.'

'Standard Arya,' Bambi whispers with a shrug. 'Everybody agrees that he's practically a vegetable. Into really hard drugs, and living totally in la-la land. Apparently can't even get an erection any more.'

'He didn't seem that bad at Cookie auntie's exhibition,' Kashi says.

'He'd cleaned up for the uncle-aunties that day,' she replies. 'This is much more his default setting.'

She says it so casually that Kashi gets angry. 'This is *nobody's* default setting! How can you be so callous, Bambi?'

'Wow! Please forgive me for having no sympathy for privileged, entitled *losers*. Shit happens to *everybody*, that doesn't mean you develop a drug habit! You're supposed to suck it up, and *soldier* on, not become bitter!'

The catch in her voice betrays her emotions.

He squeezes her arm. 'Sorry.'

She stays rigid for a moment then, wordlessly, lets her head drop sideways onto his shoulder.

As he feels the soft, scented weight land on him with a trustful sigh, Kashi is conscious of so many complex emotions that he feels his head might explode. Automatically, from sheer muscle memory, his arms goes about her waist.

Kiss her.

She wants you to.

She always has.

They stay like that for what seems like an eternity.

Finally, Kashi straightens up.

'C'mon, let's do this,' he says briskly.

He strides down the poolside and stands beside the supine Aggarwal.

'Aggarwal? Hey, Aggarwal!'

Bambi rushes up behind him, bends down and smacks the prone figure smartly on his shoulder. Aryaman Aggarwal grimaces and stirs. He manages to prop himself up onto one elbow, and agree, in a very bleary and slurry voice that yes, he is indeed, probably Aryaman Aggarwal.

'It's meee!' Bambi does her little dancing-on-the-spot routine. 'Bambi Todi! Your junior from Red House!'

He blinks, recognition lighting up the dull eyes. 'Bambi Todi. You're cuuuute. I like you.'

He reaches for her in a dim sort of way. Kashi hastily pushes her aside.

'So how's it going, bro?' he asks in his nicest man-to-man voice.

But this is too much mental stimulation. Aggarwal droops, then passes out on the deckchair again.

'What t'fuck!' Bambi mutters. 'You scared him, Kashi.'

Kashi looks indignant. '*I* scared him! You're the one who slapped him so hard!'

She leans down over the crumpled body.

'OMG, Aryaman!' she coos. 'Remember when you used to play the drums? I ogled you right through the Western Music showcase when you did that Imagine Dragons song! Didn't you used to play the drums?'

No response.

Kashi and Bambi look at each other, quite at a loss.

Bambi tries again. 'I do Zumba classes with your mum!'

Aryaman stirs.

'I *hate* my mum,' he mumbles. 'Bitch hates me too.'

'Hello, language!' Kashi rebukes him, genuinely shocked, but Aryaman has already fallen asleep again. 'Uh… should we fling him in the pool to wake him up?'

'He'll probably drown. This is all *your* fault. I wanted to zoom in on him the *moment* we got here – but you were all like, no hurry, we'll make him come to us!'

'Yeah. 'Cos Bhavani had told me to be subtle!' Kashi replies, stung. 'I didn't want people to think we'd come to the party with a one-point agenda of pumping the guy!'

'Throwing him into the pool will be subtle?'

'You have a better idea?'

She sits down with a thump. 'Oh, forget it. We'll just track him down when he's sober and get him to talk.'

He sits down beside her. 'You want a drink?'

She gives her head a quick shake. 'I talk too much when I'm drunk.'

'Really?' He quirks a brow. 'And what's all this deep dark stuff you're afraid you'll spill?'

'Oh … just … stuff.' Her eyes grow wistful. 'Like, I should never have believed Mummu-Paapu know best … I should never have broken up with you.'

Kashi doesn't reply. There really isn't anything to say.

She stares out at the party moodily. Some drunken people are moving slowly to very fast music. There's a food fight going on near the bar. Some impassive bearers are cleaning up several broken beer bottles. Birthday girl Sia Kapoor is staring down at her phone, tears streaming down her face.

'This is all *so* fucked up!'

'That's what Kuhu says too.'

'Oh *please*! Can we not talk about your perfect girlfriend?'

'That's a bit unfair,' he pushes back gently.

Bambi blinks and shakes her head, like a boxer who's just taken one on the chin. 'You're right – tell me all about her, then! How you guys met, why she didn't want to Goa with you, how soon this long-distance thread is gonna snap!'

'You seem pretty sure it's gonna snap.'

She nods. 'Uh huh.'

Anger descends in a sudden red mist on Kashi.

'Long distance isn't just about physical distance, you know,' he bites back. 'People can be doing the long-distance thing even if they're sitting right next to each other – like you and I are.'

'So you ... and Kuhu ... you're like *tight* in the head?'

'Yes,' he says steadily.

'And you and I are ... not?'

He sighs. 'No.'

She bursts out laughing. 'That's nuts! We're practically the same person! We have all the same memories and all the same ideologies.'

'We're toxic as fuck, Bambi.'

'Would you ever consider getting back together with me?'

It's a typical Bambi Todi attack, coming right out of blue and hitting him bang in the solar plexus. Completely winded, heart thudding against his ribs, he rakes hair off his forehead with slightly shaky hands and says, 'Whuh ... what?'

She was staring up at him, but now she drops her gaze at once. 'Forget it,' she says with a grimace and a quick shake of the head. 'It was a dumb, dog-in-the-manger thing to say!'

'No no, it's okay,' he reassures her just as quickly. 'You can say anything to me, you know that.'

'*No!*' she says vehemently. 'I really like this friend space we're in right now, we mustn't mess with it – I must've inhaled that damn joint accidentally.'

Kashi steps closer, his brown eyes intense. 'No, Bam, it's cool, tell me what you mea—'

'Hey Dogra! Hey Todi!'

They look around – the Doscos are back, ravaged and dishevelled and extremely pleased with themselves. Walli is wearing only a pair of bright blue briefs and Kalra's black party shirt is badly torn. There are bits of grass on their backs and in their hair, and a suspicious swollen look to their mouths.

'Have you two been banging each other in the bushes?' Bambi asks.

They just beam at her happily.

'Best party ever!' Walli declares. 'Thanks for inviting us!'

'The girls here are *too* nice,' Kalra confides. Then he blinks, 'Who's the dead guy?'

'He's not dead.' Kashi's voice is exasperated. 'Merely tripping.'

Kalra peers down at Aryaman Aggarwal's still figure then clicks his tongue sympathetically. 'Looks like a BT, bro, a bad, bad trip. He should've stuck with *us*. We met these guys, just back from a trek in Dharamshala, who were smoking the purest shit ever! Sourced directly from the hills!' He holds up his hands and gestures dramatically. 'From *farm* – to *palm*! From *farm* – to *palm*! From *farm* – to *palm*! Get it?'

'I got it the first time,' Kashi says sourly.

'We met their dealer too,' Walli adds. 'He was handing out free twenty-gram samples of weed ... really chill guy. Looked like a Citibank banker, pinstriped shirt and glasses.'

'Naice!'

Kalra nods. 'Best part was, he wasn't judgemental! I *hate* sanskari dealers, bro, matlab, in Ludhiana I used to pick from this really fucking goody-goody dealer – every time we met he'd give me a whole load of brain-freezing gyaan about how I was *ruining* my health and *destroying* my parents' happiness and *blowing away* my future and how I should stop at once.

And then he'd hand me the weed and take my cash. It was like he felt morally obliged to issue a sort of statutory warning. Twisted, sadistic bastard.'

'I feel you, bro.' Bambi nods. 'I hate hypocrites.'

'*Yeah,* Todi!' Walli swivels to face her, delighted. 'You *get* me! Anyway, I could've had a much longer chat with this dealer, but he slunk off without eating. He's keeping a low profile – the cops are chasing all the dealers nowadays, trying to figure out who supplied the Pinko Hathni to your Zumba trainer, Todi.'

'That makes sense.'

'He was sort of low-key bragging that he supplied it, TBH. But he could have just been taking the piss. Dealers take the piss a lot to scare kids into keeping their mouths shut. He said he knows that chick who's in the news – the one having an affair with that old general.'

'What … wait?' Kashi looks up sharply. 'Do you mean … *Ganga?*'

Kalra scratches his head, his eyes hazy. 'He didn't mention the name – but apparently she runs a Daily Needs at your club. He seemed pretty kicked at how high-profile "bhabhi ji" had gotten. He used to be thick pals with her husband – who used to deal to all the TVVS kids back in the old days, but then some shit went down and he had to vanish. So this guy inherited his client list.'

'TVVS kids used to pick from *Ganga's husband* three years ago and then he vanished?' Kashi asks. 'Is *that* what you're saying, Kalra?'

'People sell off their client list all the time,' Walli chips in knowledgeably. 'My dentist did the same thing when I was twelve – told my mom ki I'm off to Canada for a three-month course, my pal so-and-so will treat your son for the time being, and then he just never came back, and we realized he'd migrated to Canada and I'd been shunted off to so-and-so against my will! My top right incisor is still all crooked, look!'

Nobody looks. Kalra has wandered off to find the loo and Kashi and Bambi are staring at each other in electrified silence, words trembling on their lips.

'Shall I say?' she asks breathlessly.

He nods.

'Okay okay!' She takes a deep, calming breath. 'So, if three years ago, Ganga's hubby was the local TVVS dealer, and Arya was one of his clients, and then Ganga's hubby vanished – then that creates a direct link between Arya and the body in the kitchen patch!'

'Assuming that the body in the kitchen patch *is* Ganga's husband,' Kashi says. 'That hasn't been conclusively proven yet, has it?'

She shakes her head. 'No – but it seems logical … Oh my God, Kashi, this is *huge*!'

'I think it's probably much more likely that Ganga's husband just fucked off to Dubai or something,' says Kalra. 'Or to Canada – like my dentist.'

'Shut up, Kalra. You're right, Bambi. It's huge! We have to notify Bhavani.'

13

The Khuranas Receive Visitors

It is three in the morning by the time the Uber drops Bambi off at Aurangzeb Road. The guys are all in the backseat – Kalra and Walli had manoeuvred to make sure Bambi sat in the front seat when the Uber arrived at Sia Kapoor's farmhouse, a move that had certainly not endeared them to Kashi. Now he yanks open the back door, very tight-lipped, and gets into the front passenger seat, slamming the door shut so hard that the driver protests.

'Sir gaadi hai, truck nahi!'

Kashi sends Bhavani a long, detailed WhatsApp message, updating him on Ganga's husband's second job as a drug dealer, then drops the phone into the cupholder beside him, sits back with a sigh and closes his eyes.

A little while later, a voice cooes into his ear.

'*When Kuhu smiles at me, I feel like the sun has come out from behind a dark cloud, but when Bambi smiles at me, I feel like I am the sun itself.*'

Kalra and Walli have got hold of his phone.

'What the *fuck*, Walli!' Kashi swears, and lunges for it.

Walli chucks the phone to Kalra, who waves off the furious Kashi while sucking in his breath and shaking his head solemnly.

'Too much pressure, bro. Being somebody's sun is too much pressure. You'll burn yourself up just keeping 'em warm.'

Kashi looks at him in angry disbelief. 'Behenchod, now you're a science expert? You put the moon between the sun and the earth in the diagram of the lunar eclipse! We chutiyas copied from you and failed the class seven finals as well! Gimme my phone back!'

He is so white-faced and enraged that, after shrugging and exchanging silent looks, the pair tamely surrender the phone.

'Dirty dog, Dogra.'

'Cheating on Bannerjee.'

Kashi requests them very cordially to shut the fuck up, and they are so baked that they actually comply.

The Uber heads towards Nizamuddin in silence. Kashi glowers at the empty night roads and replays the events of the evening in his mind. Or, to be specific, one precise moment.

Would you ever consider getting back together with me?

Why, he thinks moodily, did their paths have to cross at all, all those years ago? His mother could've signed him up for horse-riding instead of swimming; he could've gone through life happily and healthily, riding horses, playing tennis, eating shakkarkandi and reading books – until the moment Kuhu Bannerjee pulled up in her little car and offered him a ride because Kalra thought he had broken his cock. How simple and untainted and uncomplicated everything would have been then.

But no, he had to bump into Bambi when he was six years old, blow air into her wretched armband, and be condemned to live forever with a hole in his heart where their relationship had been.

No more 'friendship' with Bambi Todi, he tells himself firmly. You've literally been flirting with fire. You have to get back to work soon anyway, and that can be the perfect excuse to drop casually out of her life. In fact, why wait till you get back to work – move to Noida right away, and spend the rest of your leave hanging with Ma and Dadi and Nattu. Begin the Bambi-detox *ASAP*.

Feeling a lot more sorted, he settles back into the seat and closes his eyes.

Would you ever consider getting back together with me?

Brig. Dogra is swinging dreamily on the white garden swing in his Noida kothi when Kashi's Uber rolls up at the gate the next afternoon. He looks up, and slowly stows his phone away.

'To what do we owe this honour?' he demands as Kashi approaches the gate. 'You? Here? How come?'

'Hi, Dad,' Kashi says lightly, as he lugs his rucksack down the driveway. 'Where's everybody?'

The brigadier looks at the bulging rucksack, his expression half-grumpy, half-hopeful. 'Moving back with bag and baggage, are you?'

Kashi grins. 'That's the idea. We can rig up a net on the lawn and practice some shots, I thought.'

A matching grin lightens the brigadier's face. 'Mala-D!' he shouts. 'Suna? Your ladla has ditched the fleshpots of Nizamuddin and come to stay with us!'

'For three days, Ma,' Kashi says as his mother rushes excitedly out of the house to greet him. 'I have to get back to work on Thursday.'

'Put your bag in your room,' she says. 'I'll need to put in fresh sheets and towels, and there may be a smell – we've been storing unripe mangoes under your bed! I'm making rajma chawal. Is that okay?'

'It's *awesome*.' He gives her a quick hug. 'I'm sorry I don't come over more often, Ma.'

'Stupid boy.' She kisses him soundly, then pushes him away. 'Go say hi to your Dadi. And that must be full of dirty clothes, na? Leave it in the laundry basket. And call Nattu – we can all have lunch together!'

Kashi walks slowly up the stairs to the upstairs living room, which leads off to two bedrooms. His, which has a cross-stitch embroidery sign reading 'Kashi' over the door, and Natasha's which has a matching sign that reads 'Tashi'. He enters his room and it is exactly as he had left it last. There are the same Doon School football groups on the wall, the same bunch of inter-school and college medals, the graduation picture from NLS, and a baby photo of him sitting on his grandparents' knees. Outside, from his balcony, is the familiar view of the gulmohar tree and the terrace of the Bharagavas' house next door.

He doesn't need to shower, but he does. Wearing his Jaipur House soccer shorts and an old tee, he comes running downstairs lightly, feeling suddenly revitalized and centred. He realizes with a queer little shock that he has spent the last several days free-floating about in a sort of confounded daze.

'Kashi!' Old Mrs Dogra beams delightedly when he pops his head into her bedroom. 'Come and sit here!' She pats the bed.

'Hi, Dadi!' He bends down to give her a hug.

She pats his back with gentle hands, then pulls away to gaze at him with affectionate rheumy eyes.

'How are you, beta? How's Boohoo?'

'Kuhu,' he corrects her gently.

'Your mother said Boohoo,' the old lady replies firmly.

'What! Why?'

'Because she cried so much when we all went to see *Parasite*,' Nattu's voice comes from the door. 'During the climax. She tried to hide it, but of course we noticed. Didn't you know?'

'That she cried or that you guys call her Boohoo?' he demands. 'Why are you so mean to her, anyway?'

'Shut up! You know I like her, Kashi!' Nattu says as she hugs him. 'And so does Dadi – don't you, Dadi?'

'Bengali girls are churails,' says the old lady seriously as Nattu hugs her. 'Hairy also.'

'Having quite a lucid day today, I see,' Kashi mumurs in an aside to his sister as she sits down beside him.

Nattu giggles. 'Oh yes, she's in great form nowadays.'

Presently they sit down at the big dining table before a lavish lunch.

'OG group!' Nattu says happily as she ladles steaming hot rajma into her plate. 'Yay!'

'OG means original, not olive green,' Mala Dogra explains to her fauji husband, who is looking confused. 'What should the OGs do? Let's go for long walks, and swim and drink tea on the veranda – spend a lot of *quality* time together, basically!'

'Time is time, not an ice cream,' grunts the brigadier. 'What is all this kwality and quantity?'

'Really?' His wife snorts. 'Okay, kids, imagine your father is a piece of ganna.'

'Okay,' Kashi says obligingly.

'Eww, Ma, why?' objects Nattu.

'Be quiet! Haan, so early in the morning, Balbir Dogra is this nice fresh chunk of sugar cane, tight and bursting with sweet juice! But, even before breakfast, his golf buddies get their teeth into him. Then, after breakfast, his stockbroker son-in-law phones him and has a gnaw! *Then* he goes to the gym where the trainer nikalos his juice. *Then* he comes back, showers, and sits with Amma ji who slips on her dentures and chews through whatever's left, and *finally*, at the end of the day, all that staggers into our bedroom at night is a pile of spat-out *husk*!'

She is almost teary-eyed by the end of this speech. Her voice is trembling. Kashi and Nattu exchange looks, valiantly trying to keep their faces straight.

'Aaj se dad ka nickname Husky!' Nattu says finally.

'Ma, that metaphor is problematic for several reasons,' Kashi chimes in. 'Firstly, you're objectifying your husband – he's a *person* not a plant. Secondly, it all sounds wayyy too cannibalistic—'

'Sexual too,' Nattu puts in primly. 'All this talk of juicing and chewing. Highly inappropriate thing to say in front of your children!'

'Arrey kahan sexual, we have reached the age of innocence!' snorts Mala Dogra. 'I am simply craving some quality, honest conversation. Nothing else!'

The conversation continues in this vein for a while. Finally, the siblings manage to extract a promise from their father that he will spend more one-on-one time with their mother, and, after demolishing the mighty bowls of rajma-chawal, the family regards each other torpidly across the table.

'What's the latest on the DTC murders?' Balbir asks his son. 'You've palled up with that ACP, haven't you? Does he really think Behra Mehra did it? Nobody in the fauj does. They're all saying he's being framed.'

'I think he may reluctantly be coming around to that conclusion,' Kashi says. 'I can't reveal the details because they're confidential, but there *are* other theories.'

'Reveal, no!' Nattu says cajolingly. 'Who will we tell, anyway!'

'No, no!' Kashi shakes his head laughingly. 'I can't.'

The brigadier frowns. 'Don't ask him to betray a confidence, Nattu. It's unethical.'

'Haw!' Nattu gasps. 'When it's you who wants stock market tips from you son-in-law—'

'That's not the same thing at all.'

'What about Mukesh Khurana?' Mala Dogra wants to know. 'Surely *he* has a strong motive? We all saw Leo knock him down at the club the day before he was murdered! How come this ACP isn't investigating *him*?'

'His wife was damn eager to dig up that kitchen garden,' the brigadier recalls. 'Couldn't wait to put her wretched rainwater harvester into it! Would she have done that if her husband had stuck a body in there a few years ago?'

'Maybe she didn't know,' suggests Nattu.

'Yes,' Mala Dogra remarks bitterly. 'Maybe her husband doesn't tell her anything either!'

Everybody wisely pretends not to have heard this loaded statement.

'You guys are right,' Kashi says. 'Bhavani should be following up on the Khurana angle. I wonder why he isn't?'

'Because he's being pressured to pin it on old Mehra, that's why,' the brigadier fumes. 'Typical civilian behaviour! They always get a fauji to take the hit for them!'

'But who would issue such instructions?' his wife asks.

'Somebody rich and highly placed, obviously!' is the disgruntled reply. 'Mehra's a vain, credit-hogging fool, I'm sure he's made a lot of enemies.'

My name is Om Prakash Mehra, I was born in Gurdaspur in 1954, went to school in Chandigarh and was selected to the National Defense Acadamy at the age of 16. I married my wife Savitri when I was 26 years old, served in the Indian army for 47 years, retired at age 65, and for the past three years have been a grieving widower.

On Bumper Tambola Sunday Night, I ate my dinner and went to sleep at 9 p.m. I keep no live-in help but you can check with the security guards in the building. I woke up at 5 a.m. as is my long-established practice and went for my daily morning jog.

I do not know the man Leo Matthew at all. Yes, I received a song video from him late last year, but I could make neither head nor tail of it, and so ignored it completely, and soon forgot all about it.

Yes, I did donate Rs 16 lakh, over several years, to the orphanage in Badshahpur, but I donate money to several good causes. I do not like to speak about my charitable works, but I can produce receipts, if required.

I met Ajay Kumar only once, three years ago, when he arrived at the home of his estranged wife, Ganga Kumar, and began physically abusing her, claiming she was having an affair with a rich sahib. As she is alone in the city and considers me a father figure of sorts, she phoned me and I rushed to the spot, slapped the fellow a couple of times to knock some sense into him, then marched him to the police station to give him a good fright. No formal charges were pressed, however, because Ganga did not want to destroy his life. I somehow got the impression that both husband and wife were eager to avoid the police. He disappeared thereafter and I have neither seen nor heard from him since. Nor, as far as I know, has she.

There seems to be some sort of convoluted theory doing the rounds that I was the 'rich sahib' having an affair with Ganga. This is a wild fairy tale and completely untrue.

Another wild fairy tale is that I somehow rigged the tambola game on Sunday to start an argument between Mukesh Khurana and Leo Matthew so I could frame Mukesh for Leo's murder. Apparently my motive for doing this was to discredit Mukesh's wife, Urvashi, who is my rival in the Club election, and has publicly accused me of using my position and privilege to force myself upon Ganga. Needless to say, this last is also completely untrue.

Yes, I do have an army revolver like the one found in the kitchen garden, but I misplaced it some time ago.

Anybody who knows the DTC intimately, knows that our late gardener Ram Gopal aka Guppie Ram was a phenku of the highest order, always telling vastly exaggerated tales for his own amusement. He probably found a few British-era bones in the garden, and spun an elaborate and entertaining story around them. I understand forensics is an inexact science and dating bones is problematic.

I suspect that the Opposition parties, working in tandem with Pakistani agents, are trying to discredit me because my role in the surgical strikes has made me so popular. It is their stated official position that the surgical strikes never happened at all, and now they are trying to embroil me in this DTC case simply because I happen to be a member of the Club.

As for me, my commitment to my men, the army and the nation speaks for itself. I am sure that our excellent police will absolve me eventually. Jai Hind.

END OF INTERVIEW.

The watchmen outside the Khurana residence in sleepy, leafy Panchsheel Park don't quite know what to make of the twisted, satyr-like figure who has emerged suddenly from an autorickshaw to loudly demand entrance into the bungalow within.

Exuding a powerful smell which makes them all wrinkle their noses, he leans heavily on one crutch while waving the other about like a weapon, and shouts in a thin but extremely carrying voice.

'I'm here to meet the beautiful Urvashi Khurana! She needs to explain why she doesn't love us any more! Let me in! Let me in or I will expose how the rich mistreat the crippled classes! Or—' His eyes light up suddenly. 'Even better ... I will expose *myself!*'

Dropping one crutch, he starts to fumble with the front of his pants.

'Oye, bhikari!' says one watchman. 'Keep your pants on! This is a decent neighbourhood!'

'Who're you calling a beggar?' demands the interloper, one hand poised upon his crotch.

'Nobody,' the other watchman replies hastily. 'Here, take ten rupees and git. You can't show us anything we haven't seen before anyway!'

'Who is it, Rambahadur?' Urvashi's exquisite voice speaks suddenly through the intercom. 'Who is making so much noise outside?'

Rambahadur wipes his forehead. 'Madam ji, it seems to be a crippled gent—'

Hearing Urvashi's voice, the visitor hobbles up to the security camera. 'It's me, Urvashi!' he shouts shrilly. 'Leo's friend! From Badshahpur! We sat together at the funeral, remember!'

He licks his lips and peers into the camera, an ingratiating smile upon his face.

There is a long pause.

Then Urvashi speaks crisply. 'Let him in.'

A few minutes later, an impassive manservant lets a visibly triumphant Randy Rax into the Khuranas' tastefully done-up living room. Urvashi is seated on a wicker chaise lounge, dressed in her usual flowing white, Lahore-chic outfits.

'Hello, Rakesh,' she smiles pleasantly. 'How have you been? Missing your friend?'

He stares at her, gulping unattractively. 'Yes,' he manages to say finally.

She gestures towards a comfortable couch. 'Do sit down! What will you drink? Or eat? Or both?'

He lowers himself awkwardly into the seat, throwing his crutches down beside him. 'Coffee,' he says hoarsely. 'And biscuits.' Then he specifies challengingly. '*Jim-Jam* biscuits.'

She gives a tinkling laugh. 'Well, I'm not sure we have that exact brand, but we'll organize some jammy cookies for you.'

She issues some instructions to the hovering manservant, then turns her full attention to Rax. 'Now tell me, what is troubling you? Why have you made the long trip from Sohna Road to meet me?'

Rax executes a theatrical little double take. 'You know where I live?'

'Oh yes,' Urvashi replies serenely. 'But tell me what the problem is?'

Randy Rax struggles visibly to hang onto his obnoxiousness in the face of so much graciousness.

'*You're* the one with the problem,' he manages to spit out, finally, coarsely. 'Not me!'

Urvashi's eyebrows rise. 'How so?'

He grimaces oddly, eyes darting from here to there, looking at the various expensive objects d'art in the room, the discreetly flashing diamonds at her ears, throat and fingers, the huge lawn visible from the French windows.

'It is easier for a camel to pass through the eye of a needle than for a rich man to enter the Kingdom of God. That's from the Bible!'

'That's very wise. And true.'

'It's the *Bible*. Of course it's wise and true! It's the world's biggest bestseller! Outsells Agatha Christie, J.K. Rowling and *Lady Chatterly's Lover – combined*!'

'I'm not surprised.'

He gives a low moan and starts to sway back and forth. 'Where are my Jim-Jams?'

'Coming,' she says composedly. 'You will enjoy them, you

know, my chef is quite excellent.' She smiles at him kindly, sympathetically.

He shivers visibly under her gaze. 'You're pretending to be nice.'

'Why would I pretend? Tell me, why did you say that I have stopped loving you?'

His face gives an odd sort of spasm. 'Vicky told me you've stopped donating to Badshahpur Children's Village. How are they going to manage if you don't provide for them?'

'That's not true,' she says. 'I've been giving them money for the last twenty years. Much before Father Victor Emmanuel's time. Why would I stop now? Ah, here come your coffee and biscuits!'

Rax looks at the pretty tray, steaming coffee in spotless white china, a floral Wedgwood plate piled high with gorgeous raspberry jam tarts, and produces a sound which is half-giggle, half-snarl.

'Those look like titties!'

'Well, don't hold their looks against them,' she says humorously. 'They taste really good – and that's the main thing, isn't it.'

She proffers the plate to him invitingly.

Rax takes a cookie warily. 'Not laced with Pinko Hathni, are they?'

She gives an incredulous little laugh. 'Why would I want to poison you?'

He bites into the cookie, then starts to rock back and forth again, his head cocked to one side, his eyes mischievous, and curiously birdlike.

In a thin mocking voice, he starts to sing.

'You think, your secret's safe,
You think you left no trace ...'
You think that no one knows,
You're smelling ... like a rose ...'

⚫———⚫

Chrysanthemum's night range for men is beautifully designed. There is one navy-blue dressing gown with white piping, in particular, which has been hailed as a classic by all the fashion magazines. Unfortunately, when Mukesh Khurana wears it, he looks rather like an unappetizing extra from the *Star Wars* movies.

Thus attired, he emerges from his spacious Italian-marbled bathroom and smiles at his wife, reclining on the gorgeous Malaysian cane bed with a magazine.

'Drink, Urvashi?'

She shakes her head, smilingly. 'No, thanks. How was your workout?'

'Excellent. That Thampi really is a very good trainer.'

'I'm so glad.'

Her voice is a little subdued. Mukesh looks around.

'How was your day?'

She puts away her magazine and slides lower under the covers. 'Oh! Very uneventful. Nothing happened.'

He looks a little nonplussed. 'So I'll just have my drink alone then?'

'Please do,' she murmurs, slipping on an eye mask. 'I have yoga at five ... Good night.'

He stares down at her motionless figure for a while, then nods, tightens the cord of his dressing gown a little, and pads out into the living room. He is preparing his nightcap when the security guards buzz from the gate.

'Sir, visitor.'

Mukesh peers into the security camera and recognizes the bulldoggy visage of Club Secretary Srivastava. Uttering a small exclamation of surprise, he presses the speak button.

'Haan, send him in.'

A few moments later, a manservant ushers the old man in.

'Evening, sir,' the secretary says stiffly, hovering in the doorway.

'Come, come, Srivastava,' Mukesh says with slightly patronizing affability.

'I need to speak to you urgently.'

'Arrey, I was at the club only!' Mukesh replies. 'With Thampi – you could have come in there. Why to drive all this way?'

The old man reddens. 'It's a confidential matter, sir.'

Mukesh gestures towards a plush seat – the same one Randy Rax had occupied not long ago.

'Please sit!' He points to his glass. 'Drink piyoge?'

'No, thank you, sir.'

An awkward silence ensues.

Clearly Srivastava is having starting trouble. Khurana sips his drink, and seeks about for something to say.

'Toh, how's the staff taken the discovery of the second dead body?' he hazards finally.

Srivastava unfreezes.

'Not very well, sir. The kitchen garden is right behind the office block, and quite a few of them have started saying the place is haunted.'

'Bakwas!' Khurana says roundly. 'That body's been pushing up beetroots there for the last three years and nobody breathed a word about hauntings, and now suddenly the area is infested with ghosts aur kya kya!'

Srivastava responds to this by lapsing back into an incommunicative silence.

Khurana stares at him mystified, then has another go at goading him into speech.

'So Srivastava, why you're changing sides? All this time you were supporting General Mehra. You even got me insulted me in front of the whole club on Tambola Sunday! Then why this sudden visit to the humble Khurana home?'

Srivastava presses his lips in a thin line. Then, his voice heavy with disapproval, he says, 'General Mehra has … *betrayed* my trust, sir … I was sadly misled.'

'Really?' Mukesh leans forwards, his navy-blue robe spilling open a little to flash flesh nobody wants to see. 'I thought you were a great fan of his!'

The bulldoggy old face starts to purple unattractively. 'We have a tradition at the DTC sir, that *every* year during the Bumper Tamblola, one line is always won by a proxy of the administrative staff, and all of us divide those winnings amongst ourselves.'

Mukki puts down his glass. 'Kya, kya? You have tradition that *what?*'

With even greater stateliness, the old man repeats his little speech. 'A *tradition*, sir, that every year during the tamblola, one line – top, middle or bottom – is always won by a proxy of the administrative staff, and all of us divide those winnings amongst ourselves.'

'A tradition of cheating and stealing then.' Khurana looks triumphantly vindicated. 'I knew it! Tum log rigging karte ho! You people are corrupted!'

The old man's colour heightens. 'It is a tradition devised by a president far greater than your wife can ever be, sir. To compensate for the meagreness of our salaries and show how much we are valued by all members of the Club.'

'Balls!' Khurana breathes hard. 'You buggers are well-paid enough. You have job security. Many of you are on the take for all sorts of things. You've no reason to rig the tambola and pocket one large prize every year except plain greed. How do you do it anyway?'

'It's a time-honoured system,' Srivastava explains with dignity. 'I select a particular ticket, abstract the five numbers printed on it from the ninety-nine inside the wire-frame drum, and slip them up my sleeve.'

'So *that's* why you've always resisted an upgrade to an electronic system. I thought you read out the numbers simply because you fancied the sound of your own voice.'

Srivastava ignores this snide remark. 'Then, during the tambola, I let one ball slide down from my sleeve every now and then, and announce it. A family member of one of the admin staff is in the audience with the selected ticket, and once all five numbers have been called, he claims it.'

'Bada fine-tuned system lagta hai,' Mukesh says sourly. 'Can I ask how the winnings are divided?'

'According to years of service,' the secratary replies smoothly. 'With the longest serving employees getting the most, and the newest the least.'

'So you oldies get the makkhan-malai.' Mukesh snorts, unimpressed. 'So what happened this year?' Did one of the youngsters, unhappy with his meagre share, go bleating about this grand tradition to somebody. Whom?'

'General Mehra,' Srivastava admits sulkily. 'He came to me and said he had heard of our er … little system, but was quite happy to turn a deaf ear to it – he has quite a sense of humour, General Mehra! If he became president. He said, however, that Mrs Urvashi Khurana was not similarly hearing impaired. When I pointed that she would never find out about the system, he told me that it would be his *duty* to inform her of this highly irregular practice if she won.'

'He threatened you.' Mukesh laughs coarsely. 'Serves you right.'

Srivastava's face spasms at this crude remark but he manages to continue his narration solemnly.

'As you say, sir. Then he made a suggestion which he said could help us both. You print *two* winning tickets for the middle line this year, he said. Give one to your proxy and one to Khurana – he's sure to make an ugly scene, and it will make him look ridiculous, which will help my election prospects greatly. Well sir, I didn't see any harm in doing this, even if it meant we would probably have to split our winnings with you this year, but when the ugly scene during the tambola lead to a murder the next morning, and plainclothes policemen started swarming the length and breadth of the DTC asking questions—'

'Your neat little scheme came under the police scanner,' Mukesh Khurana concludes grimly. 'Well, well, you definitely got what you deserved, Srivastava! Now why the hell have you come to me?'

The secretary clears his throat. 'I've come to make you an offer, sir.'

Mukesh's jaw sags. 'You! Offering *me* a deal!'

'Yes, sir,' Srivastava says with calm audacity. 'I will come forward and reveal this information about General Mehra coming to me and asking me to set you up if, in return, you promise that there will be no criminal persecution against the admin staff, and our tradition will be allowed to continue once Mrs Khurana is elected president.'

Mukesh is quiet for a long time. He is reluctantly impressed by the working of the old bulldog's mind. Srivastava has figured that his tale will strengthen the case against the general, but could potentially land him into trouble as well, so he's figured out a way to wriggle out of the mess.

He cocks an eyebrow at the old man. 'Got any proof?'

'I have the entire conversation recorded sir. I switched on the audio recorder the *moment* it got interesting.'

Mukesh Khurana's utters a short neigh of laugher. 'You're a sly saanp.'

A complacent expression settles on the secretary's face. 'I am just very aware of my responsibilities as Club Secretary, sir. I am in a sense, the *custodian* of the grand traditions and great history of the DTC.'

Khurana purses his lips. 'Yeh toh *too much* ho gaya, Srivastava!'

'No, sir,' the old man maintains doggedly. 'I perform exactly the same tasks Bhatti sir used to before he retired from his position as home secretary. Ministers come and go, but the bureaucrats remain forever, don't they, sir?'

'You're a sly snake,' Mukki repeats, breathing hard. 'Don't *ever* try to daso my wife or I will cook you in a Korean sauce and feed you to the peacocks in the mango trees of your precious DTC.'

'Yes, sir,' the old man replies unblinkingly. 'Do we have a deal, sir?'

Khurana sits back, and stares down at his glass, swilling its contents. This is an interesting development which can – and should – be milked well.

He nods curtly. 'We have a deal.'

'Dammit, PK, your team spent the whole day eating popcorn and binge-watching that damn footage like it was Ramanand Sagar's *Ramayan!* You must have found *something* useful, yaar!' Bhavani demands cantankerously.

Shalini, reading a book beside him in their bed, looks up warily.

Earnest squawking noises are emerging from Bhavani's phone. They go on for a while. He nods, frowning.

'And that's it? Nothing else?'

The squawking is shorter this time and regretful in tone.

Bhavani cuts the call and tosses the phone away moodily.

Shalini puts down her book. 'You're like a bear with a sore head,' she says. 'You need to eat less salt and drink more water.'

He rumples his grey hair unhappily ...

'We thought Leo's hard disk – the one we found in the Hayabusa – would give us some more leads, but there's nothing useful on it!'

'*Nothing?*'

He throws up his hands. 'Nothing that tells us anything we don't already know! The general coming out of Ganga's house late in the night, looking besotted. Aryaman describing what mixing alcohol with drugs feels like. But mostly just videos of Leo and Urvashi dancing.'

She says tentatively, 'So maybe the general *did* do it, Bhavani?'

He shakes his head. 'The general is nat guilty. That gun is just too damn convenient. It has been planted, afterwards, just to confuse us.'

'Okay ...' She hesitates, ' So who do you think would do something like that?'

'Everybody,' he replies promptly. 'You know we always suspect *everybody*, Shalu. But right now, after the discovery that Ganga's husband, Ajay Kumar, was actually *dealing* to the TVVS kids, Aryaman Aggarwal seems to be leading the pack.'

'Urvashi?'

He shakes his head. 'The dancing on those tapes is pretty sexy, but it is just dancing. Nothing he could have blackmailed her about.'

She stares down at her fingers, thinking. 'What about these youngsters of yours?' she asks. 'Your Kashi and Bambi duo? Didn't she say she has a stalker? Her supposedly dead fiancé?'

He yawns tiredly. 'That is a long shot. But yes, it could fit into this set-up. Matlab, if we were a billionaire with a scarred, psychotic son on the loose, we would pull whatever strings we could to get somebody else convicted for his crime!'

'So you think this Anshul is really alive and killing admirers of Bambi?' she asks sceptically.

'She saw an eye in the wall,' he reminds her.

'It's too ... *fantastic*, Bhavani. People would have noticed some heavily scarred man limping about the DTC, surely!'

'Agreed.' He sighs. 'But we're on a morning–evening flight to Kolkata tomorrow to meet this Anshul's father. We weren't sure he would speak to us – he's a big man – but he agreed at once.'

'And Kashi?'

'What possible motive could he possibly have, Shalu?'

'Well, you *say* he has a girlfriend, but he seems obsessed with Bambi. Maybe, if he felt somebody was trying to harm her, like this Leo, for example, then he could've—'

His phone beeps. Once. Then twice. Then several times in succession.

'That's a woman for sure.' He sighs wryly.

'Sexist!' She pulls a face, clambers off the bed and tosses him his phone. 'Dekh lo.'

ACP Brownie!

I just read the article about Ganga's husband Ajay Kumar being the dead man in the beetroot patch three years ago, and I remembered something VERY EXCITING and IMPORTANT

Oh my God!

I might have just solved your whole case!!!!

And revealed a DOUBLE MURDERER!!!

But it's all very very sad, for a VERY CLOSE FRIEND OF MINE ... so perhaps it is not so much exciting as TRAGIC!

Katoch also says it is my DUTY as a citizen to tell you.

Kyonki honestly, I am worried ki I will become too unpopular in my friend circle for doing this. Especially as none of the ladies like Mehra and my evidence (OMG EVIDENCE!!) will prove that he didn't do it after all!

But murder is murder and duty is duty. Bechara Leo.

> So please meet me at the DTC tomorrow! I do Zumba with Thinsuk in the morning now – he's not very good, but what to do?

> So 7 a.m.?

> Actually, let's meet in the Taj coffee shop. I don't want anybody to see me with you. It will be open at 7 a.m.

> This is Cookie Katoch, by the way.

> Good night.

Silently, he passes the phone to his wife. She reads, then quirks a teasing eyebrow.

'ACP Brownie?'

'Shalu, please.' Bhavani goes rather pink. 'Focus on the important thing!'

She shrugs. 'She seems to think she's cracked it.'

'Yes,' he replies. 'If this were a murder mystery novel somebody would definitely bump her off tonight.'

Shalini snorts. 'Not in her big, fat, south Delhi bungalow with security guards outside! And there's a gallant Mr Katoch in the picture too!'

'That is true.' Bhavani takes his phone back. 'Well, well, seven suits us actually – we can proceed to the airport from the Taj itself.'

The Taj Lobby is full of pink Oriental lilies,' his wife says wistfully. 'Oh, you must order a good breakfast and charge the department!' She smiles, 'Send the bill to Buckingham palace!'

He looks at her blankly.

'It's from *My Fair Lady*, Bhavani.'

'O really?' he says vaguely. 'Let us hope the "something" she has "remembered" will turn out to actually be useful ...'

14

Flames & Flowers

'Alcohol is a terrible thing,' Cookie Katoch says with a pious little shudder. 'I toh never touch a drop!'

Coming from somebody who was spectacularly inebriated the first time they met, this is pretty rich. But then, Cookie Katoch is pretty rich too – and the rich are permitted their pretty little lies.

'So great of you,' he murmurs politely

She feels the need to explain. 'I only take alcohol if I've had a terrible shock.'

'Haan, then toh it is *must*!' Bhavani agrees at once. 'All the best doctors prescribe alcohol for shock.'

Having cleared up this point, Cookie Katoch chugs down the fresh sweet-lime juice she has poured three sachets of Stevia into, then leans in conspiratorially, spilling out from several places in her pink velour tracksuit. With her chubby face, high ponytail and massively oversized D&G sunglasses, she looks rather like a Punjabi Powerpuff girl.

'Katoch is terrible with alcohol. He doesn't know when to stop, and then, once he's drunk, he insists on driving ... Even if the driver is there! We've had a few *ghastly* experiences, driving back from parties and all ...'

Bhavani nods along, giving her his full attention, wondering where this story is going.

'And so I decided, when the invite came for Bambi and Anshul's engagement party at the DTC, in the middle of the foggiest month of the year, that the best thing to do, because Pankaj Todi and Katoch are such thick friends, and they were all *sure* to get roaring drunk that night, was to book a guest cottage for the night at the Club only!'

Bhavani pricks up his ears. 'O really.'

She beams at him, nodding gleefully. '*Haan!* Now you're suddenly looking alive, ACP Brownie! Did you think I called you here just because I have a crush on you?'

Bhavani's homely features redden. 'Yes, mada— I mean no, madam!'

She chuckles. 'I'm just teasing. Where was I? Oh my God, this is *too* exciting, but scary also – my cheeks are getting so hot, uff!' She presses them with the back of her hands, then beckons a hovering waiter. 'Excuse me, beta, come here! Can you get me glass of really, really *cold* water? Thank you! So, ACP, like I was saying, Katoch and I took Guest Cottage No. 4, I think. We went in there around two in the morning, and then at around three, when I got up to go to the bathroom, I heard people arguing very loudly outside my window. Very, *very* loudly. It was actually scary – so I moved the curtains, very little bit, and I looked out into the parking lot, and of course there was so much swirling fog … Ek toh this Delhi ka pollution na, but through it all, *I saw them!*'

'Who, madam?' His voice is perfect – interested, but not intrusive.

She looks around furtively, then removes her sunglasses to reveal huge, unslept-looking eyes, part-worried, part-feverishly excited. '*Him* only, Ajay Kumar, Ganga ka husband! I recognized him in the wedding picture that was printed in that article! I've a very good eye for faces, because I'm an artist … But you know that, you came for my Shivling exhibition. My company's called—'

'ShivBling. Yes, madam,'

'It was *him* only, pukka-promise, with his French beard and his dark circles and his pink flashing gums! He was shouting, and the other fellow was shouting too. Some dhakkam dhukki also happened, and it looked like it was going to turn into mukka-mukki, which was *very* interesting, but it was also a very, very cold night, and I wasn't wearing very much, because Katoch and I were … er …'

'*Yes*, madam.'

She smiles at him gratefully. '*So* intelligent, you are. So like I was saying, I shut the curtain and got quickly back under the warm razai with my warm husband!'

'And, madam, you didn't say – did you recognize the other person also? Who was it that was arguing with Ajay Kumar?'

'Oh, didn't I say?' She looks around furtively, then leans in even closer, and whispers. 'Actually I'm not really surprised, because he was always a *strange* child – I took him to Funky Orbit once, when he was very little, along with my son and some of their friends and he *exposed* himself to me *quite blatantly* inside the red twister tunnel. I was horrified – but too scared to tell his mother, because, baba re, she's the type who *never* blames her child for *anything*! Unlike me – I toh am *very* strict! Whenever people do shikayat of *my* children, I always give them *two* tight slaps before even asking for their version of the story!'

'That is excellent parenting, madam, I'm sure your children love you very much.'

She gives a little wriggle of pride. 'Oh yes! They're well settled – my daughter's a banker in New York and my son's an engineer in Seattle. We're looking for a nice girl for him but ...'

She trails off and sips the iced water which has just arrived at the table.

'Anyway, I had started taking a video, but I stopped because Katoch was calling me back to bed. Still, it's long enough to see the two faces quite clearly! It was on my old phone, we had to stay up till three last night to retrieve it, but I have it here.'

She slides a phone triumphantly across the table.

Bhavani beams. 'That is *excellent* work, madam! You should be in the police force!'

'Hain na?' She beams back. 'I'd look so good in uniform!'

Bhavani pushes aside the mental image that has sprung unbidden to his mind. 'Madam, please, in your own words, *who* is Ajay Kumar arguing with this video?'

'Oh, didn't I tell you?'

She leans forward, beckoning him to lean forward too. Their heads meet over the Taj's beautifully polished silver sugar pot.

'Arya!' she says in an appalled whisper. 'Aryaman Aggarwal, my friend Roshni's son. I don't know what the fight was about, but it looks, doesn't it, like they had some argument that night, and Arya killed Ajay Kumar, and buried him in the composting pit?'

As Bhavani drives to the airport, deep in thought, he gets an SMS alerting him to a flight delay of half an hour. On a sudden impulse, he directs his car towards the DTC.

A few people are browsing the Daily Needs when he walks in, but Ganga seems free. She sits very straight behind the counter, sari meticulously ironed, pleated and pinned, hair pulled back into its smooth plait with not a strand out of place. Bhavani wonders what Shalu would make of her and decides that she would declare her prim.

Her large eyes widen in her glowing brown face when she sees him.

'Good morning,' he says in a low conversational voice. 'We wanted to pick up some apples. They look so fresh.'

She looks slightly confused. 'Oh but aren't you ...' She pauses, then continues haltingly, 'I mean, you're the police, aren't you, sir?'

He nods. 'We are ACP Bhavani Singh. You have met some people from our team.'

'Yes.' She hesitates. 'Sir, you can only shop here with a DTC card. We can't accept cash payments.'

'Good.' Bhavani beams genially, not at all put out. 'We will save some money. And not have to lug apples all the way to Kolkata.'

'You're going to Kolkata just now?' Her large eyes grow scared. 'Why?'

Now what is there about Kolkata to scare this girl? Or is she scared about something else?

'To meet your friend Bambi ji's ex-fiancé's family.' He explains genially. 'But before that we just wanted to chat with you – ask how you were.'

Ganga grows pale and seems to sway.

She says defensively, 'I have already been questioned by your team—'

'No, no, no.' He shakes his head. 'You misunderstand – we just wanted to apologize for how all this must have disrupted your life.'

Her chin rises. 'I'm very well, thank you.'

'And business?'

'Is booming.' Her sweet voice has a bitter edge. 'Everybody wants to have a good look at the woman whose husband was murdered and buried in the kitchen garden by her jealous sixty-plus lover.'

Bhavani looks distressed. 'We are so sorry.'

'Not as sorry as me, I'm sure,' she replies. 'My parents live in a small town in east UP, and even *they* have seen pictures of my husband and me in the newspaper! I may not have great social standing and status like the people who are members of this club, but I *do* have a small circle of relatives and customers! What am I supposed to say to them?'

'We're so sorry,' Bhavani repeats. 'We didn't realize …'

'Why should you?' she says bitterly. 'I'm not a particularly important person, why should I be on your radar?'

'The police exists to protect everybody, not just VIPs,' Bhavani replies, genuinely stung by this remark. 'Those journalists had no business printing your wedding photo. Especially when nothing has actually been *proved* yet! That the body is hundred per cent your husband, Ajay Kumar, we mean! Perhaps he will see the news in the paper and phone you?'

Ganga snorts. 'Not a *chance*! If anything, he will stay in hiding if it means making me suffer!' She throws up her hands as she speaks, hitting the lapiz lazuli bowl full of white jasmine. It starts to spin, and she settles it, repeating, more calmly, 'Not a chance.'

'That is *not* very nice,' Bhavani says decidedly, now leaning comfortably against the counter. 'Waise, what kind of a person was he? We apologize for being so curious – but we have two daughters of our own, and we are interested to know why your parents married you to him if he was such a bad lot.'

She laughs bitterly. 'Oh, Ajay Kumar knew how to put on a good act! He had a good job – assistant manager in a nice restaurant in Connaught Place – not a driver or a peon or something dead-end like that! And always smartly dressed. And spoke such good English. He impressed my family good and proper! It was only after I got to the city that I realized how jealous and suspicious he was … how violent, and moody. Bambi didi says he was a sociopath.'

'Was he a big spender?' Bhavani probes casually. 'Generous with money and all?'

She shrugs. 'Sometimes he was very generous, but sometimes he wasn't. I couldn't understand it. Maybe he had another wife, and he was spending on her too? Anything was possible with him, I don't know!'

'You depended on him for money?'

'Initially I did. But then I got a job of my own – cleaning and cooking, a servant's job – but I didn't see any shame in it. I was happy doing that for a while and being independent and sending home money, but then—' Her expressive face clouds over. 'Then *that* soured as well.' She looks up at him, her large, soft eyes kindling. 'Is there something *about* me? Do I send out some *signal?* That it's okay for men to prey on me?'

Bhavani Singh, busy staring down at his knobbly knuckles and radiating sympathy for all he's worth, takes a moment to react to this direct question. And in that moment, Ganga looks beyond him, and her eyes widen as she sees somebody in the doorway.

'Oh!' she says softly.

Urvashi Khurana is standing in the doorway. There is something oddly menacing about her stance today.

'What's going on over here?' she asks sharply, her eyes going from Ganga's expressive face to Bhavani's suddenly wooden one. 'Ganga, are the police troubling you?'

She walks into the store, and Bhavani notices that she doesn't look very well today. There are purplish smudges under the huge, beautiful eyes and the make-up seems to have been applied with a shaky hand. The expensive but airily loose salwar kameez is immaculate, but the pale, pearl coloured

nail polish on two of her nails is actually chipped. Urvashi
Khurana is unravelling fast, decides Bhavani Singh. Why?

'Hello, Urvashi madam,' he says politely.

But she is having none of that.

'You shouldn't be harassing the girl, ACP!' she rebukes
him. 'You shouldn't even be *speaking* to her without a lady
constable present. Surely you're aware of that?'

Bhavani steps away from the counter, speaking placatingly.
'Madam, we are not speaking to her about the murders. We
are just enquiring about her well-being.'

'He came to buy apples,' Ganga tries to explain.

'You are *unbelievably* naive,' Urvashi snaps. Then she turns
to Bhavani. '*Please* don't come in here pretending to buy
apples and acting all fatherly! The girl *already* has a father –
who isn't speaking to her any more, thanks to all these new
reports!'

'But the ACP is *nice*, Urvashi madam!' Ganga says
earnestly.

'You thought the general was nice too,' Urvashi reminds
her bluntly. 'Until you didn't. Then you and Bambi came
crying to me. Now *let* me help.'

Ganga stands back, subdued.

Bhavani, seeing that Urvashi is on edge today, decides to
provoke her while the iron is hot.

'So good you came, because we wanted to ask you
something too, madam,' he says genially. 'How did you
select the proposed location for your rainwater-harvesting
plant? Matlab, why did you want it to be in the kitchen
garden only?'

She gives a light, disbelieving laugh. 'I called in some experts and they chose a spot. There was nothing dodgy about it.'

Bhavani turns the screw a little more. 'It just seems to be too much of a coincidence, madam.'

'*What?*' Her exquisite nostrils flare a little. 'Do speak plainly, ACP.'

He moves about a little, half-shrugging, half-wriggling.

'That you chose the very place where the body was buried. It makes it look like you had some inside information.'

Her lovely eyes kindle.

'And how would I have that?' she asks.

Ganga's head is now turning from one speaker to the other like that of a spectator at a tennis match.

'Madam, you are right. We shouldn't be speaking to you without a lady constable present ...'

Urvashi's ante is fully up now. She slaps the counter top. '*How* would I have that, Bhavani ji?'

'We don't quite know,' he replies steadily. 'But it has worked out very nicely for you, hasn't it? Your husband and you were the top suspects, till the second corpse was found, after which the needle of suspicion shifted neatly to your rival in the election.'

'Perhaps my rival *is* guilty,' she says forcefully.

'What's all this?'

General Mehra has just walked into the Daily Needs too, dressed in checked bermudas and a firozi-blue cardigan that brings out the hazel of his eyes.

Wah, Bhavani thinks resignedly, kya timing hai! This situation is swiftly descending into pure farce. How we wish we didn't have a flight to catch!

'It is nothing,' he says genially. 'We were just leaving.'

Mehra points an accusing finger at Urvashi. '*She* was saying something about me! I *heard* her!'

'I was saying you're an unprincipled, lecherous ass,' Urvashi retorts sweetly. 'That's all.'

Ganga gasps, then giggles nervously. Around them, the entire store goes very silent.

'Excuse me?' Mehra walks right up to Urvashi, his eyes bulging with disbelief.

'But you are inexcusable,' she flashes back coolly; her eyes burning as brightly as coals in her lovely translucent face.

His jaw sags. Foam starts to gather at the corners of his mouth. 'Whuh … what the hell is this rubbish!' he roars thickly, looking around the store to see how many people are watching. 'I will haul you up before the core committee for this!'

'Oh shut *up*, Mehra,' she says contemptuously. 'I just have to tell them about the stunt you tried to pull with Srivastava and they'll bar you from the Club, along with your two sons who don't even *talk* to you any more!'

A low, cautious whoop sounds from one of the aisles behind them. Mehra's face purples.

'Who told y— I deny … I will …' He takes a hasty step towards her, clenching and unclenching his hands.

Bhavani steps nimbly into the middle. 'Please, general sa'ab, keep your cool.'

Behra Mehra's eyes bulge. 'ACP, I am *perfectly* capable of keeping my cool! I have commanded operations that require split-second decision-making in the *thick* of enemy action!'

'Oh, *enough* of your stupid little war stories,' Urvashi says curtly. '*I* have pushed out a baby without any painkillers and without any fuss, while there were rioters at our door and the entire city was burning!'

More whoops sound from the aisles behind them. An unseen female voice starts to chant.

'Vote for? Urvashi!'
'Vote for? Urvashi!'
'Vote for? Urvashi!'

Urvashi bites her lip, flushing, then smiles and bows to her unseen audience.

'Thank you.'

Thoroughly routed, Behra Mehra turns on his heel and flees the store with as much dignity as he can summon.

The Poddars' white-pillared bungalow in Alipore is set far back from the main road. The driveway is imposing and the garden beautifully lush – ringed by a high wall and topped off with jagged bits of broken glass.

Bhavani, who is having a very eventful day, smoothens his economy-travel rumpled clothes and regards the imposing gates with a fair amount of trepidation.

The Poddars prefer to keep a low profile, but they are an incredibly wealthy family, almost billionaires, with fingers in over half-a-dozen pies, and connections by marriage to some of the richest families in India. If their son and heir, presumed dead, were alive and running around murdering his ex-fiancée's paramours, they would have immediately, ruthlessly, suppressed all news of it. Pulling strings in New Delhi's Crime Branch, and pinning a crime on a mere general would be a piece of cake for their dirty tricks department.

His chief's word echoes in his ears.

'For heaven's sake, keep it *nice*, Bhavani. You will have to tread very, *very* carefully. These Poddars are not people at whose homes we can just show up, flash a police ID and say ki hain-hain-hain we are investigating a crime, please cooperate.'

A man dressed in a spotless white safari suit opens the door and looks at the chunky fellow in the crumpled clothes inquiringly.

'We have come from Delhi,' Bhavani repeats the same thing he has explained at the gate, 'to meet Shri Arihant Poddar. He is expecting us.'

A scented, white wet towel is presented to him with a low bow. Bhavani wipes his hands thoroughly, and divested off common germs, is led into a large, sunny room that looks out onto the front lawn.

'Sir aaschen,' says the man in the white safari suit, and withdraws with another of one of his low bows.

Bhavani looks around at the plump, upholstered furniture, and finally picks a large wingchair that seems to have a hard seat. Sitting down, he finds himself facing a large oil painting of a laughing, well-built, young man with broad shoulders and a deep cleft in his chin, dressed in mountaineering gear, standing against a stunning vista of snow-capped peaks.

'Anshul,' he murmurs softly as his eyes scan the expensive, gilt-framed painting critically.

Bhavani's respect for Pankaj Todi and his kleptomanic wife rises: they had definitely arranged a spectacular match for their only daughter.

He has looked Anshul Poddar up online, and the painting seems to be a faithful rendition of the original. The artist (Bhavani recognizes the signature in the corner as being that of a famous Padma Shri awardee, and nominated member of the Rajya Sabha) has captured not just the setting, clothes and features, but a remarkable amount of personality as well. Anshul Poddar seems ready to stride out of the painting to shake hands with Bhavani. His eyes ablaze with the joy of being alive, the hint of arrogance in the tilt of his chin, this is a man who knows exactly how attractive he is.

He was a little vain. He talked a lot about how good-looking our children would be. If he got ... burnt ... or scarred very badly, or became crippled in some way so that he couldn't climb mountains any more, or do any physical activity, it could have destroyed his mind.

There are several framed pictures below the portrait. One of them is a laughing candid photo of Bambi and Anshul. She is wearing the gold-and-yellow lehenga she had described to Bhavani, and Anshul is tucking a cluster of white roses behind her ear, into the loose waves of her soft, brown hair. They are both staring into each other's eyes, oblivious of the camera.

Kashi was right, Bhavani Singh thinks as he gets up to study the picture more closely, they do look like they're made for each other. Very discreetly he turns the picture around. There is a monogrammed label at the back: Flames&Flowers – Your fairytale Indian wedding.

'ACP Singh?'

It is a very soft voice, but powerful too, the voice of a man who never has to speak loudly because everybody always listens to him. It makes Bhavani turn around at once.

'Sir!'

The older Poddar is an aged version of the young man in the painting. The face is puffier, the lips thinner, and the hair grey and thinning at the temples.

Arihant Poddar gestures towards the chairs. 'Please.'

They both sit down, facing each other. Poddar is all polite attention, but it has been clearly communicated to Bhavani that the great man can spare only fifteen minutes. He has to make this quick.

'Young Bambi Todi,' he begins without preamble, 'has been receiving letters from somebody claiming to be your son.'

Arihant Poddar had been leaning forward, one arm resting on the arm rest of his chair, but at this revelation he seems to slump slightly. Taking off his rimless glasses, he massages his eyes, then sighs.

'Not again.'

'Sir?' It is now Bhavani's turn to register shock. 'She has … We mean to say, this has happened *before*?'

Arihant Poddar nods. 'She's a lovely girl, Bambi. We all fell in love with her the first time we met. Anshul was *immediately* smitten. Of course – I can be frank with you without sounding crass, I hope, ACP Singh – he had received several, far grander offers, the daughters of billionaires, of superstars. Anshul, with his height and physical attractiveness, his easy charm and, of course, our family background, was extremely sought after. But he found all the girls we introduced him to ... to be bland, boring, conventional. Just when we had started to despair of ever finding a girl to be our daughter-in-law and fill this house with joy and warmth, along came little Bambi.' Arihant Poddar's stern face softens. 'She wasn't like the other girls. She was razor smart for one, with a bloody good head for business. She was funny and warm and, most importantly for Anshul, whose one demand in a life partner was that "she must be able to camp with me high up in the mountains in a tent, and bathe with ice cold, melted glacier water", she wasn't namby-pamby in the least.'

'Why did you say "not again", sir?' Bhavani prods, very conscious of his fifteen-minute deadline.

Arihant Poddar sighs. 'You must be aware of the details of the tragedy. Neither Bambi nor my wife took the news of the accident well. Fresh from the engagement party, with the mehendi they had applied that day still blooming on their hands, they both went through a stage of complete denial. And when they found out that there was a *little bit* of a grey area – that there had been thirty people on that doomed bus but only twenty-two bodies were recovered from the water, they decided that Anshul had somehow survived. For the next three days, they kept feeding each other false hope … It was an utterly ghastly situation – I wouldn't wish such a tragedy on my worst enemy.'

He goes quiet for a while. Bhavani, on tenterhooks, resists the urge to prod him again.

'Finally, Pankaj Todi and I decided that enough was enough. There was no way Anshul could have survived the accident – the bus had rolled over twice, exploded, then plunged into the roaring river. The bodies were all so battered and dismembered that it was hard to tell their gender, let alone their identity. We zeroed in on one body – a young man, six feet tall, fair, muscular – and identified him as Anshul.'

He pauses, his eyes far away, seeing things Bhavani cannot.

'It *was* Anshul,' he says strongly. 'As a father, I felt it in my bones. I remember the moment I held my baby boy in my arms for the first time, I had such a strong sense of confirmation then! When I saw that battered body, I got the same sense of confirmation. It was a soul recognition. It *was* him. Not everybody is blessed with a long life, and Anshul's, though short, was *complete*. He had lived a full life – adventurous and successful. He had found true love, bid goodbye to all of us on that final night, and embarked upon a new adventure. Except the journey he had embarked upon turned out to be far greater than the one he had anticipated. Pankaj Todi and I identified him, cremated him, and brought the ashes back to Delhi.'

He pauses, then continues.

'We all travelled together as a family to immerse the ashes at Benaras. After the prayers were said, and we sailed upon the holy Ganges at dawn, I thought both my wife and Bambi had found their closure. They certainly seemed to settle down, stop railing against the fates, and accept that a terrible, random tragedy had ripped apart the fabric of their lives, and slowly, very slowly, come to terms with their grief.'

'That's good,' Bhavani murmurs. 'You handled it brilliantly, sir, so sensitively, so correctly.'

Poddar gives short, mirthless laugh. 'Hardly correctly!'

'Why do you say that?' Bhavani asks, confused.

Poddar raises pained eyes to Bhavani's. 'My wife still sleeps with a lock of Anshul's hair beneath her pillow. *Every single night.* And if Bambi is "receiving letters" from him, then that means that the poor child has still not found her closure.'

'Meaning?' Bhavani asks, confused.

Arihant Poddar rests both arms on the armrest of his chair and steeples his fingers. 'Don't you see, ACP Singh? It is Bambi's deepest desire that Anshul be alive. Bambi *wants* Anshul to be alive. It is her dearest fantasy. Investigate all you like, but my personal theory is that she's been sending those letters to herself.'

'Well?' the chief demands. 'How did it go?'

Bhavani breathes a heavy sigh. He is sitting outside his departure gate, eating a very soggy mayonnaise sandwich; the flight has been delayed by two hours. 'It turned out to be a bit of a dead end, sir,' he admits.

Squawking noises emanate from the other end. Bhavani winces, holds the phone away from his ear, and continues to chew.

When the sounds die down, he ventures to speak again. 'Sir, Mr Poddar was very cooperative but he seemed to be of the view that ...'

Lowering his voice, he brings his superior up to speed.

'Sending them to herself!' the chief says finally, sounding rather relieved. 'Well, that isn't so bad at all! Much better than having a crippled, demented, billionaire scion on the loose! Do you think that is what she's been doing?'

Bhavani licks the mayonnaise off his fingers. 'Well, as to that, sir, we couldn't say. Of course, her mother *is* a little unbalanced ...'

'So it runs in the family.' His chief sounds quite satisfied. 'Well, well, we did our due diligence, basis this new evidence, and now it's time to put General Mehra away!'

Bhavani registers his protest by keeping quiet. There's no point telling the chief that he has already contacted Flames&Flowers – the wedding planners mentioned on the back of the ornate Bambi–Anshul photograph displayed in the Poddar's living room. He fully intends to commandeer the recording of the entire engagement ceremony, and spend the weekend watching the footage minutely.

'Are you listening, man?'

'Sir, there is still the angle about Ajay Kumar being Aryaman Aggarwal's dealer,' Bhavani replies doughtily. 'And we've made a new discovery as well.'

He briefs the chief about his 7 a.m. encounter with Cookie Katoch.

'This woman's reliable? Not a client of drug dealers herself, is she?'

'She has provided a video recording, sir. And then there're the Khuranas too – Urvashi Khurana has been behaving very oddly lately …'

'They have no *motive*, Bhavani!' the chief interrupts. 'You've found absolutely no evidence of an affair between Urvashi Khurana and the Zumba master, and I doubt the husband, no matter how crazed with jealousy, could have been worked upon to commit a murder without *some* evidence. Even Othello needed to see Desdemona's underwear, or whatever it was, in Cassio's sweaty grasp. In modern parlance that would mean a sex tape at the very least! Besides, didn't you say the Zumba master was having an affair with the Todi girl? *And* with the woman who was making his YouTube videos? How many women could he have been pleasuring at the same time?'

Bhavani, who has wisely used this long speech to finish his sandwich, finally manages gets a word in.

'Sir, *please* can we ask – *why* is everybody so eager to pin this on General Mehra?'

'Nobody's trying to "pin" anything on anyone, Bhavani,' the chief says virtuously. 'I grant that this Aggarwal angle seems worth pursuing, but the Khuranas have no link whatsoever to the older corpse, unlike the general who *definitely* does.'

'Yes, sir. We just feel all angles should be investigated, sir.'

The chief sighs heavily. 'There is only *one* angle here. You're going to have to put Mehra away, you know. Somebody much higher than you and I is moving the pieces.'

Bhavani wipes his hands on the small tissue provided by the sandwich seller. The gesture feels very Pontius Pilate-ish.

'Yes, sir.'

'Don't sulk, Bhavani. *If* you can find any concrete evidence against these others, bring it to me. If you can't, let's just reel Mehra in. With this tambola-rigging evidence in place it should be a piece of cake.'

Flights over the low-pressure area of the Bay of Bengal are notoriously turbulent and Bhavani's is no exception. The aircraft bucks like a bronco bull with hiccups, and he has to grip the arms of his seat to keep himself from being flung about towards either the matronly lady on his left or the skinny teenager on his right, while deeply regretting the mayonnaise-laden sandwich now sitting uneasily in his stomach.

And of course, there's all the turmoil inside his head. When he closes his eyes he can see a tiny Aryaman Aggarwal flashing his privates at Cookie Katoch, the pink flashing gums of Ajay Kumar on his wedding day, Ganga Kumar's blue plate full of jasmine flowers spinning below the statue of Saraswati, a young Urvashi Khurana in the throes of labour, Behra Mehra at the frontline, the Poddars and the Todis taking a boat ride on the Benaras ghats at dawn ...

The feeling that he has articulated to his chief several times comes back to him even more strongly. Somebody is leading the investigation up the garden path – very elegantly, very smartly. This somebody, who thought to obscure the gym camera with a bunch of gas balloons, and to bury an inconvenient body in an already dug up compost pit – is the real killer. *Not* Behra Mehra who is essentially a blunt instrument, but somebody else – with a sharper, subtler mind and, perhaps, some animosity towards the general.

Judging from the scene at the Daily Needs this morning, Mehra isn't too popular anyway …

It *has* to be one of the hotties on the horticulture sub-committee, Bhavani thinks, shifting about in his seat and earning dirty looks from the matronly lady on his left.

Love … and dosti – and equal-equal trust.

Roshni Aggarwal seems a likely candidate, but she is too cold to be friends with old Guppie Ram. No, he is clearly describing a friendlier person, a *warmer* person, a person who inspires loyalty!

Urvashi Khurana fits the profile of the killer, but she seems to have no motive. No matter how hard Bhavani and Padam dig, they can find no deep dark secret in either her life or her husband's. None of Leo's many camera recordings feature her doing anything that crosses the line. The Khuranas – father, mother and the two daughters (whom Roshni Aggarwal had described rather uncharitably as buffaloes swathed in Chantilly lace) – seem to have led an entirely blameless life.

The plane hits another air pocket and everybody gasps as weightlessness sucks at their belly. Bhavani's chunky body rises a few inches into the air inside its belted seat, then lands back with jarring thud, and just like that several pieces fall into place inside his head with the dramatic *ka-ching!* of a slot machine hitting jackpot.

He sits riveted in his seat, a little thrill running right through his square, stolid frame.

Of course! There it is. Right before his nose. The only possible explanation.

He has finally divined Urvashi Khurana's 'secret'.

15

Killer on a Hat-Trick

'What d'you mean I've been writing them to myself? Are you frickking *insane?*' Bambi Todi demands of ACP Bhavani Singh at her residence on Aurganzeb Road the next day.

He sighs.

'Bambi ji … please, we are very close to cracking the case. In fact, we will go so far as to declare it already cracked. All we need to do now is tie up some loose ends. Pardon us for saying this, but you have actually been wasting taxpayers' money and our time with all this childish letter-writing. Do you know we had to travel to *Kolkata* to talk to Shri Poddar?'

She looks at him in complete horror. 'What d'you mean you've cracked it? How could you have cracked it without finding out if these letters are from Anshul or not?'

Bhavani sighs again. 'We have spoken *personally* to Shri Poddar. Face to face. We have collected handwriting samples of Shri Anshul from the house in Alipore, and had them analysed by handwriting experts. The writing is *nat at all* similar to the letters you have shared.'

She stares at him like she's talking to a moron. 'But the injuries could have altered his handwriting! Maybe he writes with his left hand now!'

Bhavani regards her with a mixture of exasperation and pity. 'Anshul Poddar is dead and cremated, Bambi ji. Please make your peace with that.'

'But I'm being stalked!' she says as tears fill her eyes and stream unchecked down her face. 'I'm being followed! I can *feel* it!'

But Bhavani just shakes his head.

Then, as she continues to stare at him in angry disbelief, he slides a pen and pad towards her. 'Write down something here, for the handwriting experts. Ideally the text of one of the letters you received. We are sure you know them by heart.'

Bambi dashes the tears from her face, gives him an angry, fulminating look, then gets to her feet and flounces out of the room.

———

'It's weak, Bhavani.'

'What are you saying, sir? We are nat saying it is the perfect solution, but it is worth investigating!'

The chief shakes his head gravely. 'No, no, no. All these … theories of yours … are too airy-fairy, and not grounded in any kind of *solid* evidence! Here we *have* solid evidence! There is a *revolver* found buried with the victim. A revolver with one bullet missing. Mehra's revolver. Ajay Kumar's body. *And* from Srivastava's phone recording, we know Mehra was trying to incriminate Khurana! It is an open and shut case!'

Bhavani, mindful of the first of his four tenets – that violence is futile – nods calmly and attempts a reasoned reply.

'But sir, we do nat even have confirmation that the body in the beetroot patch is Ajay Kumar. It is all conjecture!'

'Rubbish! We have Cookie Katoch's video of the Aggarwal boy arguing with Ajay Kumar. And Ajay Kumar subsequently vanished.'

'But he was nat arguing with General Mehra was he, sir?' Bhavani says persuasively. 'He was arguing with the Aggarwal boy. Where does the general fit into it?'

The chief gives an exasperated exclamation. 'Arrey, this Aggarwal had been arguing with Ajay Kumar – about the price or the quality of the drugs or something else drug-related – so Ajay Kumar was already in a bad mood – *then* he must have found the general canoodling with his wife, lost his cool, pounced on the wife to beat her, prompting the general to play the hero and shoot him! Everybody was clearly getting high and happy at this big engagement party! No, Bhavani, you've been given a long rope on this one, you've had your little junket to Kolkata, now the time has come to bite the bullet.'

'Sir, but what is the hurry?' Bhavani asks. 'We have only been on the case for *two* weeks—'

'Yes, but it keeps coming up in the news, and it looks bad for the department if we don't crack it soon!'

Bhavani's expression grows stubborn. 'But we are nat cracking it, sir, we are crooking it.'

'Enough!' the chief thunders. 'I have been given my orders and I have given you yours! You will arrest General Mehra tomorrow. Is that quite clear?'

'It is because he is too popular, hain na, sir?' There is a peculiar, mocking edge to his subordinate's voice.

The chief looks up sharply. The old ACP is sitting back in his chair, his expression sardonic. There is nothing genial about his face now. His eyes – wise, all-knowing eyes – are glittering strangely.

'Rubbish!' the chief says uncomfortably.

'No, no,' Bhavani says mildly. 'We completely understand. It is nat the Pakistanis and the anti-national elements in the Opposition party who want to destroy General Mehra's reputation and legacy, it is his so-called friends and supporters in the ruling party! He is invited to every news channel debate, he is hailed as the architect of the surgical strikes wherever he goes, he is applauded louder than the esteemed defense minister, Govardhan Ruia sa'ab at public meetings, and of course Govardhan Ruia cannat have that. So he himself has issued instructions to have Behra Mehra taken down a peg or two, and *that* is why the general's service revolver has ended up in the kitchen garden mud. Are we nat correct, sir?'

The chief's face is pale with suppressed rage. He looks furtively about the room, leans forward and lowers his voice. 'Bhavani, we could both lose our jobs. Just go out there an—'

'Yes, yes, we know,' Bhavani Singh replies resignedly. 'Just go out there and arrest the general tomorrow.'

In the sunny, potted-plants-filled living room of their Sector-44 house in Noida, Kashi and his sister are trying to revive a teenage ritual upon a Sikkimese carpet festooned with snow lions and dragons.

'I'm *tilting*! Kashi, I'm scared! Stop it, you choot. *Stop!* Or you'll give yourself a hernia. I'm calling Ma – Maaaaaaaaaa!'

Natasha is sitting cross-legged, precariously balanced on her brother's back as he does push-ups.

'Five … six … seh … seh …' He collapses onto the carpet with a groan. 'What the fuck, Nattu, you got fat!'

'Haw!' She tilts nimbly off his back. '*You* got weak, you poor fish, don't blame me.'

'Maybe I did,' he admits, still lying face down on the carpet, flushed and out of breath. 'Shit, I used to be able to do ten push-ups with you on my back, easy.'

She tousles his hair affectionately. 'You got older, Kashua, it happens to everybody.'

Kashi sits up, scowling. 'It's all this soft-living and drinking on the weekends. I'm going to practice—'

'Law,' she tells him firmly. 'You practice law. Not weird work-out routines, okay?'

He gets to his feet, massaging his shoulders gingerly, rotating his arms forwards, then backwards.

'Okay.'

She leans against the legs of the sofa and watches him with narrowed eyes as he walks about the room, sipping from his cup of coffee, then raising his shirt to check out his abs in the sideboard mirror.

'Spit it out, little bro,' she says. 'It's your last chance. And you know you want to. Why have you crawled back to mummy–daddy's house with your tail between your legs? Kya hui?'

He flops down on the carpet beside her, and stares up at the ceiling. 'You think you're so smart, Natti-the-tatti.'

'Is it Kuhu?' she asks sympathetically. 'D'you think she's swinging some hot tribal contractor up in the Kalahandi hills?'

His jaw drops. 'What the hell, I never even *thought* of that! Wow, thanks a *lot*, bro!'

'Don't mention it, bro,' Natasha says airily. 'She's such a smart girl, I thought she would've got bored with you. What has it been? A year?'

He nods. 'Yeah.'

'Ask her to marry you,' Natasha says seriously.

'But I'm only twenty-five!'

'Yeah, well, she won't say yes right away, obviously! Just let her know that your intentions are long-term. They are, aren't they?'

Kashi nods. 'Oh yes …'

Natasha looks at him critically. 'Then why're you looking so fucked?'

His eyes grow troubled. 'I just wish … I wish I had met her *earlier*, you know? She's so simple to love, so straightforward.'

'You make her sound like a moron.'

'She's *not* a moron. I think my whole life would've been different if I'd met her earlier. But it may be too late now …

I may never be able to love her with all of my heart – like she *deserves* to be loved.'

Natasha pokes his ribs with her big toe sympathetically. 'It's Bambi Todi, isn't it? You've been hanging out with her again. After you met at the club that day.'

He nods.

'You've had sex?'

He rears up, revolted. '*No!* I have a *girlfriend*! *Christ*, Nattu!'

'Well, thank God, *you* remember!' She rolls her eyes. 'And?'

He glares at her. 'And what?'

'And is it as bad as before?' she presses.

His eyes are agonized. 'I don't know!' He lies back on the carpet again, raking his hair off his forehead and staring at the ceiling. 'Nattu, is it possible to love two people equally at the same time?'

'It's possible,' she allows. 'But it's incredibly *painful.* You'll get completely fucked, and sucked dry emotionally, and eventually both of them will dump your sorry ass.'

'Jesus! You're not much hel—'

'Balbirrrr! Kidsss! Look! General Mehra is being arrested *on TV!*'

Mala Dogra's piercing scream brings everybody rushing to Dadi's bedroom, where mother-in-law and daughter-in-law are having their mid-morning tea. The old lady looks bemused but flattered as they all collapse onto her double bed and stare riveted at the TV. Very hospitably, she increases the volume to max. Everybody winces.

Khooni General Hai Hai!
#ArrestMehra
Fauji nikla Mauji! Hawji Hawji!

These dramatic headlines appear in quick succession over shaky footage of the front gate of the DTC, where a thin, militant-looking female reporter in a red bandana is standing next to the moustachioed guards and speaking shrilly into the mic.

'After two weeks of ceaseless, in-depth investigation, New Delhi's Crime Branch is finally set to arrest the sinister double murderer who has claimed two victims inside India's oldest, poshest and most exclusive club – the Delhi Turf Club! Our sources reveal that this cold-blooded, remorseless killer is none other than the architect of the surgical strikes and popular military hero, portrayed in last year's superhit film *Jhelum Bridge* by Amitabh Bachchan – Lt. General Om Prakash Mehra himself!'

After flashing several images of the general – in uniform, in a pink Lacoste T-shirt and tennis shorts, holding a drink in a suit and tie at a party – the camera cuts to a congested lane in Greater Kailash II, and a narrow, double-storeyed house with an ornate gate, behind which an elderly golden spaniel is drowsing in the sun.

'And here is the home of the killer general, ladies and gentlemen!' hisses a manic looking male reporter with a heroic moustache. 'A man so desensitized and immoral that he has named his dog Whisky! *This* is the den of vice he resides in!'

Whisky barks valiantly but even he cannot prevent the camera from zooming in through the gate and revealing glimpses of the Mehra front porch. There is a framed photograph of Guru Nanak, with an incense stick guttering before it, a sign in pretty tiles which reads 'Savitri & Om Mehra' and a friendly looking clay turtle sitting on a mushroom. The porch – and perhaps even the house inside – is spick and span, but somehow manages to look bereft and abandoned.

Now the shot veers sideways to capture the square homely face of ACP Bhavani Singh, dressed in unobtrusive plain clothes, speaking to the sea of cameras patiently.

'Yes, yes, we have a non-bailable warrant for General Mehra's arrest. It is for the murder of Sri Ajay Kumar, late husband of Mrs Ganga Kumar, three years ago, and for the subsequent murder of Leo Matthew, Zumba trainer at the DTC, two weeks ago.'

'Sir! More details please, sir!'

Bhavani raises both palms in a calming gesture.

'We cannat contribute anything new! You people know everything much before we do! It is all already in the public domain. Three years ago, the general was enamoured of a young lady who had a troublesome, jealous husband, so he got rid of him in full fauji fashion with his fauji revolver, misused his position as head of the horticulture sub-committee of the DTC to have him buried in a composting pit at the Club and then grew beetroot over him for three whole years! Then somebody found out about this murder and started blackmailing him, so he poisoned this person with an overdose of popular party drug Pinko Hathni. We are going inside to arrest him and we urge that the lawyers do nat let us down, but put him away for a long time nat only for these double murders but also for besmirching the reputation of the armed forces and robbing our young children of a role model they looked up to!'

Kashi frowns. 'Why is he talking like that? So insensitively? Almost flippantly? Bhavani is better than that ...'

'Being on national television does strange things to people.' Natasha sighs. 'And anyway, most cops are assholes. Just totally desensitized.'

'You can't make sweeping statements like that, Nattu! Bhavani's a decent guy.'

'Well, this arrest is preposterous!' frets the brigadier. 'Wasn't this ACP excitedly pursuing some other angle, Akash?'

'Yes, he was.' Kashi nods, frowning. 'I don't get it—'

'Oh look,' says Mala Dogra. 'They're somewhere else now.'

The scene has shifted to another – incredibly familiar – location: the back gate of the DTC. Ganga can be seen sitting inside her little red car, gheraoed by the press. The wide, looming form of Inspector Padam Kumar is in the frame, standing in front of the bonnet, frowning at the journalists.

'It remains to be seen whether Ganga Kumar was just an innocent bystander or an active accessory who attended to the amorous army man's *daily needs*! As of now, we have no details if she is to be arrested too,' an excited reporter says breathlessly. 'Madam! Madam! Why did you come to work today? Did you want to show solidarity with the general in this difficult time? Will you be visiting him in jail? How does it feel to be romantically involved with a man old enough to be your father?'

'Hullo ji, that is *enough*!' Padam Kumar's cherubic face is red with anger. 'I have already given you all the information, why are you asking the same questions again and again?'

'Ganga!' shouts another reporter. 'Ganga! What are your feelings about your sugar daddy's arrest?'

Behind the glass window, Ganga shakes her head, and seems to be appealing to the press to move out of her way. They ignore her, and the gherao continues.

'The Club is going to the *dogs*,' Balbir Dogra says worriedly. 'This is *terrible* publicity.'

'Dad, is that all you care about?' Nattu demands. 'The stupid Club?'

'Clearly, yes,' Kashi says wryly.

His mother grips his shoulder. 'Wait, what, is the story over?'

A dramatic super reading KAHANI MEIN TWIST! has just filled the screen, accompanied by music. As they watch, the camera cuts back to the studio, where a famous news anchor looks gravely into the camera.

'Viewers, a brand-new update has just been received by our intrepid reporters in the DTC Double Murder case! A *key* witness has just surrendered himself to Delhi Police and is being taken in for questioning. Sources claim that this key witness's testimony is set to change the case *completely* and *spectacularly*! Let us proceed without any further delay to New

Delhi Railway Station to unravel yet another layer in this fascinating double murder!'

The camera cuts to a grubby, chaotic platform at New Delhi Railway Station. A train is just chugging in. Announcements sound in the background. And then, from the thick of the noise and the dirt and the massive crowds emerges an undersized, adolescent reporter, clearly the last cookie in the jar, sent out in haste, probably at last moment's notice from channel headquarters.

'Oh My *Gods*!' says this young, wobbly voiced person, who has clearly decided that this is his make-or-break chance to impress all of India on national television. 'Vutt-a sensational twist in the Khooni General case! Vutt-a *dwellupment*!'

He gives an excited little wriggle at the end of every sentence, the peach fuzz on his upper lip shining with sweat, and his hair flopping up and down jauntily.

'You might have heard Madhuri Dikshit madamji's superhit song "Mera Piya Ghar Aaya, O Ram Ji", vich for the benefit of south-Indian viewers I vill explain … It means "My loved one has returned home, halleluiah halleluiah!" Have you heard this *song*? Hey, have you heard this song? No? Vul, if not, then you vill hear it *now*, because *this* is the song Ganga Kumar ji vill be singing when she hears that he is *here*, he is back from the *dead*, he was never dead at *all*! Ladies and gentlemen, General Mehra *cannot* and *vill not* be arrested after all, because the man whom he allegedly killed, is still *alive*!'

The camera turns to reveal a tired-looking man, flanked by Delhi Police constables. He has a French beard, dark circles under the eyes and a shiny rexine backpack on his shoulder.

'Vat is your name, sir?' demands the callow reporter.

The newcomer swallows, then looks to the constables for permission. They nod.

'Ajay Kumar,' he answers in a low, halting voice.

'And your wife's name?'

'Ganga Kumar.'

'Vy have you come back to Delhi?'

He licks his lips.

'To clear her name by proving I am still alive.'

ACP Bhavani Singh's eyes twinkle with quiet jubilation as he lathers his chin in front of the mirror the next morning, humming 'Mera Piya Ghar Aaya, O Ram Ji' to himself.

Shalini enters the bathroom with two cups of tea, hands him one, slams down the lid of the toilet, sits down upon it and looks at him worriedly.

'*You're* singing that stupid song? When *all* the newspapers are having a laugh at your expense this morning? What is *happening*, Bhavani?'

Bhavani clinks his teacup with hers cheerfully.

'You don't have time for your husband, busy busy Shalini ji, that is what is happening! If you talked to us more often you would know what we are up to!'

She is immediately contrite. 'Board exams are happening, Bhavani – we cannot neglect our students now. Chalo, don't be pricey, explain what you've been up to!'

'What have the newspapers called us?' he asks.

Her face clouds over. 'Clownish,' she reports reluctantly. 'And clueless and blundering. When I went out to get the milk packets, *everybody* in the colony looked at me sympathetically.'

Bhavani chuckles. 'Excellent. So basically, your clownish, clueless blunderer of a husband figured out that Defence Minister Govardhan Ruia is jealous of the general, and out for his blood. Because he's getting—'

'Too popular,' she says at once. 'Of course! That makes complete sense.'

'Yes. So, when the cief told us, in no uncertain terms, that orders had come from the top to arrest Mehra, we went ahead and complied obediently, but at the same time, we stepped up our hunt for Ajay Kumar. The drug dealer angle helped narrow the search, and we had some good pictures, so even though the fellow had no police record, we managed to track him down, alive and still peddling in a small-time way. Then we … er … *persuaded* him to show up in Delhi, and pretend that he had come forward on his own to clear his wife's name.'

She leans forward and pulls his chunky cheek. 'Clever *clever* ACP Brownie! Is the chief furious?'

Bhavani shrugs. 'We suppose so. But Ruia's scheme to discredit Mehra has failed for sure.'

Eye twinkling, he raises his teacup and clinks it with hers again.

TRANSCRIPT OF A RECORDED STATEMENT BY AJAY KUMAR.

My name is Ajay Kumar. I am a waiter at Jain Bhojanalya Restaurant in the Navi Mumbai area. I got married to Ganga Kumar four years ago. At first we were happy, but when she found out that I supplemented my livelihood by selling drugs, we started fighting.

She refused to take my 'dirty' money and started cleaning people's houses instead, saying this work was more honourable than the 'dirty work' I was doing! Then one day she came back with so much money that I knew she had started an affair with a rich man. Naturally this maddened me, because which man wants an unfaithful wife? She denied it flatly, we kept fighting, and finally I left her.

Because I still loved her, I would sometimes come back to try and talk sense into her, but she never listened.

Then she became friends with that rich Bambi Todi, who was a feminist type and turned her against me even more, with the result that the last time I went to meet her, instead of being kind to her husband and giving him a nice meal and some cash at the very least, she phoned that Jhelum-walla general who beat me up and tried to hand me over to the police. Thankfully, Ganga had the decency to not press charges.

Things were going downhill for me. I decided to leave town before the police found out about my ganja-dealing. I had started selling other drugs also, and it was all starting to get too dangerous.

*On the night of the engagement, I told Aryaman to give me
all the money he owed me, which was quite a lot. That is what
our fight was about.*

*Finally, he gave me his watch. I sold my list of contacts to a
cousin-brother and left Delhi.*

I don't know anything else.

END OF INTERVIEW.

Bhavani and Shalini have a quiet Sunday. Bhavani does his
5BX workout, then showers, cooks fluffy French toast for his
wife and himself, and settles down on the living room sofa
in front of the big TV to watch the complete and unedited
recording of the Bambi Todi–Anshul Poddar engagement
party with single-minded concentration.

Shalini prepares a big flask of coffee, and corrects her
mock-exam papers in front of the TV too, taking small
breaks now and then to watch with him, oohing and aahing
over the decorations, which feature masses and masses of her
favorite pink Oriental lilies, and asking questions which he
often ignores.

'We feel like a midwife in a labour ward,' she remarks after
a few hours. 'You are clearly pregnant and about to pop. We
would say about … one finger dilated?'

'Two,' he replies, his eyes still glued to the TV screen.
'Definitely two.'

Shalini chuckles. 'So, is it a girl or is it a boy?'

'Shush.' He frowns. 'Pre-natal sex determination is an
offence and anybody seeking it will be prosecuted.'

She sticks out her tongue at him. 'You still don't know, do you?'

He deigns to look away from the screen long enough to say, gravely, 'We are waiting for some final information that will confirm everything.'

But as the day advances, and he slowly, deliberately pieces the puzzle together, Bhavani's serene mood slowly turns restless. Something, surely, must be brewing? The twisted, elegant mind that sent the gas balloons floating up to obstruct the gym camera must be at work again ... Somewhere, the disarming charm that gave old Guppie Ram a feeling of *love ... and dosti – and equal-equal trust* must be in action! The murderer *must* have panicked when Ajay Kumar showed up, and the general was exonerated, that too on national television. Surely he or she could sense the net closing in, the noose tightening? Would he or she sit tight? Or lash out again? If yes, then where? At whom?

Each of his several calls to Dr Krishnan at Forensics is met with the same response: 'need more time'. And so he continues to watch footage of Bambi Todi in her gold-and-yellow lehenga, dancing with the dashingly handsome Anshul while Kashi sulks in the background, and the DTCs Zumba ladies air-kiss each other and cheat on their diets.

It is a slow day for everybody. At the DTC the growing heat has thinned the Club lawns of patrons, and the bearers have an easy day. Across the road, at the Todi residence, Pankaj Todi hosts Gen. Mehra and Gagan Ruia for a small celebratory lunch in honour of the general's exoneration. Gagan is all effusiveness, and presents a huge bouquet of exotic flowers to Behra Mehra, 'with dad's best wishes and congratulations', a statement which would have caused Bhavani Singh to roll his eyes like a Kathakali dancer. The phrases 'we *knew* you weren't a double-murderer' and 'now the Club election is in the bag' and 'conspiracy of the Opposition, anti-national elements and Pakistan' are repeated so many times that Bambi gets a headache and decides to walk over to the Club and chill in the Rose Garden.

Urvashi and Mukesh Khurana spend a quiet day, mostly in their bedroom, Zoom-calling their daughters and talking to each other about many, many things.

Kashi Dogra plays carrom with his grandmother, croquet with his mother, then drives up to Delhi to get some papers for the case he's starting on Monday. His three weeks of leave are almost up, and it's time to shift gears.

Cookie Katoch, dressed in an aggressively bohemian-looking smock, spends the day finishing a brand-new lingam. It is a mixed media piece, with glass, malachite and lapiz lazuli and she is very pleased with it, humming 'Satyam Shivam Sundaram' to herself as she glues glittering bit of Swarovski crystal onto the piece in her garden 'studio'.

Ganga passes the day alone, and very happy. Bambi didi has had a tough talk with Ajay Kumar, who has agreed to sign divorce papers on Monday.

And Roshni Aggarwal heads out to her favourite spa for a deep-tissue massage and a micro-dermabrasion treatment. When she finally returns home, a good four hours later, she finds her son passed out cold on the living room couch in front of a loudly playing Xbox.

Something about the extreme stillness of his body makes Roshni's heart give the most horrid thud. The sight is too reminiscent of the state in which she and Cookie had discovered the dead body of Leo Matthew three weeks ago.

As she walks slowly towards him, telling herself not to be foolish, Roshni has a sudden, sickening premonition that the same dread, malevolent presence that had been hovering in the wood-floor gym three weeks ago is crouched here, just now, in her darkened living room, over her troubled son.

Giving a frightened little gulp, she drops her bags, rushes forward and touches Arya's forehead. It is clammy and much too cold. She scrabbles about the couch for his wrist, tears stinging her eyes. The pulse is thin, a mere thread, beating unsteadily. When she pulls back his eyelids, all she can see are the whites of his eyes. Breathing slowly to calm the panic fluttering inside her chest, Roshni Aggarwal gets to her feet, finds her phone and dials the all-too familiar number of her son's specialist ...

Dear ACP Sa'ab,

This man is my very trusted assistant. He has travelled on my private jet to deliver this parcel to you. It has not been out of his sight for even a moment. And before that, the item it contains had been kept safely at our Alipore residence for the past five years. Be assured it is the genuine article. All the best with your investigations and requesting complete confidentiality if possible. God bless you.

Arihant Poddar

'Sqyooz me for asking, but in this current case you are investigating, the murdered man turned out to be alive only, no?'

The girl asking this artless question is wide-eyed and very pretty – prettier than all the other prospective Mrs Padam Kumars Padam Kumar has met so far.

Pink with embarassment, he puts down the cup of fragrant Assam tea he has just accepted from her.

'Yes,' he admits, somewhat huffily, to the little circle of people in the formal drawing room. 'But it is a *very* complicated and strange case—'

She giggles. 'Obviously!!'

Padam goes pinker than the flower he is named for. The girl is being intolerably cheeky. Humiliatingly, her mother, instead of restraining her, also giggles. 'We all saw it on TV,' she confides. 'It was *too* good! The way the murda showed up, making the mote-thaanedaar sa'ab look like *such* a fool—'

'He is *not* a thaanedaar, but an ACP and a *very* respected officer!' Padam begins stiffly, but is interrupted when his entire chest starts to thrum. It takes him a while to make his excuses, put down his cup and saucer and extract the phone, which he had buttoned away, out of sight, in the chest pocket of his formal blue shirt, fearing it may not be 'latest' enough to impress the girl's side. When he finally holds the despised device to his ear –

'Where are you, yaar PK?' Bhavani demands irritably. 'Aryaman Aggarwal ne OD kiya hai. Come to the Medicorp Emergency at once.'

It is a very disgruntled Padam who motorcycles down to the Medicorp Hospital about half an hour later and takes the elevator to the VIP suites on the top floor. He feels nothing but resentment and contempt for his unglamorous superior, with his eccentric eleven-minute workout, his womanish insistence on non-violence, and his naive, colour-sketch-penned "The Four Golden Rules".

When he emerges on the top floor, slightly dazzled by the plush décor which looks more suited to a five-star hotel than a hospital, Bhavani materializes at his elbow like a genie.

'You got the forensics report?'

Wordlessly, Padam Kumar holds out a manila envelope.

Bhavani puts on his reading glasses, tears open the envelope, scans its contents, and smiles the beatific smile of a lost child who has just found his mother again, and she is holding a packet of Lays Magic Masala chips in one hand and a Cadbury Silk in the other. As an exultant glow suffuses his square brown face, two young nurses on a tea break whisper, 'George Clooney' to each other, giggle and scamper away.

Entirely oblivious to this little by-play, Bhavani tells Padam, 'Good man! Now we know who the murderer is.'

'That's excellent, sir.' The young policeman doesn't try very hard to disguise his disbelief.

Bhavani looks up from the report for one keen moment. 'Don't believe me?'

Padam's face reddens slightly. 'Is he *dead*, sir? Aggarwal? What are the doctors saying?'

'Ah.' Bhavani gives a quick little nod. 'He's weak but he'll live.'

'Was it … attempted murder, sir?'

'All in good time, PK!' Bhavani smiles. 'Send all our guests into Suite 3. Wait inside, with the rest of the team positioned just outside. And keep your handcuffs ready. When we leave from here, we will be taking a murderer with us.'

He hurries away, moving as buoyantly as a sixteen-year-old.

The Khuranas, husband and wife.
Bambi Todi.
Fr Victor Emmanuel and Randy Rax.
Ganga Kumar.
Kashi Dogra.
Cookie Katoch.
Roshni Aggarwal.

And on the hospital bed, weak, but well on his way to recovery, Aryaman Aggarwal.

'Hai hai, it was all so *goose-pimply*, babe,' Cookie Katoch tells her girlfriends breathlessly over lunch at Olive the next day. 'Matlab, the décor in that hospital is better than Leela ka presidential suite, but there was also this total, rongta-raising, climax-wala *atmosphere*. And I toh was waise hi feeling SO much guilt, ki Roshni will hate me for telling the ACP about Arya's fight with that wretched Ajay Kumar ... Wohi jo dead ki jagah alive nikla! That is why I rushed to the hospital to suck up to her as soon as I got the news! I thought the horrid boy had OD'd because of me and my big mouth only! But then the whole story turned out to be quite different.

'Anyway, he was out of danger by the time I got there – lying on the bed and sighing like a Devdas, with a whole mehfil around him! I found out later that some of them had showed up like that only, and some had been summoned by the ACP. Rosh looked like she'd been snorting some of her son's maal, her eyes glittered so strangely. And her skin was so *stretched* over her face – if she does any more facelifts she'll get stretch marks on her face, I tell you! Mukki's eyes were darting everywhere, like a cornered chuha's, and he'd worn those wretched yellow suspenders again, this time over a black shirt! He looked like a taxicab you don't want to take. And Urvashi, dressed in white chikan mulmul, looking like Benazir Bhutto about to be assassinated! And Bambi Todi, so sweet, and Balbir Dogra's son, so cute, and my God, there was so much tension in the room!

'And then ACP Brownie stepped forward, his face ekdum *grim*, and all my chakras started whirring and jangling. All I could think was *one of us is a murderer. One of us is a murderer!* And I decided then and there ki no-carbs-after-seven rule be damned and pulled out my emergency muesli bar and started munching.'

As Cookie Katoch polishes off her muesli bar, Bhavani Singh looks about the room, his expression grave.

'Our thanks to Roshni madam for permitting us to hold this unusual meeting here. Hopefully the medical staff will continue to tolerate our presence—'

'My husband is on this hospital's board of trustees,' Roshni says in a low voice.

'Ah!' Bhavani smiles. 'In that case, all is well! Or rather, all will very soon be well!'

Khurana cocks an eyebrow. 'You know who it is, then?'

Bhavani nods respectfully. 'Yes, sir.'

'About time.' Khurana snorts scornfully. 'After all the nautanki that played out on the TV yesterday, I'm surprised you can show your face anywhere!'

Padam Kumar, standing unobtrusively by the door, winces at this public takedown of his superior. Bhavani, however, appears unmoved.

'Yes, sir,' he replies pleasantly. But the quality of his voice has changed now. It is still genial, but somehow, harder. His kind eyes seem to glint with a steely light. 'We will nat have any more interruptions, please. Speak when you are directly addressed or nat at all.'

And such is the authority his chunky figure suddenly radiates that a room full of highly influential and volatile people pipe down and listen quietly.

'We will begin from the beginning. But what is the beginning of this story, really? Did it begin almost two hundred years ago, when the DTC was established, a symbol of oppression, conspicuous consumption and class privilege? Did it begin when a little girl and a little boy met and fell in love and made vows about forever? Did it begin with an incorrigible storyteller drinking whisky in the sunshine, spinning stories which get wilder and more improbable with every retelling? Or with a very young woman who has foolishly followed her heart and ended up in trouble? Or with *another* young woman, eager to be independent, who encounters predators wherever she goes?'

He lets his words hang, his eyes moving from person to person as he speaks, observing their reactions to particular words or phrases, making mental notes about who flinches, who stays blank, who goes just a little too still as he speaks.

'But we will keep the timeline linear. When we were summoned to the DTC the day after Tambola Sunday, we were an outsider at the gates. Rather like Leo Matthew. He too was an outsider, a boy from an orphanage, growing up on scraps and hand-me-downs tossed his way by people who wanted to ease their guilty conscience and buy some good karma. Father Victor will understand.'

The priest nods silently. Seated next to him, uncharacteristically quiet and odourless today, Randy Rax nods too.

Bhavani continues. 'Let us have no secrets in this room. Several of you received a song via WhatsApp message from Leo Matthews. This song.'

He presses his phone lightly.

An insistent backbeat fills the plush, high-ceilinged suite. A husky, knowing female voice croons tauntingly.

You think your secret's safe,
You think you left no trace
You're sure that no one knows
You're smelling ... like a rose
But fate has a way of catching up with sinners
At the end of the day there are no free dinners
And I will make you pay
Oh, I will make you pay
P p p p p pay
P p p p p pay
Pay, pay, pay and stay worried,
'Cos I know where the bodies are buried
Stay, stay, better stay worried,
'Cos I know where the bodies are buried

The music hits climax and dies away.

The suite stays silent. Unnaturally silent.

Bhavani looks about sombrely. 'What made us zoom in on this particular song, from the *many* songs and videos on Leo

Matthew's phone, was the fact that this song was followed by a link to the Badshahpur Children's Village website. And everybody who had received this song, and that link, had made a donation to the BCV. This, to us, suggested blackmail.'

'My goodness!' Father Victor's face is ashen with shock. 'But I thought ... he told me that ... I mean, I marvelled and thanked God daily for the generosity of Leo's friends and clients but I had no knowledge he was doing anything like this!'

Bhavani acknowledges this disclaimer with an impassive nod. It is impossible to tell if he believes it or not.

Plump little Cookie Katoch is horrified. 'Haw! Dekho toh! And I had no clue! Whom-whom did he send that song to?' She looks about the gathering wide-eyed, but suddenly everybody seems to be fiddling with their phones.

Finally, Bambi puts up her hand. 'Me for one,' she says lightly. 'He had found out about Mammu's little ... er ... problem somehow ... and he used that to extract a tonne of money from me.'

Roshni's tight, bony face softens with sympathy. 'You silly girl! We all know about your mum's little problem! Nobody holds it against her!'

'What?' Bambi gives an incredulous little laugh. 'You guys know?'

'Sure.' Cookie Katoch shrugs. 'So sometimes your mother absent-mindedly puts some things into her purse! What's there? Everybody has mental health issues nowadays! Deepika

Padukone, Winona Ryder! You were a fool to pay him, Bambi! How much did you pay?'

'Oho, Cookie, how does it matter!' Roshni snaps before Bambi can speak. 'It's not like you know a place that's having a sale where she could've gotten a better deal!'

A few people giggle nervously. Cookie frowns. Bambi looks teary-eyed with relief.

'Thanks, you guys,' she mutters gruffly. 'This mean a lot.'

'No interruptions, please,' Bhavani says pleasantly.

Everybody quietens down at once.

'Bambi ji was unusually honest and came forward with her secret. Everybody else, perhaps because they were hiding larger, more complicated secrets, did nat cooperate with the police ... so we initiated inquiries.

'Leo's modus operandi was to befriend drivers, maids, nurses, security guards, cleaners, anybody who worked in the homes of the rich. His rags-to-comparative-riches story was inspiring to them – the way he had started off as a waiter, then a waiter on a cruise ship, then a dancer on a cruise ship, until finally his current place as a famous trainer made them think they could make the same magical leap too. These people had no clue that he was living off the secrets they betrayed unknowingly to him ...'

He looks around the room. Everybody is listening raptly.

'Through this network he managed to infiltrate the homes of several of you in this room. It was a dangerous game he was playing though – and it got even more dangerous when he stumbled upon a huge secret – something far bigger than the petty adultery and embezzlement that were his usual stock in trade. Through his network, he learnt nat about a metaphorical buried body – like Mrs Todi's kleptomania – but about a *real* dead body buried in the kitchen garden of the DTC three years ago.

'But old Guppie Ram was an unreliable source. In fact, he was notorious for taking a kernel of the truth, and spinning a fantastic tale around it. Even then, Leo decided that the kernel was worth taking a cautious shot in the dark at. So he started looking about for people who he thought *could* be the murderer Guppie Ram had helped that night, three years ago.'

Bhavani pauses, scanning the listening faces keenly. 'So what all *had* been happening three years ago?

'General Mehra was the head of the horticulture committee, ably assisted by Mrs Aggarwal, Mrs Khurana and Mrs Todi. Under their direction a deep composting pit was dug. We can safely assume that when the murderer ended up with a body on his or her hands, their mind went immediately to the freshly dug pit in the kitchen garden, and that is why the phone call was made to old Guppie Ram in the dead of night.

'There were already rumours floating around the Club about the general's alleged affair with Ganga, and speculation about the whereabouts of Ajay Kumar. Clearly Leo heard these stories and decided to take a chance, and sent the song to the general.

'That's two people who received the song so far. Bambi Todi. And General Mehra. Now let us come to the *third* recipient of the song – Urvashi Khurana.'

She's been sitting with her head bowed, but at the mention of her name, she looks up with the quiet dignity of a queen.

'Yes, let's.' She smiles evenly.

Bhavani doesn't smile back. 'Although Urvashi madam also received the song, we could find absolutely no event in her life from three years ago that could have resulted with her having a dead body on her hands. Besides, *she* was the one who ordered the digging up of the kitchen garden in the first place, to lay the rainwater-harvesting plant, so that seemed to indicate that she was unaware of the fact that a body was buried there.'

She sits with her chin raised slightly, her beautiful face in repose, her eyes half-closed. 'Fascinating. Do continue.'

'And so perhaps in Urvashi Khurana's case too, like in that of Bambi ji's, the "buried body" was a metaphorical one and nat a physical one …

'But then we learned that Urvashi madam had been very fond of old Guppie Ram too – in fact, she had even attended his funeral! He died of entirely natural causes, by the way; we checked that out quite thoroughly. Was it possible that during one of their cosy chats he told her too, like he did Leo – about the body buried in the kitchen garden? And could Urvashi ji have decided to use this body to confuse the investigating team, derail the investigation, and draw attention away from the *recent* murder – the murder she may very well have committed – the murder of Leo?'

The colour on Urvashi's face fluctuates through this speech, but she remains entirely expressionless otherwise.

Bhavani ploughs on. 'After all, it was Urvashi ji who ordered gas balloons for Tambola Sunday. It was Urvashi ji who had four bunches of them placed in the four corners of the gym – in such a position that, if a bunch was loosened – through a window left open for that very purpose – it would float up and obscure the camera completely for a few vital minutes. On a cold foggy night, no security guard would be in a hurry to leave his warm heater and trudge across the freezing, misty lawns to take down a balloon that may very well drift away itself in a while.

'Mukesh ji was already working out in the gym; how easy it would have been to offer to pick him up that day. Standing outside the gym, she could have loosened the balloons and waited till they drifted up to cover the camera inside. Then walk in, go to the fridge on the pretext of "getting some water" and slip the Pinko Hathni into Leo's protein shake, with Mukesh ji none the wiser! Then Mukesh ji would have locked up the gym – as he had promised Thampi – and Urvashiji would have walked out and driven home with her husband smelling, as the song says, like a rose!

'Yes, in the case of Urvashi Khurana, the problem was not one of opportunity, but of motive. *Why* was Leo blackmailing Urvashi ji? What was the "buried body" she was hiding? With her blameless, clean, open-book life, her loving daughters, her flourishing business, her loyal husband to whom she was a devoted wife? What did Leo know about her and how had he found out? We found no evidence whatsoever that Leo had an informant in the Khurana household, nor, in spite of all the rumours put out, we suspect by the General Mehra camp, did she seem to be having an affair with Leo.

'Fortunately for us, Urvashi ji put us on the right track herself. She was arguing with General Mehra in the Daily Needs the other day, and in reply to his statement that he knew how to keep his cool and make split-second decisions even in the heat of battle, she retorted that she was sick of his war stories, and that she had pushed out a baby without any painkillers and without any fuss while there were rioters at her door, and the entire city was burning!'

A small gasp comes from Urvashi's throat. She seems to want to speak, then thinks better of it.

'With your permission, madam, may we continue?' Bhavani asks her quietly.

She nods, very pale but composed, her eyes looking around for her husband. 'Mukesh?'

'Yes.' Mukesh Khurana steps forward, grasps his wife's hand firmly, and looks around the mystified room. 'We've discussed this,' he says gruffly. 'We don't want to hide anything and we *damn care* what people think!'

Bhavani nods. 'Thank you, Mukesh ji.' He raises his voice slightly. 'Well, it did nat take us very long to do the mathematics. The incident Urvashi ji seems to be referring to – "with rioters at the door and the entire city burning" – could only be the anti-Sikh riots of 1984. And Urvashi ji got married in 1990, at the age of twenty-three.'

'That could just be a mistake,' Bambi, who has been listening intently, leans forward to say. 'Maybe she was so angry that she exaggerated a little bit? We all do sometimes.

Maybe some chhota-mota rioting happened in the nineties too! I mean, this is *Delhi* we're talking about! She could've been flexing about that!'

Bhavani shakes his head gently. 'We checked it out, Bambi ji.'

Her eyes widen uncertainly. 'And ...?'

'And there is a record of a seventeen-year-old Urvashi Narang giving birth to a boy child in Civil Lines' Teerath Ram Shah Hospital in 1984.'

The entire room seems to suck in its breath collectively.

'A child subsequently given up to the Badshahpur Children's Village. A child christened Rakesh, and known as—'

'Rax!'

The word bursts from the crippled man's lips with pride. His crutches clatter to his feet as he raises his arms in uncertain triumph, his beady eyes still slyly mocking, but now also bright with hope, and a vulnerability which is heart-rending.

Everybody turns to look at him, slack-jawed. Even Aryaman Aggarwal struggles to sit up.

'It's true,' Rax confirms happily. 'I *still* can't believe it but it's true. This beautiful lady is my mother. She explained everything and she's going to adopt me! I met her husband, and my half-sisters already and I know I'm gonna fit right in.' He leans forward and adds confidentially, 'They're *all* as ugly as me!'

16

The A to my B

'Girls, mera mind toh ekdum *blow* ho gaya!' Cookie declares to her girlfriends the next day. 'Matlab, we all used to say ki she is in too good shape to be mother-of-two, and now we were finding out ki she is mother-of-*three*! And here I am with my bums so big after only *one* C-section delivery twenty-three years ago! It's too unfair, yaar, but what a chhupa Rustam she turned out to be, no? That woman can really keep a secret!'

Rax's statement is met with a stunned silence by the group, and then, as comprehension dawns slowly upon their faces, there are exclamations and whispers all around. In the midst of this muted uproar, Urvashi gets gracefully to her feet, walks up to Rax and stands behind his chair to face the room. Mukki follows, solemn-faced and fiddling nervously with his yellow suspenders.

'I don't owe anybody in this room an explanation except Rakesh and Mukesh and they've both already had one,' she says with quiet dignity. 'But for the sake of justice, and for the proper investigation of these crimes, I will share this much. Yes, my parents did send me away to my father's ancestral village in Punjab when I was seventeen. It was supposed to be a sort of punishment for being so wild and disobedient and flirtatious, but I decided to turn it into a punishment for *them* by having an affair with a local boy. What I hadn't bargained for was getting pregnant. I didn't have the guts to tell my parents about it till I was quite far along, and so then, of course, I had no option but to have the baby. It was given up for adoption as soon as it was born – they didn't even let me look at it, or tell me the gender, or even the fact,' her voice drops, she bites her lip, 'that it was born with some physical and mental challenges …

'The only information I had was the name of the institution that had taken the baby, and so I sent them money every year. I pictured my first child as healthy and happy, and hoped he had been adopted into a loving home, so imagine my horror when Leo showed up, and told me that this was very far from the truth. Nobody had adopted the baby, he had stayed in the orphanage all his life, and what, asked Leo, would my husband, and the world, say when they found out that Urvashi Khurana had abandoned her firstborn simply because he was not as perfect as she would have liked him to be?'

'So you paid him off,' Roshni murmurs.

'Yes,' Urvashi says quietly. 'But I didn't poison him. And the ACP can theorize all he likes, but Guppie Ram and I were never close, and I attended his funeral only out of common decency. He never told me anything about burying a dead body in the kitchen garden, and I didn't order for it to be dug up in order to get General Mehra into trouble. I had enough going on in my own life, thank you very much.'

She bends and hugs Rax, who glows as proudly as a child.

Bambi Todi jumps to her feet. 'You just put the mum in Chysanthemum!' she cries in a trembling voice, dashing tears from her face. 'Three cheers for Urvashi Khurana!'

She starts to clap. Everybody joins in. There is laughter and cheering.

Urvashi smiles somewhat tremulously and thanks everyone. Mukki beams. 'Rakesh has agreed to live with us and take the surname Khurana,' he announces stolidly. 'He's had training in accountancy and will be joining my firm.'

Bhavani, who has let the reins go slack for a bit, now effortlessly gathers them up again. Padam, watching from the door, is reluctantly impressed.

'Sach bataun toh I never thought ki Bhavani sir ki itni personality hai,' he confides to his family exultantly the next morning. 'I felt like I was watching *KBC*! Matlab how Bachchan sa'ab says *pehla padaav* and then dramatic music plays, and the camera and the lights sort of drop down and zoom in? Haan, it was same like that only! Bhavani sir's voice got ekdum heavy, and I forgot what he said, but he might as well have said *aakhri padaav*. That was the effect he managed to create!'

⬤—⬤

'Let us come back to the beginning,' Bhavani says. 'We have shared with you the details of three people who were being blackmailed by Leo Matthew, who had a motive to kill him, as well as a link to the body in the kitchen garden. Now there is *one* more thing that has a curious bearing on the case.'

He looks around the room, his steady gaze meeting every single person's face, one by one.

'Three years ago, Anshul Poddar and Bambi Todi had a beautiful engagement party to which several of you present here were invited. The engagement was tragically short-lived, because the very next morning, Anshul boarded a doomed bus to Garhwal, which went off the road in the fog, plummeted four thousand feet and crashed into a river, resulting in hundred per cent fatalities.

'Naturally Bambi ji was devastated. But she is young, and resilient, and two years after Anshul's death, she started socializing again. But this is when a strange thing happened. Every time Bambi ji went on a date, an anonymous letter claiming to be from Anshul would be found stuck under the windshield wiper of her car.'

This statement creates a sensation. Everybody turns with exclamations of surprise and concern to Bambi, who herself is staring in confusion at Bhavani.

'But … I don't understand,' she says falteringly. 'You didn't believe me when I told you about the letters. You said I'd been sending them to myself! That I was delusional!'

'What the hell!' Kashi's face darkens. 'When did this happen, Bambi?'

She turns towards him deliberately, her voice scathing. 'Oh, are you speaking to me again? How come?'

Kashi's face reddens. 'I'm not *not* speaking to you.' He mutters, 'I just … got busy…work…my mom…' He trails off incoherently.

Bambi shoots him a look of pure scorn, then faces way.

'We owe you an apology, Bambi ji,' Bhavani says to the still fulminating girl. 'Actually, we did nat want to tell you anything because we knew the stalker would be watching you all the time – perhaps it was even somebody you were coming into contact with regularly! So we thought it is better if you think the police is nat suspicious of the stalker or exploring that line of investigation at all.'

'But you were?' Hope suffuses her face.

He nods benignly. 'O yes.'

They smile at each other.

Urvashi asks worriedly. 'What's all this, Bambi? What letters? What stalker?'

'We are explaining.' Bhavani looks about the room. 'Essentially, the letters all said versions of the same thing – that the man Bambi ji was dating was unworthy, and that it would be better for her to wait till the letter writer, who signed himself as "the A" to her B came back to reclaim her.'

'That's what you called Anshul in your speech on your engagement day!' Cookie recalls. 'You said, "You're the sun to my sea, the A to my B." Kitna romantic tha!' Her face crumples suddenly, overcome with sympathy. 'Hai, bichaari bachi ... what a sick joke for somebody to play!'

'But what if it *wasn't* a joke, Cookie ji?' Bhavani says soberly. 'From our experience in the Crime Branch we know that very often bubbly girls like Bambi ji attract the attention of neurotic types. Quiet, mild fellows who underneath are a seething volcano of pent-up emotion! They are too introverted to make their move but they brood, and they obsess, and they watch, and they stare with their nose pressed to the glass – what we used to call "window shopping" when we were young! It is entirely possible that there really *is* a stalker – somebody obsessed with Bambi ji, who has been watching her for years, and is pretending to be Anshul to keep her from dating other men till he makes his move.'

'But what's stopping him from making his move?' Cookie demands.

Bhavani shrugs his chunky shoulders. 'Who knows what goes on in the head of a madman, madam? Maybe he wants to lose weight before he meets her first, maybe he is burdened with a wife and wants to get divorced first, maybe—'

'Maybe it really *is* Anshul, grievously injured, and he wants to heal completely first,' Bambi says defiantly. 'It could be that too, couldn't it?'

'Bambi.' Raw pain has made Kashi's voice very deep. 'Don't do this to yourself. Anshul is *gone*. You have to face up to it.'

Bambi's eyes grow stormy, then fill with tears. She dashes them from her eyes, then smiles blindly and reaches for a glass of water.

'Or *maybe*,' Bhavani's voice continues, now very softly, 'he has a drug habit, a very hard-to-break, debilitating, life-destroying drug habit, and he wants to kick it before he makes his move …'

His eyes travel the room till they come to rest on the reclining figure on the bed, pale and propped up on a hospital pillow.

Bambi gasps. 'What? *No!*'

The unguarded revulsion in her voice makes Aryaman flinch. Pain flashes on his face, then is swiftly replaced with a dull flush of resentful shame.

'Surely you didn't write those letters, Arya!' Bambi makes a credible effort at sounding kinder. 'Why *would* you?'

'Maybe he's an incel,' Randy Rax volunteers suddenly to the room at large. 'An involuntary celibate – as opposed to my friend Father Vicky here, who is a voluntary celibate. It's a word for men who have been sexually rejected by women for years and years – so they get all messed up, and start hating women and mass-shooting people and boasting about it to each other on the internet – kind of like in that movie … *The Joker*.' He pauses for a moment, head cocked to one side, eyes beadily bright, face sober. 'I think I was an incel for a while. But not any more. Now I'm gonna go to my stepdad's office every day and do yoga with my mum and ask a nice lady to marry me, and she will say yes, because I'm nice now too.'

'That's very nice, Rakesh,' Urvashi says softly, 'but you're interrupting the investigation. Shusshh now.'

Silence fills the room. Roshni Aggarwal has buried her face in her hands. Her narrow shoulders are shaking.

'Arya?' Bambi says apprehensively. 'I know you've been low-key stalking me. I caught you looking at me through that peephole again yesterday ... and I'm sorry I yelled at you ... especially if it made you overreact like ...' She pauses, takes a shaky breath, 'Like *this*! But I never thought—'

'I liked you,' Aryaman Aggarwal interrupts her sullenly. 'You know that, Bambi Todi, I've liked you for years – right through school and beyond. And you can deny it till you're blue in the face but you did hook up with me on the library roof that one time! I went through hell on the day of your engagement – Mom insisted on bringing me to the party, fuck knows why – you wore yellow and gold – and he ... Wow, was that alpha-male bastard a prince of choots! Maybe I'm an asshole, but trust me, an asshole can spot another asshole faster than anybody else – he wore yellow and gold too. I couldn't bear it – couldn't bear watching him put his bulked-up ape arm around your tiny waist like he'd fucking *bought* you from your fat bastard of a dad or something. So I asked Ajay Kumar to get me some shit and I went out into the garden and snorted my brains out that night. I *rejoiced* when I heard the fucker died the next day – but I didn't send you any letters and I didn't kill Leo when I found out you'd been dating him – another asshole, by the way, who got killed by *some other* asshole ... Why're you such an asshole magnet?'

Everybody listens to this rambling tirade with horrified fascination; it is like watching a animal who has miraculously been granted the gift of speech. When he's done, they all sort of blink in wonder collectively.

'Arrey wah!' Cookie Katoch says shakily. 'So nicely you can speak, Aryaman beta, I haven't heard you speak so many long sentences in years! Good boy!'

'Thank you, auntie,' he says dully.

Roshni looks up with naked, desperate appeal towards Bhavani. He nods and takes charge of the room again.

'Aryaman, because of his drug dealer contacts, had access to as much Pinko Hathni as he liked. Things were looking very bad for him indeed and so he is *fortunate* that we soon found evidence that he was nat the person we were looking for …'

Roshni's eyes widen. She steals closer to her son's bed, and sits down by his feet.

'We travelled to Kolkata,' Bhavani continues, 'where we spoke in the strictest confidence with Arihant Poddar who confirmed what you Bambi ji, and Mr Poddar's own wife had always suspected. That the battered body that was identified and cremated as Anshul's had nat been confirmed as hundred per cent his. There *had been* some room for doubt. And though the family had been in possession of Anshul's DNA in the form of a lock of hair plucked out by the roots and fashioned into a locket for his mother on her fiftieth birthday, Arihant Poddar had nat used it to confirm if the body was that of his son. He had just relied on what he called his "father's instinct" to identify the body. But perhaps he was relying more on a "husband's instinct" and his driving motive was to protect his wife from the agonies of uncertainty and give her closure.

'It does nat matter. The main takeaway from the meeting was that Anshul could very much be alive, at large, and the murderer we were seeking.'

There are gasps and murmurs from all over the room. Padam, standing by the door, braces himself, and discreetly touches the handcuffs buckled to his waist.

'And now we started looking for Anshul in earnest. We spoke to people in Garhwal. Had they rescued somebody that day? Pulled a body out of the water? Given somebody a lift? We checked hospital records all along the route of the river.

'At the same time, we checked if anybody had been stalking Bambi ji on social media. Instagram especially, where she was the most active, both on her own account and the account of the DTC. We checked Google search histories to see if anyone had been checking up on her steadily, compulsively. And slowly, a likely name started to emerge.

'Nat Anshul Poddar, no. But somebody else. Somebody whom Bambi ji had known for years. Since she was six years old, to be exact. Whom she went to school with, whom she trusted, a regular visitor to her house. Somebody she had lost touch with for a while, but who had recently resurfaced and easily recaptured the place he had always held in her heart.'

He turns to look deliberately at the handsome young man on his left, who has been listening silently to him all this while.

'Akash Dogra fit the bill exactly.'

Kashi looks up at that, utterly startled. *'What?'* He stands up abruptly.

Padam Kumar surges forward at once, handcuffs clinking.

'Stop!' Bhavani's voice is like a whip.

Padam halts.

Bhavani turns back to Kashi. 'Vakeel sa'ab, please sit down.'

Kashi slowly retakes his seat, a thousand emotions flickering over his face.

'Carry on, ACP,' he says politely.

Bhavani inclines his head. 'Very well. As we said, if Bambi Todi had a stalker, then Kashi Dogra fit the bill *exactly*. He had motive. His closest friends confirm that while he has a girlfriend who is perfect in every possible way, he is still emotionally invested in Bambi ji. Because of his constant, secretive stalking, he knew all about her dating Leo, even though nobody in the Zumba group did!'

The DTC Zumba ladies exchange startled looks. Clearly, this is news to them.

Bhavani nods gravely. 'O yes. He had easy access to Pinko Hathni from the anti-social elements he represents in the lower courts all the time. As for opportunity – he dropped in on the DTC gym on Tambola Sunday to familiarize himself with the place, which had recently been renovated. Just a short visit perhaps, but it gave him ample time to observe the placement of the security camera and note that the gas balloons could easily be released through the window to obscure it at the correct moment. Later, when an argument broke out between Mukesh Khurana and Leo in front of the whole Club, he seized the opening to establish himself as a friend and well-wisher of the very man he planned to murder the next morning! And then, late that night, it was a simple enough matter for a fit young man to jog down to the DTC from Nizamuddin with his hood up, and then in through the gates as the security guards huddled up to their heaters in their boxes – and out the same way ten minutes later!'

'You're saying Kashi killed Leo because he was *jealous*?' Bambi says incredulously. 'Have you taken a good look at Kashi? I would've picked him over Leo *any day*!'

'Bam,' Kashi mutters. 'Please. *Behave.*'

'Shut up, Kashi!' She turns back to the old policeman. 'But I *didn't* because Kashi has *a girlfriend*, and we're just friends now. Wow, ACP, your age and your moral compass are really showing!'

'Bambi—'

'He's accusing you of *murder*, Kashi!'

'Yes, I know,' Kashi replies in a low, level voice. 'And it's ridiculous and will never stand up in court.'

'You're right, Bambi ji,' Bhavani replies easily. 'Even we know that you would have picked vakeel sa'ab over Leo Matthew any day. And that is where we finally move forward out of all the fogs and confusions and come to the crux of this whole case, because you see, Akash Dogra did nat murder Leo Matthew because he was jealous of him. He murdered Leo Matthew because Leo Matthew was *blackmailing him*.'

—

'Blackmailing Akash?' Father Victor Emmanuel says blankly after the uproar in the room has subsided. 'But Lambu didn't even know Akash properly! *I* knew him! He repped some of our boys, he donated money to the orphanage because of me, not because of Lambu!'

Bhavani Singhs gets slowly to his feet and looks about the room. Everybody watches him with bated breath.

'Let us go back three years again. To the night of Bambi Todi and Anshul Poddar's engagement. A glittering, spectacular night, put together in haste because the groom has to leave for a mountaineering expedition early the next morning. A guest list comprising of the wealthy Marwari committee, business associates of the Todis and Poddars, family friends, long-time retainers, and school friends of both Anshul and Bambi. And amongst this list of school friends, there is the twenty-two-year-old Akash Dogra, fresh out of law school with nothing to offer Bambi ji but his heart, putting up a brave front after being tossed aside by his childhood friend and girlfriend of the last few years.

'We have seen the videos of that night. Akash Dogra arrives with two Doon School friends, and steers clear of Bambi ji all evening. He speaks little, eats even less, flinches when Bambi ji calls Anshul the A to her B, and drinks a lot. He meets Bambi for one short moment, hugs her awkwardly and shakes hands with Anshul, who gives him his hand in an open friendly fashion, with no suspicion whatsoever that the man he is shaking hands with has black hate in his heart.'

'You can't just say things like that, Bhavani ji!' Bambi says in a shaking voice. 'You weren't there, you can't possibly know the state of Kashi's heart from a video. You're acting like Guppie Ram, now!'

'Yes, do please cut out the filmi flourishes, ACP,' Roshni Aggarwal says testily. 'I've given you access to this space because I want to get to the bottom of this wretched business, but this situation now seems to be entering the realm of wild guesswork.'

Bhavani spreads out his hands.

'We are just now coming to the point, madam. Here is what happened that night, and we have abundant proof of it. Akash Dogra left the party after congratulating Bambi ji and her new fiancé, and went out drinking with his friends. Presumably they tried to cheer him up and so on. Eventually they dropped him to his house and left.

'But instead of going upstairs and to bed, Akash Dogra got into his parents' Maruti Swift, drove back to the DTC, parked in the parking lot, and went back into the gardens of Guest Cottage No. 1.

'Because Akash Dogra had dated Bambi Todi for years, he knew that she would do with Anshul what she had done with Akash many a time. Sure enough, a few hours later, when the party had well and truly wrapped up, and everybody including Bambi ji's parents had gone home, and she herself had retired to Guest Cottage No. 1 where she was spending the night, Anshul Poddar returned. He had stowed his bags on the bus leaving for Garhwal and was dressed in his travelling clothes. A giggling Bambi ji let him into the cottage and they were cloistered there for two hours, while Akash Dogra waited outside. When Anshul finally emerged, alone,

at about four in the morning, Akash Dogra was waiting for
him. We do nat quite know how the lapiz lazuli Shivling
Cookie ji had carried into the party so proudly as a gift to
the engaged couple entered the picture, but our guess is that
Bambi ji gave it as a "joke" parting gift to her fiancé when he
left her for the mountains.'

Kashi is staring at Bhavani with open fascination. 'Then
what happened?' he asks.

Bhavani shrugs. 'We cannat exactly say. An exchange of
words perhaps, followed by a physical fight – in which the ace
mountaineer, at the peak of his physical training, but wearied
perhaps by a night of non-stop revelry, was bested by the jilted
lover who had been waiting jealously in the freezing cold for
two hours. Vakeel sa'ab here is definitely smaller and slighter,
but they say hatred can power a man with superhuman
strength. Or perhaps he had had the element of surprise.'

'You say you have proof of this,' Kashi says in a low voice.
'Can I ask what proof you possess?'

'Perhaps you did nat mean to kill Bambi ji's fiancé.
Perhaps you had only sought to teach him a lesson. But once
you realized he was dead, sanity returned. The enormity of
what you had just done dawned on you. A man was dead
at your hands, the son of a very rich and powerful man.
Remembering the beetroot patch that you had seen being dug
up in the lawn, you made a phone call to Guppie Ram, the
old gardener, who was sympathetic to your cause, and had
always been very taken up by the idea of you and Bambi ji
getting together. Being a poor man himself, his sympathies
lay with you, the poorer suitor, and nat with the arrogant

Anshul. It was an easy enough task to persuade him to help you dispose Anshul's body into that shallow grave.'

There is a small stifled gasp from the other end of the room. Ganga has slumped forward onto the coffee table, her head in her arms.

'She's fainted,' Bambi, sitting next to her, says crisply. 'Her pulse is steady enough. She should come around in a moment. It must be all this stress.'

'What about you, Bambi?' Urvashi leans in to whisper. 'Isn't this all … too much for you?'

Bambi's face is very pale, but she shakes her head determinedly. 'I'm sure he's building up to some sort of twist in the tale,' she whispers back. 'It's okay.'

Ganga revives, looking apologetic, and asks weakly for a glass of water. Rather self-consciously, Randy Rax holds it to her lips.

Bhavani, who has not looked away from Kashi even for moment during this bit of by-play, picks up his narrative from exactly where he has left it.

'Fortune favours the brave, they say. God alone knows if you sent Anshul's expedition members a message from his phone, and what you said in that message, or what answers you dreamt up to the questions that were sure to be raised the next day, or if you even managed to get any sleep that night. But by the time you woke up, the news was in. Anshul's bus had plummeted into an abyss and all on board were dead. Nobody would go looking for him, or ask why he had nat shown up on the bus that morning. Miraculously, you were safe.'

'Please, for the sake of clarity,' Mukesh Khurana asks pleadingly, 'you're saying ki Bambi's fiancé never got on the bus to Garhwal *at all*? That he was murdered that night and buried right here in the DTC? That he's been *here* all along? You're saying the body in the kitchen garden is *Anshul Poddar*? That's your theory?'

Bhavani nods. 'Yes.'

'Fuck.' Aryaman Aggarwal turns to look at Kashi with awe in his eyes. '*Respect*, bro!'

'And so vakeel sa'ab was safe, but nat satisfied. Because Bambi Todi shunned him. Women have a special feminine intuition, they say, and perhaps, subconsciously, she sensed that the man who seemed to bear her no malice for the way in which she had jilted him, was actually the murderer of her fiancé and the architect of her grief. She did nat speak to him for the next two years.'

'But the proof?' Kashi insists again, in a low intense voice. 'What proof do you have to substantiate this richly imagined tale?'

Bhavani turns to look at him more fully. 'The shards of blue stone found in the mud correspond exactly with materials Cookie ji uses.'

'That proves *nothing*.'

'And the DNA from Anshul Poddar's hair, plucked from the root … It was sent to us by his father and it matches the DNA of the skeleton found in the kitchen garden patch exactly. We have the report here. There is no room for error at all.'

'That doesn't prove *Kashi* did it,' Bambi says hotly. 'It just proves the man in the kitchen garden is Anshul! Which,' she swallows painfully, 'is horrible, of course, but I've ... already mourned Anshul and I cannot do it again. You have no proof against Kashi, ACP!'

'But we *do*, Bambi ji,' Bhavani says softly. 'When the newspapers reported that it was Ganga's husband, Ajay Kumar, who was buried in the kitchen garden, Cookie ji came forward with a video recording of that night – a short clip of Ajay Kumar arguing with Aryaman Aggarwal in the parking lot.'

Urvashi leans forward, her beautiful brow furrowed. 'But what's that got to do with young Akash?'

'Because parked *beyond* Ajay Kumar and Aryaman Aggarwal, in that video recording, is a car we recognize very well, because we helped push it up the driveway of the DTC only very recently. An old Maruti Swift, with a Noida registration number, belonging to—'

'Me,' Kashi says, very low.

Bhavani leaps on in this confession like a large jungle cat. 'You accept it!'

Kashi's handsome face is very white about the lips. His eyes glitter strangely. 'Yes.

Everybody gasps. Bambi's eyes skitter from Bhavani to Kashi, wide with fear.

'So you were there that night, vakeel sa'ab?' Bhavani's voice is sharp. 'You don't deny it?'

Kashi throws up his head. 'No.' His voice is defiant. 'I don't deny it.'

His eyes go to Bambi's. They stare at each other, communicating wordlessly. They stare at each other in a manner that makes everybody else feel slightly embarrassed. They stare at each other like there is nobody else in the room.

'You ... came back?' she says finally, in a halting whisper.

He smiles ruefully and gives a tiny shrug. 'I came back.'

He turns to look at Bhavani then, his gaze meeting the older man's steadily. 'Bambi called me a bunch of times. But my friends wouldn't let me take her calls – they even took away my phone. We were all drunk, of course. So, after they dropped me home, I drove back to the Club to see what she wanted. I parked the car and rang the bell of Guest Cottage No. 1. When nobody answered, I left.'

Then he looks directly in the ACP's eyes. 'But I did *not* murder anybody.'

Bambi gasps raggedly and whirls to face the policeman.

'Well, of *course* he didn't! It wasn't Kashi! I tell you it wasn't him! You talked about my female instinct earlier – they say he would never do anything like that! He's too nice ... too decent ... too *clean!*'

Bhavani regards her calmly. 'Then who else could it be, Bambi ji?'

'Oh!' She pushes her hair back from her forehead, breathing hard. Her eyes travel around the room, flying from face to face. Then they light up. 'Arya! It must have been Arya – it *has* to be Arya – he said just now that he spent the night snorting cocaine in the garden and hating on Anshul! He said so! Cookie auntie has a video of him on the spot, for fuck's sake! He must have seen Anshul coming out from my cottage, got maddened with jealousy and attacked him! Yes, that makes perfect sense – you're so smart, Bhavani ji, why haven't you thought of that? Why aren't you arresting Arya?' Her young voice grows unthinkingly cruel. 'He's a waste of space, anyway! *You should be arresting Arya!*'

Bhavani Singh ignores her and steps forward. 'We have a warrant here for your arrest, vakeel sa'ab. Please come into the next room with us so we can record your statement.'

'What a shit show.' Kashi gives an incredulous little laugh, but he gets to his feet readily enough. 'I thought you were an intelligent man, ACP. Clearly, I was wrong.'

Bhavani smiles blandly. 'Handcuffs, PK.'

The cherubic inspector looms forward, clinking slightly. Light glints wickedly on the metal links of the cuffs as he hands them to his superior.

Bhavani steps closer to Kashi, with his back to the now sobbing Bambi. He looks calmly into Kashi's bewildered, furious eyes and then, very deliberately, winks at him.

For one uncomprehending moment Kashi thinks he has imagined it. Then understanding floods his eyes.

'No!' he whispers, stricken.

Bhavani nods back gravely.

Yes.

And in that moment Kashi perceives everything. What the ACP's game plan is, and what is expected of him. A soul-searing sadness sweeps over him – a wave of sorrow so strong that he almost staggers. But strangely, he feels no surprise at all.

Yes, this is where it was headed all along. This *is* how the story ends.

He holds out his hands.

'I confess,' he says lightly. 'I did it.'

Bhavani places the manacles around his wrists.

'No!!!'

The scream that emerges from behind them is both shrill and guttural. An animal scream, rising from a deep, secret darkness into the light. Heart-rending, blood-curdling and exquisitely violent.

'I didn't mean for this to happen! This wasn't in the plan at all! Kashi didn't do it! He didn't do anything! It was all me, all me! *I* killed Anshul, *I* phoned Guppie Ram ji, Guppie Ram ji came to help me and somehow Leo wormed it out of him, the slimy bastard, so I had to kill him too!'

Sobbing incoherently, Bambi Todi crumples into a childlike heap onto the ground.

17

Icky Slime

Kash, d'you remember the night you passed out from NLS? You came to my place straight from the airport so proud and happy and I made you unpack your graduation robe and wear it, and then we made love on the carpet while 'Whole New World' from Alladin *played on my red speaker, and you joked about the double meanings of 'magic carpet ride'? Well, once you sneaked out of my bedroom that night, Mammu came in and said well, I hope you enjoyed that.*

I said, wait, did you know Kashi was here?

And she said, oh yes, I knew, I always know when he's here, and what-all you're up to, but you must understand that you're older now. Just like childhood ended, and school ended, and college ended, your childish 'best-friendship' with that boy also has to come to an end.

She said everybody should marry people who are from the same faith, social standing and community as themselves because if they don't, there would be too many differences in background, and no matter how much you love each other, these differences would eventually drive you apart.

She was SO sure and SO chill about it! And Paapu and she did seem to have the dream marriage, built on all this 'logic' of hers. It rattled the fuck out of me.

They then produced Anshul out of a hat, literally. 'A prince for my princess' was what Paapu called him, very triumphantly, before we went on our first date. He was handsome, charming, thoughtful, witty, amazingly strong and, of course, crazy wealthy. TBH, what I dug most was that all the Maaru girls were panting after him — it's so fun to screw with them — so I couldn't resist making him fall for me. It was easy enough to pretend I would love to sleep in a tent and bathe in melted glacier water (As if! I'm not like your perfect little GF who I hear has turned into an actual villager, and is probably harvesting paddy as I write this) — but I swore I was up for all sorts of outdoorsy ghar-ghar games and he was hooked.

It broke my heart into a million bits to end things with you, but I swear that at that time I really thought I was adulting properly and doing the correct, mature thing. I REALLY did.

I visited him at his flat a few times, where I met his domestic help — a sweet, large-eyed brown thing called Ganga — she'd ask me for water and tea very sweetly, even though I never had any. Soon after, she randomly quit. I didn't give it much thought but then, just a few days before our big engagement, she accosted me on the road and insisted on speaking to me.

She told me that one day, while she was dusting the bottles in the bar, Anshul had grabbed her, thrown her to the ground and forced himself on her. She had pleaded with him and pleaded with him, but he hadn't listened. Afterwards, he had given her ten thousand rupees, plus her monthly salary in advance, and told her he didn't need her to work in his house any more.

Of course I was fully shook up. I asked her what she wanted me to do about it, and she said, nothing didi, you look so sweet and nice, just don't marry that man, he is a monster and will destroy your life.

I told my parents about the incident, but they pooh-poohed it. They said Ganga was making up the story, maybe in the hope of extracting money from me, maybe because she herself was obsessed with hot, hunky Anshul. They said I should ignore the incident completely.

But I couldn't get it out of my head. I started watching Ansh all the time, observing little little things – the way he spoke to servants, how curt he was with his mother when he thought nobody was watching, or even how bossy he sometimes was with me … and I started having doubts. On the night of the engagement – Bhavani ji was correct about that, I told him to sneak back to meet me after everybody was asleep – I brought up Ganga with him.

He laughed it off, of course. And then he started asking me all these questions about YOU. He said he'd sensed something between us – it was like he was trying to turn the tables on me, to put me in the wrong. So I told him, ya sure, Kashi and I had a scene, but it was always consensual – not like him, groping Ganga against her will! And then he started calling me a slut! Me! So I told him that while I'd had a few guy friends, I'd certainly never grabbed a manservant in my house and copulated with him forcibly and given him money afterwards! He made a mistake then. He said, I never grabbed her in the bar, and so of course I said, but I never mentioned the bar. He knew he'd been caught then, and, Kash, he … he just lost it.

It was like a mask had slipped from his face. He started talking all crudely, telling me it was time I stopped living in la-la land. He said all men were like this, and that he wasn't going to pretend to be goody-goody any more, that it would be hypocritical and that he was above all an honest man. Yes, he'd raped Ganga but he'd paid her, her full salary and ten thousand rupees in cash besides, so what was she complaining about?

I started feeling all panicked and sick. I was alone with a raving man and all I could do was fiddle with that blue, Swarovski-encrusted ShivBling Cookie auntie had given us – we'd opened a few presents earlier in the evening, just for fun.

Anshul kept ranting – by now I'd realized the guy had serious issues – and I just sat there frozen with horror at the mess I was in. He said women didn't mind what you did to them as long as you gave them enough money – his mum was the same and so was mine. He said Paapu was famous in whorehouses all over the world, that everybody on the Marwari network joked about Paapu and called him the human Zomato of strip-clubs. He had a rating for each club and he was never wrong. He said Mammu knew all about it.

He kept hissing and hissing in my ear, like the snake he'd revealed himself to be, and I kept thinking he's a rapist, a rapist who rapes MAIDS, not even girls of his own class, not that I'm a snob or anything, and I'm really fond of Ganga, but STILL! I kept telling him to shut up, but he wouldn't shut up, and so finally, just to get him to shut the fuck up, I swung the ShivBling, and whacked him across the side of the head with it.

It shattered with a horrible crashing sound. Ansh crumpled to the ground and didn't move. There were shards everywhere. His mouth was all slack and open and stupid – how could I have ever thought he was handsome? I didn't know what to do, so I started calling you. I called you at least six times, till I realized the Doscos weren't going to let you pick up my call. After what Ansh had just been saying about my parents, the last thing I wanted to do was phone them up. I was going to have to adult properly, and handle this one all by myself, like a grown-up.

I stared at the stupid, ugly body on the ground for a while, repeating, I've made a mess, I've made a mess, I've made a mess, to myself like fool, and then I did what I always do when I make a mess. I called Guppie Ram ji and said, I've made a mess. Come clean it up.

There must have been something odd in my voice because he came from the quarters at once.

He was so sweet! He wasn't at all psyched by the fact that Anshul was the mess. He'd never liked him anyway. I told him that Anshul had tried to rape me, which made him only too happy to roll that SOB in a sheet, drag him out of the cottage and into the patch. It was a distance of just 200 metres and it was a foggy night. We managed it easily enough.

Anshul's phone started ringing at about 5 a.m., so I sent his group a WhatsApp message saying I'd had too much to drink at the engagement party and would join them all one day late. Then I broke the SIM and the phone and told Guppie Ram ji to get rid of the bits in some manhole or something. He was always hanging out in places like that.

Then I went to sleep. I had no idea what the next day would bring or how I would cope. But I remember sleeping really well that night.

When I woke up to the news that rapist Anshul's bus had fallen into a khai and everybody on board was dead, I didn't know whether to laugh or cry. If I had left well enough alone, he would have died anyway, and I wouldn't have had blood on my hands! The thought almost drove me insane ... but the relief at not being found out kept me going ... I faked grief – faked it really well, I even pretended to believe he wasn't dead, that he had somehow survived – if I did all that nobody would think to look for him in the DTC veggie patch!

You called me that evening, remember? You'd heard about the accident, I guess – but when I stared down at your name on my phone, this sickening realization swept over me that I couldn't talk to you any more. It was like the Alladin song, I'd travelled to a 'whole new world' and I now had a 'new fantastic point of view' and I could never never share it with you and fuck up your life like I'd fucked up mine.

Besides, I had enough survival instinct to know that if you sat me down somewhere and held my hands, and I looked into your eyes, my stomach would heave and the whole story of that ghastly evening would come pouring out of my mouth like thick, foul vomit. So I avoided you.

I don't recommend murdering anyone. Even the vilest person in the world – even a person like rapist Anshul. It leaves you coated in a sort of toxic, icky slime – like your soul has blocked *pores that no amount of steaming can unclog. And there's this constant, giant lake of puke in your stomach, puke that you can't throw up, not ever. And of course, you can never be truly carefree or go drinking or smoke up ever again, in case you lose control and spill your guts to some nosy rando.*

Friending Ganga helped me cope. She never suspected the truth of what had happened that night, but she was happy for me – I had been spared a life with rapist Anshul, and he had, in a way, got his just desserts. I got her a Daily Needs franchise at the DTC, and even though her husband showed up now and then and accused her of sleeping with rich sahibs for money (he had seen the ten thousand she had come back with that day), she was happy.

I found I couldn't get the stuff rapist Anshul had said about my parents out of my head. They were flawed, and fucked up. It was high time I stopped accepting everything they said to me as gospel truth and started thinking for myself.

That made me feel a bit better.

I started gymming, and working hard at Todi Corp, and after a while, decided to start dating again. I'd burnt my boats with you, but I figured it was a big world, I'd find somebody else, equally nice.

Slowly, though, I realized that Kashi Dogras were thin on the ground in the real world …

Still, I liked Leo – he was charming, and funny and really handsome. Besides, he was wildly ineligible and long-haired and used to be a waiter and grew up in an orphanage so that would drive my parents nuts. Dating him was like sweet revenge on them for making me break up with you and getting me involved with rapist Anshul.

But then one evening in the DTC's kitchen garden Leo started giving me all this Roman Catholic, Exorcist bullshit about how he sensed a 'presence' hovering in the beetroot patch behind me. Somebody has died violently here, he said, and their blood is crying out for vengeance. Naturally, my blood froze. Then he sucked in his breath and widened his stupid, hooded eyes, and whispered that he could see a disembodied spirit floating behind me. And like a total chutiya, I whirled around and stammered, 'Anshul?'

God, I'm SUCH a little idiot!

Now of course I know that Leo got his info from Guppie Ram ji, but back then, I really thought it was divine revelation. So I blabbed out the whole story to him, and once I did, he showed me his real face. It was like the whole Anshul nightmare all over again. Except that Leo added goody-goody religious righteousness to the mix. He told me all piously that I had sinned but that Jesus still loved me and that I should repent by donating money to that freaking orphanage he was so obsessed with. The hypocritical self-righteous bastard! He didn't even have the guts to fucking call it blackmail! He called it penance!

I coughed up the damn money – it wasn't much anyway. Leo really was SUCH a small-timer, I was almost insulted when he bleated out '50 lakhs.' Anyway, I transferred the money and froze him out, and he slunk away for the time being …

But then something else happened. I realized that Gagan Ruia was starting to look more and more stupid around me. He used to totally hero-worship Anshul and after he heard the story of my tragic engagement, he began to build me up as this amaze, #goals chick or something in his brain, because one night, after he ate too much dahi kebab and red velvet cake at our house, he asked me to marry him.

Now this wasn't a bad deal at all. The Ruias are super super wealthy and very powerful. Gagan's an oaf, of course, but it was a 'Prince for my Princess' match all over again. And I was sick of the Ghia-Lauki gang feeling sorry for me. And so DONE with my parents. And with romance. Besides, unlike Anshul, Gagan is actually quite stupid and biddable and easy to control. Also, if I married him, I thought I could actually have a shot at redemption! Do something good on a mega scale with my life. For women like Ganga and all, you know? Like legit good social work, the kind you and your GF do. Something that would make you look at me with respect! Maybe I could even join politics? I'd make a damn good politician, everybody always likes me – it's because I'm so tender-hearted and sweet.

Anyway, right after Gagan and his dad made the rishtaa formally and we accepted (secretly, because I told them the Poddars would feel bad if we made a big announcement) bloody Leo bounced back into my life and told me I had to MARRY HIM!

Like, WTF?

He said he felt personally responsible for my salvation and my soul and wanted us to spend our lives together!

!!!!!

Of course, I was smart enough to recognize this as complete cock. He was just a bloody social climber – obsessed in a weird love-hate way with the DTC and being a legit member of Delhi

High Society. He had got his hooks into me, and was planning to simultaneously leech off me and preach to me till I died. So, I decided it was MUCH better if HE died.

(That's the other thing with killing people. If you've done it once, it's always on your list of available options. It's the last option, of course, if you're essentially a good person, like I am, but it's an option nonetheless.)

But I wasn't sure of how and when to do it …

Then Urvashi auntie became obsessed with her rainwater-harvesting system and wanted to instal it in the kitchen garden of all places! I couldn't have them digging that thing up and discovering the bones of rapist Anshul – whom I'd been fake-mourning for three years!

I liked Urvashi auntie, but I didn't know how to stop her – so when Mukki uncle got into a big fight with Leo on Tambola Sunday, I figured it was the perfect time. If I bumped Leo off that very night, while the memory of the quarrel was fresh on everybody's mind, there would be so much whispering about Mukki uncle having maybe done it, what with his late-night gymming and everything, that she'd be sure to lose the election!

Arya had already slipped me some Pinko Hathni in a fit of genorosity – he likes me, always has, ever since I was dumb enough to hook up with him on the library terrace that one time. He probably doesn't even remember giving it to me, he was so high at the time. I had taken it out of sheer politeness, but then I started thinking that it may be the perfect thing to use on Leo …

Meeting you that day threw me off slightly. But then you pissed me off by seeming so fond of Leo, and flexing so much about how happy you were with your new chick that I was like, okay, theek hai, I've made my slimy bed and now I'm just gonna have to lie in it.

Murder is much easier if you know you're going to commit it twenty-four hours in advance. Urvashi auntie had already placed the balloons perfectly. I had a key to the gym – it used to be the plants nursery before it was renovated into the gym and the lock on the door was the same. All I had to do was sneak out of the house over the back wall, walk across the road all bundled up in a dull shawl, release the balloons through the window that didn't lock, open the gym with my old key, pour the Pinko into the flask and walk out again. I was home in under ten minutes.

Of course, I was super lucky, but I think if you're killing total assholes then luck tends to be on your side.

I slept fitfully. At about 3 a.m. I woke up all clammy and shivering and had a panic attack, and thought about dashing across the road and emptying the contents of the flask into the bathroom sink. I even dreamt I did that, and the relief was exquisite. But then I woke up again ... and made myself think about a whole life with Leo in it, having to listen to his religious homilies, his double standards, his obsession with class and caste, his preaching and his leeching, the power he would always have over me ... and that made me strong again.

I lay in bed and pictured him riding his Hayabusa into the Club – he was as punctual as fuck – parking it, entering the gym, glugging down the Creatine ...

I was probably in the shower, getting ready to show up all innocently for the six-thirty class, when the bar rolled onto his windpipe ...

I didn't feel guilty at all, not even at the church funeral – he totally had it coming.

I was now all set to reinvent myself, marry biddable Gagan Ruia, and get on with my plan to empower deserving young women like Ganga. But then two things happened.

ACP Bhavani Singh rolled up, cute as a cheekoo and keen as a cheel, and I was rattled. I hadn't thought that Delhi Police could actually be efficient. I'd thought they were all idiots. I mean they're always in the papers for either being spectacularly incompetent or spectacularly violent.

And the other thing I hadn't bargained for was the return of my feelings for you. You know how a Chocolava cake collapses and oozes molten chocolate when you just touch it with a spoon? Ya, suddenly that was me every time you even looked in my direction. I think it's because I thought I'd burnt my boats with you – dumping you for Anshul so badly – and when I realized that you weren't bitter, and that you didn't hate me, and that you'd even found it in your heart to forgive me, I just … I fell in love with you again. I guess my class-twelve psychology teacher would say you represent the simple, innocent world I'd inhabited before I started murdering people. Or maybe I had PTSD, like the soldiers in Iraq. At the Club that Monday morning, when I'd just found out that the Pinko had worked and that Leo was dead, I felt so drawn to your sweet, clean decency that I collapsed in your arms, sobbing.

Basically, I suddenly couldn't manage without you any more. I needed you like a drug – you were the only thing keeping me sane. I knew you had a girlfriend now, and a life of your own, but I sought you out like you were my *Pinko Hathni.*

And then Cheeku-cheel Bhavani and you teamed up! What a mindfuck!

I almost told you the whole story the evening you came to my bedroom and asked me about that stupid 'Secrets' song. That song had been typical, sadistic Leo chutiyapa – he loved to watch people squirm, it was all part of his 'penance' shit – and of course Bhavani zoomed in on it at once. But I thought fast. I told you Leo had been blackmailing me because of Mammu's kleptomania – she is a klepto, of course, but only Paapu and I knew it, so I thought I might as well throw her under the bus. It worked out pretty well, because not only did you buy it, you also got all protective and gooey-eyed around me – the way you used to be before I dumped you for rapist Anshul. And Bhavani bought it too – and I was safe again.

But then Bhavani dug up that video of Guppie Ram ji talking about a body pushing up beetroots in the damn kitchen garden …

The moment I heard about that, I panicked. I knew nothing about DNA testing, I had no idea how much of Anshul's body would have wasted away, or what would be left of it. I was too scared too google it, in case somebody was monitoring my search history … I decided the only thing I could do was somehow make everybody believe that rapist Anshul had survived the Garhwal accident and was still alive. If he were alive and stalking me, he couldn't possibly be pushing up beets in a vegetable patch, could he? And so I wrote those letters, and pretended I'd been getting them for over two years.

Looking back, it was probably a silly move – it attracted Bhavani's attention to the Anshul angle, but I think he had been suspecting the body was Anshul's ever since he found those blue shards in the mud with the skeleton ...

But then I realized pervy Arya had been peeking at me through the peephole in the Rose Garden loo, and I thought he could be useful. So I worked him into my jealous stalker story.

When Ganga's husband showed up alive, I had to act fast because now everybody was asking, well, if it isn't Ajay Kumar in the beetroot patch, then who is it? And I knew Bhavani wouldn't take too long to figure out it might be Anshul ...

So I dropped something on my shorts and lured pervy Arya back to the Rose Garden loo again, then 'caught' him peeking at me through the peephole while I washed them, dressed only in a T-shirt and panties, and yelled at him so badly that he went straight home and OD'd. Just like I had hoped.

But it turns out he couldn't do even that properly!

He's SO pathetic.

I'd planned to plant a suicide note confessing to both the murders in his bedroom when I visited his home after he died – written in the same style as the anonymous 'A to my B' letters I'd stuck on my windshield. It was really sensitive and would have made Roshni auntie cry buckets and given her the perfect closure – but of course I never got to use it and tie a neat bow on this whole mess.

Arya really is quite useless!

And Bhavani Singh is really quite a chalaak cheekoo. Look how he figured out that stuff about Urvashi auntie's baby! And how he got me to confess by pretending he thought you'd done it.

He'd figured out you're my real weak spot. Not Gagan Ruia, I barely even think about him any more – he was always a dose of isabgol, anyway. Besides, his evil father's made him drop me like a hot potato, anyway. TBH, every time I talked to Gagan, I wondered how I would live out my whole life with such a boring man – but then I decided that if he became too irritating, I could bump him off in some clever way. Make a clean hat-trick of it.

Ganga still loves me. She says I'm her heroine. And that when I get out of jail I should join politics. She says that all I ever did was rid the world of a few assholes. Rapist Anshul, Blackmailer Leo. And let's face it, nobody – not even his mom – would've really missed Stoner Arya. It's not like he's going to kick his addictions and find a cure for cancer tomorrow.

And General Mehra's killed more human beings than me and he's been awarded medals for it!

I'm actually a really good person.

I'm sure the courts will see it my way.

It turns out that Bhavani didn't really have any proof against me – he was just acting on a hunch he got after snooping around in the building where Anshul used to live when Ganga was cleaning for him. If I'd kept my head, and allowed them to take you away, Bhavani wouldn't have been able to make anything stick.

But I'm glad I stood up for you.

Even if it was all a trick.

And you were in on it.

Hopefully it makes up in some small way for the shit I've dumped on you my whole life.

Leo put me off religion with all his chutiyamatic hypocritical sermonizing, but surely, confessing to clear your name was a sort of penance, after all?

Maybe it's a promo code I can use in the courtroom.

Frankly, even bumping off Anshul Poddar should count as a promo code in the courtroom. I wish Cookie auntie had taken a video of THAT. Of the blue Shivling connecting with his saanp head and the blood spurting and the shards and the Swarovskis flying every where. NGL, I would watch that on repeat. I would watch that on repeat in SLOW-MOTION.

I love you, Kashi Dogra.

I don't want to drag you into my fucked-up life any further, but d'you know any good lawyers?

Kashi folds up the sheets of paper, and hands them back to Bhavani. 'D'you think I should defend her?'

Bhavani's square, homely face is sympathetic but grave. 'No.'

Kashi rakes the hair off his forehead and looks at the ACP bemusedly. 'I think ... I don't know what to think, I guess! I *feel* foul for her – she was such a sweet little girl – entitled and privileged of course, but also so sunshiny and confident and eager to please, and then, somehow, she got so ... Shit! It's hard to find the word. So ... so *corrupted*!'

'Yes,' Bhavani says sadly.

'Poor little Bumbu Todi. And look at Leo – growing up in an orphanage, with all sorts of grudges and inferiority complexes and a twisted view of religion, with bitterness gnawing at his heart constantly! Preaching and leeching, as

Bambi puts it, and wanting to marry a murderess! The whole thing suck balls.'

Bhavani sighs. 'Vakeel sa'ab.'

Kashi looks up at him, scowling. 'What?'

'Don't take the case.'

'I didn't ask for your advice,' Kashi says shortly.

Bhavani smiles. 'Actually, you did. And so we're giving it – your problem is that you are a Mother Teresa-type. Your heart is too big.'

Kashi flushes. 'You're making fun of me.'

No.' Bhavani shakes his head. 'But we will say this – make your heart a little smaller. Focus.'

'Matlab?' Kashi glares at him with resentful, defensive eyes.

'Lighten up! Forget the world's problems! Go to Kalahandi. To the lady who is building a roof. Tell her you have taken some time off to be with her, and that she should also take some time off to be with you.'

'But ...' Kashi frowns. 'But I start work today. And I have no tickets...'

Bhavani shrugs genially, his eyes twinkling. 'So?'

Kashi stares at him, hope rising as sudden as a wildfire in his heart. Kuhu Bannerjee. Abrupt, simple, straightforward Kuhu. Talking animatedly about architecture, listening to him, laughing with him, walking with him, showing him her village, her school, her children, her famous roof.

'I could check the flights,' he says slowly. 'Fly to Bhubaneswar and drive to Kalahandi.'

Bhavani chuckles and slaps him on the back. 'Now you're talking, vakeel sa'ab!'

Galvanized to action, Kashi leaps to his feet and starts throwing things into a bag. He barely even notices when Bhavani leaves.

It takes him just about half an hour to buy a ticket online, stuff some clothes, toiletries, Kuhu's COD books, and his laptop into a cabin baggage–sized bag. Marvelling at how simple everything is if you want it to be, he calls an Uber.

Fortune is truly favouring him today. He's connected to a driver right outside, dropping somebody off, who is game for an airport drop. Kashi slams the front door shut, hefts his bag and hurtles down the stairs like a maniac.

The passenger has still not quite exited the Uber when Kashi rushes up and throws his rucksack in.

'What the fuck, bro!' She says indignantly, in a strong, musical voice. Then her eyes widen. 'Kash? Where're you going?'

And Kashi just stands there and drinks in the sight of her – travel-weary, a little sweaty, her kajal smudged, her kurta crumpled and her eyes just a little unsure of her welcome. And his heart does exactly what Bhavani Singh had advised it to do – it becomes smaller and smaller until all it can hold is her. There is a tightness in his chest and the sting of tears in his eyes as he closes the distance between them with one hasty step and clasps her firmly to his heart.

'I was going to you,' he says gruffly. 'Dammit Bannerjee! You've fucked up my travel plans *again*. Just how many tickets are you going to make me cancel?'

Meanwhile, Bhavani, almost home now, sits back in his official car and heaves a sigh of satisfaction.

The case has wrapped up nicely, all in all. The killer has been caught. The little love story has closed satisfactorily. An orphan has found a family. A hardened addict has gone back into rehab, swearing to his mother that this time he will come back clean and stay that way. At least *one* sinister plan of a megalomaniac defence minister has been foiled. A certain brand of bling encrusted ShivBling is poised to get a lot of free publicity, which will probably result in a huge peak in sales for Cookie Katoch. And judging from his chastened, sober demeanour, a certain young inspector seems to be pining for a young woman whom he considered, only three weeks ago, far beneath him.

Oh, and a hundred and eighty-year-old club seems to be well on its way to gaining its first female president.

There is just one more thing that remains to be done.

Bhavani leans forward. 'Take it from the Khan Market side,' he tells the driver. 'We have to buy five stalks of pink Oriental lilies.'

Acknowledgements.

I'll start with the clubs.

The Army Club in Dinjan, Assam, where the three-year-old me learnt how to swim, and famously ran up a tremendous bill in Coca-Cola and French fries, secure in the knowledge that '*club mein paise nahi dene padte, bas papa ka naam bataa do aur phir sab kuch free!*'

The DSOI at Dhaula Kuan, from where three of us four sisters were married. So lovely in the eighties with its kidney-shaped swimming pool, kesar-scented mutton biryani, insanely well-stocked library, and gorgeous flower garden.

The Delhi Gymkhana Club where Niret and I spent many, many Thursday nights when we were dating, and not enough Sunday afternoons once we were married.

The Press Club of India at Raisina Road, with its inverted snobbery, smiley-faced waiters, stinging Romonov Vodka-Limcas and the best 'bomb shaami kebabs' in the city.

The sunny, sky-blue Bangalore Club, the multi-balconied Catholic club, all clubs, basically!

From clubs and club culture to the king of clubs. I owe a special debt to A.S. Dulat – a cosy chat we had at the CCD in the DGC in early 2020 is what got me started on this book, in the first place.

Then the lockdown kicked in and all the clubs shut down and I wrote in a house bursting at the seams with children and dogs. Naturally I drove Niret, Niharika, Nayantara and Daivik nuts by shoving drafts in their faces and needily demanding feedback. Thank you, guys, for making it so both brutal and bang-on.

I badgered friends and family too. Many thanks to my sisters, Mini, Ruhi and Nandu, my cousin Prashant, my father, Revti Raman, and my friend Shalini Beri.

Hardi Singh, who helped me develop ACP Bhavani.

My cousin Monu Singh, the OG Pinko Hathni.

All my sisters-in-sweat at my Zumba class.

My muse Tamara Rhea Rebello, whose face and form I totally ripped off for Bambi Todi.

My friend Rishi Dogra whose surname and name (almost!) I stole for my Kashi.

Gautam Mengle, who read this manuscript and corrected my many many police procedure errors.

My incredibly talented niece, Laila, who lent voice and melody to the *Secrets* song, and performed it so beautifully for the book trailer.

Dame Agatha Christie, empress of whodunnits, whose every book I have read multiple times, and who inspires absolutely everybody who attempts to pull a murderer out of a hat.

The HarperCollins India team – Ananth Padmanabham, Swati Daftuar, Bonita Vaz Shimray, Shabnam Srivastava and Shatarupa Ghoshal, who are all so kind yet firm with my agonizing and nit-picking and general control-freakiness.

I find I cannot end this without mentioning my recent crisis of faith. After about twelve years of full-on Roman Catholism, I have become happily post-religious, deeply averse to all organized religions, believing only in the divine spark in all of us, and marvelling at the Creator's work every time I unpeel oranges, or look deep into a puppy's melting brown eyes, or see sunshine sparkling on water, or inhale the scent of harishringar flowers.

So thank you, semi-finally to this Creator, who so generously drops ideas into our head from above, and finally, to my husband, Niret, for understanding when I said, 'Heaven is not like the Delhi Gymkhana Club, Choku, you can't get me in on a spouse sponsorship. I will have to somehow find my way in on my own.'

About the Author

Anuja Chauhan worked in advertising for over seventeen years and is credited with many popular campaigns including PepsiCo's Nothing Official About It, Yeh Dil Maange More, Mera Number Kab Aayega, Oye Bubbly and Darr ke Aage Jeet Hai. She is the author of five bestselling novels (*The Zoya Factor, Battle for Bittora, Those Pricey Thakur Girls, The House that BJ Built* and *Baaz*) all of which have been acquired by major Bombay studios. She lives outside Bangalore with her three children, a varying number of dogs and cats, and her husband, television producer Niret Alva, who is a member of various clubs that shall remain unnamed here.

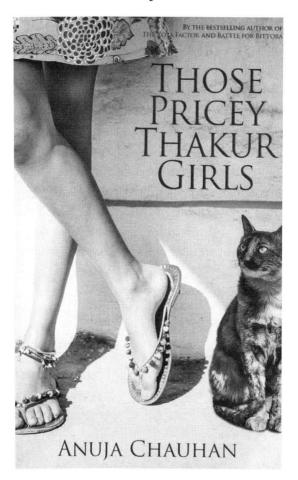

In a sprawling bungalow on New Delhi's posh Hailey Road, Justice Laxmi Narayan Thakur and his wife Mamta spend their days watching anxiously over their five beautiful (but troublesome) alphabetically named daughters.

Anjini, married but an incorrigible flirt; Binodini, very worried about her children's hissa in the family property; Chandrakanta, who eloped with a foreigner on the eve of her wedding; Eshwari, who is just a little too popular at Modern School, Barakhamba Road; and the Judge's favourite (though fathers shouldn't have favourites): the quietly fiery Debjani, champion of all the stray animals on Hailey Road, who reads the English news on DD and clashes constantly with crusading journalist Dylan Singh Shekhawat, he of shining professional credentials but tarnished personal reputation, crushingly dismissive of her 'state-sponsored propaganda', but always seeking her out with half-sarcastic, half-intrigued dark eyes. Spot-on funny and toe-curlingly sexy, *Those Pricey Thakur Girls* is rom-com specialist Anuja Chauhan writing at her sparkling best.